THE TREASON WITHIN

▲▼▲

The Muten's gaze fell directly on Phineas. Its third eye bore into his brain, deep into the place where his most secret thoughts were hidden . . .

You'd like to kill him, wouldn't you, Captain? Kill him, take his queen . . .

Phineas pulled his sword from his scabbard. He jerked his head from side to side, trying to escape the seductive whisper in his brain.

Kill him. He deserves it.

Young Tedmund's face rose before him, the ruins of Sprinfell holding, Mortmain's face the night Abelard forced him to submit, Melisande's white breasts exposed to the lust-filled eyes of the soldiers.

One stroke and she's yours.

With a cry, Phineas rushed King Abelard, sword raised. He swung and the King required both hands to block it. Sparks flew off the metal edges as Phineas attacked, again and again, and again, forcing Abelard back in an ev̶̶̶̶̶̶̶̶̶̶̶̶̶̶

•DAUGHTER•
OF PROPHECY

ANNE KELLEHER BUSH

ASPECT

WARNER BOOKS

A Time Warner Company

WARNER BOOKS EDITION

Copyright © 1995 by Anne Kelleher Bush
All rights reserved.

Aspect is a trademark of Warner Books, Inc.

Cover design by Don Puckey
Cover illustration by Thomas Canty

Warner Books, Inc.
1271 Avenue of the Americas
New York, NY 10020

A Time Warner Company

Printed in the United States of America

First Printing: March, 1995

10 9 8 7 6 5 4 3 2 1

This book is dedicated, with love, to
my mother, Frances Kelly;
my grandmother, Rose Castaldi;
and my father, Michael J. Kelleher:

Spes messis in semine

Acknowledgements: Although it would be impossible for me to name each person who, by their support and encouragement, enabled me to complete this book, I would like to thank especially: Carol Svec, Lorraine Stanton, Christine Whittemore Papa, and Juilene Osborne-McKnight, godmothers and midwives all; my agent, Sharon Jarvis, for taking the chance; my friends, both writer and non-writer, who were kind enough to listen, and in many cases, read and critique; my children, Katherine, James, Margaret, and Abigail, who tolerated late meals and sporadic wash days; and (last but not least) my husband, Ray, who didn't always believe, but paid the bills anyway.

Bethlehem, Pennsylvania
February 1994

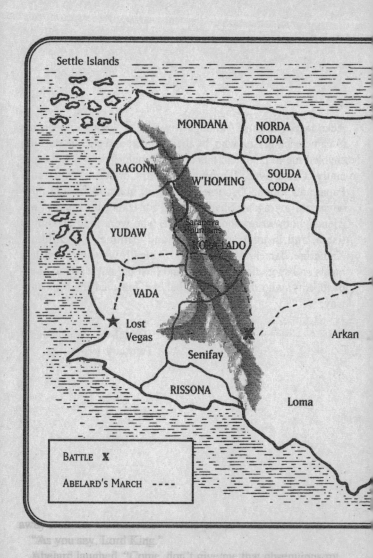

Settle Islands

MONDANA

NORDA CODA

RAGONN

W'HOMING

SOUDA CODA

YUDAW

Saratova Mountains

ROSA-LADO

VADA

★ Lost Vegas

Arkan

Senifay

RISSONA

Loma

BATTLE ✗

ABELARD'S MARCH - - - -

"As you say, Lord King."

Abelard laughed. "Come, don't give me that obsequious rot.

MHEN

North Sea

Abelard's
Holdings

Dirondac
Mountains

NOURK

Ahga

FILLAVENYA

Linoys

Pulatchian

Ithan
Ford

GINYA

Mountains

Plains

TENNESSY
FALL

X

ATLAND

Misspy
Gorge

Eldred's
Keep

MISSILUSE

D'las - Fort'orth

MERIGA

Prologue

Some say that all the words of men are in the wind, swirling perpetually through the currents, and that, if one listens closely enough, one can hear them all, whispering on forever as the years roll by. Lying alone on my litter, I listen to the voices in the wind, and I remember the days of my youth and the days of my manhood—glorious days when I rode across the plains of Meriga and called a king my friend. One might say that I could call a king my son, but such thoughts are dangerous and better left unsaid. So instead, I will whisper my story to the whining wind, with words soon lost like those days and that man, the man I once was.

I shall never forget the first sight I had of Nydia, the witch woman, when I pulled the coarse sacking off her face. Her beauty was like a sword, so piercing in its sweetness that it made a man gasp. I remember how we turned our eyes away when she let the fabric fall, as though her naked body was more than our mere mortal eyes could bear. Only the King, only Abelard, dared take it in, meeting her eyes with something like acknowledgement that in that first encounter, she emerged the victor. It was not always so between them.

There came a time finally, when he took what she offered and twisted it, made it into a thing of grief, a weapon with which he forged a future of his choosing. But that was all years from that day, years and choices later, and on that cracked and broken highway, no portent rose to turn us back from the fate we so eagerly rode to meet.

Chapter One

❧

H old!" The voice slashed through the low rumble of the small crowd with the effect of steel through flesh: the voice of a man accustomed to obedience.

The priest, a big-boned woman in coarse, sweat-stained black wool, paused at the base of the scaffold and straightened to her full height. In one thick slab of a hand, calloused from long days of labor in the fields among her flock, she held a torch. Its flames fanned out in long orange tails as a chilling wind, unusual for so early in the autumn, swept off the neighboring hills.

The villagers clustered in tighter knots, the hum of their voices increasing in intensity as the unfamiliar company of soldiers thundered into the barren market square.

They were all fully armed with broadswords strapped across their backs, sheathed daggers slapping against thighs hardened from long days spent in the saddle and on the battlefields. They wore leather armor, supple with oil, and tightly woven cloaks of olive drab.

Behind the standard-bearer streamed a white silk banner, bordered in blue and emblazoned with an eagle clutching a sheaf of wheat and a flight of arrows in its talons. The well-fed warhorses made a stark contrast with the hollow cheeks and bony limbs of the people who watched in wary amazement.

"In whose name?" challenged the priest. "Who are you?" She stared defiantly into the eyes of the tall man with a captain's insignia on his tunic. He reined his gray stallion scant paces from where she stood.

The captain did not reply. He glanced over the priest to the dilapidated huts hardly fit for human dwelling, to the crowd, shivering in threadbare clothing, to the makeshift scaffold. A young tree had obviously been hastily axed for this occasion, for a few leaves still clung to its spindly trunk. The figure tied to it was female. A dirty white shroud covered her to her bare knees. He looked back over his shoulder, his mouth drawn tight, forehead furrowed.

The priest followed his gaze. She recognized neither the men nor the colors they bore, and she squared her shoulders. The weight of the people's fear mounted to a tangible thing. "Answer me in the Name of the One! This is sacred—"

"Sacred?" Another man, as tall as the first but broader of shoulder, reined his horse beside the captain's. They were both about the same age, perhaps no more than thirty, but the ring of absolute authority in the newcomer's voice was unmistakable. He wore no obvious mark of rank, but in the hilt of the broadsword strapped across his back, three blood-red stones spat fire in the sunlight. "Since when is execution sacred?"

"Who are you to interfere with this?" The priest's face flushed an ugly mottled scarlet. "How dare you ride—"

"I am Abelard Ridenau, King of All Meriga."

In the sudden silence, the bound woman jerked her head upright. She twisted her head beneath the coarse sacking, as though she strained to hear the voice of the King.

He ignored all but the defiant priest. "Where is your writ of permission?"

"What writ?" spluttered the priest.

"The writ of execution from the Senador of this estate. You cannot execute—"

"This woman is a witch." The priest's voice regained a measure of composure, but her eyes narrowed into thin lines.

Contempt in his eyes, the King looked over the people. "Who is Mayher here?"

"I am, Lord King." A reedy man with a sparse mustache stepped out from the crowd. His voice was high-pitched, and he stared up at the young man on the pale gold stallion suspiciously.

"How has this happened? You know you cannot execute anyone—murderer, thief, or witch—without permission from the Senator's court."

"Our priest—" the Mayher began.

"Ancient scripture is clear," interrupted the priest. "You shall not suffer a witch to live."

"The law of Meriga is equally clear." The King's voice was dangerously soft.

"The law of Meriga has no dominion over the Church. The Church is separate from the State. So it was long before you Ridenaus claimed all Meriga—long before the Armageddon and the Time of Purification." The priest set her jaw.

As though emboldened by the priest's words, the Mayher squinted at the King. "There's been no court here, Lord King, in over a year—not since midyear last. The Harleyriders have raided since Gost, and the Senator has sent no men to our defense. The harvest is poor—but he took his measure. Why should I appeal to him?"

The King exchanged a concerned frown with his captain. "Have you a horse?" he asked the Mayher. "Good. Saddle it. Phineas," he nodded at the captain. "Untie the woman."

A vein throbbed in the priest's temple. Before she could protest, the King continued: "You, too, Rever'd Lady. It happens we are on our way to the Senator's castle at Ithan Ford. We'll look further into this matter there."

"She has the Magic!" The priest stamped her foot and clenched her fists into two white-knuckled knots.

"She's entitled to a hearing at a higher court than yours."

"There is no higher court."

"Rever'd Lady, in the time before the Armageddon, justice was for all. According to the ancient law, she is innocent until proved guilty."

The Mayher appeared on a rangy beast. He extended a hand to the priest, and with ill grace, she scrambled up behind him on the saddle.

The King looked up at the piled faggots, where the woman, clutching the soiled cloth to her breasts, stumbled on the uneven wood. Phineas swung her up in his arms, carried her to the ground, and set her gently on her feet next to the King. She raised her face.

She alone heard his quick intake of breath, saw the infinitesimal lift of one brow, the subtle bow of his head. Wordlessly, with eyes locked, King and condemned took measure of each other.

She knew he saw the angry red blotches raised by the rough wool and the tight leather bonds on her white arms and throat, prickled by rippling gooseflesh in the cold wind, and she made no attempt to cover them.

He reached behind his saddle, where his own cloak lay discarded. He handed it to her. She let the white shroud fall to her feet. A gasp escaped the crowd, as for a moment she stood naked and unashamed before him. Then she wrapped herself in the heavy purple cloak of wool so finely spun, of hue so richly dyed, it gave her a regal air despite her tousled chestnut hair and smudged cheeks. She looked over at a smaller pile of wood some feet away.

"What is it?" he asked.

"Please, Lord King," she swallowed hard. Her voice was rough in her throat. "My books."

At the King's quick nod, a soldier retrieved the small stack from the dry kindling on which it lay. "Come, lady." With Phineas's help, she was seated behind the company's lieutenant, who looked both dismayed and delighted at this unexpected duty. The King raised his arm, and as one, the company rode out of the village on a cloud of dust.

On the perimeter of the village, Phineas paused. The rest galloped ahead, following Abelard. Phineas looked back at the people huddled close together. Some stared with sullen eyes, some spoke in hushed voices, all clutched at their ragged cloaks and shivered as the wind blew harder. "Get back to your homes," he called, his voice pitched to carry across a battlefield. "Your priest and your Mayher will return safely, as soon as this matter is resolved."

Somewhere nearby, a door swung open on creaking, rusted hinges. The edge banged and scraped across the stony ground. The people did not move.

His practiced eye swept over the newly harvested fields, the stubbled furrows looking raw as wounds. The ramshackle huts were defenseless, and all his instincts, bred by years of waging war in the service of his King, told him the Harleys had not yet finished their raiding this year. This meager harvest, unsecured, was an easy mark. He looked again at the villagers. Their expressions of suspicious resignation reminded him of beasts of burden brought to slaughter. He suppressed a sudden impulse to order half a dozen men back to guard the village. Instead, he half rose in the stirrups. "Go on. Get along, now, all of you. And you, distribute that kindling." There was enough wood to warm the whole village for days.

They moved off slowly, shuffling for the most part in bare feet through the dry dirt of the square. Only a few of the men looked back over their shoulders.

When he was satisfied that his order had been obeyed, he put the spurs to his stallion and galloped off to join the rest.

Chapter Two

❧

"So, Lord King," Phineas asked, as they settled into an easy pace on the ancient highway, "what do you make of that?"

Abelard's face was grim. "Things are worse here than I thought. Look at the condition of this road." He gestured to the gaping holes in the black paving, cracked in places down to the stony bedrock beneath the flat surface. He shook his head and adjusted the reins. "Old Miles was a good man in my grandfather's time. Even served my father well, if such a thing were possible. But now, I'm afraid he's getting old. Too old."

"What about his heir?"

"Still a boy. Not quite twelve. Were he a few years older, perhaps . . ." Abelard shook his head.

"The villagers looked as though they've managed to survive the raids."

"What did they have to begin with?" He shrugged and glanced back at the Mayher on his nag, the priest bumping along on the rump. "The weather's getting cold early. That should encourage the Harleys to go back to their lairs."

"They shouldn't be so far north. Not this late. Not as often as the Mayher implied."

"Have you read the reports the scouts brought back last night?"

"The mountains are clear. No signs of the Harleyriders. I sent another patrol out this morning—I think we can count on the fact they'll be making their last raids of the year on the new harvests. Already the Mutens are beating their winter drums—perhaps an early winter will bring us an early peace. The scouts will meet us at Ithan Ford."

Abelard shivered as a stronger gust of wind tousled his bright blond hair.

"Will you take my cloak?"

Abelard smiled. "No, old friend. I'm not yet so soft I can't endure a few hours chill."

"Do you think there will be trouble with that woman?"

"The priest or the witch?"

"Either one."

The smile on the King's face broadened. "I wouldn't mind making trouble with the young one."

Phineas glanced at the young woman, who clung to the lieutenant's back with a white-knuckled grip. Her bare feet dangled over the horse's side, purplish with cold. Her face was hidden by the heavy fall of her dark brown hair, but Phineas knew the memory of that first sight would haunt his dreams. "Do you believe she's really a witch?"

"What's a witch? That hag of a priest is more my idea of a witch. The question is, does she have the Magic, and can she use it?"

"You would dare—" Phineas looked amazed, and the King laughed.

"I would dare anything, Phineas—you know that—if I thought I could make Meriga the realm it once was, restore the kingdom, remove those who'd have it otherwise."

"Abelard—" Phineas looked around, and this time there was fear on his face. He kept his voice low. "Everyone believes the Magic caused the Armageddon—brought about the end of Old Meriga. How could you use this, if you had it, and not bring worse upon us all?"

"What's worse than this? Look around you. The people scratch a living from the dust, if they can, and the 'Free People of the Plains' lie in wait to take it from them. That wimp-chinned Eldred still plots in his swamps in Missiluse. My father gave him a taste of Ridenau blood, and all these years, he's looked for a way to taste more."

"You aren't your father, Abelard. You've proven that many times over."

The King shook his head, and looked to the south, where Missiluse lay behind the mountains. "If Rabica had not died—" He shook his head again. "Since she died and left me the twins, between Eldred and his mischief, and my mother and hers—"

"But even so, Abelard, who among the Congress would support you, if you brought back the Magic? Too many of the troops would refuse to fight for you, I think, even if the lords themselves are not superstitious men."

The King made an impatient motion in the saddle, so suddenly that his horse threw back its head and whinnied. "Answer me this, as my friend. Isn't the prosperity of the realm worth whatever we might risk?"

Phineas was silent. When he finally spoke, his voice was quiet. "But I am not just your friend, Abelard. You are my King—my life is sworn to you. I can't forget that. You don't know that the woman has the Magic, but if she does . . ." He met the King's deep blue eyes squarely. "I cannot answer."

The King laughed. Nominally Captain of the King's Guard, Phineas was in fact second in command of the Armies of the King. No other man in Meriga held more power, save the King himself, and no other man in Meriga was less likely to abuse it. "Phineas, you know me better. You know I would never jeopardize the realm. Worry about the Harleyriders. I'll worry about the Magic." He gave another chuckle at the dour look on Phineas's face, and cantered off without another word.

Phineas followed more slowly, picking his way across the pock-holed surface where the road had fallen into disrepair. He was not a superstitious man, had never had the time or inclination to listen to the priests with their ravings and warnings. His concerns were the King's.

But Phineas was the son of one of the stablehands of Ahga, and he understood the beliefs of the common people and knew the regard in which they held the priests.

A similarity of build to the young Prince had brought

Phineas to the attention of the weaponsmaster: at six, he had been one of the few boys as strong and as tall as Abelard, who lacked experience even as Abelard did. As the years passed, Phineas grew into more than the Prince's sparring partner. At fourteen, he had pledged his allegiance into the service of the King's Guard, that elite company from whose ranks sprang the generals of the Armies of the King, and who were responsible for the protection of the King's person in battle. In the general purge which followed the murder of Renmond Ridenau by outlaw brigands, Abelard had promoted Phineas to his present rank. Abelard suspected that Eldred Onrada of Missiluse, one of those Senators who chafed under the unifying rule of the Ridenaus, had some part in his father's death, but nothing could be proven. But now, the clear evidence of the Harleyriders' raids, so far to the north, so close to the hereditary holdings of the Ridenau Kings, indicated that Eldred might no longer be keeping them from his borders, and the thought that one of the Senators could have formed an alliance with the outlaws made Phineas shudder.

As dusk began to fall, they arrived at the dark, deserted-looking keep of the Senador of the Tennesey Fall, the square central tower rising like a single black arm upthrust against the rounded foothills. The King reined his horse before the walls, frowning in the dusk at what he saw before him. "This is a disgrace."

Phineas nodded slowly. The Senador of the Tennesey Fall had been a mighty ally in the reign of Abelard's grandfather, the first of the Ridenau Kings. Ithan Ford stood beside the bed of an ancient river at the crossroads of four highways. A linchpin in the early struggles, poised between the fertile fields of north central Meriga, and the arid wastelands of the Arkan Plains where the Harleyriders roamed free, Ithan remained crucial.

As they crossed the creaking drawbridge in the fading light, Phineas squinted at the stone walls, trying to gauge the state of their repair. Like the keep of the Ridenau Kings in Agha City, the tower was of ancient origin, dating back beyond the Days of Armageddon to the height of Old Meriga. Wide panes of priceless glass stared down into the inner ward like blind eyes. As at Agha, the contrast between the smooth planes of the old tower, and the newer, rough walls of crushed rubble was stark. In the dim rushlights, Phineas noted the dirty stableyard, the equipment piled haphazardly. The men-at-arms who guided them through the first ward into the second were dirty and unkempt, several days' growth of beard darkening their chins. At the very least, discipline was slack.

At the foot of the shallow steps that led into the castle proper, a lone woman stood waiting, a dented silver cup steaming with spices in her hands. She raised it to the King as he walked with Phineas and his lieutenant, Everic, up the steps.

"You are very welcome, Lord King." She sank into a deep curtsey.

Abelard drank deeply of the welcome cup and passed it on to Phineas. He raised the woman to her feet. "Lady Kara?"

The Senador's wife, the First Lady of Ithan Ford, was no longer young, her brown hair dull with threads of gray. Although her skirts were long and full enough, as her rank demanded, stains and patches were evident, even in the flickering light. "Yes, Lord King. I am so glad to see you at last." There was a note of deep relief in her voice which made Phineas look at her more closely as he passed the cup on to Everic.

"Where is your husband?" Abelard took her arm and drew her up the steps.

With a sigh, she bent her head. "My husband is dying, Lord King, and my son—"

"Yes, lady. I understand."

"It was my husband's intent to attend the Convening of the Congress next month to ask that you appoint a warder for young Miles, but now I'm afraid—"

"Be easy, lady. We will not leave you vulnerable." In the dark hallway which led into the great hall of the keep, Abelard paused. He stripped off his gloves and wiped an arm across his face.

"You're tired, Lord King, and I've spoken of nothing but my troubles. Forgive me—a bath has been ordered and there will be food."

"No, lady, it is I who should be forgiven. I'm afraid I've brought an unpleasant situation into your house."

"Oh?" The dim light was kind to the contours of her face, but her voice was cold.

"Tell me, has anyone applied to your lord's court for a writ of permission to execute a condemned witch?"

"Lord King," she ducked her head, suddenly embarrassed, "there has not been a court held here in over a year. No one has applied to my lord for anything but the most basic needs, and those we have seen to as best we can. But a witch you say? Here in our Estate?"

"Yes. We interrupted an execution in a little village, less than five hours ride. You've heard nothing?" When she shook her head, he continued. "It doesn't matter. I brought the accuser, the Mayher and the accused with me—"

"You brought a witch here?" She drew back, with raised eyebrows.

"I'm not certain that she is a witch, lady. According to the old laws of Meriga, the accused is innocent until proven guilty. At any rate, she can be held in the outer ward, under guard, until the matter can be settled."

"It must be settled as quickly as possible. I want no witch beneath this roof. We have trouble enough without invoking the wrath of the One or the Three."

Abelard stared down at her, his mouth a thin line. Phineas suppressed a sigh. It was full dark now, and they had been in the saddle since dawn. Her talk of a bath and food had sounded like the promise of sunrise after a night's long watch.

But the King pulled his shoulders straighter and gave a short nod, as he stifled a yawn. "Very well, lady. We'll settle it now. Have you a private audience room?"

After a brief order to Everic, Phineas followed Abelard's

beckoning hand, somewhat surprised by the woman's reaction. As he watched her lead him down a long corridor, he heard her chilly voice say: "In here, Lord King." She stood aside and let Phineas pass into a small, musty chamber off the main corridor. A small fire burned in a rusted grate, and the fabric covering the clumsily carved chairs was worn away at the arms.

"Send a servant to fetch the Mayher and the priest. And, lady, some food, if you will."

She curtsied stiffly, with less grace than Phineas had expected. He wondered about her origins.

"As you say, Lord King." She withdrew with a rigid spine.

Abelard said nothing. His boots clicked on the worn tile floor as he moved restlessly around the perimeter of the room. He gestured for Phineas to sit in a chair by the fire and threw another log on the flames.

Phineas shook his head. "I think not, Abelard. Neither the Mayher nor the priest will count me as your equal. Perhaps you'd do better to speak to them alone?"

"I want you to hear them, Phineas. You're one of the only men I can trust to give me real answers, not my own words neatly packaged. Stay."

When the Mayher and the priest were ushered in, Phineas took a place in a discreet corner.

"So," began the King. "Tell me your names."

The priest looked at him with venomous eyes. The Mayher coughed: the thin, dry cough of nervousness. "My name is Tomus Chones, Lord King."

"How long has your family held the title?"

"Since before the Days of Armageddon."

"Indeed?" This was a common enough answer—and the accepted one, so long as no one challenged it. "And you, Rever'd Lady?"

"Doriunn." Too quickly, she added: "We drop our family names when we take our vows, Lord King."

"Yes. Well. Tell me. How did you manage to catch a witch in this small corner of my realm?" There was a subtle emphasis on the last two words.

The Mayher coughed again. "We found her sneaking through the woods, day before yesterday. She stole bread and one of our men caught her. Then we found the books on her."

"I see. Did you see her use the Magic?"

"Uh, no—I didn't—"

"Fool!" hissed the priest. "She admitted it, Lord King. She did not deny that the books were hers. Claimed they're her most precious possession, in fact."

"You condemned her for carrying books?"

"It was the kind of books that they were, Lord King!" The priest spread her hands in awkward supplication. "They are magic books, they contain the—" she lowered her voice "—the symbols of the blackest arts. It was those like her that brought about the end of Old Meriga. Every child in your realm," she spat back the emphasized words with stress of her own, "knows that."

"But tell me, Rever'd Lady Doriunn, how did you know it was the Magic? It's difficult to read the language of Old Meriga, similar to our own as it might be. How can you be so certain?"

"Sacred Scripture teaches us what to watch for. The beast has a number, you know."

"Mm. No, I didn't know."

"Lord King," said the Mayher with his nervous cough, "it seems the witch killed one of the men who watched her use the Magic."

At that, Abelard looked up. "How?"

"She started a fire. One of the men who watched fell over dead." The priest's voice had a note of triumph. "The other was lucky to escape with his life."

Abelard nodded, lips pursed, brows knit together. "So she's a murderer, as well as a witch and a thief."

"Exactly." The priest gave a solemn nod.

Abelard exchanged a glance with Phineas. "One more thing, Lord Mayher. You said the Harleys had been raiding since Gost. How many times has your village been attacked?"

Even in the scant light of the fire, the Mayher's embarrassment was obvious. He licked his lips and glanced down at his fingers. Surreptitiously, he glanced at the priest.

With a snort of contempt, she spoke. "We've seen them six times."

"Six raids in little more than six weeks?" Abelard frowned and made a gesture of dismissal. "That will be all."

"That's all?" Doriunn's face flushed red in the firelight.

"Ask the First Lady of this keep to see that you are given food and a place to sleep. It's much too late to send you on your way."

"What about the witch?"

"Even if I do condemn her to die, I would not send her back with you, Rever'd Lady. Surely you are glad to have this monstrous burden lifted."

The priest raised her chin and shifted on her feet. "But— what about our testimony?"

"Testimony?"

"Will there not be a court here? Why did you bring us here if we will not give testimony before the Senador?"

From the shelter of the shadows, Phineas glanced nervously at the King. This priest did have the power to make trouble here, whether Abelard realized it or not. The soldiers in Abelard's company were as superstitious as Lady Kara.

Abelard smiled, showing even, white teeth. "The Senador of this Estate is dying, Rever'd Lady. I will speak to the woman myself. If I determine that your accusations have merit, and if there is time, I will convene a court while I am here. I must tell you, however, that I am hard-pressed to return to Ahga."

"But—" Doriunn was uncertain how to respond, sensing that somehow she had been outmaneuvered. The Mayher touched her arm, and she shrugged him away. "This is a matter of utmost urgency. Don't you understand that the salvation of the land may be in danger?"

"Then surely in a matter of such urgency, this witch, as you call her, should be taken to the Bishop of Ahga."

"This doesn't sound like ancient justice to me."

Abelard rose to his feet, and although the priest was a big

woman, she was suddenly dwarfed by the breadth of his shoulders, the strength implied by the heavy muscles of his chest and arms. "You speak of ancient justice to me, Rever'd Lady?" Even Phineas was chilled by the soft voice. "You, that would burn a defenseless woman, out of hand—with no other evidence than that brought by superstitious villagers? Have you waited long enough to see if she carries a child?" When neither the priest nor the Mayher dared a reply, Abelard continued: "Then who is guilty of a greater sin? Doesn't your religion teach that nothing is more sacred than the life of a child? In your zeal to rid this land of a Magic-user, you might have destroyed an innocent life."

Finally, with a sullen mouth, the priest said, "You accept a great risk, Lord King."

Abelard bowed his head. "The King accepts all risks, Rever'd Lady." When they were gone, he sank back in his chair with a tired sigh. "Damn these priests."

"It was very clever to think that the woman might be pregnant, Abelard. It was perhaps the only argument to use against her."

The King grinned, and Phineas went on, "But the number of raids they report disturb me. Perhaps we should send a patrol south to find out if the Harleys are coming in across the mountains?"

"Perhaps. But not tonight. The sooner we get this matter settled, the better."

"Shall I bring the woman, Abelard?"

"Immediately."

As Phineas left the audience chamber, Everic approached him and saluted. "Captain, I've found quarters for our men, and the prisoner is confined in the guardhouse. The scouts have come in and are waiting for you in the barracks."

"Good." Phineas noticed both priest and Mayher standing by one of the hearths, looking lost and somehow forlorn in the cavernous hall. "Go and ask the First Lady of this house for some kind of clothing for the woman—I imagine the King wants his cloak back."

Everic saluted once more. Phineas crossed the shadowy hall, the creak of ancient floorboards announcing his approach. He bowed briefly to the two standing side by side at the perimeter of the fire's warmth. They looked like sheep without a shepherd.

"Rever'd Lady, Lord Mayher."

They looked at him warily, but Phineas recognized exhaustion in the man's eyes and despair in the woman's. "We will see you have an escort back to your village tomorrow. Have you spoken to the First Lady?"

"She has not seen us," the priest answered with a tired shrug.

Suddenly he saw that all the hostility had drained out of her. For the moment, they looked like two very ordinary, very tired travelers, confused by the events of the day. "Sit down." He indicated the low benches heaped with moth-eaten furs. He looked around for a servant, saw three idling in a corner, and raised his voice. "You—bring food and drink for these two guests. And you—find your First Lady. Tell her to attend them at the King's request." They moved slowly, with muttered curses and sidelong looks and sly smiles. "Do as I say—unless you'd like a taste of the King's discipline."

As Phineas turned to leave, the Mayher coughed. "A word, if you will, Lord—"

"I am not a lord, Lord Mayher. My only title is my rank. I am the Captain of the King's Guard."

"Your pardon, Captain—I—I have never been to court. I do not know how such things are done, but I—I wanted to thank you for your courtesy to us."

Phineas looked from one to the other and pitied them both. "We are all weary, Lord Mayher." The priest stared into the flames as though entranced. He spoke as gently as he could. "Good night, Rever'd Lady, Lord Mayher. I shall make certain that the First Lady attends to you." He gave them another brief bow and went to find the witch.

Chapter Three

❧

A silver sickle of moon had risen above the walls when the woman heard the stir in the outer room beyond her cell. She huddled beneath the King's cloak, the warmth and softness of it incongruous in the dank darkness. She recognized the voice of the man who entered as that of the Captain who had lifted her off the stake, and was struck by the immediate, deferential responses he received. Whoever this man was, he commanded nearly as much respect as the King, himself.

The heavy footfalls approached. She pulled herself to her feet, and winced as her bare soles touched the cold stones.

The hinges shrieked as the door swung open, and in the shadowy torchlight, Phineas stood, a dark bundle in his hands. He stooped through the low doorway and gave her a brief bow as he straightened. "Lady."

She blinked as he held out his burden.

"Clothes, lady. Put them on. The King commands your presence." When she did not react, he repeated, "Put them on. I am to bring you to the King."

She took the bundle, clutched it to her breasts. He nodded, as if satisfied she understood, then turned his back. His frame filled the doorway completely, though she doubted any of the other men would have dared to peer around him.

With fingers made clumsy by the cold, she pulled on the simple dress of undyed homespun. The fabric lay stiffly over her gooseflesh. The skirt barely covered her knees, and her nipples, made erect by the cold, strained against the bodice.

When she slipped her feet into the felt house slippers, she said: "I'm ready."

"Wrap the cloak around you. It's cold tonight." Without another word, he led her past the stares of the soldiers, into the poorly lit wards. As they crossed the uneven cobbled paving, where here and there piles of dung lay ignored, he took her arm, guiding her around the worst of it.

She had not expected such courtesy, and his simple kindnesses brought tears to her eyes. When finally they paused before a door, and he saw her tears, he spoke gently once more. "Take heart, lady, the King is not cruel. He will not condemn you out of hand. But tell him the truth—he hates a liar."

He opened the door and motioned her to follow. Tentatively, she stepped out of the shadows into the small audience room. A fire burned in the hearth, and several torches burned in brackets around the walls. The light was the brightest she had seen since nightfall. She blinked.

Abelard Ridenau was leaning over the hearth, gnawing on a chicken leg. He carried himself with all the arrogant grace of a man in his prime, confident of health and virility, magnified several times over by his rank. His hair was bright gold; even in the firelight it gleamed. He himself was like the flames, with a restless energy not readily contained.

He turned suddenly with reflexes honed by battle. His face with its sharp cheekbones and square clean-shaven jaw did not change when he saw her. He nodded to Phineas. "Leave us."

"As you say, Lord King." She heard caution in his tone. Nevertheless, Phineas bowed. As he passed her, he smiled and slipped the cloak from her shoulders.

Abelard watched her for a moment, saying nothing, then threw the bone in the fire and sat down. He crossed his long legs at the knee. "What's your name?"

"Nydia Farhallen, Lord King."

"You're noble." He looked surprised to hear her family name. "Where's your family?"

"I was born on the lower slopes of the Pulatchian Mountains, near the sea in Fillavenya. My family and their holding were wiped out a year ago in a Muten raid."

"I see. Are you a witch?"

"Yes." She met his eyes squarely.

He raised one eyebrow and ran his eyes down her body. His eyes lingered on her bare legs. A blush crept up her throat. Noblewomen wore long skirts as proof of wealth and standing. Only servants and farm women revealed so much. She resisted the urge to cross her arms over her breasts as she watched his gaze travel up her body. The fire snapped in the silence and a log split in a shower of sparks.

"You have the Magic?"

"It's in the books."

"Can you use it?"

"Yes."

At that he leaned forward. "You admit it."

"What good would it do me to lie?" Despite the bravado of her words, she clenched her hands in the fabric of her skirt and hoped he would not notice how they trembled.

He smiled at that—a slow, measuring smile that spread across his face by degrees. "What are you doing in this Estate?"

"I was on my way to you, Lord King."

"Why? What do you want with me?"

"To offer my Pledge of Allegiance."

"Your pledge? You, a woman? You would swear yourself into my service?"

"I would."

"Why?"

"There is no one else in all of Meriga with power enough."

"What kind of power do you seek?"

"Protection. For me and my secrets."

"Your secrets. If you do truly know the Magic, that's a powerful secret indeed. How do you come to know this?"

"Since before the Armageddon, my family kept the ancient books—as many as they could—safe from harm during the Persecution, hid them, copied them, and passed the knowledge down from parent to child. That was why we were attacked. The Mutens wanted our books."

He nodded slowly. "They have that name for themselves—Children of the Magic. Why didn't you use it to protect yourselves? Or did you?"

"No, oh; no, Lord King. The Magic is much too dangerous. We would not have dared. My father would never have allowed it."

"Even to protect your lives and your lands?"

"No one must use the Magic—it is too unpredictable. It brought about the end of Old Meriga; it must never be used again. Last spring when our holding was destroyed, my mother and I were the only ones left, and she was badly injured. Before she died, she told me to take what I could salvage and go to you and pledge allegiance. Who else is strong enough to guard this thing?"

"What about the man they say you killed?"

"He was old, his heart stopped. He would have died anyway; it had nothing to do with me. I did use the Magic that day to start a fire in the wood. It was cold. I needed to warm myself. But I will not use it again."

"Then what would the use of your pledge be to me? Do you understand what it means? It confers obligations upon us both—until death. Those who swear themselves into my service are entitled to my aid, but they must give something back. And you—you have this secret which you would expect me to guard, and clothe and feed and provide for your person, and what would you in return give to me? Lands I have in plenty, and you—you are very fair—I would have you willingly, but even your body would not be enough of an exchange."

"I don't offer you my body."

At that he raised both eyebrows and laughed out loud. "What can you offer me? A thousand horses? Five hundred bowmen? Can you lift a sword?"

"I see the future, Lord King."

"What?"

"I see the future."

"So will I marry a small dark-haired woman who will bring me three estates and bear me a fine son to be the heir of Meriga?"

"You mock me, Lord King." She straightened and un-clenched her hands.

"Lady, I have heard many plead for life before, but none with fairer face or cleverer tongue."

Angrily, she threw her head back and looked past him, just over his shoulder, where his future lay. "You will leave here in four days' time. You will leave someone here who you trust very much, and you will be attacked within three hours of your leaving. You will lose something very dear to you in the battle, though you yourself will only be slightly wounded."

He stared at her. "Attacked by whom?"

"Harleyriders."

"Where are they?"

"At the bridge over the gorge."

"The scouts have said the way is clear."

"Then the scouts either lie or the Riders have not yet ar-rived."

He leaned back in his chair, examining her closely. The flames set shadows dancing across his face. "You said you don't use the Magic."

"That's not the Magic."

"What do you call it?"

"It's—" She paused, uncertain how to explain something which was as much a part of her as the color of her hair and eyes. "What I am. A prescient."

He wet his lips. "But if you can see the future, why did you go to that village? You could have died there if I had not hap-pened along. Or did you know that, too?"

"No. The ability has limitations. I cannot see my own fu-ture."

"Yet you can see mine."

"I cannot see past places where you must make choices. I cannot see what choice you will make. I can only see up to the choice itself."

"Then if I change my mind about leaving?"

"I will see the future of that choice when you do."

He shifted in his chair, weighing her words. "Where does this ability come from?"

"It's in my family. It has been this way with us since before the Armageddon."

"Since before the Armageddon. You are indeed a witch."

Her nerves, raw and frayed, cracked, and her voice broke. "Please, Lord King, no matter what the priests say, I am not evil—I can be of great help to you—I swear—"

He stared at her outburst. "Do you think I will send you to the stake?" He laughed. "Be easy, lady. I would not burn flesh as fine as yours." He nodded at a chair across from the fire. "Sit. Are you hungry? Do you want wine?" He poured wine from a clay flask into his goblet and handed it to her. "Drink."

Nydia sat uneasily, not quite believing her good fortune. He watched while she drank, then offered her a plate with half a chicken still on it. Her stomach growled. She had not eaten all day.

Suddenly, she felt almost dizzy. Her hand shook as she reached out to tear a piece of meat from the breast. Saliva filled her mouth. She chewed, swallowed, and tore another piece of meat.

Abelard laughed. "Slowly, lady. That bird's not going anywhere. Take your time. I want you to explain everything to me about this ability, as you call it, and all you know of the Magic."

"The ability," she answered between bites, "skips through the generations and appears at random, like blue eyes or curling hair. We believe that our ancestors unfortunate enough to live through the Persecutions were at least fortunate enough not to have the ability."

"Could there be others?"

"Perhaps. But the Persecutions went on for almost two hundred years."

"And yet you say this is not Magic. Explain the difference."

She tugged her skirt as far as it would go over her knees and leaned forward, holding her hands out to the flames. "We—all of us, even you, Lord King—are the result of the Magic, indirectly. The men that made the Magic wanted to wipe out disease—and in that they were successful. All of us alive today are no longer vulnerable to the diseases which plagued old Meriga."

"What kinds of diseases?"

"You have never known illness, Lord King, but in the time before the Armageddon, no one was completely immune. There were diseases which ate away at the heart and stomach and other organs, diseases which destroyed the blood, and the brain, diseases which did not kill, but caused many great distress. So the Magic-users, these scientists, deciphered the codes within the body's smallest structures, and humankind changed." She paused. The fire was beginning to die. Abelard roused himself from his place and threw another log on the grate.

"But there were other changes, changes no one expected or could have predicted." The flames leapt up toward her fingers and she flinched.

"Such as your ability?"

"That was one. The first appearance of the Mutens was another. No one really knows how or why they came to be. But the change which most affected the fabric of society was that it became difficult for women to become pregnant. Our bodies are not receptive to the seed. Although few die as a result of illness or infection, fewer are born. It used to be that a man and woman would vow to spend their lives together, forsaking all others. It was considered a most grievous wrong to know another partner, and even worse to bear another's child."

"But what if a couple had no children?"

"Most had to try harder to prevent conception than to cause it."

"Each man took only one woman?"

"And each woman only one man. Now, no matter how many men we take, we women are fortunate if we can bear even one child." She looked up to see if he had noticed the tremor in her voice.

He only sat back and she heard him sigh. "Explain the Magic. Where did that come from?"

"In the same days, other Magic-users sought the laws which govern the universe."

"You know these laws?"

"They are not so much laws as you understand law, Lord King. They are principles, ways of understanding how the universe works. For example, although we experience time and space as two very different things, they are actually one. There is a—a place, so to speak, where space and time blur, and the boundaries which we perceive between them do not exist. So it is with the stuff of this world and energy. There is a place where these two merge, where it is possible to alter the physical world through the energy of the human will."

"This is the Magic."

"Yes. It is the most dangerous Magic of all. Just as there were repercussions for such lesser things as when the codes within our bodies were altered, there are consequences each time the greater Magic is used. And no one has ever discovered a way to predict or to control them."

The light flickered across his face, and his eyes were in the shadow. He had not seemed to hear her last words. "So how did this bring about the end? How does this work?"

"The Magic is a series of mathematical formulas and equations."

"So that's what the priest meant when she said that their scripture teaches them what to watch for? That the beast had a number?"

"Yes, Lord King, numbers, but it is not enough to simply read the equations. One must understand the formulas. The power to work the Magic is generated by the energy of comprehension."

"And you do?"

"Anyone could with enough study, Lord King. The problem is that this is dangerous beyond all understanding. When the human will interferes in the patterns of the universe, the reactions are directly proportionate to the degree of interference with the inherent order. And the order, or the pattern, has never been discernible, let alone comprehensible."

He pursed his lips and the line between his eyebrows deepened.

"It is possible," she cast about for an example, "to extinguish a candle using the equations and the force of the energy generated by my brain. One can disperse the oxygen needed by the flame to the point where the candle can no longer continue to burn. It is possible that you would not notice such an interference, because in the normal course of events, the candle would go out by itself. But to start that same candle to burning is another matter. And I cannot tell what the consequences of that seemingly minor event would be."

"But the Magic-users—did they not seek to understand?"

"By the time they realized that what was happening all around them was a direct result of their experiments, it was too late. Old Meriga was a land of plenty, but in the wake of the disasters caused by the Magic, there were simply not enough resources. Society just—fell apart." She spread her hands and shrugged.

Again, she heard him sigh. "What kinds of disasters?"

"Great waves swept off the oceans and flooded the lands. The waters rose and covered places where many men dwelled. There were earthshakes, even in places where there had never been earthshakes. Mountains opened and liquid fire ran down the sides. Whole parts of the country disappeared. Countless millions died. Not just in Meriga. All over the world."

"And so the Persecutions began?"

"All those who possessed any knowledge of mathematics or the sciences were killed, until even the priests realized that not all the uses of numbers could be eliminated entirely. But look around you, Lord King. I cannot blame the people who were forced to live in the aftermath of the destruction if they don't trust anything that even appears to be the Magic."

He got to his feet, and prowled like a caged beast. "Tell me again what will happen when I leave."

"You will leave someone here, someone you trust very much—"

"You don't know who?"

"No. There are at least two possibilities; you have yet to choose. You will take an old highway which winds along a gorge, and as you cross a bridge you will be attacked. You will lose something very precious to you—"

"You don't know what?"

"No—it's not a person—some possession that you value greatly, and you will be wounded—in the neck."

"Where?"

"Here." She indicated a place on her throat.

"Wait here." With that same restless grace, he opened the door and called "Phineas!"

"I'm here, Lord King."

"Have the scouts returned?"

"Indeed, Lord King, I've been reading their reports just now."

"Give it to me." He shut the door, unrolled the scroll and held it to the light. "There's no sign of the Harleyriders. It would be unusual for them to go that far north so late in the year." He rolled up the scroll slowly. She felt a cold chill at his unwavering gaze. He looked as if he were trying to make up his mind. "We shall see, lady, if you speak the truth." He held out his hand and she rose. His grasp was hot around her cold fingers, and his nearness made her heart beat in a slow, throbbing rhythm which unnerved her.

"If I am correct?"

"Then I will receive your pledge of allegiance when we return to Ahga. But if you are wrong—"

She looked up at him with chin high and shoulders proud.

"If you are wrong," he repeated, "I shall hand you over to the Bishop of Ahga and allow her to do with you whatever she pleases."

Chapter Four

*T*he following day, Phineas was conferring with the Captain of the castle guard when the summons came from the King. The sun was close to its zenith, the men-at-arms suitably cowed by the sight of the King's men at their morning drills, which Phineas had ordered in the face of the rampant lack of discipline. In the cold air, the ring of the weapons echoed through the dirty wards, and gradually, the Senator's men-at-arms joined in. As though galvanized by the example, the Steward emerged from whatever dim nook he frequented and set the stablehands to cleaning up the wards. Phineas noted the renewed activity without comment.

"Where will I find the King?" he asked the serving boy, who stared in fascination at the maneuvers of the soldiers.

"He's gone to the top of the tower, I think, sir. You'll find him if you take the stairs off the hall on the right and continue up."

He patted the boy on the shoulder, as he spoke to the Captain of the guard. "I think we'll be able to send you a master engineer from Ahga before the winter. I'll mention it to the King now, Captain. We'll talk again later."

"As you say, Captain." The grizzled commander managed a smart salute.

Satisfied, Phineas climbed to the top of the high tower. The sun was almost warm, but on the height, the wind whistled around the smooth planed walls. He found Abelard looking out over the battlements, his bright hair whipping around his face like a mane, his cloak held fast to his throat, the rigid lines of his body revealed as the wind molded the garment against him. His face was grim as he stared out over the land, watching the people bringing in the harvest.

"Lord King?"

"If only I could make them see all this, Phineas." The King spoke without turning.

"See what, Lord King?" He joined Abelard at the wall.

"This land—all this—what great things we might accomplish, if only we could convince men like Eldred of Missiluse to stop their endless squabbles and give me their absolute allegiance." One hand swept out from under the cloak.

Phineas followed the motion of the King's hand to the horizon, where the dark purple mountains loomed against the cloudless sky. The trees blazed crimson and saffron and flame, and in the fields, variegated rows of green and brown and pale buff were punctuated by the peasants dressed in bright blues and reds. He smiled. "I've spent this morning with the Captain of the guard. He's well-meaning, but getting old. We'd do well to leave Everic here to oversee the defenses."

Abelard nodded without looking away. He poked at a pile of rubble with the toe of one boot. "See how quickly it happens? This estate verges on chaos. The Harleyriders invade from the south and the west, the Mutens harry the eastern borders. And Eldred waits. I know he does."

"What will you do?"

"I've spent the morning with Miles. I'll be surprised if he survives to the Convening—he has asked me to take his heir back to Ahga and have him recognized by the Congress."

"Will you?"

"Have I a choice? You know at the least it's bound to raise the issue of my own heir with the Congress—and my mother. But, I am sworn to do as he asks, and so I must." He turned away from the battlements. "I want you to send a scout east."

"As you say, Lord King."

Abelard laughed. "Come, don't give me that obsequious rot. Ask me what for."

"I presumed you'd tell me. I can't send out a scout without telling him what to look for."

Abelard laughed louder. "I want information about the woman. She claims her family name is Farhallen—that their holding was destroyed a year ago in a Muten raid. It was on the lower slopes of the Pulatchian Mountains near the sea in Fillavenya. I want to know if she's telling the truth, and I want to know everything about the family."

"You're bringing her back to Ahga?"

"Don't look so sour, Phineas. You didn't expect me to send her back to the village, did you?"

Phineas sighed. He had not been surprised last night when Abelard had emerged from the audience room, calling for a room to be made ready for the woman and a servant to see to her needs. By that time, luckily, the priest and the Mayher had been ushered into chambers of their own, so they did not hear the King's loud proclamations of the woman's innocence. He was only surprised that she was not to share the King's bed. "Abelard, I'm only concerned—"

"Religion is for women and the common folk. You betray your origins. I've never heard you sound like a superstitious peasant before."

Phineas shrugged. "It's unlike you to underestimate power—especially, knowing your mother, a woman's power. If the Bishop of Ahga catches wind of this, and the women of the city spread the word, it is quite possible that our men will not fight. You might even open yourself for an attempt on your throne. There are even Senadors like Missiluse who would try to rally the Congress against you."

Abelard frowned. "There's no reason why the Bishop should know."

"Perhaps not. How will you explain the lady's presence?"

"Her story is a plausible one."

"Granted. Abelard, I don't mean to question your judgment. I'm only concerned—"

"As well you should be. About other matters. Do you think Eldred's allied with the Harleys?"

"It's beginning to look that way. This castle alone is worth a war, not to mention the valleys it protects."

"Your recommendation?"

"At the very least, we should leave Everic here to oversee the garrison, and we should send out reinforcements from Ahga. I'd want them settled here before winter. And I promised them a master engineer, as well. The walls are not in bad repair, but the outer defenses need shoring up. If Eldred has allied with the Harleys, I think we should be prepared for an attack once the weather breaks in the spring."

"You know, arming this garrison with our own troops will not make me terribly popular with some of the lords."

Phineas shrugged again. "Perhaps not. But it should tell us who to trust, and who to watch."

"Eldred or some of the other malcontents in the Congress may use this as an excuse to try to impose some limit on the powers of the throne."

"But if we do nothing, you may as well parcel out the estate at the next Convening."

Abelard smiled and clapped a hand on Phineas's shoulder. "You know, I was thinking of leaving you here. But I think I'll need you more at this Convening than ever."

"I'm at your service, Lord King."

"Even if I consort with a witch?"

"As long as I don't have to consort with her." Phineas returned the King's grin.

"Come. I want to get a look at the defenses myself. I wouldn't trust Missiluse to forget the Convening, if he thought the Ford was ripe for the picking."

They left three days later as a gray dawn broke over the distant hills. The Senador was failing quickly. Phineas did not doubt that the boy who rode with them would soon be confirmed as the new Senador. Young Miles seemed likely enough, he thought, though a little more delicately made than other boys, his dark curling hair as lustrous as a girl's. He rode a beautiful black mare with a white star on her forehead, and his clothes were carefully embellished with fine stitchwork. The only betrayal of his feelings came when they crossed the drawbridge and he did not look back when he heard his mother call his name one last time. Phineas wondered what the King's sons would think of him.

Nydia Farhallen sat upon the mediocre gelding assigned to her with practiced ease. She wore traveling clothes of serviceable gray, and her hair was bound up, as was seemly, in a white coif. Her expression was aloof, although Phineas had the feeling that her eyes, so dark their depths were purple, missed nothing. He could not deny that her beauty intrigued him, for his flesh had responded to her from the moment he had ripped the shroud off her face.

He had sent the scout east two days before, but Phineas fully expected that her story would bear the scrutiny. He had no doubt she was of noble birth.

It was not her beauty, though that certainly set her apart from more ordinary-looking women, nor even the easy grace that marked her movements, which betrayed her origins to Phineas. It was instead some more subtle quality, which she shared with Abelard. Phineas watched her as the company settled into a brisk pace on the highway leading out of Ithan, trying to define what that quality was.

It could not be characterized as imperiousness, for even Abelard was very seldom imperious. It was more a quality of—Phineas searched for the right word. Entitlement, he decided. When she spoke—to a waiting woman, a groom, even to him—it was with a certainty that her words would be listened to, her request obeyed. Abelard had that same assurance. He knew that he himself had it, too, but Phineas recognized that his was acquired. Or perhaps earned was the better word.

His eyes fell on the King. Abelard had been eager to leave. He hoped to ride north from Ahga for one more hunt before the Convening of the Congress began on the first of Vember. After that, it would be time for the Court of Appeals, and by then the weather would be too bad to permit him to hunt, even if he might have the leisure time to do it. Phineas looked from

the King to Nydia and back. Abelard made no secret of his desire for the woman. Physically, they complemented each other.
Yet Phineas felt an inexplicable twinge of apprehension every
time he looked at her, as though, like a rose, her beauty might
conceal a thorn. He wondered if he would be able to protect
his King from whatever the future held.

Less than three hours from the keep, on a narrow stretch of
broken highway where an old bridge crossed the bed of an ancient river, a long keening wail broke out from the rocky over-
hangs. The men reined in, drawing together in tight circles,
staring upward, craning their necks to see where the sound
originated. The cry was taken up until the whole area echoed.
"Harleyriders!" Phineas shouted, drawing his broadsword.
"Company, draw arms!"

The words were scarcely out of his mouth when, with
blood—chilling whoops, the attackers swept down the steep
sides of the gorge on their short-legged, hairy horses. The
cries were deafening. "The woman—" Phineas shouted,
"Emri, Bilyim, see to the woman—guard the boy!" A
broadsword with a five-foot blade fell by his side. Wheeling
his horse, Phineas raised his sword and smashed it down on a
Harleyrider's neck. As the reins slackened, the pony reared.
He gave the animal a flatbladed blow to the rump, and it
screamed and took off out of the melee, the headless rider beginning to slump off to the side.

He felt a sudden sting across his back. He turned in the saddle and swung at the foe behind him. Even in the unseasonable
cold, the Rider wore little but black leather breeches and a fur-
lined vest. The outlaw blocked his blade, gave Phineas an ugly
gap-toothed smile, and swung again. The force of the blow
shuddered down his arm. With deadly accuracy, Phineas slid
the edge of his sword down the length of his opponent's
weapon. He smelled the rank, greasy odor of the Harley's unwashed body. In one fast motion, he pierced his throat. The
thick silver chains around the outlaw's neck and across his
chest shivered and clanged as he crumpled.

Horses screamed war cries of their own, sidestepping skittishly as the smell of blood reached their nostrils, while all around Phineas, metal rang against metal as his soldiers and the Riders fought on the narrow roadbed. Out of the corner of his eye, he saw the King go down. Spurring his horse forward, Phineas rushed to his side in time to deliver a death blow to the rider who raised his ax over Abelard. As the rider fell, the ax dealt the King's stallion a final blow across the throat.

Abelard swung his broadsword over his head. A huge Harleyrider stepped in front of him, his face contorted with rage beneath his long braided beard. The King bellowed a curse, and with one mighty stroke, another head rolled down the embankment.

Phineas's darting eyes fell on the boy. His guard was lying face down in the mire, and Miles beat about himself with a silver short sword, more ornament than weapon. His mare, disturbed by the sounds and smells of battle, pranced forward and back, and the boy tugged desperately at the reins.

Phineas picked up a bow and fitted an arrow to the string, wincing at the sting of pain in his back as he drew his arm. He let the arrow fly. It landed with a thunk in the back of one of the Riders as he was about to drag the boy off his saddle. Phineas drew another arrow, and this time another Rider fell howling, the steel tip embedded in his forehead. The boy slumped in his saddle, his face a sickly gray.

His attention was caught by a lumpy figure wrapped in rags which slid off the back of one of the riderless ponies. It staggered out of the melee to the side of the road, where it crouched beneath a rocky overhang.

Phineas had time to give it no more than a suspicious glance before another outlaw bore down on him, whirling a spiked ball at the end of a thick steel chain.

The spikes bit into the leather vambrace on his forearm, and almost by reflex, Phineas drew his dagger in his left hand. He stabbed upward, scoring the outlaw's thigh.

The Harley screamed a curse and reined his pony so abruptly the animal reared up. With the outlaw's attention diverted, Phineas hurled the dagger. The blade disappeared up to the hilt into the outlaw's side. With a look of surprise and a grunt, the Harley fell to the ground in a crumpled heap.

Phineas crouched once more in a fighting stance, circling, until he realized that all the Harleyriders lay either dead or dying, or had ridden off up the steep embankment. With short commands, Phineas ordered the bodies thrown over the bridge to tumble down the steep sides of the rocky gorge, where the carrion birds would pick their bones clean. The two dead soldiers of the King's Guard were slung across their mounts. As he wiped his blade on a patch of weeds growing out of the road, he heard Abelard say: "Phineas," and straightened as the King approached.

"Lord King."

"The scouts saw no sign of this?"

"None that they reported to me, Lord King."

Abelard gave a brief nod. Out of the corner of his eye, Phineas saw the rag-wrapped figure dart from its hiding place beneath the ledge and scramble across the dusty road to Nydia, where she sat pale but composed on her horse.

"You, there!" he cried, and one of the guards, alerted by the shout, collared the ragged form and shook it.

Its hood fell away from its face, and it raised its terracotta face to the soldier who held it. "Agh!" The man fell back with a grimace of disgust. "It's a Muten, Captain!"

Phineas exchanged a shocked glance with Abelard. As the two men hurried over, the squat figure threw back the cloak to reveal more fully its deviant form. From the shoulders of his powerful primary arms, a pair of secondary arms dangled limply, the little appendages no larger than an infant's. The eyes were dark in a face scarred with tribal markings, and from the center of his forehead, a third eye stared, fixed and sightless.

Phineas suppressed a shudder, and Nydia drew in the reins of her mount. The animal reacted by backing up several paces.

Abelard returned the Muten's stare. "What are you doing here, Muten?"

The Muten bobbed its head in a queer gesture of submission. "No harm, Great Lord, no harm." The accent was harsh and guttural, his speech barely recognizable. "Found me up the hills, outlaws did—looking for the lady, I was."

Abelard looked from the Muten up at Nydia, whose face had drained of color. "And what does this lady mean to you, Muten?"

"Bring her gift of the Children."

"What gift? Why?"

The Muten ducked his head again and the tiny secondary arms twitched reflexively. "Reparation, it is. Great wrong done—never be right. What we can, we offer."

Abelard frowned suspiciously and Phineas shifted from foot to foot. Nydia looked stricken. "Give it to me." The King held out his hand.

From the depths of its garment, the Muten withdrew a hide-wrapped parcel bound with thinly stretched gut. "Only for lady, it is. Only lady must it have."

Silently, Abelard passed the parcel up to Nydia, who shook her head and refused to take it.

The Muten stepped forward and would have touched her, if the guard had not restrained him. "Bid you take, lady, bid you forgive, bid you forget."

Abelard nodded at Nydia. "Shall I open it, lady?"

Silently, she nodded.

The King unwound the thin strips of gut and tore away the soft hide covering. A leaf lay revealed, brown and withered at the edges, its center speckled yellow and green. "What's this mean?" He looked at the Muten. "What manner of gift is this?"

"Great wrong done, nothing ever enough to make it right. All we could do, we have done."

Nydia was trembling violently.

The Muten looked up at her, sorrow and contrition evident to Phineas in all the lines of its misshapen face. "By Heaven's axletree, lady, accept—" He would have touched her but his guard yanked him out of reach.

"Stay back from the lady," the guard growled.

Phineas shot the guard a look which silenced him. There was more here than he understood, and nothing would be learned by mistreating the miserable creature.

Nydia stretched out her hand. Her hand shook violently as her fingers closed around the leaf. She held it for a moment, then crushed it. She let the pieces fall through her fingers like dust. Her expression reminded Phineas of the faces of women who had lost their children, for a grief beyond bearing was etched in the lines of her face, and her voice when she spoke was as cold as the wind and as hard as the stones on the road. "I want nothing from your people. Never."

"Shall I send it on its way, Lord King?" asked the guard.

"What else do you want with us?" said the King.

The Muten shook its heavy head and Phineas felt an unexpected pity for the ugly thing and the pathetic offering Nydia had so thoroughly rebuffed. "No more to do, Great Lord. Home to return, to the hills, to the rocks."

The King gave a short jerk of his head at the guard, and with a curse, the guard dragged the Muten to the open road. He thrust it away with a loud, "On your way, filthy dog."

Abelard extended his hand to Nydia, and swung her out of the saddle. He gestured to her to accompany him. Together, they walked over to Abelard's fallen horse.

"You said I would lose something very precious to me, lady," he said. "I see you spoke the truth. I wish I had taken your warning more seriously."

"I am sorry, Lord King." Her voice was a distant whisper.

Abelard beckoned to Phineas. "Tell us, lady. Is the way to Ahga clear?"

She threw back her head a little and stared off into the distance just beyond them. "The way is clear."

"And the Harleyriders?"

"I don't see them again."

The King touched a slight wound at his throat, no more than a nick, where a thin trickle of blood ran down. He looked at the smear on his fingers and abruptly turned on his heel.

She looked up at Phineas, and the hair on his neck rose. A

chill he did not understand went down his back. He squared
his shoulders, trying to dismiss his reaction. "Don't be dis-
tressed, lady. That horse he raised from a foal and trained it
himself, in the last years before he was the King. It is not
likely he will be able to train another so, and—"

She shrugged. "It was his choice."

He recognized some sadness about her, and within him, the
instinct to protect warred with a strong urge to flee. "Lady, for
your own sake, you should know he is a good man, but he is
King first, in everything he does. He has one goal—to preserve the kingdom, and strengthen the Union. It is all he lives
for."

"And you?" Her eyes were inscrutable. "What do you live
your life for, Lord Phineas?"

"I am not a lord, lady. My rank is Captain."

"But you will be." She turned away with a puckered frown,
while a sense of foreboding so strong it was nearly nausea
wrapped itself like a snake around Phineas's gut. He put a
hand on her arm.

"I live my life for my King, lady."

"Yes, Captain Phineas. I see that you do." Without another
word, she walked back to her mount.

Phineas fell into a troubled daze until Abelard's voice interrupted his thoughts. "Come, Phineas, you've been wounded.
We'll stop at the garrison at Rivenedge. I meant to ride
through, but we'll stay there the night. Can you ride?"

Phineas ignored the question. He grasped at the King's arm.
"Abelard. What kind of woman is that?" he hissed.

Abelard gave him a distant smile. "She shall be very useful
to me, I think."

"What about all that with the Muten?" His back was beginning to throb.

Abelard looked at him with sudden concern. "Turn around,
man. Get your tunic off—Jerald, bring that kit over here."

Phineas winced as he pulled the blood-soaked tunic off his
back. The cutting wind was at least as painful as the stuff

Abelard daubed over the wound. "How bad is it?" the Captain asked between teeth clenched from both cold and pain.

"You'll have another scar to add to your collection." The King wound linen strips around the wound, then helped Phineas struggle back into the tunic.

Phineas wrapped his cloak over his shoulder and winced again as he sheathed his sword. "Abelard." His tone was uncharacteristically imperative. "Who is this woman? What is she?"

The King's eyes were steady. "Wait until we reach Ahga, old friend. I'll explain it to you then." He waved the boy over. "Miles, Captain Phineas needs a mount. Can you share until we reach Rivenedge?"

The boy's face was white, his lips blanched pale and bluish. "As you say, Lord King."

As he swung up behind Miles into the saddle, Phineas felt the tension in the young back and shoulders. "This your first battle, young lord?"

"Yes, Captain." His teeth were clenched.

"You did well. Your father would have been proud." Miles looked up with tears welling in his eyes. Phineas gave him a brief smile and tugged at the reins, as though he did not notice. With a soft sigh, the boy settled back against his chest, as they made their careful way to the garrison at Rivenedge.

Chapter Five

❧

*N*ydia shrank against an arching pillar of smooth white marble and watched, overwhelmed by the choreographed chaos around her. The great hall of Ahga Castle, seat of the Ridenau Kings and their central domain for more than five hundred years, held at least two or three hundred people. She had never seen so many beneath one roof in her life. The discordant notes of the musicians on the mezzanine above as they tuned their instruments in preparation for the night's entertainment filtered through the low roar of the crowd. All around her, voices and laughter surged up the high walls. Here and there, a future overlaid itself upon another's face, creating an indecipherable tangle with the present.

Servers hurried past, balancing platters on deceptively precarious hands, while the great company swept through the room. Men, most in the drab tunics of soldier's garb, and women, in long wool dresses dyed bright shades of yellow and green and blue, called greetings as they sought places at the long wooden tables. As the crowd parted, Nydia caught glimpses of the more expensive reds and purples, edged with flashes of lace and embroidered in contrasting designs of black and gold and silver thread.

Children darted among the throng, and were treated indulgently as usual by all—even those who sought to keep them in tow. Nydia watched as one small, wiry boy tumbled into a woman bearing a basket of long loaves of bread. Along with a mild scolding, he received half a loaf of the fragrant bread, which still steamed from the ovens.

Nydia recognized no one, not even Lady Mara, the First Lady of the castle, who had been kind but preoccupied at their meeting that morning. Nydia had been taken aback by the woman's appearance. Most of the First Ladies of noble houses were not only chatelaines but wives or consorts of the lord of the holding, as well. But Mara was a plump, elderly woman, older than Abelard's mother.

She had found a room for Nydia in one of the high towers, sent her hot water and a change of clothes, and had ordered a tailor to attend her. But beyond that, except for the appreciative glances cast by the men, she was ignored by all. Her head ached a little with the strain of jumbled patterns swimming before her. She tried to keep her eyes firmly fixed on the ancient architecture which dated from before the Armageddon. Its original use was impossible to imagine, yet Nydia knew enough about Old Meriga to surmise that it had not been built as a feasting hall. In the intervening centuries, the hall had been modified in accordance with the demands of the present. The old-style windows, with their arching sweeps of smooth glass, still soared almost to the roof. Here and there, rippled panes bore silent witness to repairs done by a less precise age. High hearths, large enough for a man to stand, had been set at intervals into the walls. The logs which fueled the roaring fires were the size of young trees.

Above her, hangings of white and scarlet silk billowed in the currents and the updrafts. At the farthest end, a raised dais draped in the King's colors of white and blue was placed perpendicular to the rest of the tables. On the wall behind the table, centered over the King's place in the middle, the gold crest of the Ridenau Kings, an eagle holding a banner in its beak, reflected the lights of the hundred torches. Nydia's eye was caught by the writing on the banner, and as the crowd jostled past her, she squinted at the faded letters.

"Faith shall finish what hope begins," said a voice in her ear. Nydia turned to see a girl in her middle teens smiling at her. "That's what the eagle says. Or did, once upon a time. It's supposed to inspire us Ridenaus when faced with defeat."

Relieved to have someone to focus on, Nydia cocked her head. "Us Ridenaus?"

"I'm Tavia," said the girl, extending her hand. "You're the lady Dad brought in with him this morning."

Nydia took the offered hand, and smiled at the frank and friendly face before her. "How did you know me in all this crowd?"

"Oh, it's easy to spot the ones who aren't used to this. Nobody is at first. Some of the Senators look as though they'd like to hack a path through the throng. Come on, let's find a place to sit." She started forward, took two steps and stumbled backward, as if pulled. "Jessie, is that you?" Behind her skirts, a child of four or five peered shyly. "There you are!" Tavia held out her arms and the child jumped into them, clasping her legs around the older girl's waist. "This is my little sister, Jesselyn. She's four. Say hello to the lady, Jess. Dad's brought her here to live with us."

A pang made Nydia lower her eyes as the dark-haired child nestled in her sister's arms. "Hello, Jesselyn," she said softly. She reached out hesitantly to caress the dark curls, which fell almost to the child's waist.

"Where's your ribbon, Jessie?" Tavia started forward once more.

"Lost it," was the soft response.

"Oh, never mind. You can sit with me if you promise not to spill. Come, lady. If you wait until the crowd thins out, there'll be nothing left but bones."

Nydia followed Tavia across the wide floor as she skillfully negotiated the throng. A ringing cheer went up as they found seats at one of the long tables near the dais. "That's Dad," said Tavia. "Now they'll bring out the meat. Here, this is good. We can watch everything from here."

Nydia's attention turned to the dais, where Abelard Ridenau, newly shaved, his bright hair still damp from a bath and garbed in a green tunic richly embellished with black stitchwork, advanced to his place. He was followed by Phineas, several of the Senators and their wives or consorts. Nydia recognized young Miles of Ithan Ford, and behind Miles, the King's mother, the Lady Agara, whom she had briefly met that morning on their arrival.

Nydia watched as the lady took the place of honor beside her son. She, too, was tall and big boned, but where Abelard's build was muscular, his mother was thin to the point of being skeletal. His face, with its chiseled bones, bore something of her stamp, yet her cheeks were gaunt, and the spare flesh sagged under her eyes. Her mouth was thin-lipped and her nose jutted. Her hair, probably once the same bright blond as her son's, was the color of the steel in his broadsword. Nydia flinched as the cold, penetrating eyes scanned the assembly. A brief look into the woman's future had disturbed her when they met: Nydia had clearly seen the violent argument which erupted between mother and son less than an hour after their arrival.

When the King was seated, Tavia pulled Nydia down beside her on the bench. As the rest of the company took their seats, Tavia waved as her father's gaze swept over the room. The King gave his daughter a broad smile and raised one brow in acknowledgement as he recognized Nydia. "Wave, Jessie," cried Tavia. "Wave to Dada!"

On the haven of her sister's lap, Jesselyn bounced and waved, nearly causing a server to spill the contents of his tray in the lap of a neighboring lady. "Ooh, careful, Jessie! Forgive me, lady, she's not usually this excited."

Nydia smiled sadly. "I'm used to children."

Tavia pressed a kiss on the little girl's head, and helped herself from a platter heaped with meat and vegetables which the server placed on the table in front of them. "This looks good. Take what you want, lady. There's enough to feed the whole city. Have you a child?"

"I did." Nydia averted her face.

"Oh. Oh, I'm sorry—I did not mean—"

Nydia sighed. "It's all right. You could not have known."

"Don't mind me and my questions. You needn't answer if you don't want. Haggy Aggie says I talk too much, and maybe

I do, but at least I don't spy on people—" She broke off as Jesselyn reached for a piece of bread.

"Haggy Aggie?"

Tavia looked sheepish. "I shouldn't call her that. I mean my grandmother, Lady Agara, up there next to Dad. But she does spy. And she's got plenty of others to do it for her. Look, see that woman over there—down a bit, eating that ear of corn? She's in charge of the laundry. She'll make sure Grandmother knows you're with child before you do—and anything else Grandmother wants to know about you. Believe me, if you've got any kind of a secret at all, you won't keep it from those two for long."

Nydia chewed and swallowed carefully. "Oh?" A finger of fear traced a cold path down her spine.

"They'll know everything about you in a week. And that's if you're discreet."

Nydia looked up at the dais, where Agara tapped Abelard's arm with a proprietary air. At this distance, it was difficult to tell whether he was bored or deferential.

"You're wise to watch her, lady. Everyone does. That's why Dad can't have our mothers here."

"What do you mean? Whose mothers?"

"Us children. Jessy's mother lives down in the city. My mother died when I was born. The rest—well, they were all serving maids or farm girls from the country, but there's no one who could tolerate life here with Haggy Aggie. Dad's got ten of us, so far, and the only ones whose mother wasn't a commoner are—see those two little boys over there? That's Aman and Alex. They're the youngest and Grandmother dotes on them. They're her pets. She wants Dad to name one of them as his heir. But he won't—only the son of his Queen, he says; and so when Rabica died, that was the end of that. So now Dad's looking for a new candidate—" She broke off and gave Nydia a speculative look.

Nydia laughed uneasily. "Oh, no, you mustn't think—I'd give your father no political advantages at all." She peered over and around the heads of the company to see the two small, delicate boys each with a nurse, dark hair close cropped on identical heads.

Tavia blushed. "Well, you are awfully pretty, and Dad wouldn't marry an ugly woman—"

Nydia offered Jesselyn a choice morsel. "He brought me here because I have no other home. The Mutens killed my family and your father was kind—"

"Mutens?" Tavia shuddered. "Those horrible things with their three eyes and four arms—" She wrapped her arms around Jesselyn. "No wonder Dad brought you here."

"I had nowhere else to go."

As Jesselyn struggled in her sister's embrace, a stocky youth dressed in the uniform of the King's Guard leaned over Tavia's shoulder and planted a quick kiss on her cheek. "Oh!" she cried, startled. "Who—oh, Drevor, it's you." A pink blush stained the girl's cheeks.

He was about seventeen or eighteen, Nydia thought, his arms and chest already heavily muscled. The slight bow in his legs bore testimony to a life spent mostly in the saddle. He tweaked one of Jesselyn's curls and paused as his eyes fell on Nydia. Despite his air of assurance, a faint blush tinged his smooth cheeks when she met his gaze in greeting. "Will I see you later?" he asked Tavia, although his eyes did not leave Nydia's face.

"Well, that depends."

"On what?" He put his hands on his hips.

"Are you eating with us, or did you just come to watch?"

"I have duty in a few minutes, but—oh, move over. Careful, little one, don't spill. Your biggest brother, Brand, won't accept even you as an excuse."

"Drevor, this is the Lady Nydia—"

"Farhallen." Nydia supplied when Tavia hesitated.

"Welcome to Ahga, lady. I hope your stay is pleasant."

Nydia managed to smile. There was a certain courtliness about the boy which reminded her of Phineas. If he was not nobly born, he was at least well schooled. "I hope so, too, sir. I hope to make Ahga my home."

"Oh, Drevor's not a 'sir,' are you? He serves under my brother Brand in the King's Guard, so he's only Drevor." Tavia poked him in the ribs.

Nydia glanced at the girl. Tavia's eyes were bright and her cheeks pinker than they had been, and just over her shoulder, Nydia caught a glimpse of two bodies, naked and entwined, on shadowed sheets. "Oh," she said softly, "I think he'll be more than that, tonight."

Tavia started and her blush deepened. "Well. Maybe."

Drevor touched her arm. "Will I see you later? After watch?"

"You mean you'd wake me?"

"Tavia, please, I've got to go. Say yes."

The girl tossed her curls. "I'll say—perhaps."

He pressed a kiss on her hand. "I'll come to you after watch." He rose and bowed to Nydia. "I've very glad to know you, lady. I am at your service, if you require anything."

"Is that anything at all, Drevor?" asked Tavia.

The tips of his ears reddened, and he opened his mouth. Abruptly, without speaking, he spun on his heel and strode away.

"You shouldn't tease him so," said Nydia.

"Oh, I know. He's one of Brand's friends, and I've known him forever. Believe me, if you hadn't been here, he would have teased me worse."

"Tell me about the rest of your brothers and sisters. How many did you say there are?"

Tavia smiled. "Nine, but not all of them are here. Everard lives across the North Sea with his mother. Her family's practically gone Muten. But there's Brand, he's the oldest—he's eighteen, and a lieutenant in the King's Guard. Not *the* Lieutenant, of course, not yet, but Dad's very pleased with him. I expect he'll be a general someday. His mother was one of Haggy Aggie's own serving women. I can imagine the trouble that caused. And then there's Vere—he's the odd one. He's not much interested in fighting and weapons like the other men. He likes books, and poking around underneath the castle. You probably won't see much of him, either."

"You have books here?"

"Lots. Maybe twenty. They're in Dad's study, when Vere isn't dragging them out. And then there's me. I'm sixteen and Dad's negotiating for a husband for me. And then—see those two over there, near the dais? That's my sister, Morgent and my brother Philip. They're both thirteen."

Nydia blinked in disbelief. It seemed as though the King had got a child on every woman he'd ever lain with. "Another set of twins?"

Tavia shrugged and blushed a little. "Dad had a busy year."

"He's taken no vows with any woman?"

"The only one he nearly swore vows with was Rabica. The contracts were all signed; it was only the formal marriage that had yet to take place. If she'd waited to die until after that, one of the twins would have been the heir."

"And that's what your grandmother wants?"

"Rabica was the daughter of one of Grandmother's cousins. It's not really the politics that interests Haggy Aggie. It's blood."

"How old are the twins?"

"Three. But you see, Dad's afraid that if he names an heir, and then changes it, there'll be a civil war after he dies. Such things have happened in the Estates. He hears cases like that all the time in the Court of Appeals. Here, Jessie, do watch out."

Nydia poked her fork into the food on her plate. She glanced again up at the dais, where Agara attacked her food with a heartier appetite than one might expect in someone so gaunt. So thin, so hungry. Nydia shivered in spite of the heat from the fire behind her.

Phineas shifted uncomfortably in his chair. The muscles across his upper back throbbed; the wound had been deeper than he had first realized. Certain movements, especially sudden ones, meant agony. It was not possible to sleep on his back, and the last nights had been fitful. His eyes ranged around the room, seeking distraction. From his place at Abelard's left, he could see the entire company. He longed to prop his heavy head on his hand. On the mezzanine above, the musicians had begun to play a soothing tune, which, although intended to aid digestion, only served to lull him further. The wine was making his sleepy, he realized, as his sleeve nearly caught in a pitcher of sauce.

"Be careful, Captain Phineas." The lady seated next to him wore a cloying perfume which aggravated the dull ache in his head.

He suppressed the urge to ignore her. Floy Wilimsin, wife of one of Abelard's most loyal supporters in the Congress, could not be insulted. He gave her what he hoped was his most polished smile. "Forgive me, lady. The hour seems late."

"I understand, Captain. You only just arrived this morning. Whenever my husband returns from a journey such as yours, he's so tired a feast such as this would be wasted. He'd be snoring into his plate before the second course was even served. And you—you were wounded, weren't you?"

He shrugged. "Nothing which will not heal."

"Yet it makes a long time at feasting seem longer."

He smiled at the sympathy, in spite of himself. Her eyes were wide and very dark, her skin a rich burnished bronze. Her gown of saffron silk was cut low, and a large topaz nestled in the deep cleft of her breasts. He met her eyes and recognized an invitation. He glanced past her at the Senador, Finlay of Norda Coda.

Without thinking, he leaned back. As the wound touched the chair, he winced, and gasped involuntarily. Abelard turned. "Are you all right?"

He gave the lady a sheepish shrug and spoke softly to the King. "So much for my skill on the field of love."

Abelard looked over his shoulder at Floy, who was leaning on her husband's arm. "Look all you please, but don't touch. Finlay grows more jealous every year."

Phineas picked up his goblet and motioned to the waiting boy behind the King's chair to fill it.

"I don't understand the man." Abelard held out his own goblet. "He has his heir. Why not let the woman—?"

"Which is more than you have," interrupted Agara.

Phineas exchanged glances with the King.

"Mother, let's not speak of that tonight. I've made my position clear more than once."

"Look at what happened to your father. Do you imagine you're so invincible the same couldn't happen to you? You think you're going to live forever, but let me tell you this, my boy, it could've just as easily been your neck that Harley sliced as your horse's. And then where would this country be—thanks to your clear position?"

"Mother." Abelard's mouth folded into a tight line. "I don't want my heir to inherit a realm such as I did. I'll make an alliance which will strengthen the throne."

Agara snorted. "You bring home stray women like puppies. Every year, another pops up with one of your children. What Senador would allow his daughter to put up with you?"

"Rabica's father was more than amenable."

"Through Eldred's good offices, don't you forget. That was arranged through my family connections. And the least you could do is name Amanander your heir."

Abelard grimaced at the mention of Eldred's name. He wiped a hand across his mouth, and clenched his fist. "Mother. If I name Amanander, and have another son by my Queen—"

"You'll never have a Queen. You can't even go off for a month without dragging in another one." Agara gestured contemptuously at Nydia.

"I didn't bring her here to bed her."

"And I'll believe that when I see it."

Abelard slammed a fist down on the table and wine splashed out of his goblet, to stain the bleached linen with drops like pale blood. "That's enough."

Agara put a placating hand on her son's sleeve. "I'm only concerned for the sake of your throne. Just as you are."

As Abelard glared at her suspiciously, a bearded man in travel-stained clothes approached the table. Phineas beckoned. The man went down on one knee behind Phineas's chair and whispered. Phineas asked a few low questions, then nodded in dismissal. He touched Abelard's arm as the messenger made his weary way across the hall.

"That's the scout I sent east, Abelard."

"Well?"

"Her story's true, so far as he could determine. Her father was the Senador of Jersy, but the estate is so small as to make the title meaningless. She was the only daughter. Her husband, who died in the raid, was the second son of some petty Mayher in the area. All that's left of the holding are the graves. There's the question of the tribute, of course, which apparently was paid through Fillavenya, and the succession of the title now that the family's gone. I expect you'll want to deal with that at the Convening."

Before Abelard could speak, Agara interrupted: "So who is this woman, Abelard? What are we to do with her?"

"What do you mean, do with her?"

"Can she cook? Can she spin? If you didn't bring her back to bear another brat for you, why did you bring her here?"

"She asked for my protection, Mother. Her family was wiped out—"

"You'll believe anything a fair face tells you."

"She spoke the truth, lady." Phineas leaned over the King. "We have verified her story."

"That still doesn't answer my question. What am I supposed to do with her?"

Abelard looked over the heads of the company to where Nydia sat laughing with Tavia. Jesselyn was seated on Nydia's lap, watching in fascination while the woman carefully peeled an apple in one long, continuous motion. The King beckoned to the boy behind his chair, gave a brief order, and settled back. "Let's ask her, shall we, Mother?"

At the servant's summons, Nydia gently displaced the child,

then curtsied when she stood before the high table. "Lord King. Lady. Captain Phineas."

Phineas picked up his goblet and wet his lips. He noted her gown, which had once been dark blue, now faded to a soft shade almost purple. Most likely, it was a cast-off Mara had found for her. Her white chemise was laced modestly over her bosom, and her hair was pulled up under a bleached linen coif. Although her face was composed, he saw the tension in her shoulders as she straightened. Abelard gave her a lazy smile. "Do you enjoy the feast, lady?"

"I have never seen the like before, Lord King."

"You remember my mother, Lady Agara?"

"Yes, Lord King." She bowed her head in Agara's direction. Agara gave a sniff of derision. Nydia looked up at her quickly, then back at the King, a wary expression on her face.

"My mother is interested in your talents, lady."

Her expression changed to alarm. "My talents?"

"And I told her she'd best ask you herself." The King raised one brow almost imperceptibly.

Nydia glanced over his shoulder. Although her face remained guarded, her stance visibly relaxed. "I can do anything you might require of me, lady." She chose her words carefully. "I—I have some talent as a singer."

Agara sniffed again. "Do you? Boy, go get the lady an instrument."

"You want me to sing now?"

Agara leaned forward with the air of a predator scenting a kill. "Is there a better time to hear a song?"

Nydia looked at the King. His face was bland. She glanced at Phineas, then back at Agara. "As you say, lady. If you have a guitar—I have some skill on that."

The King nodded at the boy, who took off up the steps of the musicians' mezzanine.

Agara clapped her hands at another servant. "You there— bring a stool for the lady. Put it there—right there, so all can hear her sing."

Nydia felt every eye in the room turn in her direction. She

took the guitar the boy handed her. The wood was cool and smooth and polished. She settled on the stool and ran her fingers over the strings. As the notes reverberated over the crowd, the voices around her gradually quieted. She glanced up to see Tavia smiling encouragement.

Nydia spoke directly to the King. "This is a very old song, Lord King, and yet, it might have been written only last year."

Her fingers shook as she found the chords, and then, as the familiar melody came back to her, she relaxed. She drew a deep breath.

"Oh, cruel is the snow that sweeps Glencoe,
  and covers the grave of my lover.
Oh, cruel is the foe that raped Glencoe,
  and murdered the house of my lover.

They came in a blizzard, we offered them heat,
  a roof, o'er their heads, dry shoes for their feet.
We wined them and dined them, they ate of our meat,
  and they slept in the house of my lover."

The crowd murmured appreciation, and Abelard smiled slowly. She sang the ancient lament with a quiet simplicity.

"They came in the night while our men were asleep,
this band of betrayers, through snow soft and deep,
like murdering foxes among helpless sheep,
they butchered the house of my lover."

As she repeated the chorus, men stirred in their seats, reaching for the women by their sides, and their hands tightened unconsciously on the daggers in their belts.

"Some died in their beds at the hand of the foe,
some fled in the night and were lost in the snow,
  some lived to accuse him who struck the first blow,
but gone is the house of my lover.

> *"Oh, cruel is the snow that sweeps Glencoe,*
>   *and covers the grave of my lover.*
> *Oh, cruel is the foe that raped Glencoe,*
>   *and murdered the house of my lover."*

She played the last bars of the song, daring a look at Agara's aloof face. Her mouth was sullen. She did not share in the applause.

Abelard pointedly ignored his mother and leaned forward. "Well sung, lady. Can you give us another?"

Nydia bowed a little in her seat. "If it pleases you, Lord King."

"Your talents please me greatly, lady." His tone was full of meaning. "Sing on, if you will."

An idea came to her. She looked up at him mischievously. "One for you, then, Lord King."

The notes rippled lightly under her hand, and her foot tapped the time. With a daring smile she sang:

> *"Willie's gone to Melville Castle, boots and spurs and all,*
> *To bid the ladies all farewell, before he goes awa'.*
> *Willie's young and blithe and bonny, loved by one and all,*
> *Oh, what will all the ladies do when Willie's gone awa'?"*

Abelard grinned with delight. Her voice was husky and a provocative smile played at the corners of her mouth. Her eyes danced around the hall from man to man.

> *"The first he met was Lady Kate,*
>   *she led him through the hall,*
> *and with a sad and sorry heart,*
>   *she let the tears down fall.*
> *Beside the fire stood Lady Grace,*
>   *said ne'er a word at all,*
> *She hoped that he might steal a kiss before he rode awa'."*

As she launched into the chorus, there were hoots of delight from the company and comments laughingly shouted from all corners to the King.

"Then through the house came Lady Belle,
  who said to one and all:
'Maybe the lad will fancy me, and disappoint you all.'
Then down the stairs came Lady Jean,
  the flower of them all,
'Oh, ladies, trust in Providence,
  and you'll find husbands all.' "

Nydia tossed her head and smiled at the King. Her voice rang out over the crowd, pure and strong and true:

"Then on his horse, he rode awa',
  they gathered through the door.
He gaily waved his bonnet blue, they set up such a roar.
Their cries and tears brought Willie back,
  he's kissed them, one and all:
'Oh ladies, bide til I come home,
  and then I'll wed you all!' "

Agara pursed her lips, folded her arms across her bony chest, and made a sound of disgust. Phineas raised his goblet, grinning despite the tension, while the court roared with laughter. Nydia's eyes locked with the King's.

"Well, Mother," he said, beneath the loud applause, "if you can't think of something to do with her, every man under this roof surely can."

Chapter Six

From the windows of the council room, seven stories above the ground, Phineas watched the white waves crest over the black ruins of the lost city beneath the sea. The incoming tide lapped at the castle walls. Winter had arrived, on this fifteenth day of Tober. Already the glass was fogged with frost in the mornings, and even the noontime sun offered little warmth. Abelard paced beside the long table with the restless strides of something caged. With a curse, he came to stand beside Phineas. "Well, answer!" he demanded.

Phineas watched the waters crash over the foundations of what had once been a tower taller than the towers of Ahga. "My answer must be yes."

"Damn your honor. I want to know what you think."

Phineas faced the King with squared shoulders. "Your mind's made up—and has been since Ithan. What does it matter what I think?" In the cold morning light, Phineas's eyes were like twin shards of flint. "Why do you insist on this pledge bond?"

"I want that woman—"

"Fine. Take the woman. But not here. Send her north—up to the lodge at Minnis."

"Then what use to me will she be?"

The two men stared at each other. Finally, Phineas looked down. "Have you thought about the obligation you take on? You'll be sworn to protect her with your life."

"Is that so different from any other pledge bond?"

"But you've never accepted the pledge of a woman. It's not

the same. What can she possibly give you in return? This special ability of hers—is it worth your life? And this Magic—even she told you it was too dangerous to be used. Abelard, think. You might protect her from the bishops and the priests, and the superstitious crowds. But can you protect her from your mother?"

It was Abelard's turn to lower his eyes and turn away. Phineas pressed on. "Are you so sure you'll be able to do all that you must promise?"

"My mother must not know." Abelard leaned on one of the heavy wooden chairs and frowned at the table. Phineas waited. Then Abelard tapped a fist on the table. "The top of the eastern tower. That's where I'll put her with her books. My mother won't go up there. She's terrified of the height. And the lady's used to being careful—"

"Are you certain of that?"

"If she doesn't want to end on the stake, she'll have to be. Mara'll help me. Summon the girl, Phineas. Let's have this over."

Obediently, Phineas opened the door, gave an order to one of the men at arms, then sat down at the council table. Abelard resumed his pacing. In a few minutes, Nydia entered. She stood with clasped hands and downcast eyes.

Abelard stopped his pacing. He raised his head and Phineas saw his nostrils flare. "Come here." When she stood before him, he said, "Kneel," then motioned to Phineas.

In one fluid motion, she was on her knees. Reluctantly, Phineas got to his feet.

"Do you know the words of the Pledge of Allegiance?" Abelard put his left hand on her shoulder.

She shook her head.

"Repeat them after Phineas, then. Give me your right hand."

When she complied, he nodded at Phineas.

Phineas hesitated. A sudden blast of wind whined around the tower. The windowpanes rattled with a sound like thrown dice.

"Go on, man," barked the King.

He pulled his shoulders straight and gave Abelard one more desperate glance. Abelard ignored him. His eyes were fastened on Nydia. Phineas took a deep breath, which might have been a shudder. "Say after me, lady. I pledge allegiance to the King—of the united Estates of Meriga . . ."

Her soft echo followed. ". . . and to the kingdom for which he stands—one nation, indivisible—"

Abelard's fingers tightened around hers. His blue eyes bore down upon her. She faltered under the hot pressure of the King's hand. Their murmuring voices intertwined, the words binding them together until death, as she swore to lay down her life, to uphold both the kingdom and the King.

Abelard raised her to her feet. "In the presence of this witness, lady, I accept your pledge, and seal the bond between us with this kiss." He drew her to him and touched his mouth to hers. His lips were cool and impassive.

Nydia lowered her eyes and smoothed her hands over her skirt. Phineas moved away from her to stand beside the window. Abelard gestured to a cloth wrapped bundle in the center of the table. "Your books, lady."

She gave a cry of delight and, seizing the bundle, unwrapped the heavy folds carefully. "Thank you, Lord King, thank you!"

"I will see that you have a room in which to keep them."

She touched the crumbling covers reverently, and Abelard looked at Phineas. "Your duties call you, do they not?"

Phineas's face was blank. He roused himself from the window. "As you say, Lord King." With a terse bow, he was gone.

Abelard waited until the door closed softly behind Phineas. Nydia was absorbed in the books. "Lady."

Reluctantly, she looked up.

"Lady, you know the Magic, do you not?"

"I do." Her face was wary, like an animal scenting danger.

"Is it possible that there is some way to predict—"

"I've told you I don't know how—"

"But is it possible?"

She spread her hands in a helpless gesture. "The ancient Magic-users believed anything is possible."

"I want you to try to find it."

"What?" She took a step backward.

"I did not ask you to use the Magic. I asked you to try to find a way to predict what the consequences might be if it were used. Can you do that?"

Nydia shook her head slowly. "I—I don't know. It is true that there is a branch of mathematics which deals with probabilities, but—"

"Will you try?"

She wet her lips. "Lord King, the Magic is not a weapon. It is the manipulation of the fabric of reality—all of reality. The use of it affects everything—even things we can't perceive. There is an interrelation between all things in the universe. The Magic interferes with it—destroys the symmetry, upsets the balance. To control it, one would have to have some sense of the pattern of the whole. I—I doubt I could fathom such a thing—"

"It is all I ask of you." He took a step toward her, thought better of it, and retreated to the window. "All is not as it might seem. I don't know what your special sight reveals. Perhaps you do not understand all that you see. I am not King of Meriga by conquest. The Ridenau Kings rule by acclamation. It was the consent of the Congress which gave us the throne—created the throne."

"I know that."

"Then do you understand that even now there are factions within the Congress which would bring down the throne? Take Meriga apart, leave her bleeding like a wounded beast for scavengers to tear off what they can?" Abelard looked out over the water. "My father, Renmond, was killed by one of those factions. I was just nineteen. I was not even here." His voice was bitter. "They hired Harleyriders and they chose their timing well. It was Phineas who held the city and the garrison long enough for me to return and assume command. My father was a weakling. The enemies within the Congress were able to play havoc under his government. I still struggle with his legacy a dozen years after his death. I could tell you such tales— My father lacked vision. He saw no future beyond his own."

Abelard faced Nydia. "But you, you see more clearly even than I. And with your help, I could restore this land. I could make this one nation—whole and indivisible as she was in the days of her glory. Together, we could make Meriga the proud nation she once was. With your help, I can overcome her enemies. I can set the past to right." He held out his hand. "Will you help me?"

Nydia felt the force of his will in those piercing blue eyes. "I have sworn to do all that I can, Lord King. But surely, you would not want me to destroy what there is?"

"No! I don't ask you to use the Magic. Take your books. I will see you have a place, a private place where you can work undisturbed. I will see that you have every comfort; I will try to provide whatever you need. I only ask that you try."

She looked over his shoulder and saw a blank; his future hinged on her response. Her eyes fell on a grayed banner hanging limply on a pole in the corner of the room. "What's that?"

"What? Oh, that. The legends say it's the flag of Meriga. It is very old."

In the silent room, she walked over and gently touched the ancient fabric. Hardly any color remained in it, and yet, she could discern thirteen stripes and a field of stars in the upper corner. She faced him wonderingly. "I had never thought to see this. They called it the Stars and Stripes. It's so very old— How did it ever survive?" Tears pricked her eyelids.

He crossed the room and took her by the upper arms. "You care enough about the past to weep for it? Then do what I ask. Help me restore this flag, this realm. Meriga was the greatest nation on earth once; it could be great again. If you will help me—think what we could accomplish. We could restore all that the Old Magic destroyed. Imagine, lady. How many would dare to make their legends real?"

She stared down at the floor, unwilling to meet his unwavering gaze. What frightened her so about this man? she wondered. She sensed his desire—knew it drew her to him. It was not the force of his physical magnetism which overwhelmed her, compelling as it might be. It was something else, something which seemed to work on everyone who came into his presence. There was something about him that made it very difficult to say no.

He let go of her arms. With the first suggestion of hesitancy she had seen in him, he drew one finger along the line of her jaw. "Do I distress you so?" She heard his breathing quicken.

He backed away and halted a few paces from her. When she raised her eyes, his arms were folded firmly across his chest. "There is a pledge bond between us, lady. Whatever more we might become, it will not be for me to say." He shrugged at the question in her eyes. "I don't order women into my bed." Bitter humor tinged his voice, and his smile held a trace of regret. "I would not have you misconstrue the meaning of your promise to uphold the King. So. What do you say? If you fail, nothing will change. But will you give me your word that at least you will try to aid me in restoring this land?"

An hour might have passed, or only a moment, as they stood facing each other without words. Finally, with a deep sigh, she nodded, and watched as the shadows of his future coalesced out of the gray void beyond his shoulder.

It was only much later, long after she was settled in the tower room which faced the rising sun, that she realized all his talk had been about land, and wealth, the security of the throne, and the past glory of Meriga. Not once had he mentioned the people.

Chapter Seven

Well, boy? What do you say?" A shaft of autumn sun reflected off Abelard's hair, surrounding his face in a gold nimbus. There was a trace of impatience in the thrust of his chin.

Miles picked at the embroidery on the sleeve of his tunic and rolled the threads into tiny balls between his thumb and forefinger. Just the day before, a messenger riding hard from Ithan had brought news of the death of the Senador of the Tennessy Fall. Now, a dull flush darkened the pale skin of his heir as all eyes focused on the boy who sat with hunched shoulders and frightened mouth. "What—whatever you think, Lord King. As you say."

Abelard's eyes narrowed and a line appeared between his brows. He shifted restlessly, but before he could speak, Phineas leaned across the table with a warning glance at the King. It was no surprise that the boy was tongue-tied. Ranged around the council table were nine of the most formidable men in Meriga: Niklas Vantigorn, First of the Lords of Mondana; Finlay of Norda Coda; Gredahl, First of the Lords of the Arkan Plains; Obayana of Kora-lado; Jarone of Nourk; Ezram of Rissona; and Tedmund of Linoys. Garrick, the General of the King's Army in the east, stood poised at one end of the table, a large hide map depicting Ithan Ford and its outlying territory pinned to a wooden stand beside him. Phineas spoke gently. "No, young lord, it's not what we think. Tennessy Fall is your estate, not the King's. Although he will help you defend it, you must request his help. Without your permission, we cannot move our men into Ithan."

Abelard tilted back in his chair. Miles furtively glanced in the King's direction. "What must I say?"

Gredahl of Arkan stirred. His heavy shoulders, hung with furs, heaved like a bear's. "Lord King, I mean no disrespect to the young Senador, but would such a request not be better made at the Convening, through his warder?"

Phineas caught Abelard's eye, and nodded nearly imperceptibly, though the matter of Miles's wardship was another dilemma for the Congress to wrangle over.

Abelard rubbed his hands together, considering. It was far more important that the defense of Ithan Ford be settled before the Congress had a chance to quarrel about it. The question of the wardship should occupy them for quite a while. When he finally spoke, his voice was kind. "Your father was a great friend, Miles, not just to me, but to my father and grandfather, as well. I would never let you lose your inheritance. When the Congress convenes on the first of Vember, a warder will be appointed for you. But the Convening is ten days away, there is other business to be brought before the Lords, and the weather grows worse. If snow closes the roads, spring may find Ithan vulnerable. I would like your consent." The King's eyes ranged around the table, meeting each man's in turn, and his voice was heavy with meaning.

"This comes at a bad time, Lord King." Niklas Vantigorn tossed a lock of his long white mane over his shoulder and pursed his lips, his weathered face a patchwork of leathery seams. "W'homing raised a battlecry last year when I asked for aid against the Chiefs of the Settle Islands—"

"His sister is married to one of them," interrupted Finlay, his gravelly voice a rasp in Phineas's ear. "And he'll never forgive you for the lands your father claimed north of Gaspar."

Abelard held up his hands. "Gentlemen, please. I know you all have concerns of your own. One matter at a time."

"But why should W'homing, or anyone else for that matter, object?" asked Tedmund of Linoys. One of the youngest Senadors in the Congress, Tedmund, unlike the others, held his lands as a grant directly from Abelard. His hair was burnished copper, his skin an unblemished cream which looked hardly accustomed to the razor's edge. His thin frame made him look much younger than his twenty-five years.

"It's like this, boy." Finlay rubbed a battle-scarred hand across his chin. "You're the only one here who holds your title from the King. For the rest of us, our lands are ours by blood. W'homing and Mondana have been at each other's throats for generations. I mean no insult, Niklas, I only speak plain. By supporting the King, Niklas tips the balance of power on his side—so he hopes; W'homing, with his sister married to one of the Chiefs in the Settle Islands, seeks to equalize it. It's a tangled coil, and you, Lord King, had better tread carefully."

Phineas wondered if the warning was not a veiled threat. Finlay's pug-dog face was innocent, but there was far more at stake than one boy's piece of Meriga. At the heart of the argument, beyond the endless intercongressional squabbles, lay the power of the King.

It came down to one issue, thought Phineas, as Garrick, at Abelard's request, repeated his plans for the defense of Ithan. There were those who sought to limit the power of the King to move in and out of estates, and those who were secure enough in their holdings that they did not care. Jarone, for instance. Nourk, on the shores of the Eastern Sea, bounded by mountains, was practically an independent principality. As long as Jarone paid his tribute, appeared at the yearly Convenings, and supported Abelard's policies, it was highly unlikely Abelard would ever set foot in Nourk. And Jarone was unlikely to ever require the King's aid, since Nourk was rich, with mountains to provide a natural defense. So Abelard and Jarone existed in a state of mutual respect and called it friendship.

Finlay, on the other hand, held the northern border of Meriga against the Sascatch Tribes. Norda Coda bordered on Abelard's lands, and Phineas wondered if that ever made Finlay nervous.

Garrick came to the end of his explanation. "Do you see, young lord?"

Miles made no response, except to glance desperately in the

King's direction. Garrick continued, "The castle is large enough to house two divisions, more if needed. I can call in reinforcements from the garrison in Atland, if I must. We need to see what the Mutens do, come the spring."

"What about supplies?" asked Finlay.

"Everic sent an inventory, and Ithan is fairly well provisioned, given the difficulties they've had down there. It will not burden us overmuch to bring the level up to what it should be." Garrick paused, allowing the words "in case of siege" to go unspoken, but every man at the table understood his meaning. "Ithan is well worth whatever resources we must devote to its defense." He straightened and cocked his head at the boy.

Miles squirmed self-consciously in his chair. "I do not want to lose my lands, Lord King. I will make it clear to all that you have my permission—my request to move into Ithan Ford."

Abelard nodded, satisfied. "Go back to your tutor, boy. Most likely your warder will be appointed with more ceremony than argument. We'll speak again if need be."

With the haste of one escaping, the boy left the room wearing a look of deep relief. As the door sighed closed, Obayana looked at the King with an inscrutable expression on his face. A small man, he appeared deceptively fragile. His dark eyes were almond shaped, his skin the golden color of the western desert sands. Nearing forty, he controlled the Saraneva Mountains from his fortress set high above the Kora-Lado Pass. "The boy is frightened, Abelard."

"He knows more's at stake than his piece of Meriga," agreed Jarone. At sixty, he was the oldest of the Senadors gathered. His dark skin was dulled with age, and his gray hair was cropped close against his black scalp. Nevertheless, his eyes were alert, his back unbowed. His left arm ended in a stump.

"The boy is likely enough." Abelard shrugged. "But he's been raised by women and old men. I've given him to Philip's tutors. It'll be some time before he's ready to assume his place."

Jarone pursed his lips. "Gredahl's right, Abelard. The boy needs a warder—who will you name?"

Abelard grinned. "You mean, who here will be most acceptable to a majority of the Congress, Lord Senador?"

Jarone spread the fingers of his right hand and smiled back with a shrug.

"What does your lieutenant at Ithan report, Phineas?" asked Tedmund.

"Some of the outposts in the southern mountains are abandoned," answered Phineas. "That could account for some of the increased raids. Scouts tell us the Riders have moved into regions in the southernmost part of the estate, and are setting up winter camps. Everic reports refugees are coming into Ithan."

"Why—" Ezram shot to attention. "Why—that means that Missiluse must—"

"Exactly, gentlemen." Abelard's voice was grim. "Eldred is either asleep, or deliberately letting them past his borders."

"But—" Ezram gasped in disbelief. "Who—why—to what end would anyone do—"

"Precisely, my lord." Phineas nodded. He tried not to smile at Ezram's panic. "That's a question I hope the honorable Senador will answer at the Convening."

"A question you might put to him, Ezram," Abelard said evenly, without a hint of guile, "given that your lands are vulnerable to the west."

"So Eldred's taken up with the Harleys?" Gredahl shook his head.

"We only surmise that, my lord," cautioned Phineas.

"Appoint me the boy's warder," Gredahl said to the King. "I'll see that his interests are protected. They're the same as mine."

Abelard shook his head. "It will be argued from too many quarters, old friend, that Arkan is too dangerous and unsettled a place to raise such an important fosterling."

"Missiluse is just as dangerous as Arkan. Surely Eldred would not—" Ezram sputtered. A thin, fussy man of middle years, given almost as much to contention as Eldred was, Ezram nonetheless was unquestionably loyal to the King. Rissona, on the southwestern coast of Meriga, was a land of stark canyons and sandy beaches, lightly populated by shepherds and fishermen.

Abelard shook his head again. "Eldred won't suggest himself. He knows we'd never consent to that. He'll just raise objections to whomever I do propose."

Niklas caught the King's eye. "Don't propose anyone, Abelard. Let the Congress settle the issue as it may. After all, other than me, Jarone, perhaps Mortmain in Vada, who are the viable candidates?"

Jarone nodded. "Niklas speaks wisely, Abelard. I think if you appear concerned, yet without a preference, the situation will take care of itself."

"And," continued Niklas, "while the Congress argues, you'll be justified in moving your troops into Ithan. For which of us, given similar circumstances, would not ask for the same help?"

"But 'which of us' are not likely to be the problem." Obayana sighed softly. "W'homing is not the only one within the Congress who will object once he finds out the King has taken a position within an Estate not his own. And with the heir of the Estate so young . . ." His voice trailed off.

A moment passed, until Garrick broke the silence. "We have a brief opportunity here, my lords. I can move my divisions into Ithan Ford within three weeks. Can you prolong the discussion over the wardship of young Miles at least that long?"

"And when it becomes known just exactly where you are, General Garrick? And with how many troops?" Ezram looked worried.

"Then we'd better be ready to expose Eldred. And put him on the defensive for once." Abelard looked at Phineas. "See that the scouts are increased in the mountains bordering Missiluse. I want as much information as we can possibly gather: where those camps are, how many men and horses, exactly what routes they're using. No Senador will look favorably on an alliance with the Harleys."

"With your permission, Lord King, I will send out the dispatches to the captains of my divisions." Garrick rose to his feet.

Abelard did not answer immediately. Phineas watched the Senadors nod gravely one by one. Suddenly uneasy, he stirred in his chair. He closed his eyes, felt his fingertips tingle. When he opened his eyes, it was as if time had slowed. He flexed his hands, or tried to, and the air felt thick, like a liquid. The air pulsed with an unseen current that rippled and shimmered around them all. As the words caught in his throat, he saw the other men held as captive as he. Only their eyes darted from side to side.

With a convulsive start, as though a dam had been released, a tide of energy careened through his body, passing through bone and sinew, reeling through his blood. His heart clutched in mid-beat and palpitated wildly. He gripped the arms of the chair. Above him, flat plates scattered throughout the ceiling flickered with a light which made the whole room seem bright as day. In the ghastly brilliance, the others sat, terror etched as clearly on their faces as he knew it was on his. Every line, every plane was illuminated by the stark, bluish glare.

Jarone's head was thrown back, his skin ashen, teeth clenched. His one hand was twined in the fabric over his chest. Tedmund's face was deathly pale; Abelard's lips were blue. Only Obayana's face was composed, although his eyes were shut, his lips compressed.

The ceiling buzzed like a swarm of angry bees and sparks arced in all directions. Then, suddenly, the unnatural light winked out. Phineas's heart hiccuped and settled into a new rhythm. He started to slump in his chair when a low roar, dulled by the thick glass, burst outside.

Those who faced the window gawked openmouthed, and Phineas twisted around. Several hundred yards from shore, a geyser spouted from the flat surface of the sea, almost as high and thick as the highest tower in Ahga. As they stared, incredulous, the water collapsed upon itself with a thunderous crack as quickly as it had arisen.

"What in the name of the Three—" Gredahl demanded.

"Look to Jarone." Phineas half rose from his seat.

"No—no." The oldest Senador was still a sickly gray, but he breathed easier, and he no longer clutched at his chest. He waved Tedmund away. "Was that Magic?"

Urgent knocking ended further speculation. "Enter!" called the King.

"Captain Phineas," gasped the manservant who stumbled into the room, "the captain of the watch requests you join him. At once. Sir." He seemed to remember he was in the presence of the King and bowed belatedly.

"Was there any damage?" Phineas stood.

"None that we see, sir. But the afterwave of that—that tower of water hit the outer wall hard."

"Summon the Captain of the Engineers. And the master masons. With your permission, Lord King?"

"Go."

Phineas paused. The King would not meet his eyes. He's not unnerved at all, he thought. And he doesn't want to deal with me.

"Lord King, this just arrived for you from the Senador of the Vada Valley." The servant handed Abelard a wooden message tube. "And another messenger from our southernmost toll plaza came in just before that wave hit. Eldred of Missiluse has arrived at the border of your territory and begs leave to continue on to Ahga."

Phineas tried once more to catch the King's eye and failed. As Abelard broke open the seal of the message case, he reluctantly followed the servant to the door. Beneath the voices of the others raised in speculation, he heard Abelard say: "Get the troops out quickly, Garrick. The Senadors will be here for the Convening in less than a week."

Chapter Eight

❧

The servant raised the lamp higher and offered Nydia an arm to guide her down the steep, narrow steps of the eastern tower. Her skirts made a heavy whisper on the staircase, and the torches set at intervals on the walls threw up grotesque shadows which shifted as they passed. Twelve days had gone by since she had made her pledge, and in that time, Nydia had seen neither the King nor his mother.

Nevertheless, he had responded immediately to her request for paper, ink, and pens, and the apartment he had given her was large and adequately furnished. It consisted of four rooms: a sitting room, a bedroom, a room which she intended to use as her study because it had a lock, and a tiled bath with a tub large enough for two adults, at least.

Twenty-five stories above the ground, the chambers were inaccessible to all but those with the strongest legs. Even the two serving women who had been appointed for her made the journey only when absolutely necessary. If it were true that Agara was afraid of heights, Nydia understood why Abelard believed his mother would not venture into this part of the tower. The outer walls, almost entirely of glass, made the rooms seem open to the air.

Like nearly everything else in Ahga, the rooms were a curious blend of old and new. The tiles in the bath were impossible shades of pale pink and mauve, colors not made in Meriga since the Armageddon. The massive bed was carved, and brightly woven rugs from the west decorated the walls in soft shades of green and blue. But the hearth was a recent addition:

it had been cut out of the vents which ran into the deep cellars
below the castle.

Tavia had visited her twice, bringing her news of the
Senators who arrived daily, some accompanied by entourages
more elaborate than the King's. She had enjoyed the girl's de-
scriptions and was grateful for the company.

The first days since moving into the tower rooms passed
quickly, reminding her of the quiet hours of study in the library of her father's house. It had been many months since she
had had the leisure to lose herself within the pages, so she had
spent most of her time reacquainting herself with her books.
But the hours grew longer as the days passed, and she remained alone. She felt more and more like one of those
princesses locked in the towers of the legends her mother used
to tell.

At this height, she could not hear the sea, and she missed its
gentle slap against the docks, the soft wash of the waves, the
scent of the salt air on the morning wind. The only sound
which penetrated the thick glass was the moan of the wind,
and even the harsh cries of the seabirds were muted as they
flapped around the towers. In the mornings, she watched the
waves break noiselessly over and through the ruins of the old
city, the bare skeletons of the buildings hung with seaweed
and the nests of the gulls like ragged graveclothes.

She was careful to hide her books, especially after she had
experimented with the forbidden formulas and been horrified
by the spectacular, immediate results. She tried not to think
about what would happen to her if they were ever discovered.
She hoped the King was right about his mother.

Now, she trailed after the manservant, obedient to the
King's summons. Yesterday, the tailors had brought her two
of the new gowns Mara had ordered made for her, and that
morning she had bathed in water heated over her own hearth.
She had twisted her still-damp hair into a heavy knot on the
top of her head. Wispy tendrils escaped and curled at the white
nape of her neck. The new gowns pleased her. It had been so
long since she had worn anything new, anything which was

not a cast off hastily made over. The fabric was soft wool, woven of so fine a thread it draped almost like silk. It fell in heavy folds all the way to the floor, to the length only the richest nobility could afford. The deep green color emphasized the reddish highlights in her hair and the creamy glow of her skin. And while she had insisted that the neckline be modest, the fit of the gown could not disguise the contours of her body.

Fifteen floors down, the servant motioned her through the narrow door. She followed him down the hall to a door where two men-at-arms stood at attention. Their faces did not change, though their gaze flicked over her bosom.

Left alone inside the room, she looked around curiously. It was a private audience room; the deep blue carpet was a thick wool, the chairs low and deep and covered in fabric dyed a rich, dark red. A small fire burned in the polished grate, and torches burned in the wall brackets. The room had no windows, she realized with a start, nor any other entrance that she could discern. She reached to warm herself over the flames. For a moment, she enjoyed the sight of her hands framed by double cuffs of cotton lace. She jumped as a click startled her.

Abelard bowed. "Forgive me, lady. I did not mean to frighten you." He seemed to have appeared out of nowhere. He gestured to the wall behind him. "There is a panel concealed in this wall—do you see? It leads directly into my chambers—that is why the entrance to this room is guarded." He indicated one of the chairs. "Please. Sit. I have not seen you for many days. Has everything been done to your liking? Is there anything else you require?"

"I have no complaint, Lord King. The rooms are beautiful. But I did wonder—Tavia says you have books. Would it be possible for me to study them?"

"I shall have them brought to you tomorrow. Is there anything else?"

She wondered in vain if there was a way to explain her isolation, the loneliness as the days seemed to lengthen. When she did not respond, Abelard went on. "What happened the other day—the light, the water—was that the Magic?"

She had expected this. From the pocket of her skirt, she pulled out a table knife, twisted and misshapen, half dark pewter, half bright gold. He took it, touching it gingerly between two fingers. "You did this? You used Magic to do this?"

"I tried to think of something small and insignificant—something where I could control the reaction, and I'm afraid I never had any control at all."

"It almost killed one of my staunchest allies, and all you did was this?"

"I warned you, Lord King. The Magic is completely unpredictable."

For a moment he stared at her. "Will you do more of this?"

"No. It was a mistake. I will not use it again—"

"But you will continue to study, as I asked?"

"If I must, Lord King."

"It may be necessary to move you—up to my hunting lodge at Minnis Saul. I would rather have you here." He broke off, looking as if he wanted to say more. "There is a matter I must raise with you—"

She looked over his shoulder and understood. "You go to meet this Eldred—the Senador—the one you distrust so much?"

"The servant told you he had come?"

"No—I see your choice."

"Ah. Yes." He took a chair beside the fire. "You see. I need your help, lady. I have reason to believe that Eldred of Missiluse has formed an alliance with the Harleyriders of the Arkan Plains, the outlaws who attacked us on our return from Ithan Ford. If this is true, it jeopardizes not only the Union but individual Senadors and their holdings, as well. You understand that the pledge bond, which each Senador has sworn to me, makes me responsible for the defense of their estates, if they call upon me for aid." When she nodded, he continued. "We are going down now to meet Eldred in the great hall. I want you to watch him—watch them all, for that matter—and tell me what you see. Now, because of your—your position here, it will most likely be assumed that you and I are—"

To her dismay, she blushed. "I understand."

He shook his head. "We will walk a fine line in the next weeks, lady. If the Senadors assume you share my bed, your presence by my side will be unquestioned. On the other hand, if we appear too—"

"Intimate?" she supplied.

"My mother will be alerted, and I do not want to rouse her suspicions, not so much that she turns her army of spies on you."

"What then, do you wish for me, Lord King?"

"Call me Abelard, when we are alone." As if he regretted the words, he went on quickly, "Say little, except to me, but encourage the attentions of all. I shall not have you near me at the feasts, but come to me immediately if there is anything or anyone—"

She interrupted him, laughing. "You give me such conflicting orders, Lord King, all will wonder whether we are friends or enemies."

"What do you suggest?"

"I will keep out of the way as much as possible—it suits me well and will keep me out of your mother's eye. As for the Senadors, let them assume what they will. If you'll forgive me, Lord King, it is generally assumed that every woman who lives in the castle has spent at least one night in your bed."

"I suppose you believe that, as well?"

"Lord King—Abelard, if you wish— it is not for me to say. Certainly you have more children than any other man I've ever known—but—" She shrugged. "I have never heard that you forced a woman against her will, and certainly you have not by word or action been less than kind to me." This line of conversation unnerved her, and she could not meet his eyes. "I think, if we are both careful, we will manage."

He smiled then, one of his broad, easy grins, and extended his hand. "Then come, lady. Let's enter the fray."

"Senifay intends to bring a grievance against Kora-lado," Tedmund's voice was low.

"What else is new?" Phineas tossed his apple core into the roaring blaze. "Senifay complains about Obayana at every Convening I can remember. He's jealous. He'd like control of the southern trade route through the Saranevas, and I suppose he thinks if he complains long enough and loud enough, someone will listen—" Phineas paused in mid-sentence as the King, with Nydia on his arm, entered the great hall.

Tedmund followed Phineas's gaze and gave a low whistle. "By the One and Three, Phineas, look at that. Where did he find her?"

"In a little village some miles from here." Phineas kept his voice carefully even.

"In what village do you find women like that?"

Despite the misgivings Phineas felt every time he saw the woman, he had to admit that the sight of Abelard and Nydia together was indeed compelling. Next to the broad span of Abelard's shoulders, Nydia's narrow shoulders seemed daintily insubstantial; compared to the flat planes of Abelard's chest, the curves of her full breasts were emphasized. The top of her head barely reached his shoulder.

Phineas saw Agara go white-lipped and narrow-eyed where she stood with Eldred across the room. "Be careful, Lord King," he murmured.

"Phineas," Tedmund interrupted his thoughts, "you don't suppose she's sworn any vows to him, do you? Is it likely he'll make her his consort?"

Amused, despite the dangerous look on Agara's face, Phineas shook his head. "Why, Tedmund, would you risk Abelard's wrath?"

"For her—" He nodded at Nydia. "Damned right, I would."

Phineas laughed. Abelard stopped frequently as he made his way across the hall, bowing and laughing. He was careful to introduce Nydia to every Senator they passed, most of whom were accompanied by their wives or consorts. To a man, they stared down at her, and even when Abelard drew her on, their eyes followed her. More than one woman tugged at the sleeve of her companion as the King went by.

"Why doesn't he bring her over here?" complained Tedmund, when it became clear that Abelard moved in Eldred's direction. "Will you excuse me?"

Phineas could not suppress a grin as Tedmund took off through the crowd.

Nydia's eye was caught by the shock of bright red hair bobbing ever closer. Tedmund broke through the men crowding around the King and reached eagerly for her arm. There was hardly time for a smile, though, for Abelard firmly shouldered past him and brought her to stand beside his mother, who was engaged in conversation.

"Mother," Abelard interrupted.

Agara broke off in mid-word. Although her smile did not leave her face, her eyes were cold as they slid over Nydia. "Here you are, at last, my son. Have you a greeting for our cousin, Eldred?"

Abelard gave his mother a smile which Phineas would have recognized as the one he wore in battle. "Eldred." His voice was a lazy drawl.

Eldred took the King's outstretched hand. "You look very well, cousin. I'm glad to see you again."

"A good journey, was it?"

"A tiring journey. It's good to be here at last."

"Let me introduce a new member of our household. This—" Abelard tugged at Nydia's arm, and reluctantly she faced Agara "—is the Lady Nydia Farhallen. Her father was the Senador of Jersy. Unfortunately, all was lost in a Muten raid over a year ago."

Eldred bobbed his head. "Lady Nydia."

Nydia took the hand he offered, amazed at the man who stood before her. This was Abelard's hated enemy? Eldred Onrada of Missiluse was a man of somewhat more than medium height, nowhere near as tall as the King or Phineas, yet something above average, or would have been if he did not stoop.

His age was equally difficult to place: he might have been anywhere between forty and sixty. He wore a beard, which set him apart in a room where most of the men were clean shaven, with wiry gray strands that poked out at odd angles from the darker whiskers. His eyes were watery blue and deep-set in sockets ringed with wrinkles. He squinted down at her. His two front teeth poked out from beneath his upper lip, giving him something of the appearance of a rabbit, and in that moment, Nydia understood why he wore the beard, and why Abelard referred to him as "wimp-chinned."

She offered a smile. "Lord Senador. I am very glad to meet you." She glanced over his shoulder and away, into his future, and saw nothing untoward—certainly nothing which would confirm Abelard's suspicions that this man plotted against the throne and the realm.

Eldred gave her the awkward smile of a man who knows that women find him unattractive and so avoids their company as much as possible. He hooked his thumbs in his belt and, glancing about the room, said to the King: "Has everyone arrived?"

Abelard shrugged. "For the most part. I don't expect the Settle Islands, of course. It's time this Congress reconsidered our treaties with them."

Eldred nodded sagely. "It would be best to encourage an alliance which would offer them advantages."

Abelard's mouth curved in disgust. "The only advantage I'd like to offer them is their lives. The Chiefs are entirely too independent and quarrelsome."

"It would be preferable to offer an alternative way of settling their disputes," he spoke with a ring of quiet authority which surprised Nydia, "if they are to be made part of the Union."

"A pity things are so unsettled in the south this year, cousin. What a fine emissary you'd make." Abelard gave him another dangerous smile.

"Well—personal allegiances must not interfere with what is best for the realm."

There was an undercurrent in the conversation Nydia could

not quite grasp. Suddenly, Abelard yawned. "You know that old Miles in Tennessy is dead?"

"Ah, yes, the reports reached us before we left."

The tension was gone. Nydia had the feeling that the King had deliberately goaded Eldred, only to draw back from open confrontation. "So, except for the Vada Valley, everyone is here."

"Owen has not come?" The new note of interest in Eldred's voice made Nydia glance reflexively over his shoulder once more. Involuntarily, she tightened her grip on Abelard's sleeve at the immediate change she saw.

"Nor will he. There is a blight on his harvest. I received his message some days ago." Abelard surveyed the hall, as if, having temporarily called a truce, he was anxious to escape Eldred's company.

"And has his messenger stayed to take back reports of the Convening?"

This time, Abelard looked at him with subtle curiosity. The King did not answer immediately. Lady Mara had engaged his mother in conversation concerning the evening's feast; only Nydia was in earshot. "No." Abelard's face was as expressionless as his voice. "I don't believe that he did. Doubtless Owen expects to receive word from a kingdom messenger."

"Oh." Eldred bowed awkwardly at Nydia. "I—I— There's some unpacking that must be seen to. I will look forward to seeing you later, cousin. Lady."

"Well?" asked the King as soon as Eldred was swallowed by the crowd. His voice was low.

Nydia hesitated. "At first, I saw nothing beyond the opening of the Convening tomorrow, but then you mentioned this Owen—"

"Owen Mortmain. Senador of the Vada Valley. First of the Lords of the West."

"Eldred intends to contact him."

"Why?"

"I cannot say. But that's where he went—to write a letter to

Mortmain. He will be late arriving at the feast tonight. He'll send the message out with one of his men."

Abelard frowned. "I've never had a reason to suspect Mortmain of anything."

"Is he an ally?"

"Mortmain is a hard man to know. He marches to his own drum—not to mine, not to the Congress's. But I'd stake the throne that he doesn't march to Eldred's, either. He supported my father—but not my grandfather, though that was when he was very young. Well. We'll see. Thank you, lady."

Nydia turned to see Agara staring at her. She hates me, thought Nydia. Agara did not flinch when Nydia met her gaze. "Will you excuse me, Lord King?" Without another word, she gracefully disappeared in the crowd. As she threaded her way across the floor, she saw Phineas standing by one of the hearths, speaking to one of his lieutenants. Uncertain of her reception, she darted over to him and touched his sleeve. "Captain Phineas?" It was the first time she had spoken to him since the day she had sworn her pledge to Abelard.

His face was unreadable, but he spoke to his companion at once. "If you'll excuse me, Jedro?"

The lieutenant bowed, and was gone.

Phineas waited.

Nydia wet her lips. "I know—I know you don't like me, Captain Phineas, so I will not embarrass you for very long, but I think you ought to know what I saw just now—"

Phineas shifted from foot to foot, and momentarily something like regret flickered in his gray eyes. "Liking you has nothing to do with it, lady. I am sworn to protect my King, with my life, if necessary, and you give me the uncomfortable feeling that you might someday make my job more difficult than it is already. I know about this ability of yours. What do you want to tell me?"

Phineas's face did not change, but he listened intently as she told him of Eldred's reaction to the news that Owen Mortmain would not attend. "What does he want with Mortmain?"

"I don't know—I cannot see that. Do you know?"

"No," Phineas admitted.

"Abel— The King did not seem concerned, and yet, I saw the change. Eldred decided to do this at the moment the King told him Mortmain would not attend the Convening."

Phineas was silent. He considered the possibilities. "When will Eldred send this message?"

"Tonight. Now. He'll be late to the feast making the arrangements." Nydia glanced desperately around the room. "Was I wrong to come to you?"

Against his better judgment, Phineas softened. "No, lady," he said after another silence. "Why was Abelard not concerned?"

"He said he had no reason to suspect Mortmain of anything."

"That's true." Phineas sighed and suppressed an urge to smile at her. "But this adds a new angle I didn't expect. Missiluse is a nuisance. Mortmain is another matter."

"Why? What is his standing in the Congress?"

"He's the most powerful man in the west. His lands extend over several Estates, just as Abelard's do. So if he has turned against the throne . . ." Phineas stared into the flames. "I will speak to Abelard. And, lady, for your own sake, no matter what he is to you, or what he becomes, he is the King—first."

Nydia glanced over Phineas's shoulder, into his future, and nodded, satisfied. "Thank you, Captain. I shall not forget that." She was surprised when he laid a hand on her arm.

"Thank you." His gray eyes were cool, but he spoke gently, and the pressure of his hand was firm.

Phineas waited until Nydia disappeared into the crowd. The servants were just beginning to lay out the places for the feast, and Phineas was certain he would not be missed. He slipped silently, unseen, out of the great hall, down the darkened corridors and into the outer ward, where the autumn night had fallen. The courtyard was deserted for the most part, animals lodged in the stables, the stablehands and grooms finished for the evening, gone to congregate in the kitchens. Only the guards on duty stood around the perimeter, and one by one, they straightened to attention as he passed.

Moving as quickly as she could, Nydia hastened from the hall. The assembly was swollen to twice the size of the feast held to celebrate the King's return, and the people pressed in on her. There was hardly a direction she could look without seeing someone's future overlain upon another's face. The images of present and future blended and swirled, creating confusing patterns which blurred her vision. Determinedly, she kept her eyes fastened straight ahead, looking neither right nor left, desperately trying the tactic she had used at the last feast.

A server hurrying by crashed into her side, and she stumbled, almost falling to her knees. "Watch yourself, my lady." The woman reached down to help her, and unthinking, Nydia glanced over the woman's shoulder. Horrified, she watched a heavy pot tip over and hot oil flood over feet only lightly clad in house slippers. She gasped, sickened at the sight of skin which blistered and crinkled.

"Are you all right?" The woman looked at her with puzzled concern.

Nydia shrank and shook off the hand extended to help her. She spun around and collided into the chest of a burly man-at-arms, who growled: "Watch out now." She looked up and into a bloody nose from a fistfight over a card game. With a sob, she broke away, and ran, out of the crazy, kaleidoscopic images, into the peace of the darkened corridor.

She leaned against the wall. Now she understood why her family had been so careful to keep her from crowds, never allowed her to go into the markets on the busiest days, why such feasts were unheard of on her father's small holding. She pressed her hot hands to her temples and breathed deeply. The pins which held her hair stabbed into her scalp, and with a sigh of relief, she pulled them out and let the long curls cascade down her back. She combed her fingers through her hair and separated the still damp strands. When she finally felt steadier, she made her way down the corridors to the staircase leading to her tower rooms.

The railing was of ancient metal, worn thin from years of handling, and she wondered whether her legs would carry her up the twenty-five floors. She took a deep breath, clutched the cold banister, and started up the steps.

"My lady!" The heavy sarcasm hit her like the lash of whip. If she did not recognize the voice, she certainly knew the tone.

Agara peered at her from the narrow doorway.

"Yes, lady?" Nydia tried to keep her voice as steady as she could.

Agara moved to the bottom of the steps. "Not staying for the feast?"

"I—I did not feel well, so I thought—"

In less time than it took Nydia to speak the words, Agara was on the step beneath her. She gripped Nydia's wrist like a manacle and touched one damp curl. "Did you think to prepare yourself for my son?"

Nydia drew back, uneasy at the glitter in Agara's eyes. "Lady, no matter what you think, I'm not—I've no desire—"

"You lie." With a final heave, Agara stood on the same step. Nydia took another step backward, pulling her heavy skirt out of the way. Agara tightened her hold. "You lie. I see your eyes when you look at him. The same way all his women look at him. I saw the way you sang that song—'he'll wed you all'—why don't you come back and sing that song to the company tonight, lady-have-some-skill-as-a-singer? Hm?"

"Lady, please, let go of my wrist. You're hurting me."

For answer, Agara gave it a wicked twist. "Think you'll get a brat from him, do you? And the pity of it is, you probably will. They all do—and he's liable to name one of them over my—"

"Lady," Nydia tried not to sound too desperate, "I'm not interested in your son. I don't want to bear his child. You're right, he has enough children."

Agara looked at her suspiciously. Nydia backed up one more step. Suddenly, Agara let go of Nydia's wrist to grasp the banister. "You see," she said, suddenly confiding, "if he doesn't name an heir, there's likely to be a civil war after he dies."

Nydia nodded, and backed up. Agara followed. "And if there's civil war, the country will be torn apart."

"And your grandsons will be too young for many years before they can claim the throne." Nydia spoke calmly.

Agara nodded and picked up her trailing skirts. Nydia tried to steal a glance over the woman's shoulder—surely she had no intentions of accompanying Nydia up twenty-five floors? The vision wavered, strands of colors and images blending in an incoherent pattern. Nydia tried to resist gently, but Agara forced her on and up.

"If only my sweet Rabica had not died. All of those women—and who had to die but my sweet girl, who bore him not one son, but two." Agara sighed. "Oh, if you could have seen her. She was tall, not a puny thing like you, so fine and graceful—like a young willow, she was, so well-suited to him."

"I am sorry for your loss, lady. I understand it was a blow to the King's plans, as well."

"The King's plans." Agara made a derisive sound. "He could still follow through on those plans. Amanander would make a splendid king—but does he listen to me?" At the top of the second landing, some forty steps above the floor, Agara paused. "Of course not." She put her face close to Nydia's, and her breath was foul with wine. "Instead he goes from bed to bed, like a bee after nectar, looking for a Queen, he says."

She glanced around and down, and gasped. The color drained out of her face, and she made a frantic grab at Nydia. "Oh, by all the gods, look how high we are—how did we—"

Nydia took the older woman by the waist and arm. "Don't look down, lady, look out. Don't keep your eyes on the floor, just look at the wall in front of you." Slowly coaxing, Nydia maneuvered Agara's wooden body down the steps.

When they reached the bottom, Agara pulled away. Even with her feet flat on the floor, she still towered over Nydia, who was on the bottom step. Agara's face suddenly contorted, and she raised her arm. Nydia flinched. "I see what you are." Agara's voice was an ugly rasp. "You're kind."

Nydia backed away, and Agara swung. Too late, Nydia turned her cheek. The blow caught her squarely on the side of the head, and she staggered and lost her balance. She grabbed for the railing, and Agara hit her again.

"That's your plan, isn't it? You'll be kind. You'll cover your breasts and make him wonder what they look like all the time he's listening to your honey words—" She raised her arm again.

Nydia scrambled back, and her heel caught in the hem of her skirt. As she fell, she heard a man's voice cry: "By the Three, lady—do you know what you do?"

Chapter Nine

*S*omething wet trickled down her neck. She opened her eyes. The room was in semidarkness, only two candles burned by the side of a high, four-poster bed. The face which peered down at her was vaguely familiar. She wrinkled her brow and tried to sit up.

"Easy, now, you had quite a fall." The voice was young.

"Who—where—?"

"I'm Tedmund Allcort. You smiled at me in the hall. I looked for you after you left the King. I checked with the Steward, and since you weren't to sit at the high table with the King, I hoped you'd sit with me at the feast. But—well—I'm glad I found you when I did."

In the dim light, she struggled to sit up. The room was unfamiliar, though large and carefully appointed. Tedmund sat back. He was not as young as he appeared at first; he was in his mid-twenties, she guessed, but his wiry frame made him look no more than sixteen. "Where am I?"

"I brought you to my room. I hope you don't mind—I don't know where yours is, and I wanted to get you away from Agara as quickly as I could."

"Agara. Where is she?"

"She went off, back to the hall, when I—interrupted her. Forgive me, lady, but, what did you do?"

Nydia shrugged. "Helped her down the steps." She wiped at her cheek, which was damp from the wet rag he had placed on her forehead. Immediately, he leaned over and patted her face with a linen towel.

"Imagine what she does to people who hold doors open for her."

Despite the pain in her head, Nydia laughed. Tedmund smiled back. "That's better." He watched her for a moment. "Seriously, what did you do?"

Nydia shivered, and felt tears well. "She's—she thinks the King and I . . ." Her voice trailed off and she wrapped her arms around herself.

Tedmund looked around, grabbed a cover from the bottom of the bed, and dragged it around her. "Warmer? Agara was beating you because you're the King's companion?"

Miserably, Nydia nodded, and the tears spilled over and down her cheeks. She turned her head away, mortified that such small kindnesses could garner such a reaction. Tedmund peered at her uncertainly. She wiped futilely at the tears.

"I think you should go to the King. He won't let his mother treat you this way—"

"No." Nydia shook her head. "You don't understand. There's nothing between me and the King." She bit her lip at the lie.

"But I thought surely when I saw you with him today—"

"Everyone's bound to think that about any woman the King is seen with, aren't they? I don't really care what people think, but I certainly don't want Agara—"

"The woman's mad. It's not you she hates. It's been going on as long as I can remember. The King refuses to make Amanander his heir, and so she strikes out at anyone she can. Would you like me to speak to him about this? He must be told."

"You're very kind, but who are you, sir? What influence have you with the King?"

"I'm the Senator of Linoys. That's just south; it's part of the hereditary lands of the Ridenaus. My family was given the title by Abelard's grandfather; we hold the land directly from him." He spoke so earnestly, like a boy reciting a history lesson, and stared at her with such unabashed admiration, she smiled.

"Well, Lord Senador, I do thank you, but I'm not certain what's best—"

"Your name is Nydia?"

"Nydia Farhallen. My father was—"

"Senador of Jersy. I overheard Abelard tell Eldred." Hesitantly, he brushed a curl out of her eyes.

His touch made her conscious of the dim light, the wide bed.

"Forgive me if I stare, lady. You are the fairest woman I have ever seen."

She did not resist when he took her in his arms, cradling her as if she were a child. With the tip of one finger, he traced the path of a tear which leaked from the corner of her eye. "Why do you weep?" He tightened his embrace.

She heard his heart pound through his thin chest. She held her breath, scarcely daring to move. For the first time in many months, she felt protected, secure. A little sigh escaped involuntarily as she relaxed, the grip of constant fear finally loosened by the strength with which he held her. It felt so good to lie in the arms of a man who wanted her only for herself, who was gentle, brave enough to confront Agara, and kind enough to offer to question the King. She did not turn away when he bent and kissed her mouth.

She gasped, and he withdrew. Desire sparked through her body, catching her off guard, and she arched her back, lips parted. Her breath caught in her throat. His eyes narrowed, and he bent his head once more.

This time her hands reached up and caressed the back of his smooth neck, her fingers twining eagerly in his short red hair. His hands shook as he pushed the heavy blanket aside, frantically searched for the lacings of her bodice. She moaned against his mouth as he brushed her nipple. Through the thin chemise, he caressed her breasts, thumb flicking her nipple, and she turned in his embrace, pulling at the lacings of his trousers.

They came together still half-clothed, and she strained against him, demanding satisfaction of a need she had not known she had.

Finally, breathless, they collapsed in a tangle of sheets and cast-off clothes. He rolled off her onto his side, still breathing heavily. A light sheen of sweat covered her breasts. "By the Three, lady, when I brought you here, I did not intend—"

She smiled, a lazy languor seeping deliciously through her body. "But you hoped . . ."

"I wouldn't be a man if I didn't hope." He touched her cheek with the back of his hand. "Why do you smile?"

"You remind me of someone."

"Who?"

"My husband."

"Gods, lady, you're married? Has he an heir?"

Nydia smiled in spite of herself at the sudden panic. "He did. But it doesn't matter anymore." Her smile faded. "He's dead—they're all dead."

"You've no one left at all?"

She shook her head.

"This heir—was he your son?"

She nodded, feeling tears well once more.

"Ah, lady. For your loss, I grieve." He rose up on one elbow, and tenderly tucked a blanket around her shoulders. He cupped his hand around her face. "Come with me."

"What?"

"Come with me. Back to Linoys. I'll make you my consort; if the King allows, I'll make you my wife. I'll swear fidelity to you for the rest of my life. Say yes."

She was touched by the reckless urgency. "That's not possible."

"Not possible? You've nothing to keep you here, surely. Say the word, and the sun will set on your command."

"I can't leave Ahga."

He dropped his eyes and spoke softly. "I understand. I'm only a junior Senador, and a woman like you deserves a King."

"Oh, no, Tedmund, it's not that. There's something I must do, promised the King I'd do—"

"But would you join me at the feast?"

She pulled his arm across her body so that she lay encircled. "It would by my very great pleasure."

Phineas returned to the great hall to find Abelard seated and the feast just beginning.

"Where've you been?" Abelard asked as Phineas slid into his seat.

Phineas smiled pleasantly and nodded at the Senators and their ladies gathered at the table. The hall was packed tonight; although Nydia was nowhere to be seen, if indeed she was present at all, and Agara's place of honor next to Abelard was empty too. As he leaned over to pick up the napkin he deliberately dropped, he muttered, "I don't see your favorite relative."

"He'll be here," growled Abelard.

"I've arranged for his man to be followed."

"How?"

"Nydia told me. I think we'd better keep informed. There's too much she can't tell us."

Abelard nodded over his goblet and moved closer as a server deposited a huge haunch of roasted meat on a platter in front of them. "And in the meantime, Phineas?"

Phineas smiled. An observer might have thought that the question was whether the meat was done to his liking. He nodded at the far corner, where Eldred of Missiluse slipped into the hall, and slouched up the side aisle toward his place on the dais, looking neither right nor left. "We wait, and we see what happens at the Convening."

Abelard stabbed his fork into the platter of food, and stopped. From the opposite entrance, across the hall, Nydia entered on Tedmund's arm. He steered her through the long rows of tables with a possessive hand on her waist. Someone shouted a remark; he responded, laughing, and Nydia blushed. They took places side by side among the junior Senators. Tedmund raised his goblet and brushed a loose curl behind her ear.

"Yes." Abelard did not take his eyes off the couple. "We'll wait. And we'll see."

Chapter Ten

*T*wo gulls wheeled in the updrafts of the gusts between the high towers. Nydia watched them swoop close to the window, graceful sweeps of dark gray against the leaden sky. Rain clouds gathered over the sea and the wind blew hard in the west. The momentary respite from the pelting Prill rain was over.

She put her pen down and went to stand against the windowed wall. The shoreline stretched north and east; the beaches beyond the town were slim lines of white sand against the dark green water. A spring haze of green was on the trees and the far hills to the east. Immediately below her, on the docks, the fishing boats rocked on their moorings as the storm began to whip the waves into a frenzy.

Her neck was stiff from a morning spent bent over her books; her hand sore from writing. She rubbed ink-stained fingers on her black apron, knowing that the dark fabric would hide the smudges. She picked up Tedmond's latest letter. More than a month had passed since he had left Ahga. With his characteristic enthusiasm, he described in great detail his plans for the spring planting. She shut her eyes, envisioning the green fields rolling across the landscape even as she massaged her temples and felt the blood throb beneath her skin. She tried not to wonder if her work of the last few months was futile.

The only known method of controlling the Magic required more from her than she was willing to reveal. She would not yield her ultimate secret to Abelard any more than she would give it to the twisted Muten who'd almost taken her life. She remembered the day on the way to Ahga, when that wretched Muten had accosted her with the leaf. What courage had been needed to leave the security of their hiding places, to venture out into the hostile world. Perhaps she should have received it with more grace. After all, not all of them were responsible—

The knock startled her. She closed her book, carefully covered it with the heavy folds of unbleached linen which protected it, and shut the door of her study. She was surprised to see Tavia when she opened the outer door of her sitting room.

"Tavia. Come in." Nydia held the door open and gestured to a chair by the hearth. "Sit down."

Tavia's face was flushed and beaded with sweat. She gasped a little, as though she had run most of the way. With a sigh, she threw herself into the chair. "I'm sorry to burst in on you like this. I know you're busy, but just now, I overheard—" She stopped, looked away and bit her lip.

"What is it? What's wrong?" Nydia's heart began to pound.

Tavia hesitated, then the words spilled out in a rush. "It's my grandmother. She's saying terrible things—that you're a witch—that the reason you stay up here in this tower is that you're practicing the Old Magic. And Dad's so busy getting ready to leave for the spring campaigns— Lady, I didn't know what to do."

Fear clawed at Nydia's heart, made her stomach clench. The King was leaving Ahga. Of course he was. She thought of her books, her papers carefully stored in the other room. The lock looked flimsy all of a sudden, the door nothing but an obstacle easily torn down, both nothing but a momentary deterrent. She shuddered at the expression Agara would wear if she knew that her accusations were correct.

Tavia looked at her with a mixture of concern and bewilderment. "Lady, where are you going?"

Nydia dashed down the steps, her full skirts bunched in her arms. On the floor of the King's audience room, she ran down the hall to the guarded entrance. The guards crossed their spears in front of her. "I must see the King," she pleaded.

They glanced at each other. "In the council room, lady," one murmured under his breath.

Put not your trust in princes. The ancient warning, so old its source was forgotten, echoed in her skull. Of course the King would leave. Of course the coming of spring meant that fighting would recommence, the ceaseless bickering and raiding that set the tenor of the times. What had she thought, all those months ago, when she had first decided to find the King? What vain hope had so addled her wits she had pledged allegiance and bound herself for life? She should never have sought the King, should have stayed where she was and lived or died according to fate's whim. Had she cheated death only to find it waiting for her in the only place she thought safe?

She burst into the council room without knocking. Abelard, Phineas, the captains and the lieutenants of the King's Guard, were clustered at one end of the long table around maps and tally lists. They all stared, and Abelard broke off in mid-sentence.

Nydia glanced around wildly. The men were gathered close, faces over faces, and as her eyes sought the King's, her gaze was directed into the future of the soldier who leaned in front of him.

She gasped. Blood ran down the sides of his head, clots hung from his forehead. His arms had been torn from their sockets. His torso was bound with rough ropes to the branches of a great tree, a tree whose trunk was thicker than six men together. Bubbles gathered on his parched lips, flies crawled unimpeded over his face. With her fist pressed to her mouth, she crumpled.

Phineas was the first across the room. He caught her as she fell and lifted her easily. Her face was sickly pale, sweat gathered in cold beads on her upper lip and laced her forehead.

He turned to Abelard, a question in his eyes.

"To my audience room," Abelard said.

"What ails the woman?" asked one of the lieutenants.

"Probably breeding," another answered as Phineas started down the corridor. "Funny things, these breeding women are.

Before my son was born, his mother fainted all the time." The voices faded.

In the King's audience room, he laid her on one of the low couches.

"Send for wine, and find Mara," said Abelard. "Wait for me in the council room. I'll be back as soon as I know she's all right."

Nydia stirred, opened her eyes and struggled to sit up. Abelard pushed her back down gently but firmly. "Lie still. What's wrong?"

She would not look at him. Flushed and embarrassed, she turned her head away. He took her chin and forced her face to his. "Weeks have gone by and I would not even know that you exist, and then, without warning, you barge into my council room? Are you breeding? You know Linoys isn't here. What do you want with me?"

His grip on her face was firm but gentle, and Nydia felt a tug of the inevitable response his presence always roused in her. With effort, she swallowed and hoped her voice was steady. "Tavia says your mother's telling everyone I'm a witch."

With a curse, Abelard rose to stand over the cold grate. "I told Mara to come to me if she heard anything like this."

"Perhaps Lady Mara hasn't heard. And Tavia said you were busy making plans to leave." Nydia sat up.

"Surely you realized I would be gone much of the time?" The gentleness in his voice surprised her.

"I don't know what I thought. I know I've done my best to avoid your mother, but it seems that my very existence—"

Abelard held up his hand. "And even the young Lord of Linoys cannot protect you." This time he sounded almost triumphant. Then, with that abruptness which she had come to expect from him, he changed the subject. "What did you see in the council room? What made you faint?"

She closed her eyes against the awful vision. "I saw that man—that man who leaned over you—I saw him crucified."

"Crucified?"

She nodded as the bile rose in her throat. "He'd been scalped, his arms torn from his shoulders. There was so much blood."

"War's not a game, lady. Tell me, is this bound to happen?"

"You mean, is there anything which can be done to prevent it?" She took a deep breath. "Certain choices can affect those around us in ways we don't immediately understand. It is the Harleyriders who crucify." When he nodded, she continued. "If you now change your mind and send him to a place where there are no Harleyriders, he will not die. But if you do not, the consequence will be that he will end on that tree."

"Do you know where it is?"

She looked down, threading her fingers together. "It's the tree the Mutens call the Axletree of Meriga—the one they say will not die. Its trunk is as thick as six men or more."

"I know that tree. I would wager it is the only tree still standing in all of Arkan—even the Harleys consider it sacred." He stared moodily into the cold grate and did not notice how she trembled, or how her hands shook in her lap. "Can you tell me when?"

"The tree was in full leaf."

He looked up at a knock. "Enter."

Lady Mara swept into the room. When she saw Nydia half-reclining on the couch, she stopped in the door. Color crept up her cheeks to the white edge of her coif.

"Come in, damn it." Abelard motioned. "Why didn't you tell me about my mother's latest mischief?"

"Lord King," Mara gestured helplessly, "I did not wish to disturb you—"

"Never mind. Tell me. All of it."

With a quick glance at Nydia, Mara said, "It began after the New Year—after you began to receive the dispatches from the outposts. Agara's been very agitated all winter, you know that. The more likely it seemed you would be leaving soon, the more she talked. It's true, after all, that Lady Nydia keeps to herself, but I never faulted her for that. Her work—the sewing and the spinning I give her are always done quickly and well—"

Abelard waved his hand impatiently. "Yes, yes. But my mother, what does she say?"

Mara swallowed hard. "She says that Lady Nydia must be a witch. That the books which she brought with her to Ahga are ancient ones of Old Magic. She says that the episode last year in the autumn, when the great wave came up, was the wrath of the One, and that the lady should be punished lest we all suffer." She looked at the King, distress plain on her plump face. "Lord King, what would you have me do?"

Nydia's face drained of color and she looked at Abelard in mute appeal.

"All this because of Amanander," muttered Abelard. "All right, Mara," he said after a silence. "Thank you. Come to me at once if my mother says anything more."

Mara looked at him with such a blatant desire to please that Nydia nearly smiled despite her situation. This man could make anyone do anything he asked. Except, apparently, his mother.

"Lord King," Mara said hesitantly, "I think for the lady's sake that she would be safer at Minnis while you are gone."

He nodded. "We'll see."

When Mara was gone, Nydia sat with hands clenched tight. Abelard threw himself into a chair. "So. What are we to do, my dear? If I leave you here, I may as well sign the death warrant. If you go to Minnis, there's still nothing to prevent my mother from sending an armed guard after you. And even if I leave a regiment to protect you—which at the moment I can't spare—she could send another from the city garrison. I would not have my men at such a stalemate. I'm afraid that in my absence they would obey her immediate orders. So. What are we to do?"

A moment passed. "Take me with you."

"To war? Lady, do you know what you suggest?"

She wet her lips. "I think I do."

"You fainted just now at the semblance of something which

by your own admission may not even come to pass. Believe me when I tell you that such sights are more common than not."

"There are women who accompany the army—"

He crossed the room and loomed above her. She raised her chin and met his eyes, abruptly aware that this was the first time in months she had been alone with him. His thigh muscles rippled beneath the supple leather breeches. His jaw was rough with faintest haze of beard. She kept her face carefully blank.

"Those women provide certain services." His eyes roamed across her face and down her throat. "Hardly appropriate for a woman like you."

She blushed in spite of herself. "Could I not be of some use to you, at least, Abelard?"

His eyes locked with hers. His voice, when he finally answered, lulled and excited her, like honey poured into wine. "I have no doubt, my dear."

She thought he might touch her. Her heart beat faster and her lips parted.

"But there is the question of your books. My mother is more accurate than she realizes, hm?"

"Perhaps Vere could look after them?"

"Vere?"

"Your son. He's very interested in such things—"

"I know all about Vere." There was disgust in Abelard's voice.

"He's a wonderful boy, so curious and eager to learn—"

"Though not so eager to learn to use a sword," interrupted Abelard dryly. "He's the least likely of all my sons. Very well. You may come. There will not be room for a great deal of baggage, you understand?"

"My needs are not so very great."

"I have noted that."

"May I ask where you intend to go?"

"We have received urgent pleas from Gredahl in Arkan. The Riders launched an attack from the Loma deserts. Ithan is braced—there are refugees pouring in from the Plains. Gredahl has even appealed to the Lords of Mondana."

"Is there word of Eldred?"

"He spent last winter entertaining the Harley Kahn—their lord, if you can call him that. Thanks to you, we knew to watch him carefully, and our scouts have reported almost weekly."

"And Mortmain?"

"Eldred's man reached Vada. But we don't know if there was ever a reply."

"Surely—"

"There must have been? We think so, too, but I doubt Mortmain would align himself with the Harleys. That's Eldred's notion. But we don't go to war against either. Not yet. We go to answer Gredahl's plea."

Nydia raised her head and looked over his shoulder, into his future. She saw the bitter clash of armies and frowned. There was something wrong with what she saw, but she did not understand what it was. "Not yet," she echoed.

Chapter Eleven

❧

*N*ydia peered uncertainly into the murky blackness, holding her candle high. The tiny flame did little to penetrate the almost palpable dark. She felt, rather than saw, the cavernous roof disappear down long tunnels which stretched for miles beneath the city. She clutched the steel doorframe. Scabbed rust flaked off onto her sleeve.

Behind her lay the burial chambers, dim light filtering through dusty windows set high in the walls at ground level. The crypts held the tombs of the Ridenau Kings and their ancestors, the Senators who had risen to power in the terrible years following the Armageddon and the Persecutions, who by marriage and treaty had forged the largest and most powerful estate in all of Meriga.

On the oldest tombs, the names of ancient estates long ago absorbed into the hereditary holdings could be vaguely understood, names she dimly remembered from her father's books. Names such as Wisconsin, Michigan, Iowa, Missouri, Indiana, Nebraska, Ohio. Names lost and long forgotten, even as these tunnels were.

She held her candle higher. Only the Mutens knew the secret of cold fire, light generated by cylindrical cells filled with chemicals.

At the thought of the Mutens, she shivered and the memory of childhood was gone. Another, darker and more terrifying, rose in its place. Deliberately, she suppressed it, pushed it down into the dark recesses of her mind. A dank breeze made her candle flicker, and she wrapped one hand protectively around it. She looked down at the lichen-covered floor of broken tiles. "Vere?" Her voice echoed off the high ceilings, bounced off the cracked floor. It reverberated down the empty distances. In the dark, it seemed unnaturally loud.

No answer. She sighed and gathered up her skirts in one hand, her eyes adjusting to the gloom. Above her, something stirred and flapped. She glanced up, saw nothing. A chill of disgust ran down her spine, made the hair at the back of her neck prickle. Holding the candle higher, she stepped out of the entrance and picked her way across the uneven floor. "Vere?" She thought she saw a dim light bobbing ahead. "Vere?" She started forward.

An arm wrapped around her waist, and she gasped. "No, lady, no further—" She was wrenched backward. She spun around to stare up at a tall, thin youth dressed in ragged clothes.

"Vere." Her tone was half reproof, half relief.

"Forgive me, lady." He released her and stepped back awkwardly, pushing back a long lock of unkempt hair from his narrow face. "I meant no disrespect, but—look. If you had gone maybe another two steps . . ." He gestured with a long arm.

The broken tiles ended abruptly perhaps eighteen inches from where she stood. A shallow chasm gaped beyond, a long well of black which disappeared down two tunnels. "A subway," she muttered. "Of course."

"Lady?"

She broke away from Vere and gingerly crept to the edge of the platform. She peered over and down, then backed away when she heard the soft clatter of debris. A reflection of the candle flame gleamed dully in the oily water and some small creature darted out of the light with a splash. She looked across the chasm to where the opposite wall must be and realized that the light she thought she'd seen had been a reflection of Vere's tallow lantern off old glass.

Vere extended an arm. "Do you know what this place was, lady?"

"These are subway tunnels. The men of old Meriga used them to go from place to place throughout the city at speeds of sixty, seventy miles an hour."

"An hour? Almost a whole day's ride in an hour?"

"Maybe even faster. I don't know."

Vere looked around, his thin face so like his father's expectant in the gloom. He was tall like Abelard, but his frame was bony, his shoulders round and hunched. His clothes were a motley assortment of frayed tunics and cast-off shirts, layered over each other for warmth and ease of movement.

"Look." His sudden shift in interest reminded her of Abelard. He held out a rusted metal case, perhaps a foot square. "Look what I found."

He put the box on the floor and picked up the lantern he had set behind them. "I smashed the lock getting it out. I was going to bring it to you upstairs, but let's look now."

She held her candle over the box, and he worked at the lock with a small knife, running the blade along the edge, scraping away the accumulated rust of centuries. The top opened with the squeal of ancient hinges.

"Look, lady!" He sounded as excited as a child on his birthday.

She peered over his shoulder into the container, as curious as he. Bright colors, impossibly red and yellow and blue, lay jumbled in heaps. Gingerly, Vere touched one of the small, rectangular-shaped pieces. It was hollow, smooth-sided, with cylindrical protuberances on top, and matching depressions underneath. She heard his swift intake of breath, and his expression suddenly made her want to laugh. "What is this?"

She reached over him and picked up two of the little objects. Carefully, she fitted them together. "See? Like this?"

"But, what are they? What are they for?"

"Blocks. Toys. What the children of old Meriga played with."

"These? Colored so bright . . . why, lady, after all these centuries they have not faded. Surely such precious things are not suitable for toys."

She shrugged. "But they are. See—" She picked up another piece, fitted it with the first two. "You build with these."

Vere looked more closely into the box. A tiny hand poked through the jumbled mass. He lifted a doll from beneath the shapes. It was naked, with an incredibly tiny waist, narrow hips and large breasts. Red hair had been hacked clumsily around its head. "And this." He turned it over, examined its every crevice. "Is this what women looked like in old Meriga, lady?"

Again she shrugged, amused by his scrutiny. "I hardly think so. I've never seen a woman look like that before—it's just a doll."

He sifted through the box, the little building blocks rattling around his fingers. "Ah, look!" From beneath, he drew a small metal object with four black wheels, faded green paint chipped in spots and a number discernible on its top.

"That's a car—a fuel-powered vehicle they used to use on the streets above. That's what they looked like, only bigger, of course."

He turned it upside down, his index finger tracing the outline of the engine. "What a world it must have been!"

"Where did you find this?"

"Back there—" He gestured toward a tunnel. "There's a room, full of bones and rocks. I found this under the bones."

"A child's things. Must have been caught down here in the earthshakes during the Armageddon. You mustn't bring them up, you know that?"

He shook his head in disgust. "I know, the priests." Suddenly, he seemed to remember where they were, and he looked at her with a puzzled expression on his face. "What are you doing down here, lady? Why did you come?"

As abruptly as if he had doused her with cold water, she was yanked back into the present. Reluctantly, she put the blocks into his hand. "I was looking for you. They told me in the kitchens that this was probably where you'd be, or in the crypts, so I—"

"Why me?"

"I need your help." Her white hand on his ragged sleeve made an odd contrast.

Vere blushed. "What—what do you want with me, lady?"

"When your father leaves this spring, I will go with him. Lady Mara doesn't think it's safe for me here, in Ahga—"

"Because of my grandmother." Vere's voice was flat.

Nydia nodded. "When I leave, I need someone to look after my books—they are too precious to take on a campaign."

"You go to war, lady?" Vere was incredulous.

She dropped her eyes.

"Do you know how dangerous—what do you owe my father that you would risk . . ." In the young voice, she was amazed to hear the unmistakable note of jealousy.

She looked up, then, and understood. This tall, thin youth was more than a boy, and he responded to her as a man. She took her hand from his arm and picked up her skirts. "Come. Let's talk."

He followed her back through the low doorway and watched with narrowed eyes as she seated herself on one of the stone crypts. She wedged the candle into a crevice. Shadows flickered on the old brick walls.

Silently he sat and waited.

"You know under what circumstances your father found me. And you alone, besides your father and Phineas, know what is in my books. I pledged allegiance to your father when I first came to Ahga—" She held up her hand at his astonishment. "He swore to protect me with his life and I swore to use my abilities in his service."

"You use the Magic for him?" Vere whispered.

"No! I have another gift. I see the future."

"A prescient. You're a prescient. I thought they were all dead, killed in the Persecutions—is it true that a child born of a prescient is an empath?" His expression changed from awkward desire to something like worship. "Is such a thing really possible? Can you really see the future?"

In as few words as she possibly could, she explained her ability. "But the future depends upon the choices of each individual. Everything I see can be changed."

"No wonder you fear the priests."

"So, please, Vere, will you guard my books, care for them? They are all I have of my old life, and they are very, very dangerous."

He nodded without hesitation. "With my life if I must, lady."

Tedmund used that same tone of reckless devotion. She touched his hand and smiled. "Thank you." Nydia dusted off her skirts as she rose.

"When will you leave?"

"Soon, I think. Your father has not yet made up his mind, but I understand that the raids in Arkan are worse every day."

He nodded, dragged one foot through the gravel on the floor. For a moment his face was bitter.

"Vere?"

"There is a certain irony in this, lady. Do you see it?"

She shook her head.

"You go on the campaign with my father while I hide here—in the ruins of an ancient city—down with the bones and rubble. Anything so I don't have to go to war."

"It was not always so," she said, uncertain of his meaning. "There were many men who did not fight in Old Meriga."

"But as my father would say, this is not Old Meriga, is it, lady? And there can only be a new Meriga if every man is willing to give his life for it."

"I—I don't know that that's true, Vere. Not every man fights—there are merchants and farmers and—" She sat down next to him and picked up his rough hand. The fingers were long and delicate; the nails, though dirty, were cut neatly. "There is more in Meriga than war, Vere. There is music and singing and poetry. There are the fine arts of the gold- and silversmiths. And think of the woodworkers, the weavers, the dyers who draw the most beautiful colors from the most unexpected places. Or the stonemasons and the engineers, who from the ruins of Old Meriga have raised up castles and towers and bridges. There are a hundred things or more which have nothing to do with fighting."

"All made possible because of men like my father."

"I suppose that's true to a certain degree. There is more here in Ahga than in many other places because the Ridenaus have kept the peace so long. But perhaps our way, of son following father, is not always for the best. Do you know that the Mutens have a peculiar custom—though I suppose it is as sensible as ours, maybe better. When a child is ten years old, they take that child and test it, see if he or she has any particular talents or abilities. And depending upon what the results of those tests are, the child is allowed to become whatever he or she wishes. It has nothing to do with what the father or the mother is."

"The mother?"

"In the Muten tribes, it is not unheard of for a woman to do more than spin or sew or cook. In fact, some of their greatest Pr'f—" She broke off, biting her lip.

"Tell me," he demanded, and in that moment she remembered he was a prince of a warrior race.

"It is forbidden to speak of such things."

"Forbidden by whom? Who cares?"

"I care," she said, so softly he nearly could not hear.

"Why?" This time the tone in his voice was unmistakably his father's.

"I should not have said so much. Please, let's—"

"No, wait, lady. I've heard the old women say that the Mutens have the Old Magic—that they know more about Old Meriga than we do."

She heard the plea, understood the desperation, the need to find a place where one belonged. She hesitated, shot a glance over his shoulder, looked as far into his future as she could. She saw nothing more than an apple hastily stolen from the kitchens. "It's true."

"Have you ever talked to them? Do you know them? Could you tell me where to find them?"

"Vere, no, you don't understand. There are certain things which I cannot reveal—things I am sworn never to tell. Don't ask me any more—and don't try to find out for yourself. You'll be as sorry as I am if you do."

He stared at her, thin face pale in the flickering light. She reminded herself that this was a boy, no matter how sympathetic or how kind he seemed. But when he spoke at last, after a brief pause, he did not sound like a boy. "Truth can't be hidden, lady. Not forever. I will do all I can to keep your books safe. For now. But someday I will go and find these Mutens. If they will teach me what I want to know, I will learn what I can." He leaned against the cobwebbed crypt which held the bones of his grandfather, Abelard's father.

"Listen to me, Vere. I know things are difficult for you—I know you feel you don't fit in—"

"Fit in?" He spun on his heel so suddenly she was startled, and again the intensity of his expression reminded her of the King. "Lady, do you know you are the first person I have ever met I can talk to? The only person in my entire life who does not laugh but listens?" The hunched shoulders fixed in frustration. "Can you imagine what it's like for me? The only one out of the whole litter that's too clumsy to swing a sword—too clumsy to even fight with quarterstaves?"

She held out her hand. "Vere, I didn't mean—"

He took a deep breath as if with a great effort. He looked up at the great crest over the tomb, then back at her. His shoulders sagged. "Forgive me. Of course I will do as you ask. Come. It must be nearly dinnertime."

She smiled, remembered the filched apple. She allowed him to guide her through the crypts and up the ancient stairs to emerge into the warmth and light of the great kitchens of Ahga. He took her to the passage which led into the hall, and with the merest touch of his father's grace, bowed and whirled away, slipping an apple out of a basket on the floor as he melted into the confusion.

Nydia stepped into the dimly lit corridor. Even in Ahga, wax candles were too expensive for the kitchen staff, and the walls were lined with sconces set with rushlights.

Her conversation with Vere troubled her. If the boy should try to find the Mutens, she would hold herself responsible for whatever happened to him. She halted in the center of the corridor. Should she go after him—try to explain what had happened to her at greater length? Her flesh crawled at the memory of the squat Muten, its long-fingered hand caressing her flesh, black eyes boring into her skull, as though it sought to enter . . .

No. She would never disturb those memories. They were laid to rest as surely as the bones of Abelard's ancestors in their quiet crypts. She felt very weary. Should she stay down here, she thought, and eat in the hall? Perhaps she would return to the kitchen and let the staff know that she would not need a tray carried to the high tower room. Her waiting woman would be glad of that. Still musing, she turned and collided with Agara.

Agara smiled down at her, thin lips drawing back over her large white teeth. "Lady Nydia," she drawled. "At last you grace us with your presence. A month or more's gone by since we last saw you—and you've not joined us in the chapel since the New Year's Rites."

Nydia glanced around Agara. The woman was not alone. Two black-clad priests, hands tucked into the long sleeves of their gowns, stood behind her. One wore the green, white, and blue surplice of the Three, the other the purple surplice of the One. Before, she had glimpsed these priests only at a distance.

Agara did not wait for Nydia's reply. She turned back to the priests. "Rever'd Ursla, Rever'd Renn, I expect that you know the Lady Nydia Farhallen."

Nydia stiffened.

The priest on Agara's left, Ursla, cleared her throat. "From a distance, my lady. I saw her at the New Year's Rites, among the other women of the castle."

"Then you, Renn, surely you know her?"

Renn's face was expressionless, her voice flat without inflection. "Nor I, my lady. The last I saw her was in the great hall at the King's birthday."

"The King's birthday. Of course." Agara took a step forward, and Nydia tried to stand her ground. "You have not come for Absolution or Atonement, lady? You do not feel the need to beg the Three or the One for forgiveness?"

Nydia bit her lip.

"How shall we ever make reparation to the One and the Three?"

"For what, lady?"

Agara exchanged an arch glance with her priests. Renn raised her eyebrows. Her flat moon face was expressionless. "For the sins of our fathers, which shall be visited on the children, even unto the hundredth generation."

"My father did not believe we are guilty of anything."

Agara snorted. "What could a man know? Did your mother not teach of the necessity for the Absolution or Atonement?"

"Under certain circumstances." Nydia clenched her hands in her skirts. The servers were beginning to bring in the dinner, and the passageway was becoming crowded. Nydia moved to one side, but Agara stood her ground. The servers hurrying past were forced to scurry around her or run the risk of jostling her with their great platters and baskets of linens, plates, and cutlery.

Agara's eyes bore down on her, Nydia felt herself shrink. "Or is there something more, my lady? Do you know something which we—the rest of us—do not? Something which you keep up in that tower room of yours—the one you so seldom leave?"

Desperately, Nydia glanced over the woman's shoulder into the future. The picture shifted, tilted, figures wobbled before her eyes, grew solid, then indistinct. "There's nothing, lady. I know nothing." She gasped. The pattern crystallized. Agara was going to order that her rooms be searched. She did not intend to wait until her son was out of Ahga.

Agara threw her a look of something like triumph and raised her chin. She took a breath and Nydia knew what her words would be before she spoke.

Another voice, young and fresh, rang down the passage, and before Nydia's disbelieving eyes, the vision disintegrated. "Lady Agara, the King commands your presence."

Agara paused in mid-breath, her mouth open to give the orders for the search. A woman stood at the doorway of the long corridor which led from the hall. She was young, perhaps five or more years younger than Nydia. She sauntered toward them, a lazy seductive stroll calculated to infuriate Agara even more.

The light reflected off the top of the girl's smooth blond head, for she wore no coif. Her hair cascaded freely down her back in long waves. Her gown, cut low over her bosom so that her heavy breasts threatened to spill out, rustled with the heavy whisper of silk, and the fabric seemed to shimmer in the rushlight. Her skin had the same silky texture of her gown. "Well?" Her voice was low and husky, and Nydia caught the scent of her perfume. "The King said at once."

Agara's thin mouth tightened. "Where did you get that pearl?"

Around the girl's neck, a tear-shaped pearl dangled on the end of a silver chain. With two fingers, she stroked the jewel delicately, caressing it as she raised her chin and smiled. "You know where, lady."

Agara made what might have been a snarl and pushed past Nydia, hand outstretched as though she might tear the pearl off the girl's throat. With a graceful gesture, the girl sidestepped, hand curled protectively around the chain. "Don't even think of it, lady," she taunted. "The King himself bid me wear this tonight—if nothing else."

Something like madness blazed from Agara's face, something dangerous and unleashed. But the girl stood her ground. Her expression reminded Nydia of a cat found licking the last drops of cream from its whiskers.

Without another word, Agara rushed past, the two priests hurrying to keep up with her.

When they were out of sight, and even their footsteps had faded away, Nydia sighed in relief and nodded at the girl. "Thank you."

She shrugged. "I only obeyed the King."

Nydia remembered her name: Liss. A farmer's daughter, Tavia had said, who'd caught Abelard's eye when her father came to plead a case in the King's Court of Appeals. If her father's intention had been to gain sympathy by displaying his beautiful daughter, he had succeeded in that, at least. Liss had remained behind.

"Your name's Nydia, right?"

Nydia nodded.

"You need to learn how to handle that one."

Nydia smoothed her skirts. "I doubt I'll ever be able to do that."

"It's easy. You're much too afraid of her—give her too much power. Why should she be able to terrorize us all?"

"She is the King's mother. She has the Bishop's ear, and that of every priest in Ahga."

"And I'm the King's favorite, and I've got a lot more than his ear." Liss laughed. "And so could you, if you wanted it."

Nydia dropped her eyes.

"Oh, I don't mind. These last two months have been like a dream for me—who would ever have thought I'd be wearing anything like this?" She held out her wide skirts, and the silk flashed. "Who are you? You are a lady, aren't you? Even if he hadn't told me—you've got it written all over your face."

Nydia started. What else had Abelard told the girl?

As if she heard Nydia's thoughts, the girl cocked her head. "He doesn't say very much about you, but I can tell by the way he watches that he wants you. Sometimes at night, when he holds me, I think it's you he's holding. And you are very beautiful—prettier than me." She came a little closer, and Nydia saw a curious kindness beneath the flippant exterior. "Look," Liss said impulsively, "if you need help with that woman—that witch—come to me. She doesn't like me and I don't like her, but I'm not afraid of her."

Nydia tried to smile, although her lower lip quivered. "Thank you."

"Ah, don't be upset." Liss put an arm protectively over Nydia's shoulder. "She's not worth it. We're leaving in a few weeks—"

"We?"

"The King doesn't travel so far alone."

When Nydia said nothing, Liss smiled. "I'll be frank with you. I don't know why you don't want him, but I don't mind at all."

Aren't you afraid of him? Nydia wanted to say. Afraid he'll make you do something you don't want to do?

Liss fingered her pearl protectively. "Come. It's time for dinner. We'll talk about what to pack."

Chapter Twelve

❧

They left Ahga early on a May morning as a rosy dawn broke over the eastern sky. Despite the hour, the twisted streets of the city were lined with cheering crowds, who endured the early morning chill to watch their King ride to war. They showered him with the first spring buds, waved evergreen branches and white linen squares as he rode past.

Abelard, tall in his saddle, basked in the admiration. The broadsword strapped across his back threw off glints of light from the jewels in its hilt. He nodded and smiled in acknowledgment, and here and there paused to accept a drink or choice morsel offered by women in the crowd. He bowed to every woman from whose hand he accepted a favor, no matter how young or old, plain or pretty. It was not until they were at last clear of the city walls that they made any kind of progress at all.

Phineas rode by the King's side, surrounded by the lieutenants of the mounted regiments of the King's Guard. As they reached the open road, and the company spilled out in looser formation, Nydia rode up with Tedmund of Linoys by her side. Phineas noticed the tension in Abelard's face, the subtle narrowing of his eyes and the sidelong glance he gave the couple. If Tedmund himself had noticed the King's displeasure, he gave no sign.

Instead, he seemed blissfully unaware. He reached across Nydia's saddle and picked up her hand. "Quite soon, now, sweetheart," he said, quite oblivious of Abelard's sudden scowl. "Do you see that toll plaza up ahead?"

When she nodded, he went on, "That's the border of Linoys. Those are my colors those guards wear, and those are my fields they guard."

Abelard did not seem to have heard, but Phineas saw her glance in the King's direction. He met her dark eyes with concern, then turned away with a puckered frown. Abruptly, Phineas remembered the change he had been told by the King to make in Tedmund's orders and was suddenly uneasy. Phineas narrowed his eyes, watched Abelard's gaze linger on Nydia. Was it only a disruption in the usual routine, understandable under the circumstances? Or was there some darker purpose? Abelard had insisted that Tedmund was to believe that the order came from Phineas. He was unwilling, he said, to undermine the boy's self-confidence.

Nydia gave Tedmund a wider smile.

Encouraged, he continued, "The prettiest land in all of Meriga, my land is. The people of Ahga feed on the bread of my fields. Is that not so, Lord King?"

"Indeed, Lord Senador," replied Abelard, "and for the privilege of raising the crops for the King's table, you pay the lowest taxes in all of Meriga."

Tedmund's smile disappeared.

"Lord King." Phineas edged closer. "I have been thinking that we must reinforce our supply lines into Arkan."

Abelard gave Phineas a moody stare. As he drew the King into deliberate conversation regarding the campaign, Phineas watched the byplay between Nydia and Tedmund. Stung by the King's rebuke, Tedmund looked dejected, though he brightened when Nydia touched his arm and asked him some question about his holdings.

Phineas listened with half an ear. Like most of the professional army, he tended to hold the Senadors, whose main occupation was farming, in something which bordered on contempt. Still, the farms of Linoys did indeed supply not only the markets of Ahga but many of the army's provisions, as well. And Linoys was a pretty estate, all soft rolling hills and gentle fields, tinged with the first green of the new crops.

He did not believe the boy deserved Abelard's reproof or disdain. But the King seemed determined to make a soldier out of Tedmund. Phineas thought again of the new orders Abelard had insisted he give Tedmund before they left Ahga, and shrugged. Perhaps Tedmund was the product of a sheltered upbringing, the favored son of doting parents. Perhaps Abelard was correct. A journey into southern Arkan, a scouting expedition, would give Tedmund a chance to acquire the experience he lacked. Still, Phineas had doubts. He was careful to keep Abelard engaged in conversation.

As the shadows lengthened toward evening, they reached Tedmund's keep at Sprinfell. The little castle stood perched on a gentle rise by the far banks of a lazy river. It was of ancient design and perfectly placed upon the hill, as beautiful now as it was when new.

To the right, one square tower rose five stories high; behind it, and perpendicular, another stood perhaps three. The years had buffed the stone to a soft gray, and the setting sun cast a rosy light on the walls. To the right, on the other side of a small courtyard, a low rounded building stood, with guards posted on the roof as lookouts. Tedmund spurred his horse on to a gallop, letting out a loud haloo as he rode across the bridge.

He was greeted by answering shouts from the men atop the roof, and as the rest of the company crossed the bridge, a long silk standard was raised over the battlements, the red and silver of Linoys. Tedmund had halted at the base of the hill. He turned back to the company, and a broad smile lit his face. "Welcome," he cried. "Welcome, Lord King, my lady, honored guests. Welcome to Sprinfell. Rest and be honored."

Phineas glanced up to see another banner unfurl, Abelard's white and blue, the eagle plain in the center. He reined in beside Nydia. "A fine sight, isn't it, lady?"

"Yes, indeed. No wonder Tedmund loves his home and hates to leave it."

"It wouldn't remain his home if he did not learn to leave it.

Shall we go?" Politely, he held back, allowing her to ride on ahead. And so Nydia entered Tedmund's keep just behind the King.

At the feast that evening, Nydia sat on Tedmund's left who, as lord of the holding, occupied the central seat. Abelard, the guest of highest rank, sat on Tedmund's right. Liss was beside the King on his right. She toyed with the food on her plate.

Although the hour was late, Tedmund had ordered that a feast be laid for the King, and the meal had been elaborate as any she had ever seen at Ahga. The remains of a great haunch of meat lay in front of Abelard, and platters which had been piled high with fruits and cheeses, breads and vegetables were nearly empty. Abelard and Tedmund were laughing together over some joke; Liss leaned on Abelard's arm and giggled. There was an empty space for Phineas next to Liss; some problem with one of the horses had occupied him since their arrival.

Nydia listened to the banter between Abelard and Tedmund, relieved that the hostility Abelard had displayed on the journey seemed to have dissipated. She was tired as much from the tension as from the journey. When Tedmund turned to her, trying to draw her into the conversation, she only smiled quietly.

The company grew so loud the musicians had to strain to be heard over it. Abruptly, Abelard rose in his seat, goblet in hand. "There you are, Captain Phineas. We'd begun to miss you. No doubt a mare required your attention?"

Nydia looked up to see Phineas striding down the center aisle toward the high table. The captain shrugged and grinned.

"Is she well settled for the night?"

Phineas bowed briefly. "I guarantee she'll sleep till morning, Lord King." There were snickers of laughter around the hall.

"Let all the mares and fillies rest so well." Abelard raised his goblet and drained it. The rest rose, some less steady than others, and drank.

Without pausing, Abelard turned back to Tedmund. "Our

host informs me that as a boy he had some renown here as a singer—isn't this true, Lord Tedmund?"

Tedmund shrugged, looking both pleased and abashed.

"Then come, Lord Senador, give us a song—a song to your lady."

Without more encouragement, Tedmund rose, bowed to the company, and took the harp handed to him. He ran his fingers over the strings, and the crowd murmured. Abelard held up his hand for silence, and the company quieted.

"As far as the plain is wide, my love
As long as the sky is high,
As deep as the forest is green, my love,
As constantly as the tide.

Whatever you would ask of me,
My answer shall not change,
As long as life beats in my blood,
My love for you remains,

As far as the plain is wide, my love,
As long as the sky is high,
As deep as the forest is green, my love,
As constantly as the tide."

Nydia bent her head. Tedmund's voice was not unpleasant: a wistful tenor as plaintive and sweet as his song.

As the harp faded into silence, Abelard set his goblet down heavily and clapped. Tedmund blushed like a girl, and under cover of the applause signaled for the musicians to begin to play a dance tune.

"Yes," cried the King, "let's dance and be merry this night—for who knows what we go to find tomorrow?"

Nydia raised her head at that. Something in Abelard's reckless tone disturbed her. She met the King's eyes with a little puckered frown. Abelard pushed his chair back and stood. "Will you open the dancing, lady?" He held out his hand to Nydia.

She glanced at Liss, who shrugged. Nydia was the lady of highest rank, without question; it was her place to open the dancing with Abelard. She could not refuse without offering an insult.

Tedmund, still glowing from the applause, nodded and urged her on. Nydia rose unsteadily. Surreptitiously, she wiped her hands in her skirts before she laid her fingers on Abelard's open palm.

The King's hand closed around hers like a glove cut to her measure. He swung her out into the center of the wide, polished floor. The candles and the torches reflected on its surface like stars. The music was wild, as though it dared her to fling all caution aside. As she danced, the ribbons in her hair loosened and her curls tumbled down her shoulders. She remembered they were a day's ride away from Agara's prying eyes, and suddenly she looked up to meet Abelard's gaze with unaccustomed daring. Her heart beat faster.

Abelard swung her practically off her feet. She gripped his hand, startled, and looked down. Instantly, he settled her, his touch gentle and reassuring. He pulled her closer. Through her skirts she felt the hard muscles of his thighs, and her cheeks pinkened.

"You're out of step, my dear," he whispered, and his hip thrust against hers.

The music throbbed through her, as demanding as his arms. She threw her head back, tossed her hair over her shoulder. Her long white throat was exposed and his eyes followed the curve down to the modest neckline of her gown. His hand pressed her forward, against his body, and she gave herself over to the music's insistent pulse. Their bodies molded, all sleek lines and curves, meshed in the rhythm of the dance. Some of the other dancers stopped to watch.

The musicians sensed the change in the King's mood and without missing a beat, slowed the tempo.

She raised her eyes to Abelard's and caught her breath at the heat she saw there. "Do you know this dance, Lord King?" Even to her ears her voice sounded soft, wanton.

"Certainly I do—do you?"

"If you'll lead, I can follow."

"But will you follow wherever I lead, I wonder?"

"Would you lead me where I wouldn't want to go?"

His smile narrowed and lifted the corners of his eyes. His hand moved lazily down her back to rest with gentle yet insistent pressure just above her hip. "I think not, my dear. I'll only take you where—and when—you wish."

There was obvious pride on Tedmund's face as he led Nydia across the smooth slate courtyard to his chambers. As the heavy door closed behind them, she turned into his embrace. The dance with Abelard had aroused her. Her body felt liquid, as though her bones had dissolved in the heat of passion. She wanted to wallow in this moment, savor each second of the present before it passed. She shut her eyes against her visions.

"Why do you close your eyes? Am I so ugly, you can't stand the sight?"

She glanced up, careful to look anywhere but over his shoulder. "No, not at all." In the months since she had shared his bed, she had never shared her secrets. Lest he continue to question, she tugged at his tunic. "Come, let's to bed. We won't have many nights like this—"

"No," he agreed, nuzzling her neck, "in fact, tonight will be our last together for quite a while. I leave at dawn—Phineas has changed my orders and is sending me south."

She pulled back, out of his embrace. "South? Ahead of the army? Why?"

"There've been reports of an outlaw massing in the deep desert south of Arkan. Up until this afternoon, one of the other captains was supposed to lead the expedition, but Phineas has decided to hold his company in reserve."

"But why you? Why the change?" Memory flared on the edges of her awareness like the flicker of a flame in a breeze. She twined her fingers in his tunic.

"Why not me? I'm to lead my own men. Don't you think I can handle it?"

Steeling herself against what she might see, Nydia looked deliberately into his future. He stood on the banks of a muddy river, dark brown under a sky of piercing blue, his fair skin sunburnt, freckled and peeling. The light was so intense it hurt his eyes. He wore a length of fabric wound around his head to protect himself against the sun. He had to make a decision, she thought. There, beside that sluggish water. "Please, you will be careful?"

"Of course I'll be careful. Do you think I want to die?" Gently he disengaged her grip. He kissed her, forestalling any more objections.

At the mention of death, the warning flared again, brighter and more insistent, the memory of some knowledge struggling to the surface of her consciousness. She shut her eyes, pressed closer into his chest. He smoothed her hair, whispered reassurances. "Don't you know I'll always come back to you?"

If you can. She pushed that thought aside, turned her face up to his and opened her mouth to receive his kiss. He guided her to the bed, his fingers fumbling with laces and bindings as he laid her on her back, and their clothes slithered heedlessly to the floor. The sheets were cool in the twilight. The only sound was the gentle snap and hiss of the fire. He stretched out beside her, and the mattress creaked under his weight. He touched her cheek with tentative fingertips, as though he weren't quite convinced she was there. "I sang that song for you tonight; I meant every word of it. Even if I were to die tomorrow, I've been happier these months with you than ever before."

His mention of death frightened her. "Don't say that," she whispered. "Don't talk about dying." He cupped her breasts, and she reached around his neck to pull him down. Inexplicably, she thought of Liss, who had left the hall on Abelard's arm, and of the two of them entwined.

She thought of Abelard's hands—the coarse gold hairs which curled on the backs, the palms smoothly callused. She thought of how those hands would feel if it were he who pressed her breasts to his mouth. She forgot Tedmund and her fears.

As passion overwhelmed her, it seemed as though a ghostly image of the King overlay the man who rained light kisses on her belly. She groaned as he spread her legs, and against her closed lids the tongue which teased the wet mound between her thighs was Abelard's. She twined her fingers in his hair, hair which was gold, not red. Let it be the King, her mind screamed, and she lifted her hips.

Later, when he had fallen asleep, she rose and gathered the folds of her nightdress about her. She stood, troubled, by the window.

The full moon had risen above the castle walls, and the courtyard below was bathed in silvery light. She heard the guards who kept the watch muttering among themselves. From the direction of the stables, she could hear the whicker and stamp of the horses. The earthy odors of the stables mingled with the tang of herbs in the kitchen garden and the sweet scent of the roses climbing the trellis on the wall.

Despite the peace which lay around her like a cloak, something was not quite right—something she had seen from that day in Abelard's audience room, when over Abelard's shoulder she had first looked into a future at once both obscure and obvious.

Why? What was wrong with what she had seen? She pressed her hands to her temples and tried to remember. Two armies—mountains rising steeply all around—was that it? Surely on the plains of Arkan there were no mountains. And the men—Abelard's men, dressed in the uniforms she was accustomed to, but the men they fought, what standard had they carried? A white field—an orange sun rising behind a green hill? Did the Harleys carry standards? Who fought under such a flag?

She looked back at Tedmund, now softly snoring into his pillow. Foreknowledge was not the blessing one might suppose it to be, she thought. There was too much she would rather not know, episodes of human suffering which were the results of thoughtless choices made carelessly, heedlessly. And how, she wondered, would she cope with the scenes she was sure to see—these men who would ride to their deaths upon the orders of their captains and the King. Did Abelard ever remember, she wondered, when he reviewed the ranks of the regiments, that some would not return? Did he ever meet a man's eyes and think, "This day, I send this man to die?"

A soft breeze ruffled her hair. It brought the scent of the newly turned earth, the first buds. The window faced southwest: the direction they would take in the morning. The horizon lay flat in the distance—no mountains for hundreds of miles. Where then, she wondered, were the mountains ocher and brown, sharply rising into high peaks capped with snow? And what army marched under that standard?

She shivered as the breeze blew harder.

"Nydia, sweet." Tedmund rose on one elbow. "What's wrong?"

She turned without thinking, and in the gloom she saw it again—his future where it lay over his shoulder. She saw him at the time and place of his decision. She could not see beyond it. With a sigh, she went back to bed and brought his outstretched hand to her lips. "Nothing. Nothing's wrong." Then added to herself, "I hope."

Chapter Thirteen

*Gost, 47th Year in the Reign of the Ridenau Kings
(2715, Muten Old Calendar)*

*S*omething is wrong, thought Phineas. In the hot glare of the midday sun, he shifted restlessly in his saddle and squinted at the western horizon. Beyond the river, which wound like a silver thread at the base of the sepia foothills, Senifay lay in the mountains. According to the reports of the scouts and the messengers from Gredahl, the Harleys were in full retreat. He had expected to see some sign of them, but as the army pushed further and further west, the Harleys had apparently melted into the deserts like spring snow. Abelard drove relentlessly across the desert, certain that at last they had some chance of corralling their ancient enemy.

The bridge was a curious blend of old and new, for the changes wrought by the Armageddon had carved a new channel into the land. The surface of the bridge had once been a highway arching over another road. The supporting piers had been scoured by the relentless wind and water of passing centuries, but the wooden railings on either side were hardly weathered. Now dark water flowed sluggishly through the steep, high banks on either side of the bridge, and the late summer air was thick with heat.

The camp spread out in the shadow of the bridge, where the ancient pillars provided some shade against the blazing sun. From his vantage point, Phineas could see the men at their ease in the heat of the day. Some sat gnawing on the camp rations, which they supplemented by hunting; others polished weapons, washed or mended uniforms. Light glinted off the edges of swords and pikes and spears.

Heat shimmered off the sticky black surface of the bridge. Phineas's horse tossed his head and snorted. Absentmindedly, Phineas patted the side of his neck and clucked a reassurance. He had not expected the army to come so far west. The supply lines were stretched thin—and here, in this no man's land of fumbling foothills covered with wind-whipped trees and stunted, parched pines, they were vulnerable to unexpected raids. Phineas was glad Senifay was so close. If the scouts did not come back soon with some report of the outlaws' position, they would cross the bridge in the morning and send word to Senifay. With reinforcements, they could launch an attack from the far side of the bridge.

He flapped his reins and the horse slowly clopped down the incline, head low. In the center of the camp, he could see Abelard's command tent, his own beside it, and the tents where the captains were quartered. Pitched a little apart was the tent which Nydia ostensibly shared with Liss.

Nydia slept alone, he knew. The King did not. Neither did most of the men, for here and there was a flash and swirl of the short, cropped skirts of the camp followers. Occasionally, one or two of the bolder ones approached him, but Phineas rarely took advantage of the favors they so freely offered. Their eager faces saddened him, made him pity them for reasons most of the men would find inexplicable. Lacking land, he had no great need to father a child. And to Phineas, who had spent most of his life engaged in systematic killing, who had seen human flesh mangled and maimed in ways more terrible than he cared to remember, a human body was too precious to exchange for the mere promise of a hug in the night, an arm to lean upon, a meal or a place by a fire.

But he could not deny the thoughts of Nydia, which came unbidden in the drowsy moments before sleep, memories of the sight of her as she danced in Abelard's arms at Sprinfell Castle, glimpses of the rounded curves of her breasts beneath the thin fabric of her light summer gowns. And the act of will which had forced him to turn his back upon her that cold night nearly one year ago at Ithan Ford, when he had ached to see if her body was truly as perfect as he remembered when she had let the rude shroud fall to her feet before them all. He shut his eyes deliberately against that memory.

He wiped the sweat from his face. The land rippled in the heat haze. A cloud of dust rising out of the east over the hills caught his attention.

He urged the horse forward at a faster pace. Dust billowed and finally disgorged a rider who clung to the bare back of a horse with foam on its flanks and at its mouth. A sentry caught at the rough rope bridle, and the rider rolled off into the arms of another, who flung aside his spear.

They shouted for water and a doctor. Phineas slid off his horse and pushed through the curious men who pressed in closer.

A rank odor like old cheese rose from the prone form, the stench of one kept in close confinement for a long time, given barely adequate food, and forced to lie in his own excrement. The horse he had ridden was lathered, eyes rolling widely, chest heaving in great labored breaths. The white foam on its mouth was flecked with blood.

"See to this animal," Phineas ordered the closest soldier. "I'll be surprised if we don't lose it in this heat." He dropped to his knees beside the man and recognized what remained of the tattered uniform as he did so. This was no scout. This was one of Tedmund Allcort's men—one of the ones who had ridden out of Linoys with Tedmund over three months ago.

His chin was dark with a straggled beard. Dirt caked the deep lines of the exhausted face. One arm dangled uselessly by his side.

"Is he conscious?" Phineas propped his head while the sentry poured a little water from his flask between the man's colorless cracked lips.

For answer, the man moaned. The sentry poured a little more water in his mouth and waited. Red-rimmed eyes fluttered opened, closed, and finally opened. Recognition dawned. "Captain—" It was a weak whisper.

"The Lord of Linoys?" Phineas resisted the urge to shake the man.

"Dead. They were waiting for us—south of Arkan. Crossed into Loma. Outlaws got us there. Dragged us back. To the Tree. Crucified him on it. Don't know why they let me go."

Silence had spread through the ranks when he began to speak, and now, as the faint whisper died, a mutter rose, gradually intensifying as the news spread. Despite the heat, Phineas went cold. Something like rage closed around his heart, made his mouth go dry. He remembered Tedmund's face on the day he rode from Sprinfell—so full of purpose, proud and eager to serve his King. He did not feel the tap on his arm the first time.

"Sir?" The gray-bearded face of the camp doctor peered down at him, brow wrinkled in concern.

Reluctantly, Phineas rose, stepped back. "Do what you can." He watched the sentries lift the injured man as gently as possible and carry him away.

His eyes ranged once more over the empty horizon. Two thoughts sprang clear: anger at the senseless waste of the life of a young, loyal supporter, and growing realization that the Harleys must be somewhere very close. Heartsick, he stalked with grim purpose to the King.

Abelard was sifting through the dispatches on the long wooden table which served him as a crude desk. He looked up when Phineas stuck his head through the tent flap. "Well?"

"One of Tedmund's men came in. Tedmund's dead and his whole company with him." If there was accusation in Phineas's voice, Abelard chose not to hear it.

"How?" Abelard's voice was flat, completely devoid of expression.

"Does it matter?"

Abelard shot Phineas a dangerous look, calculated to cow a man less brave.

Phineas cleared his throat. He understood immediately that Abelard, his friend, was gone. It was the King of Meriga who sat before him, eyeing him with cool detachment. He straightened to attention, his posture that of a subordinate reporting to his commander. "The survivor, who's more dead than alive at this point, said they were attacked when they crossed into Loma."

"Loma?" Abelard's voice rose in disbelief tinged with anger. "Why'd the fool go there? He should've known the Harleys would be waiting—"

"At the time his orders were changed"—Phineas chose his words carefully—"it was pointed out that the young Senador had only limited experience fighting the Harleys." He did not say by whom.

"Yes, I remember." Abelard laid the rolls of parchment in ordered progression. He stared moodily at the hide map stretched out and pinned to the tabletop. "Anything else?"

Phineas took a deep breath. "Abelard, this changes things, don't you think?"

Abelard raised his head and stared out the tent flap. The words did not seem to register.

Phineas broke his stance. "Damn it, don't you see? We've been lured into a trap."

Abelard did not respond.

"But where are the Harleys?" Phineas asked. "According to our reports, there should have been a large host holed up somewhere west of Fort Dodge. So where are they?"

"Where do you think they are?"

"I think they're behind us. I think unless we get some promise of reinforcements and supplies from Senifay and Rissona, we'll be cut off very quickly."

"Have you sent a dispatch to Senifay?"

"Not yet."

"Then you'd better do that, don't you think?"

Phineas spun on his heel. "As you say, Lord King. As soon as I tell Lady Nydia the news. Unless you'd rather?"

Abelard ignored the question. "You will make it clear to her that the Senador of Linoys went south on your orders." The King's eyes bore into Phineas's with such intensity Phineas felt as though surely Abelard could see inside his skull.

Phineas gazed back, every fiber of loyalty he possessed stretched to its limit. So Abelard would accept no blame and expected Phineas to assume complete responsibility for Tedmund's death. Unbidden, the words of the oath he had sworn to the King echoed through his brain like the throb of a funeral drum. It was the code by which he lived his life: it defined and shaped him. He knew nothing else; without it, he was no more than the son of a stablehand. Finally, he dropped his eyes, and his shoulders sagged almost imperceptibly.

Abelard nodded, satisfied. "I think," he went on, "that under the circumstances the dispatch had better come from me. Send a messenger by in one hour."

Phineas paused. Abelard pulled a fresh piece of parchment from a low stack on his table, picked up his pen, and began to write. Phineas knew he was dismissed. Without another word, he left the tent.

Hesitation in the face of unpleasant duty was not part of his code, reflected Phineas. Despite his deep disappointment in Abelard and his own sense of loss, he went directly to Nydia's tent. He found her seated in the shade, rolling strips of linen into bandages.

She looked up at his approach. He did not wait for her to speak. "Where's Liss?"

"She's gone to fetch more water."

"Good. I need to speak to you alone."

She rose and beckoned him into the tent. Although the flaps were open, the air inside was stifling, but she hugged herself as though she felt a chill. Phineas himself shivered under the cool regard of her dark eyes, wondering if she knew what he had come to say.

"I'm sorry to tell you this. A few minutes ago, one of Lord Tedmund's men came in. Lord Tedmund is dead."

He heard her draw a shuddering breath and waited for her tears, but she only turned her back and walked to the opposite entrance of the tent. "I see." There was another silence, and then she asked: "How?"

"I would rather not say, lady."

"Was he crucified?"

"Is the ability to see the past part of your gift, as well?"

She met his eyes with disdain. "No. It doesn't matter how I know."

He waited a few more minutes, struggled to find adequate words to express his sympathy. When it appeared she had nothing more to ask, he bowed and cleared his throat. "If there is nothing more, lady, shall I call for a woman—?"

"No, wait, Captain." She faced him with squared shoulders and raised chin. "Why did you send him?" Her voice quavered only a little.

"All the squadrons of the King's Guard were needed elsewhere."

"But why Tedmund? He was young—he had no real experience with the Harleys. Surely there were others—"

"Young? He was twenty-five. I swore my allegiance at fourteen. I am thirty-three—I have spent nineteen years in this life. I am not to blame if the old Senador of Linoys chose to coddle his son, kept him safe by the hearth while younger men risked their lives."

"But why—"

"Many decisions are made in war that in retrospect are wrong." He cut her off with a brutality he did not feel. "I don't have to justify my choice to you. I am sorry he is dead—both for your sake and the sake of the realm." With a harsher voice than he intended, he spoke as though his rough words could rub out his own grief. "He took the same oath we all take—the same oath you've taken. Do you think those are only words, lady? When we swear to uphold the kingdom and the King with our lives, it means we die if we must."

She lifted one eyebrow. Suddenly, he wanted to take her in his arms, shake the contempt out of her eyes. With only the greatest effort, he controlled himself. "Don't you understand? Don't you ever wonder if someday the King will demand something you aren't willing to give?"

The remark struck home. She jerked her chin as though he

had hit her with his fist. This time the pain in her eyes was raw. Instantly, he regretted his words. "He was a fine man," he said by way of apology. Before she could ask him more, he spun on his heel and ducked out of the tent.

Nydia stared after him, struggling with the numbness that was descending on her like a cloak. In his moment of hesitation, she had looked into his future and seen something at once both familiar and strange. She understood, at last, something of what she had seen on that day back in Ahga when she had first looked into Abelard's future.

"No!" She ran after Phineas out into the blinding light. Her footsteps stirred up a cloud of choking dust. She grabbed his upper arm and tugged on his sleeve. "You mustn't—you can't."

It was his turn to stare down at her in amazement. "What are you talking about?"

"The river—you intend to cross the river. Don't. Please."

"Why not?"

"There's danger there—an army waits—"

"I hope so, lady. I think the outlaws have tricked us— they'll attack from our rear and cut off our supplies. We've got to get over the river to where Senifay can reinforce us."

"No! We must not cross the river."

"We have no choice." He tried to make his voice gentle. "You must be mistaken, lady. You aren't familiar with this part of the country, are you?" When she shook her head, he nodded. "Perhaps what you see is wrong. We have no choice." He picked up her hand. Her fingers were so small, he thought, so fragile. Almost at once, he felt nothing but the wish to protect, to console.

She pulled her hand away as though his touch stung.

"Forgive me, lady," he muttered. Tears blurred his vision, and he left her standing in the middle of the camp. He walked away feeling very old.

The survivor died a few hours later. Phineas stood, staring at the mounded grave covered with rocks to keep the scavengers away, then across the shallow hills to the horizon.

How had this man found his way to them? he wondered. Was it luck alone that led the poor wretch? Nothing moved beyond the perimeter of the camp except a few listless tumbleweeds.

Nydia's warning gnawed like a toothache. Abelard's strategy of feint and dodge relied on the army crossing this river on the border of Arkan and surrounding the outlaws with the reinforcements from Widgidaw, as well as those from allies like Arkan and Senifay, if necessary. Senifay's closest holding, a border outpost, lay over the mountains, perhaps a day's ride away. Abelard's messenger should be well on his way. But what army had Nydia seen? Could she have meant their own? No, he decided almost at once, that made no sense at all. And in the highlands over the river, they would have more control over the movements of the Harleyriders, not less. Unless— Phineas froze. Unless there were another enemy Abelard had not counted upon, and the Harleys had.

Senifay. Senifay who complained at every Convening. Senifay who claimed the southern trade route through the Saraneva Mountains. Senifay who hated Obayana of Kora-lado with undisguised passion. Yes, Phineas thought grimly, Senifay hated Kora-lado enough to take up arms against the King. At least, it was possible.

And the Harleys delighted in making extravagant gestures. If the return of Tedmund's man was an implied threat, it might mean the outlaws were closer than any of them realized. With an increasing sense of foreboding, he snapped his fingers at the closest soldier. "Find the Lady Nydia and request that she join the King and myself in his tent. Immediately."

He did not wait for the answering salute. He threaded his way through the confusion of the camp and was brought up short when he noticed one of the sentries leading a dust-covered man on a strange horse from the direction of the western perimeter of the camp. In the fading light, he squinted a little. "Soldier. Who's this?"

The guard came to attention. "Messenger from the Senador of Senifay, sir."

Phineas frowned. "Senifay? Where's our messenger?"

"Senifay's man came in alone."

Warily, Phineas inspected the newcomer and repeated his question.

"I am to report to the King of Meriga. Sir." There was a trace of impudence in the man's manner.

"I'm the Captain of his Guard. Get off that horse." The man slid—reluctantly, Phineas thought—to the ground. He stared up at Phineas. "Where's our messenger?"

"Your messenger had an accident."

"What kind of an accident?"

"He—fell off his horse, broke his ankle."

His eyes darted right and left, skirting the edge of Phineas's vision. Phineas frowned. "Where did you come from?"

"From my master—"

"I know who sent you. I asked you where."

The messenger licked his lips and glanced at the guard, who kept a tight hand on the horse's bridle. "What do you mean, where?"

"Your master's closest holding is at Lahunta, which is at least a day's ride or more. How did you get here so quickly? Where did you come from?"

Phineas took another step closer. The messenger backed up against the horse's flank, and the animal snorted. "I don't know what you're talking about. I have a message for the King—"

"I asked you a question. I expect an answer."

The messenger's eyes slid from right to left, and he opened his mouth once more. Before he could speak, an eerie cry went up, echoing in the still, hot air.

The hackles rose on the back of Phineas's neck. Harleyriders. He gripped the little man by the collar of his tunic, twisting the fabric around his fist and half lifted him off his feet.

"Did you know anything about this?" He shook the little man so viciously his teeth rattled while he shook his head.

"No, no, Captain, my lord—I swear—"

Phineas flung him away with enough force to send him sprawling on the ground. Reflexively, Phineas reached for his broadsword, then realized it hung in his tent. "Guard that man—don't let him escape."

The guard saluted smartly.

Phineas dashed past, first to his tent to grab his sword from his frantic serving boy, then into the melee. The outlaws had taken advantage of the late afternoon lassitude. They rode in on shaggy, shortlegged ponies, grinning at the confusion. Fiery arrows flew through the air, landing with a whoosh and a thunk in tents, men, and tethered horses. The animals screamed and reared as the smell of burning reached them. The cavalry horses reacted instinctively to the howls, the reek of blood and burning flesh, and the glint of metal. Hooves lashed out indiscriminately, as dangerous as the flying arrows.

Phineas vaulted onto his horse's back without taking time to saddle it. He gripped the animal's flanks with his thighs, and it responded perfectly to his signal. Without spurs, he urged it forward with his knees, one hand wrapped in its mane, the other around the hilt of his sword.

The Harleyriders surged through the camp, heavy silver chains whirling above their heads. At the end of each chain was a heavy steel ball studded with spikes. They dealt blows right and left as they galloped past. The wild howls rang through the still air. Dust billowed from the ground, and Phineas choked even as smoke from a burning tent made his eyes water. A soldier stumbled past, wailing in agony, his back aflame, an arrow protruding from between his shoulder blades.

He heard the captains frantically try to rally their men and he turned, half-blinded. Out of the watery blur loomed a Harleyrider, a man almost too big for the short pony he rode, brandishing a double-bladed ax. Gripping the stallion's sides between his thighs, Phineas grasped his broadsword with both hands and swung.

The outlaw blocked the blow with the handle of his ax and forced the axhead forward. The stallion danced backward, reared, and struck the pony a blow to the chest. The animal stumbled; the outlaw was forced to grab the reins. His guard faltered.

Phineas crashed the heavy broadsword down on the outlaw's shoulder. The blade bit deep, severing bone and muscle, driving hard into his lung. For a moment, the outlaw looked surprised as dark blood spurted and arced, and then he fell. Phineas shoved the pony's head aside and cantered past.

As suddenly as it began, the fighting was over. As if some signal had been given, the war cries ceased, and the outlaws retreated, one or two shouting threats over their shoulders.

He found Abelard a short distance away, listening to the reports of the captains. He slid off the horse's back and beckoned to a groom to lead the animal away. A thin line of blood ran down the animal's right front leg.

"They may attack again at first light, tomorrow," one of the lieutenants was saying. He dragged an arm across his forehead, and in the fading light, Phineas saw a red burn on his forearm.

"Get that looked at," said Phineas. He turned to the captains of the regiments of the King's Guard. "I want an accurate accounting of all the wounded: who can still ride, how many horses we've lost."

"Do you think they'll come back tonight?" asked one.

Phineas hesitated, thought of Nydia's warning, and shook his head. "I doubt it."

"That's all for now, gentlemen. Double the watch. I want those reports within the hour. Get your wounds looked at—see to your men. Thank you." As the men moved off, cradling wounded limbs, flexing tired muscles, Abelard turned to Phineas. "Well?"

"I think they think they have pinned us between them and the river. They let that poor bastard go—a message for us, I suppose. I've got to talk to you—I was on my way to your tent when the attack came. There's something Nydia said—something you need to know."

Abelard stared at his second in command. Phineas was conscious of a change. He no longer felt the easy friendship between himself and the King, and he wondered if the King sensed it as well. Abelard spoke first. "Send the Lady Nydia to my tent. And come as soon as you've washed."

Phineas turned away, then stopped in mid-stride when Abelard spoke again. "I know you're angry about Tedmund."

"He would have served you loyally for a lifetime."

"He lacked judgment."

And once, so did we all, Phineas wanted to say. But force of long loyalty and his sense of duty silenced him. This was the closest to an apology he would get from Abelard. There was nothing else to do but put the matter aside. Once again, he thought, you've gotten exactly what you want. But he said nothing more. As the King moved off toward his tent in the lengthening shadows, a cool breeze began to blow. It ruffled Phineas's hair. A weight seemed to have settled on his back, which he could not entirely ignore.

Nydia twisted her hands in her lap. The King's tent, larger than most, was nevertheless stifling, and the evening wind, which blew the smoke away, had not reached into the tents. She pushed tendrils of damp hair out of her eyes.

She had just reached the King's tent when the fighting started, and the startled guard had thrust her into the King's sleeping quarters. She had huddled inside, listening to the screams of the wounded and the shouted commands, the crackle of the flames and stamp of the horses, the whistling arrows. Every now and then, she heard the thunk of a blade finding flesh. She had tried to remember the calm displayed by the other camp women during other attacks.

Now, even in the sudden silence, she was not certain she should leave the comparative safety of the King's tent. She hoped either he or Phineas would come soon, and hoped they would believe what she had to say when they did.

She recognized Abelard's footsteps, heard his low whistle under his breath. The surprise attack had not unnerved him; indeed, he seemed invigorated. He strode into the tent, looking neither right nor left, and over to the bucket of water in the corner. He tore his sweat-stained shirt off to splash water on his face, chest, and arms.

She could smell the acrid odor of the smoke mixed with sweat on his body. She rose from the low camp stool and reached for a linen towel. As he surfaced, shaking drops of water from his hair, she handed it to him silently. He jumped, startled by her presence.

"By the gods, lady." He straightened.

Something quivered deep in her belly. She swallowed hard, trying to ignore the sight of his damp chest, water-darkened hair curling tightly on his wet skin. His muscles were swollen from his exertions.

Her heart sped up at the sight and scent of him, standing so close, well within arm's reach. He was so very male, she thought, and something in her wanted to step back; something else shivered in anticipation that he might, just might, pull her toward him. She wondered how it would feel to be bent back in his embrace, mouth and throat and breasts exposed to meet his lips.

She clutched her hands together and hoped her voice would not betray her, although her knees felt weak. "I came—"

"Yes?" He took one step toward her and she quailed.

If he touches me, she thought, I will never say why I've come.

"Were you frightened?"

She looked down at the hard-packed dirt and refused to look up. "Of course. But that's not it. Phineas—before the attack—Phineas sent for me. I—I think you ought to know what I have seen."

At that, he withdrew, reaching for a clean shirt from a small wooden chest at the foot of the cot. "Well?" He laced it slowly. She felt a vague sense of disappointment.

"Do not cross the river. Death waits behind those hills."

He frowned, reacting even as Phineas had. "We have no choice, lady, surely you understand. These blasted outlaws—they've trapped us. If we don't get across the river and join with the reinforcements from Senifay—"

"No!" Her voice was shrill. She took a deep breath and forced herself to speak calmly, for she knew he would never listen to a hysterical woman. "There are no reinforcements—"

"Senifay has betrayed us, Abelard." Phineas spoke from the entrance.

Abelard turned slowly, still frowning. "You think he's in league with the Harleys?"

"I'm not sure. But this dance they've been leading us across Arkan—now here, now there—it seems almost too convenient that we should end up here, just a few miles from Senifay's camp."

"How do you know that?"

Briefly, Phineas told the King of his exchange with Senifay's messenger. "We ought to question this messenger and find out what he has to say. But Senifay isn't here by chance."

Grim-faced, Abelard turned once more to Nydia. "Tell me what you see. All of it. What waits?"

She lifted her eyes. "Over the ridge, in the valley, I see a white flag with an orange sun rising, or setting, behind a green hill. Do you know that standard?"

Both men hissed, dismay plain on their faces. They glanced at each other and Nydia was frightened by the look she saw pass between them.

"Mortmain." Abelard said the name as though it were a curse. "So that's the way it is. A blighted harvest, indeed. No wonder Eldred was so eager to contact him last Vember."

"Lord King!" A guard burst into the tent, tripped and sprawled on the dirt floor. "The messenger—the messenger from Senifay—he escaped in the attack, killed his guard."

Abelard hauled up the man, or boy, for he was very young,

by the arm. For a few long seconds, he said nothing, mouth drawn tight. Finally, he nodded a dismissal. The soldier saluted, nodded to Nydia, and scrambled away.

"The messenger lied," Phineas said flatly.

"Yet we can not stay here—" Abelard broke off, and she heard him sigh. He picked up her hand and brought it to his lips. She felt the heat of his body and she wondered why the damp curls around his ears did not steam. "Thank you." He released her hand. The skin burned where he had kissed it. "Get your things together—only what's most essential—what you could carry if you had to. And extra water. You understand? Good. Go now. I'll send someone as soon as we've made plans."

She nodded silently. She knew they both watched her as she threaded her way through the camp in the falling dark.

Chapter Fourteen

❦

$\mathcal{I}$t was Abelard who came for them as night fell. He silently motioned for Nydia and Liss to follow him, holding the tent flap wide. Two guards held horses saddled and waiting. Abelard handed their bundles to the men and assisted first Liss, then Nydia, onto the horses. By the light of the flickering torches, Nydia saw that the horses' feet had been wrapped in rags.

Abelard stood between them, a hand on each bridle, dressed for battle. A breastplate reflected winks of firelight, and a broadsword was strapped across his back. "Our scouts tell us that just off the highway, on the other side of the river, there's the ruins of a roadhouse—not much shelter, but better than nothing. It's protected, up on a hill. It will be easy to defend."

"Lord King," Liss said without her usual flirtatious lilt, "what's happened? I don't understand."

Abelard sighed, and his cloak flapped around his shoulders in an unexpected hot gust. He raised his face to the sky, squinted at the clouds which had begun to move across the pale cloud-streaked moon. "We're trapped, my dear. We've been outmaneuvered—and we've no time to lose."

Nydia clung to the reins. The muffled hooves made an eerie shuffling sound in the silent night. The road was dark and the wind blew harder as they reached the crest of the bridge.

Like an army of shadows, they followed the scouts off the main highway into the foothills of the Saranevas—mountains which Nydia knew would be ocher and brown in the morning, with high, sharp peaks. She wondered if there were anything she might have said to have averted this crisis. Would the King have listened to her, she wondered, if she had told him the day he had agreed to take her that she had seen two armies joined beneath these very mountains in battle?

Her attention was distracted as they picked their way across an ancient track, once paved as smoothly as the highway, now broken and nearly erased by time. Walls loomed suddenly out of the blackness. She heard the order to halt.

A captain materialized out of the ranks. At his terse command, their escorts helped them out of the saddles. For a moment, she stood disoriented in the dark, almost dizzy with fatigue.

Then she felt a hesitant touch on her arm, and she and Liss were guided into the ancient roadhouse.

It had not been built for the ages, reflected Nydia. The roof had long ago caved in; the wide windows gaped like open mouths. The place had been ransacked many times, and whatever could be carried off and used elsewhere was long gone. What remained was not much more than a shell.

As if across a great distance, she heard Abelard's voice and recognized Phineas's as they rose above the muffled babble. The wounded moaned as they were moved from the wagons. She and Liss were taken to a room which was little more than a sheltered niche—no roof, no windows, only three walls which rose perhaps ten feet into the air. The smell of decay and mold was strong on the damp night air. The guard left them the lantern. Its feeble light barely penetrated the shadows in the corners of the room.

"I don't suppose this place has been swept out." Liss sounded more aggrieved than tired.

Nydia smiled in spite of the situation. Something crunched under her feet and she hoped it was only eggshells of the birds which nested in the ruins. "Let's make the best of it."

Liss yawned. "I hope they remembered to bring the brooms." She moved slowly in the dark, feeling her way to the packs the guards had left. "Here—this one's yours—"

Nydia reached out, took the heavy bundle, and felt for her blanket.

"Let's try to sleep, shall we? Maybe tomorrow we can get this place straightened out." Liss yawned again and Nydia murmured agreement.

The two women moved awkwardly in the dark, feeling their way around each other. Liss made little noises of disgust when her face brushed cobwebs.

Phineas startled them both. "Will you come with me, Lady Nydia? The King requests you join him." He spoke with his usual grave courtesy.

Liss made a little noise, at once a protest and a question. Nydia straightened slowly. She made her way unsteadily across the dark room, where Phineas stood like a ghost in the doorway. "Now, Captain?" It annoyed her that Phineas could behave as if the knowledge of Tedmund's death had changed nothing.

"Immediately, lady."

"Liss, will you be all right—"

"Lady, please come." He grasped her arm gently but firmly. Without another word, she followed him down a crumbling passage to another room. A tree had grown into the room and its boughs hung low. In the light of the small fire which burned in the center of the cracked floor, the branches threw up weird shadows on the walls. Abelard crouched in its light, peering at a hide map stretched out before him. He looked tired, she thought, shadows under his eyes, a night's growth of beard on his chin.

He beckoned her closer. She knelt by his side and looked at the map. Phineas knelt beside her. She recoiled a little, wondering if he would have sent Tedmund south if she had told him of her vision in the council room that day in Ahga.

Phineas's sense of duty was so great, she thought, that it would not have mattered. He would do whatever Abelard required, whatever in his judgment would best serve the King.

"I have sent the men to rest."

Abelard sounded older than she had ever heard him, his voice slow and hoarse in his throat.

Phineas only nodded.

She waited.

Abelard stared at the map for what seemed like a long time. The wind gusted through the branches of the trees, and the leaves dipped low. The fire flared, sparked. Twigs snapped and broke.

Finally he sighed. "Forgive me, lady. You, too must be tired." He fell silent again, brooding.

"What do you want of me?" Her shoulders ached and her head felt heavy.

"If Senifay has indeed betrayed me, then we must assume that either Rissona is with him, or will be of little use. So the only hope we have is Kora-lado."

"A messenger has gone out, Lord King."

She heard the formality in Phineas's voice and fleetingly wondered what had happened between the two men. But she was too tired to consider it for long. She stifled a yawn.

Abelard rose and began to pace. The top of his head almost touched the tree branches. "Can you show me where they are?"

She hesitated over the map. The orientation was unfamiliar. She tentatively touched a point on the hide. "We are here?" When he nodded, she tapped a spot a few inches to the left. "Here, I think. This is not what I am used to."

Phineas nodded, examining where she pointed. "It makes sense. Abelard, look here."

The King stopped pacing long enough to peer down. "What more can you tell me?"

Nydia shrugged. "You have not yet made a decision."

The tree shivered suddenly as a cool wind shook it. A shadow suddenly appeared in the door. "Lord King. Captain Phineas." The man saluted, straight at attention.

Phineas recognized the scout. "Come in, Ronal. What can you tell us?"

The scout bent down beside the map. Bits of leaves and

twigs clung to his clothes. Unerringly, he pointed almost to the very spot that Nydia had. "Here, sir. I found the enemy camp. It's about two hours from here, though it's hard to be sure in the dark."

"Well?" Abelard's face betrayed nothing.

The scout hesitated. "There's more than the Senador of Senifay, Lord King. Vada, Ragonn, and I think I saw W'homing's standard, though in the dark it was hard to be sure—"

"What about Yudaw?" interrupted the King.

"I didn't see his standard, sir."

"That's not to say he's not there," murmured Phineas.

"Yes," Abelard nodded. "If he's not there yet, I wager he will be. Go on, man."

"I got close enough to hear some of their sentries talking. I don't think they know yet that we got across the river—and I don't think they are planning to attack. Not yet."

"Why not?"

"They want the Harleys to soften us up—those were their words—and then, when we retreat across the bridge, they expect to be in a position to force terms without a fight."

"Terms?" Phineas repeated. "What kind of terms?"

"I'll make no terms with traitors." Abelard's face was murderous. His hands flexed. "The only term I'll negotiate with any of them is on the blade of a sword." He jerked his head toward the scout. "Go. You've done well. Get something to eat—then sleep. If they don't expect to attack, perhaps we have a little time."

When the scout was gone, Nydia shifted uneasily by the fire. Her muscles were growing cramped. Abelard stopped pacing and stared up at the night sky. Here and there a star shone through the cover of clouds. The wind ruffled his hair. "Don't they understand?" He spoke so softly she wasn't sure she heard him correctly.

"No," answered Phineas. There was a hard edge in his voice which Nydia did not understand. He looked at Abelard with a grim satisfaction. "The Meriga you envision—a Meriga united and at peace—is beyond what most of them can imagine. And

even the ones who do, laugh and call you a hopeless dreamer."
He stood up, slinging his cloak over his shoulder, and he
pushed his broadsword across his back. "If you'll excuse me,
Lord King, I have yet to give the orders for the watch." He
bowed, barely, and stalked out.

Nydia was shocked. She had never heard anyone, not even
Agara, speak to the King in that tone of voice. She half expected him to hurl his dagger after Phineas. Instead, he only
stared at the stars. "Yes," he said, after a long time. "I know."
He looked so alone, standing there, that for the first time since
she had known him, she felt pity.

There was another long silence. The flames danced on their
faces, and the wind blew harder. She shivered in spite of herself. It was that which roused Abelard.

"Do you stay for comfort, lady?" He gave a short, bitter
laugh. "I have none to give. Look here." He dropped down on
one knee, motioned her closer. With the point of his dagger,
he indicated the map. "The Harleys stand between us and our
reserves. There is nothing but open desert for five hundred
miles or more east and south."

"But how—"

"Did this happen? Phineas is right. It was my fault. I assumed too much, you see. I took it for granted that all the
Senators felt as I did—as Arkan and Tennessey Fall—though
I shouldn't count him, he's only a boy. We knew they were
there, now following, now luring—I thought we played a
clever game of cat-and-mouse. Only it wasn't very clever after
all. Because here, you see, are all the Senators in western
Meriga."

"What do they want?"

"Oh, I can guess. Senifay wants the southern trade routes.
W'homing wants the ancient territory he claims for his against
Mondana. Yudaw wants a chunk of Kora-lado—most likely
this chunk, here—this pass into Vada. I'm not sure about
Ragonn."

"And Vada?"

Abelard shook his head slowly and stared into the fire. "For all I know, it could be my crown."

"What will you do?"

"If we could hold the Harleys on the other side of the river, there might be a chance that we could strike at this western alliance first, before they know where we are or what we're about. They may not be as cohesive as they look. Vada and Ragonn are hardly the dearest of friends. Senifay and Vada have been at each other's throats for generations. They may all be warm in bed tonight, but I'd wager their men have longer memories. We may have fewer troops, but there're no jealousies, no scores to settle, no ancient wrongs to right. We may have a chance." He gave her a crooked grin. There was regret in that smile and sorrow, but there was also courage and cool determination. He would not go down easily, and he would bring a great many enemies down with him.

And in that moment, Nydia understood what made men and women love him, why so many swore to follow him unto death. If he stood beside her, she thought, it did not matter who might stand against her. And here they were, she thought, wildly, recklessly, with half of Meriga against him and she beside him, she who had more power at her disposal than any of them reckoned. "If the bridge was destroyed?"

He gave a short laugh. "That's an idea, but that bridge has stood a thousand years or more. If we had weeks, perhaps, we might tear it down. I appreciate your suggestion, but I don't have that kind of time."

She put her hand on his, heard his swift intake of breath. He turned to her so quickly she started back. His eyes blazed in the flickering light. "By all the gods they claim exist—" He turned away, shaking his head. "Ironic you would choose to come to me now—when I haven't even a bed to offer you."

She touched his shoulder, wondering at her boldness. "Abelard, I don't offer you comfort—not that kind. I have something else to give. I know the danger and I know what may happen, but I would not—"

He grabbed her upper arms. His gaze bore into hers, and she

felt the force of his will penetrate to the core of her being, as though he reached down into her soul. She squared her shoulders and raised her chin, met his eyes with all the pride she could muster. She wet her lips. "I understand what you want for Meriga. I don't believe it's beyond anyone's imagination, and I don't believe you are a hopeless dreamer." Something in her tolled a warning, but she went on, lashing out at Phineas, at his words which had struck her as immeasurably cruel, at a world where someone as kind as Tedmund could die so painfully. Had it only been today that she had heard of his death? Well, he would not have died in vain; she could give him that, at least. She could offer some measure of hope to Abelard, and let Phineas, that superstitious peasant, squirm on his own hook. Let them all mumble every prayer they ever knew. This was the King, and she had sworn allegiance, pledged to uphold his kingdom unto death.

She reached up, took his face in her hands. Desire shivered through her, but she ignored it. Now was not the time. The day would come, she knew with sudden certainty, when she would hold out her hand and bring him to her bed. But not now. Not here among the dilapidated ruins of an ancient inn. "I offer you the Magic."

"You would use it now, to help me?"

She nodded, swallowed hard. Her hands shook. He wrapped his fingers around them and brought first one, then the other, to his lips. "But I thought you said—"

"It's dangerous? It's the most dangerous thing in the world. I don't do it lightly. I would not do it at all, if I believed there were any other way—and I cannot use it indiscriminately."

"What will you do?"

"The bridge is old. If it's destroyed, it will cut off the Harleys from Mortmain's forces. Surely there is some weakness in the supporting pillars—all I need do is take advantage of it. If the supports fall, the cables will break, and the bridge, at least that part of it, will collapse."

"Can you really do that?"

She smiled at the disbelief in his voice. "We must go now,

quickly. Surely there're only a few more hours until dawn. I mustn't be seen."

Abelard pulled her up as he got to his feet. He reached for a cloak, wrapped it around her shoulders, and drew another around his. He seized a torch from a makeshift bracket on the wall. "Let's go."

She felt like a fugitive as they slipped from the roadhouse. The sentries who challenged their passing fell back without question when they recognized the King. The wind had picked up, clouds scudded across the sky, and the stars had disappeared. The flames fanned out, blew wildly. Abelard swore beneath his breath.

When they reached the causeway leading up to the bridge, the torch winked out altogether, just as the light attracted the attention of the guards posted at the bottom of the bridge. Their horses were tethered out of the wind, and a small fire flickered in the remains of what Nydia knew had been the tollbooth where the bridge tax was paid. The guard on watch rose to his feet, spear lowered, peering suspiciously out into the wild night.

His challenge died on his lips when he heard the King's voice, and he resumed his place at the fire readily enough at Abelard's command. They were alone in the black night.

Nydia shivered, pulled the cloak tighter. Abelard wrapped his arm around her and tugged her around to face him. For a moment they stood, the outline of the ancient bridge rising between them like a ghost. As he tilted her face up to his, she caught her breath, realizing his intent. Her eyes closed as his mouth came down on hers.

She was not prepared for the riptide of pleasure which surged through her. It made her breasts ache to be touched, her legs tremble, her center liquid with heat. She clung to him, and his arms held her as easily as if she were weightless. Time slowed, ended, all urgency dissolved, and nothing mattered on this dark night but this man. She made a little sound of protest when he released her. He traced the line of her cheek with one finger, and his touch was a promise, unspoken but understood.

Her heart thudded in her chest, and her blood was a dull roar in her ears. Still shaken, she took a deep breath. "Is there a place to get out of the wind?"

He looked around, pointed to a stand of scrubby pines nestled in a hollow off the road. "There?"

She looked back at the bridge and nodded finally. "I think so."

She settled herself next to one of the little trees. Its branches made a soft whisper in the wind; the scent was clean and fresh. There was going to be a change in the weather, she thought. He took a place behind her, as though he understood instinctively that she must not be distracted. She heard him shift, sigh.

Then there was silence. She waited a few minutes, listening to the low sigh of the wind, the rush of the water slipping beneath the bridge. It slapped against the piers.

She took a deep breath, then another, and shut her eyes. As the moments slipped away, she reached down into the well of her mind, stretched, pulled up from her memory the first, the most basic equations of the Magic, equations she had memorized long ago before they had any meaning.

But this time, she did not simply run through them like a road so often traveled its landmarks are no longer noticed. This time she thought each through, savoring the forbidden progression. Flashes of light shot through her mind, darting here and there, as a pattern revealed itself, slowly, certainly, inevitably. She reached the second level of the equations, delved deep, pulled from places she never thought of, remembered formulas that, ordinarily, on a conscious level, she would not have thought she knew.

But the equations were like arrows, each pointing the way inexorably to the next and the next, as the order of the universe lay revealed, peeled off like the layers of an onion, deeper and deeper, yet greater and greater.

And then she was there, in that place where the hard edges of matter were frayed like a piece of cut fabric. Her mind flitted over and through a hundred, thousand, million fractal curves, turning in and over until infinity beckoned.

The molecules of her brain flared like beacons, the energy of her will firing along the synapses, and conscious thought took shape. Borne on the infinite line between chaos and order, her will achieved a form, surged like a wave over the borders dividing matter from energy, and wrapped itself through and between the infinitesimal spaces of the atomic structure of the bridge.

She felt the molecules of the stone shudder, and something like a ripple, like that from a pebble dropped into a pond, shivered through her. It spread out and over and through in all directions, and she knew that the ripples would shift in some random, unpredictable way, out of her reach or control. She let it go and pulled back, ducking her mind out of the backlash.

Abelard, lying beside her on the ground, wrapped in his cloak, was aware of nothing except that her breathing slowed and deepened. Her body was perfectly still. He lay, watching her face, almost hidden in the shadows of the night.

He tried to sigh. His lungs would not expand. He tried to sit up and something weighty seemed to press him down. He remembered the day in the council room and forced himself to relax. His eyes were all that responded to his brain's frantic commands.

Nydia was very pale. Her eyes flew open, her lips moved once, twice, muttered something in a low, moaning chant he could not understand, but it made his skin prickle as though pierced by a thousand needles and his stomach lurch with sudden nausea.

From very far away, he heard a groan and then a grating noise. Something shifted, beyond his vision, and he strained in the dark, tried to see. Without warning, there was an enormous crack, as if lightning struck the very tree he sat beneath. The entire bridge swayed, and as he watched, awestruck, one tower fell, lopsided, as the supporting pillar beneath it crumbled, the stone fragmenting into dust. There was another crack, and then a crash, as though the earth would split.

With every ounce of will he possessed, he pushed up through air which felt thicker than water and grabbed Nydia. The spell broke as he swung her up in his arms, just as the cables severed and the entire side of the bridge fell into the water. He ran. At what he judged a safe distance, he stopped to watch, cradling her in his arms. Debris rained, chunks fell from the sky like huge hailstones. White water shot into the air as the massive structure toppled into the river with mighty splashes and heavy creaks.

She clutched at him, twisted the fabric of his cloak. "Get down," she whispered. "Can't you feel it coming?"

He dropped down on one knee. The hair on the back of his neck rose. The bridge slumped to one side, a crazy wreck of ancient stone tangled with broken cables. The night went still, absolutely silent. The wind died. From the tollbooth behind him, he heard the cries of the guards calling for him, and then suddenly they, too, fell silent. He tried to speak, found the words stopped in his throat. Of its own accord, his dagger shifted in its sheath like a living thing, seeking some direction of its own. Something like a rustle of wind lifted the hair on his head. A vise seemed to have caught his temples in its grip.

A tree branch dipped into their line of vision. As if that were the signal, a great wind suddenly roared out of the clouds, swirling in relentless gusts. It tore at his cloak, lifted it over his head, and covered his face. He shook it out of his eyes, relieved he could move. As the wind increased to a mighty whine, he thought he heard the guards cry out once more, and then there was nothing but a raging wail. Nydia shuddered, holding on tightly.

"Get down," she shrieked.

Together they watched, fascinated and horrified. A swirling gust of wind reached down from the clouds. It touched down on the river upstream from the bridge. For a moment it wavered, as though making up its mind which way to go, dancing almost lightly upon the surface. Waves pounded the shoreline.

The cyclone took off, straight for the bridge, a little off-center. On the other side of the water, abandoned tents ripped off the pegs, discarded equipment went flying into the air, sucked into the center of the whirlwind. It skirted the bridge on the far shore and continued on, until only the dull howl told them it had not yet disintegrated.

Nydia sat up. Sweat laced her forehead. A few drops of cold rain stung her cheek, and she stared southeast in the direction the thing had gone. "Thank the gods it went the other way," she breathed.

"Are you all right?"

Before she could do more than nod, two of the guards from the tollbooth ran up, lanterns bobbing in the dark. "Lord King!" they cried.

Abelard rose. "I'm here—unharmed."

"What was that thing, sir?"

"A twister. Such things are common on the Plains, but I never saw one so close before."

In the lantern light, Nydia saw the concern on their broad faces. "Look what it did to the bridge, Lord King!" One of them pointed.

"Let the Harleys try to get across now," said the other with a satisfied nod. "Nearest ford's what—ten, fifteen miles to the south?"

Abelard extended a hand to Nydia and drew her up beside him. Their eyes seared her with speculative interest, and she pressed against his side, embarrassed. Abelard was completely unperturbed. "If you would let us have one of your lamps, sergeant?"

"Certainly, Lord King."

"Get back to your posts. I believe the storm is over. It will be dawn in a little while."

They saluted and trudged back to the tollbooth, calling to their fellows.

Together, Abelard and Nydia picked their way back to the roadhouse. As they came closer, but before they were in sight of it, Abelard stopped, set the lantern on the ground. She saw again the fatigue in his face, and suddenly she wanted nothing more than to lay her head on his broad chest and sleep, curled beside him in some wide bed where neither the present nor the future could intrude. He kissed her hand, touched her face. "We still aren't out of danger. You understand that? At least the balance isn't tipped quite so much against us."

"Will the Harleys try to cross the river?"

"I don't know. I expect that the reserves I left in Wigidaw will come, especially if they don't hear from us within a few days. It's been almost a week since the last messenger went out—even if the outlaws intercepted him, Gredahl will come looking for us. I'd say the Harleys will be busy—not beaten, perhaps but busy."

"What about us?"

"Us?"

"Here, now. What will you do? Will we retreat north?"

Instead of an answer, he pulled her close. Exhausted as she was, her body thrummed in immediate response. He kissed her with unexpected tenderness. "Leave the strategy to me."

He saw how very weary she was and swung her up in his arms. She was much too tired to do any more than nestle her head in the hollow of his shoulder. She did not see the look of triumph he wore as he bore her inside.

Chapter Fifteen

❧

 $\mathcal{I}$ n the beginning, Phineas believed they had some chance. The tornado which destroyed the bridge was considered by most to be a sign of divine favor. The scouts watching along the river reported that the Harleys, who staged a dawn raid as expected, cursed when they found the camp deserted and the bridge gone.

But Phineas, who detected a change between Abelard and Nydia, suspected something more. The reports of the sentries from that night seemed to suggest that the bridge collapsed before the cyclone had been spotted. But he had found that the limits of his loyalty could be stretched further than he had thought possible and still hold strong as ever.

She blamed him for Tedmund's death; he understood that and accepted his responsibility. She treated him with cool disdain, as though he were nothing more than a pack groom or a scullery boy, who existed to serve at her pleasure. It only rankled when he thought of it, but he accepted it as fitting penance for his part in Tedmund's death. Besides, Phineas had many more immediate problems.

Of the fifteen hundred men who had left Ahga, there were less than nine hundred still battleworthy. The army they faced numbered in the thousands. Kora-lado was more than four weeks away. With winter coming on, and the days beginning to shorten, even Abelard acknowledged the wisdom of a withdrawal north into the mountains.

So now Phineas guided his horse across the rough, once-paved tracks which led around and through the highest peaks of the Saraneva Mountains. He knew, by the rigid set of Abelard's shoulders, by the furrowed lines across his brow, that the forced retreat chafed the King. Abelard preferred to meet obstacles head-on. Now, their best hope was to reach Obayana's keep above the Saraneva Pass and wait for spring to consolidate their forces.

The sun was warm across Phineas's shoulders, and he silently thanked whatever gods might exist that the heat had broken and the cold had not yet come. But the rough and rocky terrain made the march slow, and Mortmain's camp was only four days behind. Phineas stared ahead at the first of the great peaks rising in their path. A tunnel cut through the very heart of the mountain—the only route into the north and Obayana's lands. Once they were through the tunnel, he would rest easier, and the march need not be so hurried.

They paused at noon only long enough to refill their canteens and waterskins from the mountain brook which tumbled across the road, and to pull salted meat and flat bread from their ration packs. Phineas took the opportunity to confer with the sergeant in charge of the squadron who guarded their retreat and talk with a returned scout. "Has there been any sign of Rissona?"

The scout shook his head and paused to take a long pull of water. Dirt was smudged across his face, the better to obscure it in the shadows, and his clothes were full of pine needles. "None at all, Captain. It looks as though the Senador is cut off completely. Even if he has not allied with the traitors, there is no way he could break through and come to our aid. Not now. There's no sign that Mortmain intends to leave his position, either. They seem to be waiting for something."

Phineas looked over the man's shoulder, where the cloud shadows scudded across the hillsides and the road threaded through dark green stands of spindly trees. "Or someone," he finished. He glanced up as a boy of about fourteen, whom he recognized as one of the standard-bearers, ran up and saluted.

"Captain Phineas, sir."

"Well?" The boy was breathing hard, as though he'd run all the way from the front of the company.

"The King, sir. He requests you join him. Immediately."

Phineas looked back at the scout, and the man, as though he heard the thought, shook his head once more. "I saw nothing more to report, Captain."

"Go, boy. Tell the King I'm on my way."

"No, sir. He said not to come back unless I brought you with me."

Phineas raised an eyebrow. "All right, I'll come." He waved a dismissal to the sergeant and the scout, then started back through the ranks. "What's wrong?"

"I don't know, sir. But the lady—not the King's companion, the other—I heard her tell him she'd seen something, and the next thing I knew the King was calling for me to find you as quick as I could."

Uncertain fear kept him silent as Phineas shouldered a way through the crowd of men and wagons and horses behind the boy. When they reached Abelard, the King impatiently motioned the standard-bearer away. "What is it?" He noticed Nydia standing a little apart.

"It's Yudaw." Abelard gestured to Nydia. "Tell him."

"Over the farthest ridge—past the next valley—there's an army coming this way. If we go through the tunnel, we'll run into them about a day's march farther on."

"How many men?" Phineas tried to keep his voice carefully neutral.

She twisted her hands in the fabric of her gown. "I don't really know. I have no way of estimating—"

"More or less than what you saw across the river?"

"Less. I think."

"But more than our own?"

"Yes."

Abelard took Phineas's arm and led him a little distance away. "She wants us to take another road."

"But there isn't another road. And if we don't go through the tunnel, we'll be pinned between two armies."

"I know that."

"So?"

"We'll go through the tunnel, find a place, and make a stand. What choice do we have? We can't turn back." Abelard put his hands on his hips and scanned the horizon. "Send out the scouts, Phineas. You know what to look for. If we can't avoid a fight, at least it will be on our terms."

In the gray predawn light, only a few clouds were gathered on the horizon, and the wind was fresh and from the west. From his place on the hillside, surrounded by squadrons of the King's Guard, Phineas could see the standards of the regiments of the Senador of Yudaw flap sluggishly in the morning breeze, as though they had woken from a night's long sleep. In the center of the camp, he could see the makeshift stables where the horses were penned. They moved restlessly, as though scenting danger. Here and there, among the trees, Phineas caught a glimpse of the King's archers hidden in the boughs, and now and then a soldier coughed softly, or stamped his feet against the chill and nerves.

The sentries at the periphery of the camp were drowsy, their night's long watch nearly over. Phineas drew the reins tight, lest his stallion, caught up in the excitement of the moment, leap ahead before the time came.

Abelard sat his dark gray mount as though the animal were part of himself. He went into battle dressed in the same leather armor that the men wore, but his bright gold hair made him an unmistakable target. Phineas looked over at the young boy who bore the King's standard. His lips were blue, and Phineas thought of young Miles, the Senador of the Tennessy Fall, safe with Jarone in Nourk. He guided his animal over to the boy, who clutched the long staff with white-knuckled hands.

The boy straightened to attention as Phineas guided his horse nearer. "Stay close, boy. With luck they'll never get near you, and if they do, well, I'm here, and so are the rest." He gestured to the riders of the King's Guard, all veterans of years of campaigning, men with hardened faces, mouths set in grim lines, weapons drawn.

Once more, he thought, Nydia's foresight had given them a chance they would otherwise have not had. They had come safely through the tunnel, and as Nydia had predicted, the scouts had found Yudaw's army just ahead. Abelard began to plan their attack with grim determination.

As the first orange crescent of the sun edged over the eastern horizon, the archers concealed on the hillsides loosed the first volley of arrows. Phineas, watching their flight, noted with grim approval the effectiveness of the first stage of attack.

Many below fell without a sound, only a few realizing what was happening. As the first alarm went up and spread through the camp, the King raised his arm. With a mighty cry, the company swept down the hill, and into the camp.

The familiar heat of the battle rage swept through Phineas like a tide, sharpening his senses, quickening his pulse. His cloak billowed in the wind behind him, and with one smooth motion, he drew his broadsword from its scabbard. The hilt fit as though it were an extension of his hand. He tightened his grip on the stallion's flanks and the horse whinnied a challenge of its own. In his peripheral vision, he saw the other riders pull up as they met the first of the contenders, some still struggling into armor, still reaching for weapons.

Then there was nothing but the foe in front of him. In the light of the rising sun, his blade was a gray blur, slicing right and left. He hacked away, the heavy blade biting into limbs with a vicious thud. Blood spurted, splashed, and men fell, screaming.

Through the early morning hours, the battle raged. Gradually Phineas began to realize the futility of the attack—whatever advantages surprise and terrain had lent them had dissipated in the face of an enemy who would crush them by sheer numbers.

He rose in his stirrups, ready to give the order to fall back into the hills, where the highlands might give them some protection in a retreat. One look around showed him nothing but a sea of men engaged in the deadliest of hand-to-hand combat. Many of Abelard's cavalry had been unhorsed, their horses killed by enemy soldiers who had not time to mount their own.

A spearman planted himself in front of Phineas and, before Phineas could pull up on the reins, drove a six-inch spearhead deep into his stallion's chest. As the animal fell to its knees with a heavy groan, Phineas rolled out of the saddle. He came up crouched in a fighting stance. The spearman drew the spear from the horse's chest and feinted at Phineas. With a fast parry, Phineas shoved the head of the spear aside and drove his blade into his opponent's chest. The man fell, dark blood fountaining from his mouth.

"Captain Phineas!" A young boy's voice rang out behind him. He half turned and saw the standard-bearer. A dagger missed his arm by inches. He grabbed the reins as the boy rode up, the King's standard fully unfurled in the breeze.

With the ease of long custom, he swung into the saddle behind the boy. The horse reared. Phineas took the reins and brought the animal under control. The sun flashed in his eyes. Had it been so long that they'd been fighting? It seemed like only a few minutes since the battle had begun.

"Captain Phineas," cried the boy, "look there, sir!"

Phineas followed the line of the boy's pointing finger in time to see Abelard surrounded by three of the enemy. The King handled his broadsword with one hand, and the blade whirled and flashed in a blurred dance of death. Beneath him the warhorse cavorted and pranced, nostrils flared.

"Stay down, boy!" Phineas urged his horse forward. As he sliced through the neck of one enemy from the rear, the rider behind Abelard brought his blade down in a mighty blow over Abelard's shoulder. Phineas heard the sickening crunch as the blade bit into the King's flesh, slicing muscle and bone. Abelard sagged. The man raised his sword to finish the King, but Phineas stood in his stirrups and threw his broadsword straight at the man's chest. It landed with a satisfying thunk, and the man slumped out of his saddle, hands wrapped around the blade embedded in his ribs.

Abelard's face was pale, his lips were drawn with pain, but he managed to bring the edge of his sword up with his good hand and cut down the last assailant. Phineas slapped the dying soldier out of the way and reached for the King. Abelard crumpled, his breathing shallow.

Phineas dismounted and threw the reins back to the boy. "Don't let the standard fall." He pulled himself onto the King's horse. "Our men mustn't know the King's down. I'll get him to safety—stay close to our men." Without waiting for a reply, he cruelly spurred the horse on, reins entwined in one hand, holding Abelard with the other. He galloped out of the battle, up the hill, back to the camp where he had left Everic and a company of twenty men to guard Nydia and Liss.

He eased out of the saddle and half carried, half dragged Abelard into shelter. The women rushed forward with cries of distress. Two guards eased the King out of Phineas's arms and laid him on a pile of blankets. His face was pale, his breathing shallow. Phineas knelt, felt beneath Abelard's jaw for the pulse which beat erratically under his fingers. Satisfied that the King still lived, he stood and grasped Nydia by the arms. "Bind his wounds as best you can and go north. North, do you understand?"

She nodded, eyes wide, saying nothing. Liss already knelt beside the King, her face white, her eyes huge as she gently pulled the blood-matted fabric back.

Phineas swung around to Everic. "You've got to get out of here as soon as you can move him. Don't wait for me, or for anyone else."

"But—but, Captain—"

Phineas shook his head. "No buts. There's no time. I'll hold them back as long as I can, but don't wait. Get moving and don't stop until you reach Obayana's lands."

"He'll die," murmured Liss. She pressed a linen square against the King's shoulder.

"If you stay here, you'll all die. Go now—as quickly as you can."

He had his hand on the reins when he felt Nydia touch his arm. "Is it that bad?"

He looked down into her dark eyes. Tears clung to her lashes like pearls, and he thought she had never looked so beautiful. "We're outnumbered at least four to one." He smiled ruefully, picked up both her hands and pressed them between his own. "I put the King's life in your hands, lady. It is not a charge I hand over lightly."

"But, where will we find you—how will we—"

"If I can, I'll go to Kora-lado. The men know to rendezvous there. But don't wait. This is your only chance, and it's been bought with blood." Impulsively, he pressed a kiss on her mouth, grinned at her startled expression. "Go. And don't look back."

It was not for a long time afterward that she remembered there was nothing over his shoulder but gray shadows.

Chapter Sixteen

❧

$\mathcal{A}$utumn fell like an ax, with a rush of cold wind out of the north that cut through Nydia's thin clothes like a blade. Overnight, the deciduous trees burst into a crazy quilt of color, all crimson, flame, saffron, and cinnamon. In the late afternoons, as soon as the last red edge of the sun dipped behind the purple peaks, the temperature plummeted; in the mornings, Nydia noticed that the white caps of snow on the highest mountains had crept further down the slopes.

As best they could, they kept to an old trail which wound through the mountains, the remnants of an old blacktopped surface nearly obscured by the heavy growth of underbrush. In these mountains it was too costly to maintain the secondary roads. Only the old highways which looped over and through the high peaks were important enough to warrant the endless hours and expense necessary to keep them in repair. But they could not afford to take the highway, for they would be too vulnerable, too exposed to attack from the enemy soldiers whom they had to assume pursued them.

Horses' hooves crunched through the thick layer of fallen leaves as the makeshift litter which bore the King scraped and dragged over the rocky track. In the mornings, a light layer of frost covered his blankets as well as the ground. Ten days had gone by since that last battle, and they had no way of knowing what the outcome had been. But they had seen none of the King's soldiers or even any of the camp followers on their slow trek north, and Everic looked anxiously south each day, grimly searching for some signs of his fellows.

Abelard lay, feverish and unconscious most of the time, wrapped in as many layers as they had, his wound still slowly seeping blood. Nydia and Liss watched closely for signs of infection: foul odor, pus, reddened skin. So far the King's constitution was strong, but it would not remain so forever, Nydia knew. Without adequate nourishment, the King would weaken, and without the attention of a physician, who could set the collarbone, Abelard might lose the use of his arm, even if he did survive.

"How much further, Lieutenant?" Nydia approached Everic one evening as they stopped in a little valley near a brook to make camp. He had tethered his horse beneath a tree and was staring moodily north.

He shook his head. "The borders aren't well marked up here; we could be in Kora-lado already for all I know. But then it's likely to be another three or four days until we meet anyone. Obayana's got patrols in these mountains, but where they are, or how we find them, is anyone's guess. Another messenger did go north a day before the battle, but who knows if he made it to the pass? All I know is that we're heading in a straight line for the keep. And that could easily take another week to reach."

Nydia nodded. Everic turned to his men, gave a few brief orders, and looked back at her. He was older than the King; there were streaks of gray in his dark hair, and his beard, which had grown in during the last days, was grizzled. His eyes were hooded, but his face was kind. "And the King?" He spoke softly, as if he feared her answer.

"He needs a physician." Nydia said nothing more. There was no use in saying what they both knew to be true: Abelard would not survive more than another few days without attention.

Everic scraped the edge of his boot in the ground. "Is there anything we can do for him?"

"If you could have someone bring us water?"

"That's all?"

"I'm afraid that's as much as we can do for him."

"We'll get a fire going, too."

Nydia smiled her thanks and made her way back to Liss. They had cut their skirts off at the ankles to make bandages for

the King, and cold air swirled up and around their bare legs. If
the weather got much colder, their light cotton dresses, worn
against the summer heat on the Plains, would be inadequate.

Liss crouched beside the King, her drab brown blanket
wrapped like a shawl around her shoulders. His face was very
pale, the flesh drawn, and he looked so much like Agara that
Nydia caught her breath. Liss did not look up. She smoothed his
hair, now darkened and damp with sweat, back from his brow.

Nydia knelt beside her, touched her arm. Liss was pale, too,
her skin a dull, pasty white, dark circles under her eyes, her
mouth drawn down with fatigue. Her shoulders were slumped
beneath her blanket. Liss looked at Nydia with miserable eyes.
"What if he dies?"

Nydia drew a deep breath. She could not see the future beyond a few hours—there were too many variables at work.
She looked hard at Abelard as he shifted and muttered in
fevered dreams. He would live through the night—more than
that, she could not see.

"What if he dies?" Liss repeated in a hoarse whisper. She
pushed back a lank lock of hair. "What will happen to us all?"
Her hand trembled as she touched Abelard's hot cheek.

Nydia preferred not to consider what might happen were the
King to die. Of all his sons, only Brand was old enough to
even consider assuming the throne on his own. Brand—the
son of a kitchen maid, born of a liaison when the King was
fourteen. There was Vere, of course, whom Tavia said had
been born of a Mayher's daughter from a village near Ahga,
but who in the Congress would support Vere? And there was
Agara, always Agara, who would press for Amanander. But
Amanander was a child—and that meant a regency. Who
would govern for him? Agara? Nydia shuddered. "Let's not
think about it, now," she said. She wrapped an arm around
Liss. The girl sagged against her.

"You don't understand," whispered Liss. "I bear his child. If
the King is dead, his mother will kill me and the baby if it's a
boy."

Nydia froze. "Are you certain?"

Liss nodded miserably.

"Listen to me," Nydia said. The girl responded instinctively to the tone of command. She blinked the tears out of her eyes and sat straighter. "The King won't die tonight. Sooner or later, we're bound to run into Obayana's men, and when we do, they'll get us to safety. But we mustn't give up now, or waste time worrying about what might not come to pass, do you understand? That's not going to help any of us—not you, not your baby, not the King. Go rest. I'll bring you some food when I've tended to him."

Liss's wan smile was more a token of obedience than belief. "I should tend him—"

"Hush. Do as I say. Look, the fire's built—go lie near it and stay warm."

Liss stood up with a heavy sigh. "As you say, lady."

She shuffled off, and Nydia was left beside the King, watching his chest rise and fall with every shallow breath.

The following day dawned behind a thick mist. Fog rolled down the mountainsides through the trees in palpable waves, muffling all sound. Visibility was less than a few yards in all directions. The party moved slowly, a little island in a gray sea. The road they followed was a dim trace of broken stones swallowed by the drifting leaves. Everic stopped many times to curse. Without the sun and the neighboring mountains as landmarks, it would be easy to travel in circles.

Liss huddled miserably beneath her cloak. She did not look up when Everic swung out of his saddle and walked over to Nydia.

"I think we'd best make camp here, lady, I dare not go any further. I'd hoped this fog would burn off, but it seems like it's bound to stay with us. We'll rest now and go on in the morning."

"No," Liss moaned. She wrapped her arms around herself and rocked back and forth in her saddle.

Everic spread his hands. "Madam, you must understand. I can't tell which direction we're going in this soup. We could double back, take the wrong turn—if we rest now, and the fog lifts in the night, we can follow the stars. But without the sun, or some other guide to tell me which direction to go, there's—"

"No!" This time Liss was shrill. "The King will die! We've got to go on."

Everic looked up at Nydia helplessly. She grimaced in resignation, and motioned him to help her dismount. She walked over to Liss and reached for the girl's hand where it plucked at the reins. "Liss, get down. Please, it's better this way. I know—"

"No," cried Liss again, louder this time. "You don't know. It's not your child who'll die—"

Nydia saw the soldiers exchange startled looks. Everic jerked around with a curse. "Liss, come down now."

"No! If you fools won't move, I will. I'll go find help myself. I won't let him die!" She slapped at Nydia's hand and kicked her heels hard into her horse's sides. Startled, the animal jumped forward.

Nydia watched, stricken, as horse and rider crashed into the underbrush and disappeared into the fog. Everic strode up, hands on his hips, his face registering exasperation. He was swearing under his breath. "Now what, lady?"

Nydia looked up and saw, horrified, what Liss's unthinking actions would bring upon them. "Oh, by all the— Stop her!" She clutched Everic's arm. "She's got to be stopped—"

Everic stared at her. "Dom, Kyle, go after her." He looked down at Nydia's white frantic face. "What ails you, lady?"

"There's soldiers close by," Nydia hissed. "Mortmain's men. Quickly, we must prepare—"

"Mortmain? Lady, you see ghosts in the fog." He patted her arm patronizingly.

Nydia ripped her arm from his grasp and drew herself up. "No, I do not," she said emphatically. "Mortmain's men are near—her screaming brought them closer. Arrange your men, Lieutenant, they'll be upon us very soon."

Everic stared at her, something like fear on his face. The men shuffled and the horses whickered and stamped.

"Listen to her." The hoarse mutter cut into the uncertain silence.

Everic whipped around. Abelard lay on his pallet, head raised painfully off the rolled cloak which served as a pillow. "Lord King!" gasped Everic.

"Listen to her." The King rasped once more and fell back, sweat lacing his forehead.

Nydia hurried to the King's side. Without another pause, Everic beckoned to his men. They leaped off their horses, galvanized into action. He paused long enough to ask Nydia, "Which direction are they coming, lady?" His question was half sarcastic, but Nydia raised her head and pointed. "That way," she replied.

There was barely time to drag Abelard into the underbrush. Everic handed Nydia a long dagger. "Here," he said. "I don't know if you can use this or not, but you may need it. Try to aim for—"

But Nydia never heard Everic's advice, for one of the men gestured frantically for silence. "Lieutenant," he whispered from his position in a tree, "I think I hear something."

Everic drew a sword and hid behind a tree, head cocked. Muted by the mist, the sound of hooves came through the tangled undergrowth. Everic nodded, holding his finger to his lips.

Camouflaged by the thicket, Nydia hunched over the King. His eyes were closed, his breathing shallow. She touched the back of her hand to his forehead: the flesh was hot. His eyes fluttered and focused. His mouth curved in a weak smile when he recognized her. "Thank you," he mouthed.

She pressed a finger to her lips, shook her head as a warning. Suddenly, Liss crashed into the clearing, bent low over her reins, Everic's soldiers in hot pursuit.

With a curse, Everic grasped the bridle of Liss's horse as it swung by the tree where he crouched, sword at the ready. The animal reared, screamed, and Liss tumbled off the saddle. One of her pursuers hauled her off the ground, and she staggered. Almost at that same moment, a company of fifteen or more soldiers burst into the clearing, wearing the green and orange colors Nydia recognized from her visions. The King's Guard attacked.

Liss shrieked. Nydia pressed her hand against her mouth. She gripped the hilt of the dagger, unable to move or go to the girl's assistance. A guard thrust her into the underbrush, behind a tree, as much out of the way as possible. Nydia saw her collapse in a heap.

And then her attention was distracted by the battle. The men fought at such close quarters that the two companies were nearly indistinguishable from each other. One after another, they fell, bloodstains blooming on their clothes. Everic fought about fifteen paces from the thicket where Nydia crouched with the King. He swung his broadsword in both hands, desperately trying to prevent any of the attackers from noticing the King's hiding place.

Everic slashed the throat of a warhorse looming over him. The animal collapsed with a shriek and a heavy thud, its rider crushed beneath its weight. Another mounted soldier rode up, blade in hand, and Everic dodged and parried. An arrow flew out of the nowhere beyond the mist and landed in his chest with a soft thud. A groan escaped his lips, and he turned, one hand clutching the haft, an apology on his face. He slid to the ground.

From her own hiding place, Liss screamed a protest. The soldier on horseback looked up in the direction of the sound and spied Liss crouching in the undergrowth. He smiled evilly, sheathed his sword, and pulled a dagger from his belt. He slipped off his horse and advanced.

Nydia half rose to her knees and pressed a white-knuckled hand to her mouth, for all the men of the King's Guard were either fighting or fallen. There was no one to protect the woman who had brought the enemy down upon them.

"What have we here, sweetheart?" He reached for Liss. Nydia watched, horrified, as he gripped Liss by the forearm to drag her out. She sank her teeth into his wrist. With a yelp, he let her go, only to grab her by the hair, wrapping her long blond strands around his hand like a rope. "None of that, darling," he snarled. "I can be rough, too, if that's how'd you prefer it."

With a vicious yank, he pulled her out. Nydia winced, felt her own scalp flair in pain.

He tilted her face up to his with the point of his dagger. "Look at you," he said softly. She struggled, and he yanked her head back, her long white throat exposed. "Now you'll be still," he said. In one fast motion, too fast for Nydia to see from her position, Liss's bodice was split to her waist, so that her breasts tumbled into view.

Liss screamed and tried to break away.

With a laugh, he wrapped his arms around her waist and threw her facedown, flat on the ground. He dragged her closer, her bare breasts and nipples scraping across the ground. Everic's lifeless body lay ignored twelve or fifteen paces away. Nydia fingered the hilt of the dagger and remembered what her father had taught her about using one. Thrust underhand, aiming for the soft belly beneath the ribs—he'd never said anything about throwing it across a clearing full of fighting men. But if she didn't do something—

Liss struggled, her skirts lifted over her haunches as she tried to rise to her knees, but the grip which held her was firm. With one hand thrusting cruelly beneath her skirts, the man rose to his knees behind her, his back to Nydia. Nydia saw Liss's white thighs forced apart, the curve of her rump as her underlinen was torn away. Liss raised her head, crying out weakly, but the King's men were engaged in desperate hand-to-hand combat.

As Nydia watched, the man's hips thrust forward. Liss screamed, and Nydia rose as high as she dared. Before the soldier could thrust again, she hurled the dagger, praying that her aim was true.

It struck home, straight between his shoulder blades. He grunted, shuddered, and collapsed over Liss. Nydia withdrew hastily, back as far into the thicket as she could, huddled against Abelard's litter. Her hands shook.

His eyes were wide as he tried to raise his head. "Nydia," he breathed, "Nydia—" Over his shoulder, she saw his future— her future—and closed her eyes. She covered her face in both her hands and wept as the mountain patrol of the Senador of Kora-lado swept into the clearing.

Chapter Seventeen

❧

$\mathcal{P}$hineas opened his eyes to gray gloom. All around him were the silent forms of sleeping men. Some moaned a little in their sleep, others were unnaturally still. He struggled to sit up, winced at the stab of pain in his leg. Under the odor of unwashed men and blood, the air smelled like morning. He put the time as just before dawn.

"Captain Phineas."

He looked around when he heard his name. Across the dirt floor, a slight figure sat up. He recognized the young standard-bearer through a whirl of dizziness. The boy's face was white in the dim half-light.

"Captain Phineas. It's me, Roderic. Are you all right, sir?"

He rolled on one side, propped himself up on one elbow. He tried to remember how he had gotten here and shook his head. "Where are we?"

"We're prisoners, sir," came the young voice. "One of them smashed you on the head—don't you feel it?"

As he tried to raise his head, another wave of dizziness hit him, and he put one hand up. A thick crust of blood had formed over one eye. Cautiously, he felt around his head. A lump was under the new scab. The edges of the wound were raw, but it did not seem very large or very deep. Certainly his skull was intact. He settled back with a sigh. "Where are we?"

"This is Mortmain's camp. They brought us here after the battle, but you've been asleep most of the time."

"How long have we been here?" Phineas lay back and tried to remember.

"Since last night."

"Are you hurt?"

"No, sir, just a few scratches—nothing much."

Phineas was suddenly too exhausted to do any more than nod. He heard the boy shift, move, and then suddenly he knelt over him, a tin cup in his hand. "I saved your water for you, sir. They gave us some last night—I thought you'd want it when you woke up."

Gratefully Phineas accepted the cup and was alarmed to see how his hand trembled. The boy held it steady, helping him bring it to his lips. "My thanks, boy."

He lay back with a sigh.

"What do you suppose will happen, Captain?"

Phineas opened his eyes, tried to think. "It depends. If the King got away, they may hold us for ransom—try to bargain with us. If not, and he's dead—who can say?"

"Do you think they'll kill us, sir?"

He looked at the young face above his in the gloom. He did not want to lie, and yet, how to tell a boy too young to shave that the day just dawning might be his last? "I don't know," he said finally. "Lie down, boy, get some more rest. Who knows what this day will bring? Prisoners or not, we're still soldiers of the King's Guard, right?"

Roderic sat up straighter. "As you say, sir."

Phineas watched the light under the tent brighten, heard the first stirrings outside as the camp woke. He lay still, hoping to husband his strength for whatever was to come.

Three soldiers entered, pulling the tent flap back. For a moment they stood, surveying the men lying on the ground at their feet. One pointed here and there, and the men who had died in the night were dragged out. When the bodies of the dead had been cleared away, less than one third of the original occupants of the tent were left.

Phineas raised up on one elbow as a bucket of water and three loaves of bread were placed near the entrance. Roderic jumped up at the sight of the food. He hesitated, looked at

Phineas. He nodded at the boy to break the food up into shares.

He was munching on a crust of the hard bread when the guards returned. They squinted into the tent and focused on Phineas. "You there." The speaker wore a captain's insignia embroidered on his tunic sleeve. "You the Captain of the King's Guard?"

Phineas pushed himself up slowly, fighting the waves of dizziness. "Yes." His voice was hoarse, hardly as firm as he would like it to have been.

"Bring him," said the captain.

The other guards jerked him to his feet, and he bit his lip against the cry of pain as his weight fell on his injured leg. Nausea whirled through him, and he fought to keep the bread in his stomach.

"Easy with him," said the captain. "Lord Mortmain wants him alive."

They half dragged Phineas into the sunshine. He squinted in the light.

They brought Phineas to another tent, much larger than the one in which he had awakened. Two guards at the entrance pulled back the tent flaps and Phineas was surprised as he stared into the face of a short, dark man who was pouring wine into two goblets. "Give him one," the man said, gesturing to a goblet. He took the other and raised it to his lips. "Your health, Captain Phineas."

Phineas staggered a little as the men released him and a goblet was thrust into his hand. He tightened his lips, willed himself to stand straight. "And yours, Lord Senador."

Mortmain smiled. "You remember me, Captain."

"Of course." Phineas tried to remember all he could about the little man who took a seat behind a long plank table and smiled over the rim of the goblet. He was one of the few staunch supporters Abelard's father had claimed in the Congress. His Estate stretched from the thickly forested acres south of the Summer Lake region on the border of Ragonn, east into the western edges of the Saraneva Mountains, and south almost to Rissona. It encompassed the richest farmland, the most fertile valleys in all of Meriga. The cities of Vada, the most prosperous of all the cities in Meriga, were known for the quality of their goods and the liberal practices of their markets. He was at least fifty-five, with a slight paunch that hung over his leather belt, but it was clear from the ease which marked his movements that he was still a vigorous man. Phineas wondered what had turned this man against the throne he had once supported so steadfastly.

"You wounded the Lord of Yudaw rather badly. It's been four days since the battle, and he still hasn't regained consciousness. A seat for the Captain." Mortmain beckoned to a guard, and a three-legged stool appeared. The man pushed Phineas down, and he winced as new lancets of pain flashed up his leg. "Gently," admonished Mortmain. He waved one hand. "That will be all for now."

The soldiers saluted, bowed, and left.

Phineas stared up at Mortmain.

"Drink your wine, Captain. It's not poisoned, I promise, and it'll help your head." Mortmain drained his goblet to the dregs.

Phineas sipped, sighed, shifted on the stool. His injured leg throbbed and his head wound pounded. He looked at Mortmain over the rim with the dangerous eyes of a caged animal.

"I have to congratulate you, Captain. You've done quite a bit of damage. Not enough to stop us, of course, but enough to make me think twice about pursuing Abelard."

Phineas did not respond, but inwardly his heart leapt. The King was not yet captured.

"And I won't insult you by asking you where he went."

Phineas looked into the goblet. The wine was bracing. He felt it warming his veins.

"You've lost quite a lot of men," Mortmain continued. "My estimates are already at about two-thirds of your forces. Abelard must have been feeling desperate, indeed, to throw so few against so many, just so he could escape."

Phineas considered Mortmain's words. First, he didn't

know Abelard was wounded. Second, he didn't know how many men they had to begin with, or he'd have known that Abelard had thrown everything he had against him.

"But you managed to purchase your King's escape and did it with a significant loss to the opposition. I salute you." He raised his cup.

Phineas raised his in return, hope beginning to surge through him. Mortmain believed Abelard had an army with him—certainly a force more menacing than the small company he had in truth. So Mortmain hesitated because he wasn't certain, and that might buy more precious time. However, Mortmain did not seem too perturbed about the "significant loss," which meant that he had plenty of ready reserves, if not at hand, at least where they could be mobilized quickly.

Mortmain was watching him closely. Phineas decided the best course of action was to simply say nothing. He sipped the wine.

"I expect you're wondering what will happen to you, Captain. You know you're too valuable to be killed. We'll hold you for hostage."

"What about the rest?"

"The ones that survive the march back to Vada will be hostages like yourself. The rest . . ." Here he shrugged and spread his hands. "More wine?"

Phineas felt sick again. He shook his head and the room seemed to spin with that weak effort.

"Will Abelard attack before winter?" Mortmain's voice was soft.

"If you remember anything about me at all, Lord Senador, you must know I take the vows I swore to my King very seriously. Far more seriously than you apparently did."

The retort struck home. The ghost of a flinch passed across Mortmain's face. "I deserved that," he murmured.

Phineas stared him straight in the eyes, wondering why that remark should bother the Senador so much and what had driven Mortmain to raise arms against Abelard.

"But our vows are somewhat different, are they not, Captain? You pledged to die for him. My vows are slightly more complicated. At least as I interpret them."

"I see no difference."

"No. And I don't expect you to, either. Have you ever studied history, Captain? Not the mealy-mouthed rantings of the priests, but real history? History as it's found in books?"

Phineas shook his head once more.

"I didn't think so. There will be plenty of time for debate in the winter, if you are so inclined. But let me leave you with this thought: your Abelard Ridenau is a very dangerous man. And the Meriga he's so intent upon creating, the throne he so rabidly seeks to strengthen, runs counter to every ideal ever espoused by the men of Old Meriga. There were no kings in Meriga."

He gestured to the tent flaps. "I'll have a physician attend you. You will find I am not a cruel man, Captain, and that while you may think me disloyal to your King, you will find me very faithful to my ideals."

"I'll have to hope so, Lord Senador."

Mortmain frowned. "What do you mean by that, Captain?"

"A man who's broken his word once could conceivably do so again."

"I don't blame you for not trusting me."

"But what about the others? Senifay, Yudaw, and Ragonn? We've seen little of you at the Convenings these past years, Lord Senador, but the rest have attended faithfully. And by their words and actions there, I find it hard to believe that they've adopted your ideals—or any ideals at all."

"It's not for you to judge my allies." There was a faint edge to Mortmain's voice that told Phineas the Senador may have entertained similar doubts.

"Perhaps not, Lord Senador. However, I cannot help observing that the men you've chosen as allies are among the most contentious in the whole Congress. Your ideals must be very compelling, indeed."

"Perhaps compelling enough to sway you, Captain."

Phineas made a slight gesture of dismissal. "And who else embraces your beliefs? The Harleyriders? Missiluse?"

Mortmain held up his hands. "Captain. You know you don't expect me to answer those questions." He looked toward the door. "Guards!"

When the soldiers entered, he nodded at Phineas. "Take Captain Phineas to the tent next to mine. Summon a doctor to see to his wounds. Treat him with all respect—any complaints from him and you'll answer to me. Understood?"

They saluted smartly and stepped forward. Phineas rose. They were courteous enough, Phineas noted. He was not pushed or shoved; rather, they seemed to make every effort to accommodate his injuries. At the tent he paused. A sudden wind blew out of the north, and he looked up, toward the mountains which loomed like sentries in all directions. He hoped whatever gods existed had Abelard in their care.

Chapter Eighteen

$\mathcal{L}$ ike the shadows of the future, snow swirled, pattern upon pattern, blown about the heights on the ever-present wind. From the high windows of the keep overlooking the Kora-lado Pass, Nydia hugged herself and shivered. She could see nothing but a few dark rocks upthrust through the drifts. She had never seen so much snow in her life. Snow lay twenty or thirty feet deep in some places. No one could get in or out of Kora-lado.

The fortress of the lord of the Kora-lado Pass was a haven, a place of comforts unheard of even in Ahga. Room after room was furnished with articles from before the Armageddon, heated by hot water forced through a complicated system of pipes in the walls. Nydia had never seen such things as water flushed through the toilets, and hot water which flowed at the turn of a tap, and was amazed.

Obayana bowed courteously when she exclaimed over his keep, obvious pride on his clean-shaven face. Kora-lado was one of the best kept secrets in all of Meriga.

"The priests and the persecutors did not care to come too far into these mountains, lady," the Senator told her. "With the Armageddon the land changed, and the old maps were useless. The men and women who fled here found the passes easy to defend. And their descendants found it easy to take what they wanted from those who tried to journey through the mountains."

She was a little shocked at the easy way he admitted that his ancestors were thieves. Most of the Senators went to great pains to prove their lineages dated back before the Armageddon and that their families had held the title for at least that long.

But Obayana simply smiled. "The past is over and done, lady. If my great-grandfathers were resourceful enough to carve a life for themselves out of these rocks, who am I to deny it? It was an achievement which needs no embellishments. I am what I am because of them. I would do them great dishonor if I denied the truth."

On a wintry afternoon while the King slept, he took her on a tour of the keep. They began in the deepest cellars, where fires roared within ancient furnaces, day and night, fueled by logs and black rocks called coal, mined from the bowels of the very mountains upon which the castle stood. "They were the last, you see, the last of the Magic-users, the last of the scientists, the last guardians of what they called technology. They came here, and they used what they knew to build all this—" He waved his hand toward the ceiling and the massive steel girders, which dripped with condensation from the steam.

Sweat beaded on her forehead. Her gown of light wool hung heavily on her shoulders. Her skin prickled beneath her linen undershift. "But, what if it breaks? Wasn't that one of the greatest problems caused by the Persecutions? When the technologies began to break down, there was no one left who knew how to fix such things."

Obayana gestured courteously for her to precede him. "Are you warm?" he asked, as she paused to pat her damp cheeks.

She smiled wanly. "Hot."

"Come, lady, let me try to answer your question."

She followed eagerly at his heels, up twisting staircases and winding corridors. Kora-lado was a patchwork of many buildings, just as Ahga was, built with steeply slanted roofs and smaller rooms to accommodate the climate. Few lived here; besides the garrison, Kora-lado sheltered no more than forty souls.

At the top of one of the highest towers, he had opened a door for her and stepped aside to let her enter. She gasped.

Shelves rose from the floor to ceiling filled with books and leather sheaves containing parchment copies. Cold light filtered through the high windows. She wandered down the center of the library, hardly able to believe what she saw. The oldest books were protected in wrappings of heavy canvas, stored in locked glass cabinets. She could see the tiny keyholes in the wooden frames. Obayana leaned against a massive desk in the center of the room and smiled as Nydia gave delighted cries of recognition. Many names of the authors were familiar, but here were works her parents had thought long lost.

"You see one to your liking, lady?" asked Obayana softly from the shadows in the center of the room.

"John Milton," she murmured. "Is this truly the complete work of *Paradise Lost?*"

He smiled. "The story

*'Of Man's first disobedience, and the fruit
Of that forbidden tree, whose mortal taste
Brought death into the world, and all our woe,
With loss of Eden.'* "

She faced him, smiling, and quoted:

*"'What in me is dark
Illumine, what is low raise and support;
That to the highth of this great argument
I may assert eternal Providence,
And justify the ways of God to Men.'* "

"You know it well."

She shook her head. "No. Only the beginning. And the end. The rest of the copy which my family kept was lost, ages ago."

His eyes narrowed, he watched her with renewed interest. "And did your family keep the books as well, lady?"

For a moment, she almost told the truth, then stopped. "We

had a few bits and pieces gleaned over time. But nothing like this."

"And yet you know the language—these names are familiar to you, are they not?"

"Some," she admitted. She turned her back against further questions. She continued around the perimeter of the room, forgetting Obayana at the realization that she stood in the midst of what was perhaps the greatest collection of the lost literature of old Meriga, and the world to which it had belonged. She realized as she completed her circuit that there were no books of science, no mathematics. Not even a child's primer. Whoever had brought these books here had chosen carefully, and with a purpose.

"Are you looking for something in particular?" Obayana's voice cut through her reverie.

She started. "Oh, no. It is only that I have never seen such a collection before—"

"No. Nor are you likely to."

She ventured a question, although she suspected she already knew the answer. "The last of the Magic-users came here and built this place? But I see no magic books, nothing of theirs. Surely they must have also brought their books—"

Obayana shook his head. "They did, lady. Do you see the leather-bound parchments? Ostensibly those are copies of these books here, made by hand, done painstakingly over the years. But if you look through them, you will find, inserted into the texts, directions, instructions, carefully disguised. You know that during the Persecution whole libraries were burned without thought if any magic books were found in them."

"As though the rest were contaminated by proximity."

"Yes. Doubtless my ancestors tried to ensure the safety of these by hiding the knowledge within the copies. Let me show you." From a ring on his belt, Obayana selected a tiny key. He turned the key in the lock and withdrew a thick sheaf of parchment. "I suppose this one will do. Note the poor quality of this parchment. However, look here. This is, for all appearances, a copy of a play by one William Shakespeare, whose diction is

nearly unintelligible. But see, can you make anything of this?"
He laid the copy gently on the wide desk and carefully
smoothed the pages.

Nydia peered closely at the hand-lettered text. She squinted
and read slowly, aloud: "Study is like the heaven's glorious
sun/ That will not be deep searched with saucy looks; Small
have continual plodders ever won,/ Save base authority from
other's books. These earthly godfather's of heaven's lights/
That gave a name to every fixed star—" Abruptly the blank
verse ceased. The next lines read, without any attempt at poetry: "The Earth is the third planet in the Solar System. Nine
known planets orbit the Sun, which is the star at the center.
The sun is composed primarily of hydrogen and helium. Refer
J. Donne, Sn Rsng. Known planets: Mercury, Venus, Earth,
Mars, Jupiter, Saturn, Neptune, Uranus, Pluto. The circuit of
the Earth around the Sun is the duration of the year. Refer Wm
Shasre, Jls Csr, I.ii.15."

Nydia looked up with wonder on her face. "Are all the
copies like this?"

Obayana nodded silently. "For the most part. The references
are generally obscure and require some effort to locate. If one
were to take the time, I have no doubt one could piece much
knowledge together."

"You've never done it?"

"Lady, it would take years of doubling back and forth. Certain things make no sense unless one has read the text before
it. And there is the question of context. It may be there is significance in the placement of certain facts. It would take a man
his whole life and more to decipher it all."

Vere, thought Nydia. What would he make of such a place?
"So the Magic may even be here?"

Obayana raised his eyebrow. "Have you an interest in
Magic? It is a dangerous pursuit, is it not?"

"Indeed, my lord," Her voice was chilly. "It is hardly an acceptable pursuit for a lady."

He said nothing more. A little time passed as she circled the
library once more. Finally, he said: "You may read what you

like, as long as you will be careful with the originals. The copies are sometimes hard to read, and the sense of the texts are often interrupted as you have seen. I know you keep a lonely vigil with the King."

He opened the shelves for her and allowed her to choose two volumes to carry back with her to the rooms where the King lay sleeping as his wounds healed.

Now she stood alone in the library on a gray Sember afternoon, watching the snow fall. Time was heavy on her hands these days. Liss spent her time preparing for the birth of her child, and Abelard no longer required constant attention.

When the fever finally abated, Abelard was left very weak. But he had grown stronger rapidly, and now, less than six weeks since their arrival, he chafed to try a sword. Although he was permitted to get dressed and to walk about, the doctor refused to even consider allowing the King to lift so much as a dagger.

With another sigh, she curled up in one of the deep leather chairs set on either side of the fire. The flames hissed and snapped gently, and the book grew heavy in her hands. Her head drooped against the high winged back, and she drowsed.

"Nydia."

She thought at first she dreamed, and then she realized that the King did indeed stand before her, his arm pinned to his chest by a white bandage, his bright hair reflecting sparks from the fire. Unbidden, lines from *Paradise Lost* ran through her mind:

Who in the happy realms of light,
clothed with transcendent brightness didst outshine
Myriads though bright.

She rubbed the sleep from her eyes and stretched in the chair. "Lord King," she murmured. She would have risen, but he held up his hand and took the chair opposite her.

His eyes reminded her of the summer sea beneath the towers of Ahga. "So this is where you spend your time since I have no longer required your constant attention." He looked around the room.

There was a new timbre in his voice, and something about the way he looked at her sent a shiver down her back. It sparked a sensation deep in her belly at the base of her spine. She sat up straighter and clutched the book in her lap.

Under his gaze, she felt the blood rush up to her cheeks. "Is there something you require?"

"I spent the morning with Obayana. He told me you might be here." Abruptly the corners of his mouth turned down into a bitter scowl, and he stared into the flames. "Phineas is lost."

"Dead?"

He shook his head, eyes on the fire for a few silent moments. "The scouts think they saw him riding among Mortmain's men. If that's true, he's a prisoner."

She searched his face. "What will Mortmain do with him?"

"Try to use him to bargain with me, I expect. Mortmain won't kill him—not yet. But when he realizes I won't bargain, he won't have a choice. He'll have to kill him."

"But, Phineas—"

Abelard sighed and held up his right hand. "No, I don't want anything to happen to Phineas. But there's very little we can do about it until this weather breaks." He looked beyond her, up to the windows where the snow blew like lace against the pale gray sky. "So we wait." He gestured to the book. "What's that? More Shakestaff?"

"Shakespeare. No, it's another—"

"Read it to me." He settled back in the chair.

She wet her lips, found her place. His eyes swept over her and she blushed again, remembering his kiss on the night before the battle when they had stood at the bridge. Suddenly the flames hissed loudly and the wind whispered with renewed insistence. The heat seemed to be intensifying. "It's very old—the words are hard to understand—"

"Do the best you can, then."

She fumbled with the pages and took one more deep breath.

"Had we but world enough, and time,/ This coyness, Lady, were no crime./ We would sit down, and think which way/ To walk, and pass our long love's day./ Thou by the Indian Ganges' side/ Shouldst rubies find; I by the tide/ Of Humber would complain. I would/ Love you ten years before the Flood,/ And you should, if you please, refuse/ Till the conversion of the Jews./ My vegetable love should grow/ Vaster than empires and more slow. . . . /

"But, at my back I always hear/ Time's wingèd chariot hurrying near;/ And yonder all before us lie/ Deserts of vast eternity." She glanced up. His eyes were fastened on the ceiling, and she thought she heard him sigh. "Thy beauty shall no more be found,/ Nor, in thy marble vault, shall sound/ My echoing song; then worms shall try/ That long-preserved virginity,/ And your quaint honor turn to dust,/ And into ashes all my lust:/ The grave's a fine and private place,/ But none, I think, do there embrace. . . ."

He chuckled.

She did not dare look at him. "Let us roll all our strength and all/ Our sweetness up into one ball,/ And tear our pleasures with rough strife/ Through the iron gates of life;/ Thus, though we cannot make our sun/ Stand still, yet we will make him run."

"What is the name of that work, lady?"

"The title? It's called 'To His Coy Mistress'—the poet attempts to induce his lady to—"

"I know very well what he's attempting. Look at me." He shifted his weight, uncrossed his long legs, and leaned forward.

She raised her eyes hesitantly.

"Nydia." His voice alone was a caress, and she felt it shiver down her spine as surely as his touch. "I know what you think."

She looked up, surprised at his words.

"You think that in the old days, before the Armageddon and all the changes wrought by the Magic-users, when men and women swore themselves one to another, it was a better world then. And you think I would laugh, that surely I, with ten children, who woos every woman in Ahga, surely I must disagree." He leaned closer, reached out his good arm. "You think I could never understand why any man would possibly be satisfied with one woman for a lifetime. I tell you now you are wrong."

She drew a quick breath, but he continued before she could speak. His eyes held hers. "Perhaps I might have thought that way. Once. But I believe I could swear fidelity to one woman for a lifetime, if that woman were you."

She made a little murmur, but he held up his hand. "I have wanted you since that day you stood naked before me with your little chin so high, and your shoulders so proud, your breasts lifted, as though you would dare me or any other man to touch you. I'm not a boy, Nydia. I will not tell you I would throw away half my kingdom for one night in your arms, or that my throne is worth a lifetime of your love. I can be no more than I am. But I told you the day you swore your pledge that whatever more we might become would be for you to say.

"I want you, Nydia, I dream of you at night. Even when I have lain with other women, you are the woman I hold. I have waited for you as I have never waited for any other."

She closed her eyes as though that could stop the flow of his words, his voice like a warm wind blowing through her body, rousing her, reminding her of the taste of his mouth, the musky masculine scent of his body, the strength in his arms as he cradled her.

"Why do you look so frightened?" His voice was low and sweet. "Haven't I lived up to the pledge between us? Done all in my power to protect you and your secrets?"

She made a little noise in her throat.

"Is it Tedmund?" A new note, like the knell of a mourning bell, crept into his voice, tingeing it with regret. "I, too, mourn for him. I know you've lost much, and I cannot know the depth of your grief, but surely, you will not spend the rest of your days . . . ?" His voice trailed off, and she stared into the fire for she could not look at him.

She thought of Phineas, remembered the words he had spat at her the day he told her Tedmund had died. Aren't you afraid, he had said, that someday Abelard will ask you to do something you do not want to do?

As if he could hear the words in her mind, Abelard spoke as he rose to his feet. "I will not force you to do anything you would not want to do. But I won't pretend I don't want you— and I have thought once or twice, that you wanted me as well."

She twisted her hands together. His presence pinned her to the chair. Her legs felt weak, and she doubted she could have stood if she had wanted to. Her blood felt thick, like honey in her veins, her pulse a deep throb.

Suddenly he was standing, long legs poised to leave. "When you decide, lady."

He was halfway across the room when her voice stopped him. "Abelard—" It was only a whisper, but it was enough to make him turn back with that swiftness born of battle. "Shall we go chase sun?"

Faster than she would have thought possible, he was beside her, crushing her against his chest with his uninjured arm, massive muscles hard against her back. She braced herself, expecting the violence of passion long held in check suddenly unleashed. He only touched her forehead with his lips. Her knees went weak, as though her bones dissolved in the heat which radiated from breast to womb. She clutched his tunic, her face tilted up to his, lips parted, mouth soft.

His eyes were no longer the drowning blue of water but the hot blazing azure of summer skies. He dropped gentle kisses down her cheek, up to the curve of her earlobe, drew the flesh between his teeth and sucked. Delight rippled through her like a wave. His breath was hot in her ear. "I shall not always be gentle, sweet, but by the throne of my father, I will love you until I die."

And when, finally, he brought her out of the library, nothing else mattered for a very long time.

Chapter Nineteen

$\mathcal{T}$he unexpected disturbance in the outer room brought Phineas to his feet. The day had begun exactly like any other since his arrival at Mortmain's keep in the southernmost part of the Vada Valley. His rooms on the third floor of the eastern tower were adequately furnished, certainly with more comfort than he had expected. Except for the guards posted outside in the corridor, he was treated much like an honored guest. Roderic, the young standard-bearer, had been allowed to attend him as his serving boy.

His meals consisted of generous portions, and he and Roderic were allowed in the inner ward each day for a period of exercise. The sudden commotion set his pulse racing. He recognized Roderic's voice. The boy had gone to take their tray back to the kitchen over thirty minutes ago, and Phineas wondered what trouble the boy had managed to find.

He stole to the door, his soft leather boots making no noise, and peered cautiously around the doorframes. He was relieved when at first he saw only Roderic, but became alert when he saw the boy had brought a companion.

He stepped into the room, a frown beginning to pucker his forehead, wondering why the guard outside had allowed such a thing. Although they were not mistreated, and Roderic could come and go with a fair amount of freedom, he was not allowed visitors. Not that there was anyone to visit him.

"Roderic, what in the name of the—" He broke off when he saw the fresh bruises on the boy's face. One eye was swollen almost shut, and bits of straw and dung clung to his torn clothes.

Roderic leaped to his feet, leaving his companion on the low couch. "Captain! Please, help—" He gestured toward the figure on the couch, who sat clutching one upper arm with the other hand. Phineas stared in horror as he realized that the boy had brought a woman to their chambers.

"Roderic, what's this mean? How could you bring—"

"Please, Captain, I'll answer your questions later. You've got to help her."

Phineas looked from Roderic to the girl, who seemed about sixteen. He drew a quick breath as she raised her face and he recognized Mortmain's daughter. "Lady Melisande!"

"Captain." Her voice was steady, but her face was pale, and her loose-fitting trousers tucked into high boots and wide-sleeved shirt beneath a belted tunic were as dirty and disarrayed as Roderic's. They both looked as though they'd been in a yard fight.

With a little shake of her head, she indicated her upper arm. "Roderic says you have experience with field dressings, sir. I'd appreciate it if you'd look at this."

Phineas saw that the fabric of her left sleeve was ripped, and blood was seeping beneath the hand she held clenched against her upper left arm. He dropped to one knee beside her. "Roderic, fetch that pitcher of water and those towels in the other room." Gently, he removed her hand and tore the sleeve away from the wound, ripping the fine white linen all the way down to the embroidered cuff. He inspected her arm. A long red slash ran from her shoulder to just above her elbow.

Roderic hovered in the background, flitting behind him like a nervous butterfly while Phineas washed and bandaged the wound. The girl made no sound, even when he gently probed the edges to determine its severity. Finally, Phineas rocked back on his heels. "There, lady, that should do you well enough. The wound is not so wide or deep you need it stitched, though it may leave you with a pretty scar." He looked over his shoulder. "Roderic, sit down. Now, how did this happen? This is from a dagger, isn't it?"

The girl looked away.

"Roderic?"

"Captain, she was wonderful." The boy's voice was breathy with admiration. "You should have seen her—"

"I see the results of whatever she did," interrupted Phineas dryly. "And the results of whatever you did are all over your face, as well. Would either of you please tell me plainly what happened?"

"It was those ruffians in the kitchens, Captain," said Melisande. "They went after your boy when he brought the tray down to the kitchens. It wasn't the first time. I was coming back from the stables, and there were ten of them waiting for him. I've seen him do well enough against three or four, but ten was more than I thought he could handle."

Roderic nodded. "They jumped me, sir, and one of them had a knife—not a real dagger, a kitchen knife—and the next thing I knew, there she was with a stave in her hands. Before they knew what was happening, she knocked at least five of them silly."

Phineas looked at the girl, who still cradled her arm close to her chest. "How did that happen?"

She shrugged, an exact replica of her father. "The one with the knife went after me."

"And they didn't recognize you?"

"It happened too quickly."

"What's your father going to say about this, lady? Surely—"

She stopped him with another shrug. "My father's away, Captain. It's my mother who'll go off if she sees this."

"That's why I brought her here, Captain. I knew you could bandage it, and I thought I could give her one of my shirts."

Phineas regarded the girl before him, a half-smile tugging at the corners of his mouth. "Lady, is this a common practice in your house? Who taught you to fight with staves?"

Melisande made a little sound of dismissal. "My father has no sons, Captain. Perhaps he indulged me."

"He taught you to fight like a boy?"

"I can handle a dagger and short sword, as well. I have not the strength to manage a broadsword."

He ran his eyes frankly over her shoulders, a more appraising look than he was accustomed to giving women, and he wondered briefly at his boldness. But the girl did not seem to mind. She shrugged again and got to her feet. "I could not let them kill him. And they would have—given half the chance. But I think they'll not bother him again. I will speak to the Steward and the Chief Cook."

"Thank you," said Phineas. She had an air of grave self-possession about herself which gave the impression she was older than her years.

She tilted her head back, and he saw that she greatly resembled her father. "I will tell you quite honestly I wanted to meet you, Captain."

"Why?"

"My father says you are the King's right hand."

"Your father does me too much honor, lady. I think he'll find Abelard not as crippled by my capture as he might like to think."

"You think the King still has a chance against my father?"

Phineas smiled at the proud set of her shoulders, the indignant tilt of her head. Her hair was black, coiled into a braid and knotted at the nape of her neck. Little tendrils escaped and curled around her temples. Her eyes were hazel, her face an almost perfect replica of Mortmain's, the features feminized and softened. Yet the square jaw and tip-tilted nose were the same, as were the dark eyebrows. "It is never wise to underestimate the enemy." Melisande's face was suddenly ashen, and beads of sweat had broken out on her forehead. Without taking his eyes off her face, he said, "Roderic, in my room there's still some wine in the flagon. Go fetch it. Bring a goblet for the lady."

"Shall I get one of my shirts, too?"

Phineas nodded. "Come, sit down." He guided her back to

the couch and gently pressed her head down between her knees. "Breathe deeply."

She did as she was told. When she finally raised her head, her color was better. "Forgive me, Captain—"

"There's nothing to forgive. You lost a fair amount of blood. And battle, whether a brawl with kitchen toughs or another army, is always distressing."

She looked at him with eyes so clear they reminded him of the crystal depths of mountain streams. "Surely you don't mean to tell me battles distress you?"

"I find the thought of killing another man very distressing, lady."

"But you're good at it."

"I'm a soldier. If I weren't good, I'd be dead. But I don't kill for pleasure."

She cocked her head at him as though weighing his words. "That's what my father says."

Before Phineas could say more, Roderic touched his arm. He bore a tray with the wine and a goblet, and over his shoulder he had thrown a linen shirt. "Put it down—then go wash."

"But, Captain—"

"Go." Abruptly Phineas realized he very much wanted to continue his conversation with this girl alone.

With a resentful scowl, Roderic disappeared once more.

"He's very fond of you," Melisande smiled.

"Oh?"

"Whenever I've seen him, in the kitchens or the halls, it's always the Captain says this, the Captain says that, Captain Phineas wants this, Captain Phineas needs that. He tries to be just like you."

"How well do you know Roderic?" Phineas was taken aback.

Melisande shrugged, a much more girlish gesture than before. "I've seen him in the wards, you know. Seen you both, for that matter. He's very kind, more so than the other boys—ready to help even the old women in the laundries with their burdens. And he's brave—he would have faced all ten of those animals today."

"Why haven't I noticed you?"

"I suppose because I did not wish to be noticed. You would not expect to see Melisande Mortmain dressed like this, and so you don't. It's very effective."

"Does your mother know about this?"

"She tries not to notice." Melisande smiled at the frown he wore. "Don't look so stern, Captain. I like you better when you smile."

Disconcerted, Phineas stepped back and thrust the shirt into her hands. "Here. You can use the room in there. I'll have Roderic mend the other—he can do quite a reasonable job when he sets his mind to it. That way, not even your maid need notice."

She dimpled suddenly and tossed her head in a way that, if her hair had been unbound, would have set the black curls dancing. Despite the smudges on the creamy skin of her cheeks, she was beautiful in a spirited way that made him think of a half-tamed filly. "That must be the chess set Roderic says you're carving." She gestured toward a table against the opposite wall covered with scraps of wood. Small tools were neatly laid out on it.

He raised an eyebrow. The boy's infatuated with her, he thought. Well, why not? Despite the almost defiant stare, she had a gentle mouth. And she had gone to the defense of a stranger when the odds were five to one against her. The wound she'd taken wasn't serious, not really, but certainly more than any other woman he'd ever known would have suffered.

"Do you play, lady?"

"A little—not much since my father left. I have heard of your skill, though."

"Oh?"

"Roderic says Captain Phineas is the best in all of Ahga."

"Roderic is inclined to exaggerate."

"Perhaps you'll allow me to judge for myself someday, Captain." She went to the table and picked up the largest of the little figures, one about eight inches high. "This is my father," she exclaimed.

She turned back to Phineas, a smile playing at the corners of her mouth. "And the other—Abelard Ridenau? You're not only skilled at working with wood, Captain, you have a sense of humor." She picked up the pale wooden piece carefully.

Phineas cleared his throat, feeling more and more uncomfortable in the face of this feminine approbation. "The nearest approximation I could manage. The time is sometimes heavy on my hands."

Fascinated, she picked up the golden queen. "And this lady? Is this your sweetheart?"

"No," Phineas admitted. "She is a lady of the court."

"But not yours? This beauty is not a gift of your memory?" Melisande peered at the image of Nydia's tiny face.

"No," he said again. "She is more beautiful than I could ever make her."

"And yet you have not given her your heart?"

"She belongs to the King."

"And you would not compete with your lord for such a woman?"

"I would not compete with my lord at all."

"Never?"

"I pledged my allegiance to the King when I was fourteen. In nearly twenty years I have not broken my word."

He noticed how thickly her long black lashes fringed her hazel eyes while she appraised his words. For a moment, he thought she would speak, but the minutes passed, and all she said at the end of a brief silence was: "She's beautiful. And here—this is you, no?" Her fingers skimmed delicately over the knights. "And look, here's Roderic as a pawn—these are extraordinary, Captain. Your work is beautiful."

"The days pass slowly."

She nodded. "Is it very tedious?"

"Only when he's trying to teach me to play chess," said Roderic as he entered the room.

Phineas smiled ruefully.

She turned back to the table, delicately fingering the little pieces. "Time hangs heavy for us all, Captain. I wonder—" she hesitated, then turned to face him and said in a rush, "Would you be good enough to play chess with me? I doubt I am good enough to be much of a challenge, but as I said, there's hardly anyone here since my father left and took my tutor—"

Phineas held up his hand and bowed. "I am in your debt, lady, for saving my serving boy as you did. It would be my very great pleasure—but would it be a problem with your lady mother?"

Melisande smiled suddenly, a wide grin which lit her face and gave it real beauty. Color rose in her pale cheeks, and she winked at Roderic. "I managed to handle ten scullery boys, Captain, armed with sticks and stones and knives. I can handle one woman."

Despite his misgivings, Phineas smiled back. "Indeed, lady, I believe you can."

He thought of her for a long time after she had gone, as he sat musing at his table over his carvings. No wonder Mortmain had never brought her to court. Mortmain knew what he had—and he would not show his hand too soon. Abelard would have noticed her long ago. A pawn, an heiress of a tract of land almost as great as his. Abelard had forgotten about Mortmain's heiress, or so it appeared. Doubtless, he still thought of her, if he thought of her at all, as a child still. But Melisande was not so very young, Phineas thought; she must be seventeen or eighteen, of marrying age, certainly. Something inside him recoiled at the thought of Abelard married to Melisande.

Despite her half-tamed nature, she would never be won by brute force. He sensed a gentle heart beneath that spirit. Abelard would eat this little one alive. And Phineas would not like to see that brave, bright heart discounted beside the worth of her inheritance. Melisande should have a man who loved her for herself.

He picked up a new scrap of wood and began to carve Melisande's face on the figure of Mortmain's queen.

Chapter Twenty

❧

*Prill, 48th Year in the Reign of the Ridenau Kings
(2716, Muten Old Calendar)*

*S*pring arrived brutally in the Saranevas, a gush of melt-ing snow and falling icicles, which crashed like splintering glass to the ground below. Mountain streams became torrential rivers as the warm west winds swept over the heights. Passes which had been blocked for months opened nearly overnight, and roads which had disappeared in early Tober suddenly lay revealed beneath thin sheets of brittle ice. High above the Kora-lado Pass, Nydia watched as Abelard paced, ever more restlessly, as the days slowly lengthened.

On a warm morning in Prill, Nydia turned on her side, sighed and stretched. Her body felt swollen and replete. Her breasts ached pleasantly, her thighs were sticky where Abelard's seed leaked in a slow stream from the cleft between her legs. She felt him touch her mouth with a fingertip. With-out opening her eyes, she smiled, tugged gently at the finger with her teeth.

"Lazy woman," he whispered, bending over her. He swept the hair off the nape of her neck and grazed the white skin with his lips. "Will you sleep all morning?"

Reluctantly, she opened her eyes to the bright light which streamed through the open windows. The morning breeze was fresh and pleasant, without the biting smack of the winter wind. "What else should I do, when you've exhausted me, Lord King?"

"Hush." He gave a little frown. He did not like her to ad-dress him so, especially in bed. He pulled her closer, so that her head lay in the hollow of his shoulder. His nipple was next to her mouth, and the tip of the long, red scar of last year's wound was before her eyes. He had healed well over the winter with no lasting effects, but he would carry that scar for the rest of his life.

Her hand crept up to his face, caressed his cheek. His growing restlessness often found release in bed, for at times his lovemaking was almost savage.

She shifted her position. In the months since she had begun sharing his bed, he had used her in ways she had never dreamt of, made her do things she had not thought men and women could do to each other. But beyond her initial shock or shame was hot pleasure, which brought an end to all her protests and carried her away in a heady flood of passion such as she had never known.

She listened to his heart beat in slow measures beneath his chest, the thick mat of gold hair tickling her nose. For the first time in many months, she thought of Tedmund, whose lovemaking, no matter how impetuous, was nearly always tinged with hesitation and a kind of fumbling tenderness, as though he could not quite believe that she was truly real. And she remembered the boy who had been her husband. He had been a boy, she thought, with a brief pang of something like regret— the two of them not much more than children. How old had he been? She had been sixteen and he not much more than that, chosen by her father for his gentle, pliant nature, a boy who would not ask too many questions, so enamored was he of her beauty.

And for the first time in many months, she thought of the son she had borne her husband, a boy with soft brown curls and gentle eyes, heir to the secret which made him so valuable and so vulnerable. The secret for which he died.

As if Abelard heard the echo of her thoughts, he traced the faint, silvery lines which ran from her nipple down the rounded contour of her breast. She shuddered at the touch. He knew what they were, of course; he had too much experience with women not to recognize the marks left by the weight of pregnancy, when her breasts had been swelled with milk. "Tell me," he said, his mouth coaxing her eyes open.

Her lids fluttered. She met the intensity of his blue gaze with guileless grief. Could he, she wondered, who had seeded nearly a dozen women, could he understand the sorrow of a woman who had lost the only child she was ever likely to bear? How could any man, for that matter, understand what the loss of a child meant to a woman? It was impossible to think that in the time before the Armageddon women actually tried to prevent conception.

Was it two years now, or three? She swallowed hard and spoke in a low voice, so softly he had to bend his head to listen. "He was conceived almost at once," she began. "Perhaps the first month or two of our marriage." She paused, wondering briefly why she could not remember the act which had brought the child into existence.

"So it often happens," murmured Abelard.

"When he was born, there was great rejoicing in both our families, you understand?"

He only nodded, pressed her head closer to him.

"When the Mutens came—" Her throat thickened, threatened to close. Tears suddenly welled, and she remembered the small face, the little brown hands clenched in hers.

"I'm sorry," Abelard whispered.

The pain wrapped around her like a shroud. It had been so long since she had let herself remember, ler herself feel the loss, the empty ache in her breast where a child's head had lain, the empty arms where a child's still body— She gasped as the sobs overtook her, racking, shuddering cries. Abelard gathered her closer, held her as she clutched at the broad expanse of his chest, stroked her hair as her body shook in the grip of a grief too long suppressed.

He said nothing for a long time. Finally, her sobs diminished. He reached across her to where the linen shirt he had discarded the night before lay on the chair beside the bed, took it, and gently wiped at her face. "Forgive me," he murmured again and again, until at last she lay quiet in his arms. "I would not willingly cause you pain—even the pain of memory."

She swallowed, sniffed, and wiped her eyes. "I—I never really mourned—there was no time, you see."

He said nothing more but held her closer, and finally the slant of the sun told her it must be nearly noon. Her stomach growled alarmingly.

She sat up, ran her fingers through the thick fall of her hair. Life went on. She had decided that long ago, and there was no use dwelling on the memory of what had once been. She wiped her eyes once more and drew a deep breath. "I suppose we'd better eat something before we devour each other." It was a thin joke and they both knew it, but he smiled broadly.

"Are you all right?" He touched her cheek.

She met his eyes and nodded. "Yes," she answered with only a little difficulty. "I will be."

He was gentle with her as they dressed and called for breakfast. He was washing her back in the great tub when a knock on the outer door disturbed them. "At last." He stood up, pressing a kiss on the wet nape of her neck. "You'd better hurry out of there, or there'll be no breakfast left for you."

He shut the door behind him and left her to dress.

She was nearly dressed when she heard him swear. She hurried out, twisting her wet hair into a knot, in time to see the top of the table shudder as Abelard's fist slammed down in the center of it. The hapless messenger did not dare look his King in the eyes. He kept his face down, as though he very much regretted being the bearer of bad news.

"Go!" raged the King. The boy escaped with a sigh of relief. Nydia looked after him with a worried air. She had been half afraid that Abelard would take his wrath out on the boy. And it was not his fault that the news pouring into Kora-lado, with the same speed as the thawing mountain streams, was uniformly bad.

"Look at this," Abelard thrust the dispatches across the table at her. "And here we sit, surrounded by these godforsaken mountains and this everlasting snow."

Nydia forbore to mention that it was these same mountains and snow which had provided the protection Abelard had needed over the winter. He glared through her as though he did not see her. And in this mood, she reflected, it was probably better that he did not. With a soft sigh, she turned back to the door. "I'll be in the other room."

At once he was beside her, one of those lightening quick moves which never ceased to amaze her. He had her in his arms, and he pressed a kiss on the top of her head. "It had nothing to do with you, sweet, you know that. I'm not angry at you."

She pulled back. "What's wrong?"

He tightened his embrace and would have kissed her mouth, if there had not been a discreet cough from the doorway behind them. "Excuse me, Lord King."

Abelard turned and released her. Obayana stood in the doorway, watching them with a bemused smile tugging at the corners of his lips. "I understand that the messenger did not bring happy news."

The scowl returned to Abelard's face. "General Garrick is still in command at Ithan, but the Harleys raided Ahga. My family was forced to retreat north this winter. And the Army of the Plains is engaged with the outlaws already—it will be a miracle if they can join us at all. At least there's one piece of good news: the Harleys killed the Bishop. At least that's one less woman to meddle in my affairs."

Obayana nodded, lips pursed. "We must appeal to Mondana for aid."

"And the M'Callaster."

"Will Cormall take arms against W'homing? Isn't W'homing's sister married to one of the Chiefs?"

"Perhaps not W'homing. But maybe Ragonn. After all, if this coalition or alliance, or whatever they call themselves, were to succeed, who knows where they will turn next?"

Obayana nodded, and Nydia thought he knew all too well in what direction the Western Alliance would turn if they succeeded. She moved off and took a seat in the far corner underneath a window, and watched the melting ice stream in little rivulets down the windowpanes. She accepted a cup of warm milk and a plate of bread and cheese from the servant who brought their breakfasts, and nibbled as she listened to Abelard and Obayana discuss the news.

"Perhaps what is most remarkable," said Obayana, "is the report from Garrick stating that it was the Mutens who appeared out of the hills and drove the Harleys away from Ithan."

Abelard dismissed it with a wave of his hand. "The Mutens hate the Harleys—and why not?"

"Would it be worth trying to open negotiations with the Mutens, Abelard?"

"You aren't serious?"

Obayana shrugged. "What of Eldred?"

"It seems that the Kahn took every advantage of Eldred's hospitality this winter—Garrick received a plea from the fool requesting aid. Hah. There's justice in that, if nothing else."

Leaving the men still discussing strategy, Nydia slipped away to knock on Liss's door. She cautiously opened it when she heard the girl's voice say "Enter."

"Liss?"

Liss sat in a wide wing chair, her burgeoning belly providing support for her sewing. Her hair was carelessly caught at her neck with a length of blue ribbon. She smiled tiredly when she recognized Nydia.

"How do you feel?"

"Large." She shifted her bulk into another position. "What brings you here?"

"A messenger's finally got through."

"So that's what all the shouting was about." Liss sighed and thumped at the pillow behind her back. "When do we leave?"

"I'm not sure that we will leave, you and I."

"Things are that bad?"

Nydia nodded. Briefly, she told Liss the news.

Liss put the little garment aside with a sigh. "I wonder

where my parents are. Their farm is due south of Ahga, you know, probably right in the way of the Harleyriders attack."

Nydia took the other girl's hand between her own. "Surely they'd be safe in Ahga. They must have had some warning of the Harleyriders attack—"

Liss looked at her skeptically. "Did we?"

Nydia looked at the floor. "No," she said finally. "We didn't."

"What will he do?"

"I don't know. He intends to appeal to Mondana."

"Don't you know what he'll do?"

Nydia froze. "How could I know that?"

Liss persisted. "Because you know things. I've watched you all this winter. You know things will happen before they do— not everything, but you know exactly when the dinner will be served, and who will arrive late, and sometimes you even know why. And you know if someone will fall or hurt themselves somehow. I've seen you warn servants not to carry this tray or that bucket, or to watch the fire or the ovens. Don't deny that you know things, I know that you do."

Nydia bit her lip.

Liss clasped her hands over her belly. "There was truth in some of the things Agara said about you, wasn't there? That's why Abelard brought us with him—not because he was bedding me and wanted you, but because he was afraid of what would happen to you if he left you with his mother. And with the way things are in Ahga, I'd say he was right. She'd have had you burnt as a witch when the Harleys came calling, if not before."

"How do you know this?" Nydia said faintly.

"Because I watch and I see. Sometimes I see things that other people don't just because I'm paying attention and others aren't. Or maybe they think that no one is paying attention, and they don't realize—"

"That's spying—"

"No, it isn't. I don't listen at keyholes like Agara and her crones. I just watch and listen. It's amazing the things people say and do, and no one notices because they are so caught up in what they are saying or doing themselves." She leaned over and picked up Nydia's clenched hands. "I'm not trying to scare you. I don't believe any of that priestly garbage, you know that."

Nydia looked up into Liss's eyes, glanced over her shoulder. She saw only the intent to eat dinner in her room and sleep. There was no indication of any secret plans or schemes. "You must understand that I don't speak of this to anyone—"

"But Abelard knows."

"Yes."

"No wonder he brought you along."

Nydia glanced around helplessly and forced a laugh. "I didn't realize I was that obvious."

"You aren't. But I've had more time on my hands this winter, and so I just watched."

Nydia sighed. "Liss, I'm sorry. I never meant—"

The girl smiled and held a finger to her lips. "Hush. Don't apologize. If you never meant for it to happen, Abelard did. I told you a long time ago that you were the one he wanted. Even when I shared his bed I knew that. Did I tell you he used to mutter your name in his sleep?" She touched her belly. "I got as much from him as any other woman was likely to get. I know he'll provide for me and the child, there's no shame in having borne a child to the King—at least, there didn't used to be. Agara hated me before. And now she has a reason. I wasn't born a lady, not like you, and never hoped to be. So don't mind about me. You have enough to worry about."

She heaved her awkward bulk out of the chair and pressed a fist against the small of her back. "I never thanked you for what you did that day last Tober—when Mortmain's men found us. You saved my life, and my child's. I'll never forget that."

"No need," Nydia whispered.

Liss shrugged heavily. "My baby . . . do you see anything?"

Nydia shook her head. "All will be well—he'll be born

healthy in another month's time." She had not realized she'd known that until the words were out of her mouth.

"Will he live to manhood?"

"I can't tell you that—I'm not a soothsayer. My ability depends on choices people make. Only rarely does a choice have such far-reaching consequences that I can see beyond a few days or maybe weeks."

Liss nodded. "But you know what Abelard intends to do?"

"Not until he has some plan in mind will I see what the future might hold."

They walked slowly to the door. As she opened the door, Liss spoke again. "I meant what I said, lady. No matter what happens, if you need me, I'll help you. Any way I can."

Chapter Twenty-One

❧

"L ord Mortmain." Phineas paused near the door and inclined his head.

Mortmain turned from his place by the empty fireplace and beckoned. "Good day to you, Captain. I trust your stay with us has not been too unpleasant?"

Phineas shook his head. "Your guards and your servants have treated me with all courtesy, Lord Senador."

Mortmain gave him an enigmatic smile. "Servants gossip, Captain. You've heard of the dispatch I sent to your King?"

"I heard of it." Phineas forced a deep breath. Whatever Mortmain wanted of him, it would be best if he kept his head.

"So you know I've been elected King by the western lords?"

Phineas nodded silently.

"Come, Captain, don't look so pained. I know you believe that what we did is treachery of the worst kind, yet have you examined the reasons for what we did?"

"What reason could there be to justify breaking a pledge? According to the law of Meriga, you've all committed treason—and as far as I'm concerned, understanding of any reasons which you might offer is secondary to that fact."

"Of course, Captain." He moved away from the hearth and gestured to a table set up for chess in the corner of the room. "My daughter tells me you are a chess player of considerable skill. She credits you with what she learned this winter."

Phineas raised one eyebrow.

"Are you surprised, Captain, that I should know about your

association with my daughter? The first evening I was home, as soon as I sat down to play with her, I realized her game had improved. And so I asked who her master was, and she answered readily enough. For you see, Captain, the one thing I demand from everyone around me is the truth. I will not tolerate a liar—or a hypocrite."

Phineas returned Mortmain's gaze evenly.

Mortmain threw himself into a chair and gestured to Phineas to take the seat opposite. He poured wine from a silver flagon into a silver goblet and held it out to Phineas. "Drink with me, Captain."

"To what?" asked Phineas as he gingerly took the cup, twisting the stem around in his fingers. The cup was cold, moisture condensed on it, and the scent of the wine was crisp and fruity.

"No, I don't ask you to drink to the success of my campaign, Captain. It's begun, did you know that? Senifay and Yudaw wait just beyond the Wolvgreek Pass, south of Drango. Ragonn's men sit in reserve just a little to the west of them—Abelard is walking into a vise from which he'll not escape easily. By this time next week, he'll be wiggling like a worm on a hook. I think he'll regret refusing my offer to negotiate peace." Mortmain poured a cup for himself, nodded, and did not wait for an answer. "I sent a messenger last month to your King—he's at Obayana's keep, above the Kora-lado Pass—but you knew that, didn't you? I offered to meet with him, parley for terms."

Mortmain drank from the goblet slowly, savoring the taste. "I told your King that if my army crossed the Saranevas, we would not stop until we stood before the gates of Ahga itself."

"And he replied?"

" 'If.' " Mortmain laughed again, shook his head. "If, indeed. Typical. Abelard always had too much confidence. He'll have a surprise waiting for him when he reaches Drango."

Phineas only nodded, sipped the wine, and thought of Nydia. He doubted that Abelard would ever be surprised again.

"You aren't interested, Captain?"

Phineas took another slow sip of wine. It was excellent. "Lord Mortmain, do you expect that I would say or do anything which might betray my King to you? Doubtless you've made the battle plan you think best. Doubtless Abelard has, as well. But I don't intend to remark upon either."

Mortmain smiled, a smile of grudging respect. "If you are as worthy an opponent at chess, Captain, as you are at debate, you must be a formidable master, indeed. And if you are as adept at war, Captain, as I think, I know Abelard Ridenau is seriously disadvantaged by your loss." He set the cup down on the polished surface of the table. "Even though Abelard refused to parley, I don't intend to kill you yet."

Phineas leaned back in his chair. "Lord Senador," he said with calm deliberation, "I'm quite certain my King counts me dead already. I don't flatter myself that my life is worth a throne, and I'd bid you not overestimate its value either."

"What a cool head you have, Captain. You talk of your own death as easily as you might a chess move. Are you really so fearless? Or are you convinced your King will force me to release you?"

"You'll have to decide that, Lord Senador."

"I would prefer it if you addressed me by my new title, Captain."

Phineas said nothing.

Finally, Mortmain shook his head. "You won't believe this, Captain, but I did not bring you here to wrangle. More wine?"

Phineas silently pushed his goblet across the table and watched the purple liquid flow over the lip of the silver flagon and into the goblet. "Then what do you want of me? A game of chess?"

"Perhaps. I wanted to talk to you, Captain. I remember you, you see, from the Convenings. You said little, but what you did say always had merit. Your father was a stablehand, wasn't he?"

"Yes."

"And you were picked out of the stables because—"

"Because I was as tall as the young Prince, and as inexperienced. It was the weaponmaster who picked me."

"You needn't speak so defensively. I salute you, Captain. You've served your King better than he deserves."

"I'd leave the judging of the quality of my service to my King, Lord Senador."

"Point scored. But you never studied history, did you?"

"I studied what I needed to know. I can read and write, and I have read the ancient treatises on warfare—those that remain."

Mortmain shook his head and sighed. "So much was lost in the Armageddon and the Persecutions. In Old Meriga, men like you would have been given an education worthy of their talents."

"Much was lost, Lord Senador, and it has ever been my King's goal to restore—"

"Ha!" Mortmain gave a derisive snort. "In Old Meriga there were no kings. No kings, no hereditary lords—"

"Then who ruled?" asked Phineas, shocked and curious despite himself.

"Men were governed by the rule of law. It was written that governments are instituted by men to secure the rights of the people. The people elected their representatives, who sat in the Congress and called themselves Senadors, and they governed by the will of the people. In Old Meriga, the Senadors did not inherit their titles. They were granted them by the people of the Estates, and if the people did not approve of the policies they enacted, or the ways in which they governed, the people were free to choose other men to lead them. It was not until the Persecutions and the Armageddon that the titles became hereditary."

Phineas sat back. The wine stung the roof of his mouth.

"A great man once wrote that custom reconciles us to everything, and that the greater the power, the more dangerous the abuse."

"So you seize power for yourself?"

"It's the only way to prevent Abelard Ridenau from becoming a tyrant. For if not Abelard, it will be his son, or his son's son. It is inevitable. Unless there are limits imposed on the power of the crown, it will grow like a poison vine run riot. Those who have been once intoxicated with power can never willingly abandon it."

Phineas stared at Mortmain. "So you choose to use Abelard's own methods against him?"

"His own—"

"You seek power by force of arms."

"I defend my country against a hostile invader."

"But you seek the same end as Abelard."

"You don't understand what I am trying to tell you. Do you know that once the men of Meriga rebelled against a king? Indeed, Captain, they declared themselves free and independent from all kings, all tyranny—they fought against a power far stronger than themselves and won. And it was not a victory of the nobility, Captain, but a victory of the common men."

"Like myself?"

Mortmain stared, the light still bright in his black eyes. "Yes," he said after a short pause. "Like yourself. Why can't you see what Abelard will become? Can't you see he'll become a tyrant, that there are no checks on his power—nothing to balance him, nothing to gainsay his will?"

Unbidden, an image of Tedmund of Linoys flitted through Phineas's mind. A shadow must have crossed his face, for Mortmain leaned forward eagerly. "You do see, don't you?"

Phineas drew a deep breath, and controlled a shudder with effort. "I will not betray my King."

"I don't ask that of you, man!" exclaimed Mortmain. "But you do see it, don't you? Abelard isn't like his father, for Renmond—"

"Renmond Ridenau was a weak man and a weak king. The country nearly disintegrated into ruin under him."

"No," Mortmain shook his head. "Renmond wasn't weak. He didn't have that trick of Abelard's—of getting people to do his bidding and making them think it was their idea all along. But he wasn't weak at all. He trusted people. He tried to con-

vince the Senadors to work together, rather than constantly at
cross purposes. He had some sense of the balance of things,
and I supported him. His death was only timely from his son's
point of view."

Phineas stared, shocked by Mortmain's implications. "Are
you suggesting that Abelard was responsible for his father's
death?"

Mortmain shrugged. "The facts speak for themselves. Renmond was killed by brigands very conveniently just before he
was to sign a treaty, which would have limited the power of
the throne and brought back a large measure of the checks and
balances which existed in Old Meriga between the Chief Executive and the Congress."

"The what?"

"The Chief Executive. The leader—the Chief Executive as
he was called—was not a member of the Congress. He was
apart from the Congress—he controlled no lands, he repre-
sented no people directly."

Phineas frowned, trying to digest the information. The idea
of a government without a king was so foreign, it was nearly
incomprehensible. Surely there could be no peace between the
Estates without a strong government in place? And who could
be stronger than the King? His mind rejected Mortmain's no-
tions and seized instead something much more tangible. "How
can you suggest that Abelard had something to do with his father's murder? Abelard was nowhere near Ahga when it happened."

"Ah, yes, on a campaign in the Pulatchian Mountains, wasn't
it? And you, Captain, held the city for him, and the garrison,
until he could get there and take control. How very convenient. Did it never occur to you that he might have simply
used you? Used your loyalty, your love?"

"Abelard was nineteen years old when his father was killed.
What you suggest is monstrous."

"Monstrous, indeed, Captain. But not outside the realm of
possibility?"

Phineas was silent. He remembered Tedmund, and

Abelard's insistence that the boy be sent into a situation for which Phineas had well known he was not really prepared. Doubt raised its ugly head. His automatic denials died unsaid.

"Captain." Mortmain's voice was quiet. "I don't expect you to betray your King. I understand the importance of the oath you swore. And I understand your contempt for me, who broke the pledge which you hold most dear. But it is not because I am a hypocrite that I seek to change Meriga. I see the way the future leads, and I fear where it heads."

He faced the windows and beckoned Phineas to stand beside him. The valley rolled away, north and west, green rows of crops stretching peacefully under the spring sky. "I love this land, Phineas." He did not seem to notice that he called his prisoner by name. "My father taught me to cherish it, and to respect the men and women who worked it. He said to me it was a sacred trust between me and my people. I cannot countenance or support the reign of a tyrant who would not respect or cherish anything but his own desires."

"How do you know for certain that my King would not?"

Mortmain looked at Phineas and their eyes met. The room was so quiet that Phineas heard the chirp of the birds outside the window and the shouted commands of the guards in the kitchen yard. "You know him better than any other man in Meriga. Do you believe he will?"

But Phineas, heartsore and troubled, could not meet Mortmain's gaze.

Chapter Twenty-Two

On a warm evening in late Prill, the newly combined forces of the lords of Mondana and Kora-lado emerged from the last of the high mountain passes into the southern foothills of the Saranevas. They marched beneath the banner of the King of Meriga, and the eagle blazoned upon it seemed a living thing as the white silk snapped in the light wind. The sky, which had been a clear, cloudless blue all day, blushed rose and lavender over the western horizon. Above them, the first star of evening shone steadily.

The road wound down in a gentle curve between the mountains, which rose steeply on both sides, and gradually rounded into a small valley. Ancient oaks spread their branches overhead, hazed with the first faint green of spring. From the thick mulch of old leaves on the ground, small green shoots were just visible in the fading twilight. Nydia took a deep breath and glanced at Abelard. The air was a rich blend of the sun-warmed earth, the woodsy smell of the trees, and a scent she could only define as that of green growing things. She sighed a little and patted her horse's neck.

When they reached the other side of the valley, Obayana nudged his mount over to Abelard's and trotted along beside him. "Over there, Lord King, just over that last ridge, is the first of my border garrisons. It's a small garrison, but enough to house us for the night."

Abelard looked back over his shoulder at the troops who jogged along behind them. "Enough to house us all?"

"The men may have to camp beneath the stars, but it's a

fine night. Certainly there's room for us and the captains of the regiments."

Abelard nodded, satisfied. "Send a messenger on ahead. We'd better let the garrison commander know to expect company for dinner." He grinned at Nydia. "How does a bed tonight sound, sweetheart?"

She smiled and lowered her head. She felt a little uncomfortable, the only woman of any rank among the whole company. Obayana had provided two women to wait on her. Liss had remained behind. The week before they left the Kora-lado Pass, Liss had given birth to a son, whom she named Reginald. Abelard had smiled approvingly on his seventh son and cuddled the baby with more expertise than Liss.

Nydia realized suddenly that she missed Liss, missed the girl's forthright demeanor. She gazed ahead in the fading twilight and wondered again if she had made a mistake in trusting Liss. There was nothing to indicate that she might betray her, but Nydia had been taught from infancy to be cautious.

"How much farther, Lord King?" The voice of Niklas Vantigorn jarred her back to the present. "Perhaps we should stop here?"

"Obayana says there's a garrison just ahead over that ridge. A messenger's gone on ahead—"

Nydia looked casually over at Niklas and Abelard, and froze as she glimpsed a shadow of the future. She gasped involuntarily, and her hands tightened convulsively on the reins. Her horse whickered in protest.

At once, Abelard looked up, eyes narrowed. "Lady?"

Nydia squinted in the fading light, looking over his shoulder. The images were indistinct, and yet she had quite clearly seen an arrow fly over the King's head and pierce the chest of Mondana's heir. In the gray light, the vision swirled and shifted.

Abelard brushed past Mondana and guided her gently aside, out of earshot. With one hand, he reached over and covered both of hers. "What is it?"

His trust was implicit. Between Nydia's foresight and

Obayana's knowledge of the mountain trails and passes, they had managed to cross Kora-lado in less than two weeks and avoid the trap Mortmain thought so cunning. Mortmain's army south of Drango waited in vain; guided by Nydia, they had come due west.

She squinted past his shoulder. It was nearly full dark, the men were bringing up the lanterns to light their way, and it was nearly impossible to see the road ten yards in front of them, much less the future. But he was looking at her intently. She said quietly, "When you spoke to Niklas, I thought I saw an arrow land in his son's chest."

In the gloom, Abelard's face was white with dismay. "Is it Yudaw, lady? I thought Mortmain's army was massed south of Drango—"

She took a deep breath and nodded. "When you decided to send a messenger to the garrison, I saw nothing wrong then— is there some animosity between Kora-lado and Mondana?"

Abelard shook his head. "None. Mondana and Kora-lado are the best of allies. Could you see colors?"

"No. Just a long arrow—long enough to be a spear, almost, fletched with long white feathers, tipped scarlet."

Abelard stared. "The M'Callaster!"

It was Nydia's turn to look puzzled. "Who?"

"Cormall M'Callaster, Chief of the Chiefs of the Settle Islands. He's entitled to call himself a Senador, and sit in the Congress, but he scorns both. No one else uses such arrows. You should see the longbows—nearly seven feet high—a man needs the strength of one of these oak trees to bend it. The white feathers come from the white eagles on one of the islands, and each family has their own colors. The M'Callaster's colors are white and bright red." There was excitement in his voice that made her sit straighter. "Come, lady, let's ride ahead. Perhaps if we can get there ahead of the rest, we may avert disaster."

"But—"

"Mondana and the Settle Islands are bitter enemies. They have wrangled for generations, and only in the last years have

I managed to establish a peace which is tenuous at best. If Mondana's heir is killed by a stray arrow, this alliance of mine will vanish like morning fog. Come, I must ride. Or, is there a reason we should not?"

She looked hard into the night past his shoulder. "No," she admitted.

"Then come. I want to see what the best of Obayana's stables can produce." He shouted a few orders to the others riding behind them, then turned back to her while the others were opening their mouths to question the King's intent. "Are you with me?"

"As you say, Lord King." She touched her heels hard against her horse's flanks as Abelard leapt ahead, riding down the dark road. They disappeared into the night, leaving Obayana, Mondana, and the captains of the cavalry gaping in astonishment.

When they reached the crest of a hill, Nydia could see the road rolling down the gentle incline and, perhaps a mile in the distance, a cluster of low buildings, the highest no more than two or three stories tall. Light flickered, and the odors of smoke and roasting meat drifted toward them on the light evening breeze.

Further beyond the buildings lay what appeared to be no more than a pool of deeper shadow. Abelard tugged the horse to a stop and pointed to pinpoints of light shining here and there at ground level. It looked to Nydia as though a hundred stars had fallen to earth and found a place on the black ground.

"Campfires," he said, with no more explanation. "A lot of them. Too many for a small garrison such as Obayana described." He looked back at Nydia. "Is there danger, lady?"

She shook her head helplessly. "It's too dark." Above them, a million stars or more wheeled in the dark heavens, casting the only light. There was no moon.

"Let's go," he said.

Somewhere beyond the farthest reaches of the foothills, Yudaw lay like a ripening peach, all rolling fields, thickly forested woodlands and gently meandering rivers running into the Western Sea. This road led into its heart, and it was this route Abelard intended to take to the walls of Mortmain's keep.

The land lay quiet around them. The night wind was warm and Nydia fancied it carried with it a tang of the salt sea. The horses' hooves slapped softly on the black surface of the road. Obayana spent a lot of time preserving the roads running through his domain. Without them, thought Nydia, the Saranevas would be nearly impassable, even in the summer. The horses carried them closer and closer, and the walls of the garrison loomed above them, blotting out the stars and the campfires. The odor of roasting meat grew stronger, and Nydia's mouth watered and her stomach growled.

They were still at least two hundred yards from the dark walls of the garrison, close enough to see the torches flaring in the guard towers, still too far to distinguish much else in the shadows, when Nydia heard a high whine pass close to her ear. Instinctively, she ducked low in the saddle, while Abelard swore loudly. "Those war-hungry devils—" He reached over and grasped her hand. "Are you all right?"

"Was that an arrow?" She turned, squinted down the dark road behind them.

"Their idea of a joke. Doubtless that's what might have ended in Nevin Vantigorn's chest—and then there'd be a fine mess to deal with."

Shakily, she straightened and urged her mare on. "They do that—"

"By way of welcome."

"Some welcome."

"Indeed. Only a friend would venture on much further, they reckon. Come on, we'd better hurry. I think they allow a count of fifty or so before they loose a volley."

"What?" But his answer, if he had one, was lost in the clatter of hooves as he galloped off.

At what she hoped was a safe distance, Nydia followed warily and arrived before the walls of the garrison in time to see Abelard vault out of his saddle, the flash of metal in one hand.

In front of the garrison, a large crowd of men stood, and from the walls of the garrison, more craned their necks over the battlements to watch. Nydia reined up, horrified to see the messenger they had sent on ahead struggling in the grasp of two burly men-at-arms who wore dark trousers and tunics covered with long cloaks woven in intricate patterns of color and design. She looked up at the walls, drawing in a quick breath at the sight of so many men, each with longbows an arm's length taller than they.

Her mare pranced and shied a little as the torches flared and the crowd of men pressed closer. Stricken, Nydia saw Abelard stride through the crowd, dagger in hand.

"Lord King!" cried the messenger. A hand was clapped over his mouth, but still he struggled in the hard grip of his guards.

With slack hands on the reins, Nydia watched as the crowd parted to reveal Abelard squared off against a black-haired giant who was easily a head or more taller and, to Nydia's eyes, at least, twice as broad as well. The men shouted encouragement and called out wagers.

Nydia gasped, fist pressed to her mouth. The King's opponent lowered his huge head and raised his fist. The long metal blade in his hand threw off glints of light, and Nydia saw clearly the barbs along one edge. A heavy hand fell across her reins and Nydia started. The horse shied and would have reared, but the man held the reins with a firm hand and spoke gently. "There, there, what have we here? Abelard out to bring the lords to heel with only one small missy by his side?"

Nydia looked down on the man by her side. He was at least as tall as the King and huge in the chest and shoulders, like his fellows. His beard was full and fell to his chest, his hair was long and curled about his shoulders. He wore a braided leather circlet around his forehead to hold the long hair off his face. His hands on the reins were large and brown, covered in coarse black hair, and a thick gold ring gleamed on the middle finger of his left hand. His teeth were broken in places, and a ridged scar ran across his forehead and down the bridge of his nose. It made his nose red and misshapen, even in the torch-light.

At Nydia's silence, he smiled broadly. "Don't you mind, my girl." To Nydia's ears, it sounded like, "Duncha mind, m'g'rl." His accent cut the vowels short and clipped his speech, so that she had to think a moment in order to understand. "The boys are only having their fun—he'll not be harmed. I give you my word."

"Your—your word?" she stammered. "And whose word might that be?"

He grinned and swept her a low bow in a swirl of plaid. "The M'Callaster's, missy. Chief of the Settle Islands and Lord of the North. Cormall M'Callaster, that's whose word it is."

Nydia could only stare at him a moment before her attention was drawn back to the two men who circled each other warily, like fighting cocks looking for an opening.

Abelard ducked the first attack. He rolled to one side as the other rushed forward once more, then came up crouched in a fighting stance. Nydia realized he held the dagger in his left hand, the arm which was so severely wounded in the autumn.

"That's your man, Lord Senador?" She gave him the title before she remembered that the Chiefs scorned the mainland titles. "Can't you stop them?"

Cormall shuffled his boots in the stones of the road. "I hate t' interrupt. Looks like the fun's just getting started. The King looks like he's holdin' his own just fine—"

"The King almost lost that arm last fall," she hissed. "What kind of barbarians are you that you'd welcome your King with a knife?" Anger overrode any caution which she might ordinarily have felt in the presence of so many apparently armed and dangerous men.

The M'Callaster apparently did not hear, or did not choose to acknowledge that he had heard. He was watching the fight with pursed lips. The Settle Islander had managed to nick his blade across Abelard's cheek, and a thin stream of blood trickled down the King's face. Abelard retaliated with a fast series of low slashes which laid open a wound in his opponent's thigh. "Ah, well, I suppose we'd best save the blood lettin' for Mortmain and his pack o' traitors."

He winked at Nydia and shouldered his way through the crowd, his cloak of vivid red and green and blue plaid swirling in his wake. Nydia watched in amazement as he fearlessly caught the younger man easily by the waist and swung him around, dodging the wicked thrust of the dagger as he did so. He drew back one huge fist and swung.

The blow hit the other squarely on the chin. For a moment he stood, dazed and blankfaced, as the dagger quivered in his fist. Then, as the M'Callaster stepped back, the soldier muttered something incoherent and crumpled.

Abelard straightened, his breathing hardly faster than it had been when he was seated on his horse. He wiped absentmindedly at the blood seeping down the side of his forehead.

"I see he bloodied ya, lad," said the M'Callaster.

Abelard nodded, the beginning of a grin lifting the corner of his mouth. He touched his temple gingerly. "A scratch." He sheathed his dagger. "You shouldn't have stirred yourself, Cormall. I would have had him down in another minute or two."

Cormall jerked a thumb over his shoulder toward Nydia, who still sat on her mare in tight-lipped silence. "The nurse-missy you brought with you sent me out to look after ya." He shrugged. "But if you'd rather, we can wake Jonny-lad here, he'll be all right soon enough, sooner if someone douses him with water."

"And sooner than that if it's ale," cried some anonymous wit.

Abelard joined in the general roar of laughter and emerged from the press of the crowd with an arm around the M'Callaster's shoulder. Together they walked over to Nydia. "Don't look so worried, my dear." He bowed. "I should've warned you about this particular custom." He swung her out of the saddle. "Shall we go in?"

On Abelard's arm, she entered the garrison. He casually

strolled through the crowd which had been calling for his blood just a moment before, greeted the flustered captain of the garrison with nonchalance, as though this were the welcome he expected. The little garrison was crowded, indeed, thought Nydia, the stables overflowing with horses and equipment of every description. The inner ward was packed with men and barrels of provisions, weapons stacked in high piles neatly against the walls. Everywhere she looked, it seemed, there was a grinning bearded face.

Suddenly, she was seized by the queer dizziness that overtook her whenever there were too many crowded around her. She clutched the King's arm and stared at the ground, drawing in deep breaths, trying to still the whirling before her eyes.

"Nydia?" Abelard stopped and frowned down at her in concern. When he saw her white face and blanched lips, he was suddenly all seriousness. He circled her shoulders with a firm arm and forced a path through the press of the crowd. "Make way," he cried in the voice she had never known anyone to disobey. She heard Cormall make little clucking sounds through a haze of nausea, and she knew that they were inside before a bright hearth. She was pushed into a low chair, and a goblet of strong ale raised to her lips. When she would have turned her head away, she heard Abelard say, "Drink it."

Obediently, she took a swallow or two and closed her eyes. When she opened them, she saw only Abelard kneeling on one knee next to her. "Are you all right?"

She took another deep breath. "Yes. It was just that there were too many people out there—all pressing in too close—"

"Yes," he said, "I understand. Will you be all right here?"

She nodded.

"I'm going to see that those fools don't repeat that performance with Mondana and the others. I've given them their fun for the evening. They can just wait to cool their hot heads in Mortmain's blood."

He pressed a quick kiss on the back of her hand and was gone. She lay back in the chair, the goblet of ale still in her hand. She shut her eyes with a little sigh.

It looked as though the M'Callaster had brought at least five hundred of his fellows with him. She wondered how Niklas and Obayana would react, and if the long history of enmity between Mondana and the Chiefs would complicate the alliance Abelard so desperately counted on.

She looked around the small hall. No wonder the garrison commander had appeared so flustered. He would be hard-pressed to find lodging and food for them all, and it was a good thing the Settle Islanders appeared to be well provisioned.

The roof was low—no more than a few feet above the heads of the men who stood around drinking and talking. The architecture was pre-Armageddon, she guessed—here and there the roof was shored up with a more recent repair. The floor was dull and scuffed with age, the finish long worn away.

At the far end of the hall, a long sign, brightly repainted again and again, advertised in the language of Old Meriga, "Breakfast at Roy's—3.99 All You Can Eat." Around the hall, near the ceiling, curious shields were hung, obviously metal and, equally obvious by the precision of the design, very ancient. Here and there, they were scabbed with rust, but effort was obviously made to keep them in repair. A bright red octagon proclaimed STOP in bold white lettering. A yellow triangle warned YIELD. Most of the backgrounds were yellow or white, and the lettering or the figures black or red. A few were orange, the largest at the opposite end from the "Breakfast" sign, was green with white letters. Someone had painstakingly repainted it, and it proudly announced for any who might have cared:

GRAND JUNCTION	25
DENVER	186
PROVO	90

She wondered idly if any of those places yet existed, or if any remembered where they might have been. Obayana might understand the significance of these decorations, but for the rest . . . She looked around the hall again, at the burly men who quaffed their ale in clay goblets and gripped the daggers in their belts, or caressed the hilts of their swords so carelessly. These men cared nothing for the past and its mysteries. And the words of an ancient writer, which she had briefly skimmed in Obayana's house, came back to her: "Those who forget the past are doomed to repeat it."

Loud voices told her that the rest of the army had arrived, and before much longer, the captain of the garrison appeared before her, bowing earnestly, begging her leave to allow him to escort her to her place at the high table beside the King.

She felt as if a hundred eyes watched her process down the makeshift aisle, masculine eyes that looked at her as hungrily as they might a haunch of beef. A blush crept up her throat to burn her cheeks a warmer pink.

Abelard looked up as she approached. She saw Mondana, seated tactfully to his left, Obayana beside an empty chair on his right. Cormall was next to Obayana. He raised his cup in a salute when he saw her.

She managed a smile and moved behind the table to take her place. The food, great haunches of what looked like the giant oxen that roamed freely through the mountains, and platters of spring vegetables, as well as fresh bread and cheese, were carried out. The wine was poured, the ale was passed, and the feasting began in earnest.

She could not see Mondana's face, but she heard his low murmur in Abelard's ear. The King's face was carefully neutral, betraying nothing of his own thoughts, and Mondana's drone went on and on. Finally, Abelard turned away with a nod and smiled at her. He raised his goblet to her and looked past her to the M'Callaster, who sat gnawing a great hunk of meat. "So, Cormall."

"Lord King." Cormall did not pause in his eating. His eyes flicked up and met the King's in a glance full of meaning.

"Your journey through Ragonn—"

"Easy as a walk in the clover, Lord King. Ragonn's got other matters on his mind just now."

Abelard beckoned to the serving boy who stood behind the chair, back pressed to the wall by the tight quarters. "More wine, Cormall?"

"Ale for me, Lord King. It's the only thing takes the edge off the nip in the nights." He winked at Nydia and kept on eating.

"So an army might find Ragonn easy pickings, you'd say?"

"True."

Nydia glanced quickly from Cormall's grease-smeared face to Abelard's. In the russet light of the fire, his hair glowed gold, his rugged cheekbones highlighted, his skin flushed a healthy rose.

Obayana caught her eye and smiled. "The meat to your liking, lady?"

"Yes," she replied, startled. "Everything—everything is delicious."

"As it should be, missy," declared Cormall, pausing long enough to reach for another hunk of cheese. "That's one of Yudaw's finest herds you've got there." He winked at Obayana and resumed his steady consumption of food.

"According to our scouts," Abelard spoke slowly, and to no one in particular, "Mortmain and the main body of his forces are massed just south of Drango on the other side of the Wolvgreek Pass. Senifay has troops held in reserve a few days' march to the east, presumably to cut us off if we attempt to rejoin our regiments in Arkan. Yudaw's reserves are held just to the northwest, on the other side of the Rado River. W'homing apparently withdrew over the winter and has attacked Mondana from the south. However, both Norda Coda and Souda Coda have joined the Second Lord of Mondana against him." Abelard idly traced a knife dipped in gravy over the linen. "And Ragonn—"

"Ragonn sits at Owen's side and behaves as though he were the next heir." Niklas's voice was bitter with enmity for his ancient rival.

"Which well he might be, gentlemen." Cormall spat a bone onto the floor. "Mortmain's heiress is of an age to marry—oh, indeed, we hear more of you mainlanders than you may think—and Ragonn of the whole traitorous pack is unmarried."

"If Ragonn's lands were threatened—" began Obayana.

"He'd hightail it back to his holding." Niklas tossed his long white braid over his shoulder.

Abelard looked from man to man, his face blank. Mondana was already feeling the brunt of the campaign, Nydia knew. He had troops here, and because of W'homing's attack, troops engaged in the defense of his own holding. He could not carry another front.

Cormall wiped his cheek with the back of his hand and met Abelard's eyes with a knowing smile. She could not read all that passed between them, but Nydia understood that Cormall had known all along what Abelard wanted of him, and that Niklas must be brought to the same realization. He cleared his throat, scratched the side of his face, and ran his tongue over his teeth before he spoke. "Well," he said finally, "I could take these boys back and harry Ragonn. We'd be pleased to do a bit of raiding on his side of the water."

"As long as you stay on his side of the water," growled Mondana.

The M'Callaster raised his heavy head. "Niklas, I thought we were here for the same reason. Surely our first allegiance is to the King—"

"Without question," retorted Mondana. "But let your boys, as you call them, set one foot or hoof over my border—"

"Gentlemen." Abelard held up his hands. "If you would honor your pledge to me, I would hope you'd first honor a pledge to each other, as allies in this allegiance. Can't this be so?"

Mondana's glare slid from Cormall to the King. "You need have no fear of that from me, Lord King."

Cormall's brows were lowered. He reminded Nydia of a bull about to charge, and hoping to defuse the situation, she tapped Abelard's arm. "A song, Lord King," she suggested. "Perhaps the men might enjoy a song or two? Surely they are weary of thinking of nothing but war. Perhaps a song—"

"Yeah," cried Cormall, beating his fist on the wooden planks. "A song, missy, give us a song!"

The cry was taken up by the others and soon the whole place echoed with the sound.

Nydia knew she blushed, as once more she was the focus of everyone in that crowded room. Abelard grinned, cool and appraising, and nodded. The captain of the garrison, cheeks flushed with too much wine, and grease spots on the front of his uniform, thrust a small stringed instrument, something like a guitar but smaller, into her hands.

Tentatively, she ran her fingers over the strings, testing it, and was pleased with the gentle twang. She plucked a melody out experimentally and the men quieted expectantly. She looked up into their eager, laughing faces—flushed with wine and ale and food, and the knowledge of certain battle, if not on the morrow then sooner rather than later—and the song that came to her was ancient and sad, a song of a warrior race long forgotten.

Her foot tapped the time, and the little guitar thrummed beneath her fingers as she sang:

"I must away, love, I can no longer tarry,
This morning's tempest I have to cross,
I must be guided without a stumble
Into the arms I love the most."

The hall gradually quieted as her silvery voice reached out, full of longing and regret. Abelard leaned against the back of the chair, toying with his goblet. His face was unreadable in the flickering light of the torches. A little smile played across Obayana's face, and the M'Callaster stared with unabashed admiration.

Even Mondana listened, a look of bleak loss on his face. And Nydia wondered what these men thought of, alone in their thoughts.

The ancient melody pleased them. They understood intuitively the old songs with their simple rhythms, for their lives

were not so very different from those long ago days. With fists
and the flats of their palms, they beat out the time. Time's
wheel had come full circle, thought Nydia, as she looked up at
the low-peaked roof of the feasting hall.

She looked back at the crowd, at Abelard who leaned back
in his chair. The blood had clotted, the wound was nothing
more serious than a scrape. His eyes were intent on hers.

> *"And when the long night was passed and over,*
> *And when the small clouds began to grow,*
> *He took her hand, they kissed and parted,*
> *Then he saddled and mounted, and away did go."*

The notes died away. In the silence, not one man moved. As
though held by a spell, the crowd was rapt, faces usually hard
and resolute almost tender.

Then Abelard rose, and the spell was broken, and the looks
on most of the faces changed to envy as the King held out his
hand.

She put the little guitar down. Without a word, he led her
away.

Chapter Twenty-Three

J'ly, 48th Year in the Reign of the Ridenau Kings
(2716, Muten Old Calendar)

"H as the man the Old Magic?" Owen Mortmain demanded as soon as the servant had closed the door.

Phineas did not answer. Mortmain stared out the low window. The glass was rippled, not flat and smooth. The lands west of the Saraneva Mountains had suffered most in the terrible days of the Armageddon. Few buildings of more than two or three stories remained standing, and those that did had been seriously damaged. Mortmain's castle at Lost Vegas was one of the few which remained relatively intact.

Through the rippled glass, Phineas could see the wide green fields of the fertile Vada Valley. It was said that the grain of the Vada Valley could feed the whole of Meriga. Mortmain swore softly beneath his breath. "They outmaneuver us at every turn. If I position my troops to the west, they swing east. If we try to attack from the north, they surprise us, instead. How does he do this? Do your scouts have eyes in the backs of their heads? Ears like lycats?" He turned back to Phineas. "And all the time he heads west and south. I think he means to come to the very walls of this keep itself."

Phineas hid a smile, remembering what Mortmain had threatened to do once he stood before the walls of Ahga.

"We've looked for spies, informants—but nothing, no one. How can he know where we wait for him? How can he slip so easily and so smoothly through every trap, every net? If I didn't know better, Captain, I'd say you were getting information to him somehow."

"I know nothing of your plans."

"I know you don't. But do you know what Abelard does as he advances? He burns, destroys—the swath of destruction he has left in his wake is crippling my people."

Phineas cocked his head. "I'm sorry for your people's sake, Lord Senador. But you brought this on yourself. Surely you knew that Abelard would fall on you like a summer storm."

"Indeed." Mortmain stroked his chin and nodded. "A summer storm that falls only on certain places and at certain times."

Phineas spread his hands wide. "The intelligence network of the King is very capable."

"What network? There is no one within a hundred miles who would be loyal to the King, save perhaps your—" Mortmain looked past Phineas, and Phineas turned to see Mortmain's daughter standing in the doorway. "Yes, Melisande? What is it?"

"Forgive me, Father. I would not interrupt—"

"Come, child, what do you want?" answered Mortmain with a tired sigh.

"Perhaps it had better wait till you are finished with Phin—Captain Phineas."

Something in her voice made both men look up. "What's wrong?"

The girl's eyes flicked over at Phineas, then back at her father.

Mortmain waved his hand. "Say what you must, Melisande."

Melisande drew a deep breath. "Lewis is asking for an audience with you. Immediately."

"Why?" Mortmain's brow arched sharply over his left eye.

"A messenger just came from Ragonn—he's received a plea from his steward."

Mortmain's face was harder than stone. He glanced at Phineas as if he would say something, and then strode from the room, his boots making a loud click on the tiled floor.

Melisande was dressed in women's clothes today, Phineas

noticed, and her breasts rounded out the low bodice nicely. Her lips were tightly pressed together.

"Is anything wrong?"

She shot him a vicious look from under dark brows identical to her father's. "You know there is."

"Surely you realized there would be setbacks—that if your father wants to wear a crown, he has to do more than make one."

"I did not think the men who—" Suddenly her face crumpled, and she looked as though she would burst into tears.

Phineas made a move toward her, but she controlled herself with an effort and stalked past him with a loud swish of her skirts to stand in the very place her father had just left. "You did not think that Abelard Ridenau would command such loyalty from such far-flung supporters?"

"I thought the men who swore to support my father would stand by him, no matter what Abelard Ridenau did." She spoke over her shoulder and did not look at him.

Phineas forbore to share with her his observation that a man who could go back on one oath could as easily go back on another. Instead, despite his growing certainty that Mortmain's forces were doomed, he felt a deep sympathy for Melisande. She pressed her cheek against the glass. "I am sorry, lady."

At that she faced him, arms crossed over her breasts. "Are you? I find that hard to believe."

"Why?"

"I know you think my father and his supporters are traitors to your King. You think they'll only deserve whatever it is he does to them and their lands. It doesn't matter to you if crops are ruined, if the work of centuries—yes, centuries—is destroyed, if good and decent men who believe in something greater than themselves are killed, or worse. I don't know why my father lets you live." She turned her back on him again.

"Perhaps it's because he does believe in something greater than himself."

"What do you mean?" She sounded very weary.

"I—" Phineas hesitated, searching for the right words which

would neither compromise nor betray but yet would hold some comfort. "I do not agree with what your father has done, lady, and I do not agree with his methods. I don't trust the men who have sworn to support him, but your father never asked me for advice, and it is not mine to give. But I do believe, from what I have learned this past winter, that your father is very sincere, and that the things he seeks are not wrong, in and of themselves. These things he speaks of—ancient ways of governing, of justice, of establishing law for all men—I can not disagree with, not in theory."

"What then?" She turned back to him, and her face was achingly vulnerable. "If he is right in theory, why do you say he is wrong?"

"Wrong in method. It seems to me he attempts to raise ancient concepts long lost and impose them upon a new world that does not yet understand. It is as though he speaks another language."

"But you understand it."

"Not entirely, lady. Ideas have very little power in this world. Look at the Church."

"Religion means a great deal to the people."

"True. But if the Harleys raid or the Mutens threaten, it's not to the priests that the people turn. And as much as the Church says that they who live by the sword shall die by it, it is only by the sword that we maintain any kind of order."

"You know your scripture."

"My father was a stablehand in Ahga."

"And you reject everything he taught you?"

"No. But I have often thought that the scripture is outworn. If this is indeed a new world as the priests claim, perhaps we need a new creed as well."

"I don't think my father's wrong. I know what he wants is just and true and right." She lifted her chin and stared at him defiantly. "And I will never stop believing in what he says. Never."

She reminded him of an angry kitten.

"Don't you dare laugh at me."

"I'm not laughing at you. I smile because I've never met a woman like you."

"Oh?"

"I admire the strength of your conviction. I've never heard a woman speak of the things you do, or—"

"Fight like a boy?" A smile hovered at the corners of her mouth.

"Nor that, either."

"I admire you, as well, Phineas. You're honest and kind and thoughtful, and—" She broke off and faced the window again. "I often thought these last months—"

She spoke so quietly that he moved closer.

When he stood beside her, she continued, her eyes fastened on the horizon. "I have regretted we must be on opposite sides of this—" she searched for the word "—this dispute. I have often thought that if things were different, then—"

He held his breath, scarcely believing what he heard. "Yes?" he prompted gently.

"Things might be different between us," she finished in a rush.

He opened his mouth, uncertain what to say, but she hurried to the door. "You aren't like any other man I've ever met, and no matter how this ends, I wanted you to know that."

He stood by the window, staring after her, until the guards came.

Chapter Twenty-Four

Nydia slid off her horse by a brook which meandered through a little stand of trees marking the boundary of some unfortunate farmer's property. The water sluiced over and around the stones in the stream bed with a loud gurgle that still could not mute the screams and the cries of the battle which raged a few hundred yards away.

It was cool beneath the trees. She dipped a linen square into the clear water and pressed it to the back of her neck. Battle was the wrong word. It implied a clash between equal but opposing forces, and there was nothing equal about the conflict now occurring. A puff of wind blew smoke into her nostrils, and her eyes watered. Her horse neighed a warning, and Nydia tied the animal to a tree limb.

She tried not to think about the hungry gleam in Abelard's eyes as he'd led the charge on the little garrison, or the blood lust which burned on the faces of the soldiers as they rushed in his wake. A woman's scream, high and wailing, cut through the calm rush of the water, and Nydia bowed her head, shut her eyes, and tried not to remember that it was she who had guided Abelard's army into this pleasant valley.

More smoke, this time black and acrid, gusted through the wood, and she heard harsh, commanding voices. Abelard had been right that day in Ahga, when he had told her that horrible sights were more common in war than not. She shuddered at the rape of this temperate land, and tried to block the sights and sounds and smells of the last weeks from her mind.

Abelard moved across Yudaw and into Vada with grim and

deadly purpose, sparing nothing and no one, weaving in and out and between Mortmain's forces with the uncanny certainty provided by Nydia's foresight. Galvanized by victory after victory, the army of the King followed him with single-minded loyalty. And she was proud to ride by his side, most of the time, she thought, as she wiped her linen square across her face. Except when his lips curled back in something like a snarl, and he did not look quite human. Then there was a ruthless light in his eyes, and his face was unyielding, unrelenting, and the force of his will to succeed was like a tangible thing, even without the Magic. The thought that Abelard might ever possess the ability to use the Magic himself made her shudder again. If a man like Abelard ever learned to use it—perhaps it was better that the Magic was lost. She leaned against a tree.

"You grieve, lady?" The soft voice seeped through her concentration, and Nydia looked up into a pair of almond-shaped eyes that at once held pity and remorse and the promise of peace.

"How did you know I was here?" Nydia managed, although she knew the answer.

"Followed you. Felt the pain." The girl was young, no more than twelve.

"You shouldn't say such things, child. It's dangerous."

"To most I wouldn't. But you're like my father." It was a statement, not a question.

"Who is your father?"

"He's dead. Mother said the priests took him before I was born—they did not know I was conceived, or they would have taken my mother, too."

"You never knew him?"

"Only what my mother told me of him. But when I saw you, a little while ago, watching, I felt the pain your sight brings, and I followed. I'm sorry if I frightened you."

A long scream sliced through the quiet, and the girl's frame reverberated as though the sound were a sword stroke passing through her body.

"They don't know what they're doing out there—" Nydia

half rose to her feet, and would have put her arms around the girl, but she backed away, hands pressed to her ears.

"No, lady. They know what they do—oh, such pain—" Her face contorted.

"Child, sit—"

"I can't—ah—" Between clenched teeth, she said, "Do you know—is it better, ever? Is it always like this? Must I feel it all?"

Nydia tore her coif off her head and wrapped her hands in the cloth. Careful not to touch the girl's bare skin, she gently put one arm around the thin shoulders and led her to the water. She dabbed the linen square on the pale bloodless cheeks and forehead. "It gets better as you grow older, I think. Empathy is not my gift, as you guessed, but from what I was told, as you age, you will become better able to control it. But with something like that—" she jerked her head in the direction of the garrison "—I doubt that even the oldest empath would be able to block out all that pain."

The girl sank down and leaned against the thick trunk of a drooping willow. Her eyes were shut and she breathed deeply. "I should not have followed you."

"You couldn't help yourself, could you?"

The girl shook her head, eyes closed.

"It's like a magnet, isn't it?"

"A what?"

"A magnet—the pain. It pulls you, like a moth to the flame."

"Yes."

"Don't be afraid of it. If you surrender to it and give yourself to the pain, you will be stronger once past it, do you understand?"

"I—I think so. How do you know these things?"

"My family prepared me. Since the child of a prescient is always an empath, I suppose they thought I'd better know what to say when the time came."

The girl reached out with two fingers tentatively, and Nydia recoiled. "No, no, lady, let me touch you." The fingers were soft, gentle, the pads thick and smooth, not worn by life and living. Nydia shut her eyes as the two fingers brushed the side of her face hesitantly, as though seeking, finally settling just above her brow. "So pretty—but you've suffered for it, haven't you? It brings you no joy—and the love you have for the King? Yes, the King himself, brings you no joy either. Poor lady, so fair and so hurt."

Nydia shut her eyes, felt the burden lift, imperceptibly at first, and then, for the first time since her childhood, she felt all pain, all loneliness, all fear, lift like a fog at dawn. She sighed and opened her eyes. The girl was deathly pale; sweat beaded her upper lip and her forehead. With a cry, Nydia broke away from the gentle touch, and simultaneously, everything crashed back like a falling wave, and the girl jolted against the tree. "Stop." The girl looked at Nydia, not comprehending. "You have limits. You cannot take away my pain—you're too young."

There was agony in the girl's face as she raised her head to stare into Nydia's eyes. "As best you can, let no one know what you can do—do you understand?" Nydia said. "It may mean watching people that you love get hurt or die—but you must at least live long enough to bear a child. This ability must pass on, do you understand?"

The girl withdrew, and nodded quickly. "My mother says that someday—there will be a king—like me—that he will free us all—and heal the world of all its hurts. Lady, is this true?"

Nydia glanced over the girl's shoulder in the direction of the farmhouse, where the agonized screams had faded out of hearing. "I don't know. I have heard—others speak of such things, but empaths are always females. I never knew of a male empath, save one, and he is dead."

"Your son."

Nydia flinched at the uncanny perception. He had died long before he was of the age to manifest his power, and to experience something of what his ability could have been was doubly painful. "Yes," she admitted. "My son. He was the first in

I don't know how many ages. But—it doesn't matter. He would not have grown to be a king." She raised her head, hearing the shouts of Abelard's men. "Go. It may not be safe for you if the King's men find you."

"You fear the King."

"No, not really." She looked over her shoulder. She did not want to confront her deepest feelings any longer. "Child, please go."

Reluctantly, the girl rose to her feet and paused, looking down at Nydia, her hands clasped nervously together. "I shall not forget you, lady."

"Nor I, you." Tears rose in her eyes as the girl darted through the trees and disappeared into the woods on the other side of the brook. Overwhelmed by something she could not name, Nydia sank to the ground.

So there were others. The Mutens had not lied. And the tale they told—that was known by others, as well. She listened to the sounds of Abelard's men crashing through the trees, coming to find her, as though from a long way off. A male empath—born to be a king. Long awaited. She had born one son—was it possible she could bear another? A king to free all who had the ability—whether foresight or healing, or who carried it in their families? And heal all the world's hurts. That would have to be a mighty empath, indeed. She thought again of Abelard and the joy he seemed to have in killing, the look on his face while he watched men tortured to death, men who would rather die than swear allegiance to a foreign lord. Could such a man father such a son? What irony there would be in that. She grimaced. And the Bishop of Ahga was dead. If Agara could be sent away, somehow, perhaps Nydia could not be Abelard's Queen, but his consort.

She did not speak at all through the evening meal. She sat a little apart by the fire, not paying attention to Abelard and his men. She was startled when he stood before her, hand extended, and she realized that they were alone. The others had gone to their tents. "Come, my dear, let's to bed. We have many miles to cover tomorrow. I want to reach Lost Vegas as quickly as possible."

Nydia sighed as she got to her feet. In the firelight, he frowned down at her. "What's the matter?"

"Nothing."

He caught her by the shoulders and jerked her chin up to his. "Tell me. What is it?"

She kept her face low and did not meet his eyes.

"I told you, didn't I, before we ever left Ahga, there would be many unpleasant sights?"

"I expected that."

"Then what's wrong?" There was an edge of exasperation in his voice.

She threw her head back and stared up at him. "I didn't expect to see you enjoy it."

"Enjoy it," he echoed. The exasperation was replaced by bewilderment.

"You do enjoy it; I see it in your face. When the soldiers torch the fields and the houses, and leave the people to starve, I've seen you laugh. When they kill those poor men, who are only trying to protect their homes and their farms, you urge them to it. You allow them to rape the women. The only ones you spare are the children, and even those, you— Why do you do these things?"

"This is war, lady." There was a hard edge in his voice, although he spoke patiently as if to pacify a child.

"Yes," she agreed, "it's war. But does it need to be slaughter and ruin and rape?"

"Mortmain must be crippled. The people of Vada must learn the lesson—"

"But they aren't rebelling against you."

"Then they must bring pressure to bear against their lord."

At that she laughed. "What are you talking about? Could any of the people of Ahga make you do one thing you would not want to do? Could all the people of Ahga and Minnis, and all your holdings, matter one iota to you in any decision you would make?"

"If the people withheld their grain, I could not eat. If my soldiers refused to fight, I could not hold this nation. If the merchants refused to bring their goods into my cities I could not collect my taxes. Of course the people can influence me. Of course they can force me to do things I might not want to do."

"Do they know it?"

A shadow flickered across his face, and it might have been nothing more than the light of the fire. "Maybe it's something I don't always admit. But what has this to do with it? These men are not mine; they are the armies of Mondana and Koralado. They are entitled to carry off what they will—if this is the arrangement that Niklas and Obayana have with their men—"

She shook her head and broke away, moving out of the firelight to stare into the shadows beyond. The camp noises were all around them; she heard the whicker of the horses, the grunts and mutters of the men as they settled for the night. Beyond the circle of tents and fires, she saw the shadowy movements of the sentries, as they kept the watch.

"Perhaps you're right. Perhaps I just don't understand."

He laid a gentle hand on her shoulder and coaxed her around to face him. "I am sorry if what you have seen has caused you grief. Surely you know that I would not want anything to upset you, sadden you. You've been invaluable to me on this campaign. We could not have come so far, or done so well without you—"

"Stop." She turned away and tears pricked her eyes.

"What is it?" His voice was soft and wooing, infinitely patient and kind.

"When you say that—how much I've helped—you remind me that I have a part in these people's suffering. That I'm to blame, as much as if I'd raised the sword or lit the torch myself—"

"Hush, now," He drew her into his arms and pressed her head against his chest. "Hush now. We won't think of these things tonight. For just a little we'll forget." He pulled the coif off her hair, which tumbled free down her shoulders in lustrous living waves. He stroked her hair, twined his fingers in it, and buried his face in its depths.

"Besides," he crooned as he parted her hair to touch the soft white skin below her ear, "there'll be no more of what happened today, unless we're forced to it."

She pulled back, disbelieving. "Why not?"

"From here should be a straight line, more or less, to Lost Vegas. Owen's troops are cut off, now that we control the road, and Rissona's men have attacked from their rear. I intend to lay siege to Owen's castle. And I'll need the provisions of the countryside. Who knows how long we'll be here?"

"Oh." She surrendered to the seduction of his kiss with a little sigh. He bent her back, and her hair fell almost to the ground. He tugged at the laces of her bodice, untied them with one hand.

"However," he murmured, against her throat, as the lacings loosened, "there is a way to make the siege much shorter. So we can get this over with and all go home."

"How?" She tried to straighten, but his arms were strong. As he swept her off her feet, her breasts spilled out of the bodice. He started toward the tent.

Halfway there, he bent his head and took one nipple in his teeth. She gasped so loudly she was certain the men nearest could hear, and twined her fingers in his hair. His tongue lashed the hard brown-pink tip, and his mouth opened, greedily, to encompass as much of the heavy rounded flesh as he could. She moaned, and he laughed low in his throat. "Does that please you, my dear?"

"Don't stop," she gasped, when he would have raised his head and continued on his way.

He rolled her nipple delicately between his thumb and forefinger and little arcs of delight raced through her like shooting stars. "But if I don't stop, I'll take you here, in full view of the army, my dear, and surely that wouldn't please you?"

She quieted instantly, nestled her head against his chest, and he chuckled.

Once in the tent, though, he laid her on the low frame which served them as a bed. She lay, watching as he drew the tent flaps closed and returned. He threw his shirt off and sat beside her, unlaced his boots and kicked them aside. She sat up and wrapped her arms around his naked torso, savoring the strength in the thickly muscled chest, and combed her fingers in the mat of golden hair.

She found his nipples and rolled them between her fingers as he had done to her. She half knelt behind him and teased his earlobe with her tongue. With a smile and a groan of pleasure, he turned in her embrace and lifted her so that she was cradled against his chest. "What witchcraft do you weave, my dear? You are the only woman I think about—the only woman who haunts my dreams. What spell have you cast that no woman exists for me, but you?"

His breath was hot on her ear, and she moaned again, turned her face so that his mouth covered hers. She wanted nothing more than to lie naked in his embrace, nothing in the world but this man filling her, easing the empty craving in her womb, an ache that no one had ever satisfied but Abelard.

She tugged at her clothes frantically, pulled the chemise off her shoulders, shrugged off her dress, kicked off her shoes and stockings.

"Easy, my dear, easy," he breathed, and she gave a little sigh of protest as he pulled away and stood beside the bed to undo his trousers. The hard length of his erection sprang free, and she arched a little as he quickly peeled the tight fabric off his hips. He was on her so fast she did not quite see him move.

"Please," she whimpered just before he plunged into her. And then nothing mattered, nothing existed, only the exquisite sensations of their flesh as they cleaved together, arms and legs and tongues entwined, long, slow strokes teasing her, luring her, bringing her into ecstasy.

Afterward, she drowsed in his arms, her head pillowed on his chest. She listened to the slow, rhythmic beat of his heart, the gentle rise and fall of his breathing. He caressed her cheek absently. "Nydia," he whispered. There was an urgency in his voice that made her look up. "Do you want to go home?"

She shrugged, pushed the heavy fall of her hair off her face. "I have no home."

He gripped her shoulders, brought her face close to his. "Your home is with me. What other home do you require?"

She smiled then, and traced the lines of his muscles beneath his skin with one careful finger. "No other, I suppose."

"What I meant was, do you want this war to be over?"

"Of course I do. You know I do."

"Then, would you—"

She pulled away, sat back. "Would I what?"

"Use the Magic. Level the walls of Owen's fortress—surely that would not be so difficult? Not much more difficult than the bridge? If we could get into Owen's keep—"

She was shaking her head in disbelief, her legs drawn up, her arms wrapped around her knees. "Didn't you realize that night how dangerous it is? It was the Magic—the consequences of the Magic—which raised that cyclone. We could have been killed if it had come in the other direction or headed at us—"

"But it didn't." He rose up on one elbow.

"It didn't, but I don't know why. The Magic isn't some secret weapon to be used at your whim. I used it that night because we were trapped and there seemed to be no other way out of the situation. Believe me, if it had not seemed so hopeless, I would never have suggested it, never even thought of it. And even so, it only bought us a little time."

"If you level the walls, you'll do more than buy us time. You'll help me end this—once and for all."

"Abelard, I can't believe you ask this of me. I can't believe you would even think of it."

"It may take weeks or even months to tunnel beneath the walls and bring them down. Mortmain's keep is well constructed—we may even have to starve them out. Meanwhile, the rest of the country—have you forgotten Garrick, and Ithan and Missiluse? The Harleys have raided Ahga. Do you forget?"

She stared at him, dismay plain on her face. "Abelard," she whispered, "don't ask this of me."

He did not answer, but his eyes bored through hers, and she felt more naked and vulnerable than she ever had, as though she were some object without life or will or desires of her own. For a long moment they stared at each other. "Very well, lady," he said at last. "I won't."

She held out her hand, a helpless gesture of contrition. "Abelard, you said I'd helped you—led you here—that without my foresight you would never have come so far so quickly or eluded Mortmain's army at every turn. Surely I have upheld my pledge?"

His eyes softened, and he grasped the tips of her fingers. "Yes," he said, as though he would rather not admit it. "Yes, you have. Come here, let's sleep. We have a long way to go tomorrow."

With a long sigh, she stretched out next to him. But she lay sleeplessly long into the night, wondering it if were only a matter of time before he asked her to use the Magic again. And the next time he asked her, would it be a request or a command?

Chapter Twenty-Five

❦

$\mathcal{F}$rom the windows of his prison, Phineas watched the construction of the siege engines. It was only a matter of time before the outer walls were breached, before Mortmain was forced to admit defeat. Rumor ran rampant through the halls of Mortmain's fortress, gnawing more steadily than rats through corncribs at the hearts of Mortmain's men.

Roderic's movements had been severely curtailed in the weeks since Abelard's appearance outside the walls, and now a grim-faced sergeant brought their meals at regular intervals. It had been ten days since Phineas had been permitted to exercise outdoors, but the sounds from the courtyard below still reached him. Nor was he permitted to see any of his fellow prisoners, who he no longer even glimpsed from his windows. From scraps of overheard conversations, Phineas gleaned the information that Ragonn was irrevocably lost, his forces crushed in a vise of the M'Callaster's devising. The forests of Yudaw were in flames. Thousands upon thousands of acres of woodland burned, the result of Abelard's last act as he entered Vada.

Curiously, the farms of Vada had been spared for the most part. Phineas heard the grooms and stablehands discussing the progress of the campaign as they exercised Mortmain's horses in the narrow wards beneath his windows. So complete was their demoralization that it appeared they believed resistance was futile.

Phineas heard, too, the tales of Abelard's march into Vada, and although he dismissed some as servants' tales, most he be-

ieved. The talk was of the King's uncanny knowledge of his
nemy's movements, the accuracy of his battleplans. He knew
hat Abelard had no need of spies while Nydia rode at his side.

Sometimes he saw Mortmain directing the defenses, though
n the last days his attention had been caught by the banners
nfurled on the other side of the walls. He recognized the
reen and silver of the Lords of Mondana, the gray and purple
f Kora-lado and, floating lazily overall, the blue-bordered
tandard of the King, the eagle's talons outstretched as though
t reached for Mortmain's walls.

A commotion in the outer chamber made him leave the win-
low. He heard Roderic's young voice raised in protest and a
nuffled curse. He whipped open the door. Guards crowded the
oom. One had Roderic by the collar. He shoved the boy
cross the room as soon as he saw Phineas. "Let's go."

"No, Captain!" Roderic cried. He launched across the room
nd fell bodily against the soldier, who shook him off as
hough he were a puppy.

"Be still, Roderic." Phineas looked at the guard. "Let's go
vhere?"

The boy looked up, tears streaking down his cheeks. "But,
Captain—"

"You'll find out."

Phineas said nothing as the guards dragged him away. They
ushed and shoved him up a winding set of steps until at last
hey emerged into the bright sunshine. A soft wind ruffled his
air, and he blinked in the glare of the strong noon light.

He heard quick, light running footsteps, and Mortmain
poke from behind him. "Over there. Hang him over the
vall—let him dangle. Make sure he's well-displayed—I want
Abelard Ridenau to know we've got this one."

Before Phineas could react, they hoisted him off his feet and
orced him over the side of the eastern gate, with ropes wound
round his chest, under his arms and at his wrists. His shoul-
lers ached with the strain, but the ropes held him firmly
gainst the crenellated stone of the battlements. Fifty feet

below or more, the ground lay hard and rocky. Abelard's camp was spread out below.

Mortmain moved to the edge of the wall. He cupped his hand around his mouth and called for the King's attention.

In the camp, Nydia heard the hoarse cry, heard the shouts go up in answer. She ran through the camp, following the men, as they crowded near the walls of Mortmain's keep.

She stared in dismay. Phineas dangled over the edge of the wall from ropes which looked too flimsy to hold the weight of a man. A small, dark man leaned over the battlements beside him and bellowed for Abelard. She looked back for the King. He was shouldering through the crowd, followed closely by Niklas Vantigorn and Obayana.

Abelard broke through the press of the men and walked almost to the walls of Mortmain's keep, well within arrow range. Nydia sucked in her breath, and her eyes darted to the walls where she knew an archer might be waiting for just such an opportunity.

From the top of the gate, Mortmain leaned over and addressed the King. "Abelard Ridenau!"

"I have come, traitor." Abelard stood with his legs planted firmly on the ground, hands on his hips, one hand gripping the hilt of his dagger.

"Do you recognize your Captain?"

"I do." Abelard's voice echoed off the walls.

"If you leave my lands within the next twenty-four hours, I shall send him, as well as all the other prisoners, back to you. Will you agree to leave my lands?"

"Whose lands?"

"Mine."

"These lands are part of Meriga, and while I have breath in my body, I will not allow one yard to be stripped away. I will not leave until you have renounced your claim as King and sworn your pledge of allegiance to me again."

"I have over thirty of your men, Abelard Ridenau. If you are not gone from these walls within twenty-four hours, I shall drop them, one by one, off this gate—one for every hour that you linger. And this man will be the first."

Abelard gave a snort of derision. "Then you've got a corpse dangling there, Mortmain. You'll not dictate terms to me." He turned on his heel and strode back to the crowd of soldiers.

Nydia turned in disbelief to Obayana who stood beside her. "How can he—" She could not believe what she had just heard. Abelard's words seemed immeasurably cruel. No matter what she thought of Phineas, he was the Captain of the King's Guard; he had never been anything but loyal to Abelard. How could Abelard so readily abandon him?

"The King has no choice, lady," murmured Obayana. "What could he say otherwise without appearing weak?"

"But there's only twenty-four hours, then, until Mortmain—"

"Captain Phineas understands that. Understood it when he took his oath. If it is required that he die in the service of his King, I am quite sure Phineas, of all people, is ready."

Nydia could only stare. Abelard pushed his way through the crowd and beckoned to Obayana and Niklas. Reflexively, Nydia started after the men. Once inside Abelard's command tent, she took a seat in the corner as she was often wont to do—the men had become accustomed to her presence and thought nothing of it any longer. But her own assessment of the situation was confirmed by the first words spoken by the King himself as he faced his councillors.

"We have twenty-four hours, gentlemen."

Niklas Vantigorn shook his head and rubbed his fist over the hilt of his short sword. "Our assault on the walls, Abelard, while it has proven to be of some success—we will never break through the walls in time."

"There must be another way in," said Obayana. He walked to the tent flap and stood half in, half out, staring at the long low structure of Owen's keep behind massive walls.

"We can starve them out eventually," said Mondana.

"But not soon enough to save Phineas." Abelard stared down at the hide map stretched across his makeshift desk. "If

we can't think of another way in, we'll have to watch him
die."

Nydia stared at Abelard. He looked up at her pointedly, and
she knew what he wanted of her.

Obayana shifted in the door, as though watching something.
"Abelard," was all he said in a low voice.

Instantly the King was by his side, peering over his shoulder
into the maze of tents and men and supplies of the camp.
"What is it?"

"Over there—do you see—" Obayana broke off in mid-
sentence and dashed away from the tent, short sword drawn.
From beneath a wagon piled high with supplies he dragged a
ragged boy of perhaps thirteen. The boy immediately saluted
and put up his hands. "My name is Roderic. I was the King's
standard-bearer. Please, sir, take me to the King."

Obayana stared at the boy in amazement. "Where did you
come from?"

"From there." The boy pointed to Owen's castle. "I was captured with Captain Phineas last year, and I've been his waiting
boy. They'll kill him—please, I've got to see the King."

"The King's right here, Roderic," interrupted Abelard, striding forward. "So you survived the battle."

The boy straightened and saluted. "Lord King. Accept me
into your service once more, sir." He would have gone down
on one knee if Abelard had not stopped him.

"Enough, boy. How did you get out? Did they let you out?"

The boy grinned. "No, sir. I have a way of getting in and
out, and I thought you ought to know about it—given the difficult position Captain Phineas is in." He gestured back toward
the walls where Phineas had disappeared.

"Can you show us how to get in?"

"Yes, Lord King. I know a way."

Abelard put his arm around the boy and urged him to keep
talking as they walked toward the tent.

The whispers rose in a ragged chorus as the guards half-
dragged, half-shoved Phineas down the narrow corridor of the

dungeon. He grimaced in sudden pain as a heavy elbow thudded between his shoulder blades and he was thrust forward into a dim, subterranean room.

Apparently, with Abelard nipping hard at Mortmain's heels, all show of courtesy was lost. Or maybe, thought Phineas, as he staggered to his feet and tugged his tunic into place, it was because Mortmain did not quite like the idea of killing him.

"It's the Captain."

"Captain Phineas!"

"Are you all right, Captain?"

From the shadows, dark shapes coalesced into the forms of men. Phineas recognized the faces of the other prisoners. He rubbed his wrists where the ropes had left raw red burns and nodded his greeting.

"What news, Captain?"

"Is it true the King has come?"

Phineas drew a deep breath as his eyes adjusted to the lack of light. The men who crowded around him looked healthy enough, though he soon learned they had been in the cell for more than two weeks. "Gentlemen," he began. Instantly they quieted, and he was gratified to see them come to attention.

Tersely, he told them all he knew, that the King had indeed come to Lost Vegas, that Mondana and Kora-lado and Rissona as well as the M'Callaster had risen against the alliance, and finally, he told them about Mortmain's ultimatum.

"So we're to die, Captain?" The first man to speak was probably the oldest—Phineas recognized him as a veteran of many campaigns. He had been an old soldier when Phineas was young.

"Unless the King can find a way in, or force Mortmain's hand in some way . . ."

"Well, I'm ready," grunted the speaker. He turned away, leaving the rest to crowd closer, voices raised in speculation.

"Gentlemen," Phineas raised his voice and the babble ceased. Before he could continue, however, the heavy steel door swung open, and a slim shape was tossed into the room. It landed with a heavy thud on the floor.

"Roderic!" Phineas hurried over to the still form. He cradled the boy's head, squinting in the shadows. Black blood flowed over his face from a wide wound in his forehead, and white bone gleamed dully in the dim light. "By the One, who did this?"

The boy was unconscious. Someone tapped his arm and handed him a grimy piece of damp linen. Gently, Phineas dabbed at the blood, pressed the edges of the wound together. Roderic's face was puffy and bruised and his arm hung at a crooked angle. "Who did this?" he repeated more to himself than to the onlookers.

"Is it the young standard-bearer, Captain?"

"Yes." He handed back the blood-soaked rag. "Is there a place I can lay him in some comfort?"

"Over here, sir."

The men withdrew to a respectful distance as Phineas carried the boy's inert form over to a pile of ragged blankets beside a wall.

"Things have changed," muttered one of the men.

"Yes." Phineas felt for the boy's pulse. It was weak and fluttered under his hand. "I should have expected this."

The steel door creaked suddenly on rusted hinges, and Phineas half-rose to his feet, expecting some other blow. He gasped to see a slight form peer into the room, a torch held high, a basket over one arm. "Phineas!" It was a whisper, high and stealthy. "Phineas, are you here?"

He was beside her before the others could react. "Melisande! What are you doing here?"

The torch made her large eyes luminous. "I saw what happened to Roderic. I knew they'd brought you here and I hoped he'd be here, too."

"He's here." Phineas gestured to the makeshift bed. "What did you see?"

"That gang of scullions—they jumped him. He didn't even know what hit him, I think. I tried to stop it, but they were too many. And by the time the guards came, well, there wasn't much I could do." She glanced over to the wall. "I—I brought some water, and bandages. I—I don't know what to say."

"It's not your fault." He spoke for her ears alone and they both knew he did not refer to Roderic's beating.

"I've tried to speak with my father, but he won't listen."

"I don't expect he will." He guided her over to the door. "You'd better go. How did you get past the guard?"

"There isn't—" she began, and stopped. She looked up at Phineas, pleading.

"Go." He took her basket, listening as the heavy door clanged shut behind her, heard her soft footfalls fade in the corridor. No guard. Just a locked door. A locked steel door. One narrow window, set so high up in the cement wall escape by that route was unthinkable. But no guard. Mortmain's men were stretched thin, then. If only there was a way to get to Abelard. . . .

He went to Roderic's side, dropped on one knee and opened the basket. He uncorked the flask of clean water and moistened a white linen bandage. He touched it to the boy's lips.

"Captain." It was less than a sigh.

"I'm here, boy, lie still."

"The King."

"I know, the King's very close." Fleetingly, he wondered if the boy was hallucinating.

"Is it dark?"

"Yes, yes, boy, it's dark. We're in a basement, a cellar, somewhere beneath the keep—"

"King—after dark—be ready." Roderic groped for Phineas's hand. "Told him—"

"Lie still, boy, rest."

"Listen!" The whisper was harsh with urgency. "Went to King. After dark—expect—rescue—be ready."

"What's he saying, Captain?"

"Did he say he went to the King?"

"He's dreaming, right?"

Hope made the voices breathy with agitation. The men moved restlessly behind Phineas's shoulder like leaves blown by a breeze. Phineas sank back on his heels, scarcely daring to believe what the boy said. "Roderic."

The boy's lids fluttered, tried to open, and were still.

"Squeeze my hand, if you understand me." At the answering pressure, Phineas continued: "Good. Once for yes, twice for no, understand?" Again the firm pressure, once, then twice, then once more. "Good. Now, are you trying to tell me you went to the King?"

The fingers tightened, then relaxed.

"You found a way out of here?"

Again a squeeze around his hand.

"You made it to the King?"

Yes was the answer.

"And he'll be here sometime after dark?"

Yes.

Phineas smoothed the boy's rough hair back from his forehead. That was how the kitchen toughs got to him, he thought. Roderic had not been in the kitchen yard for weeks—they must have come upon him as he was sneaking back in. And why had he come back? So Mortmain would not be alerted, of course. He sat crosslegged on the floor next to the boy and listened to his labored breathing. The evening wore on as he kept the vigil.

Gradually the darkness thickened around him, so that he could no longer distinguish the forms of the men from the blackness of the room. Noises seeemed preternaturally loud: the grunts and snores as men slept against each other, coughs, throat clearing, a few muttered conversations. He might have drowsed, but suddenly he was wide awake, alerted by loud crashing outside. The men straggled to their feet as the ceiling above their heads shuddered under the force of some massive blow. In the corridor on the other side of the steel door, there was the sound of running footsteps, and faintly, Phineas heard a horn cry an alarm.

He's come! he thought, and he looked down at Roderic. The boy was still. His flesh was cold, and Phineas fumbled for a pulse. There was none. He let out a deep breath, and his shoulders sagged.

"Captain." In the dark, one of the soldiers groped for his shoulder.

Phineas stood up. "I'm here."

"Is it—Captain, do you think—"

"Yes. I think the King has come."

The men let out a ringing cheer, but Phineas was silent. He stood by the body of the dead boy. Even when the door slammed open and light flooded the dungeon, he turned reluctantly, squinting as he did. The men crowded out the door, greeting their rescuers with loud cries.

"You—over there!"

Phineas did not at first realize that the soldier was speaking to him. He turned, pulling his shoulders straight as he did so.

"You—what's your name? Your rank?"

"My name is Phineas. I am the Captain of the King's Guard."

"Sir!" The soldier snapped to attention and saluted. "Engus Greentree, Lieutenant of the First Company of Mondana, sir." He came a little closer, pushed past the last of the prisoners, who were rushing out to grab swords and staves and anything else to use in the battle. "Is that a prisoner, sir?"

"Roderic, the King's standard-bearer. He served me this winter."

"Is he injured, sir?"

"He's dead."

"Oh. I'm sorry, sir." He gestured over his shoulder. "The King's in the main hall, I believe, sir. Would you care to join him?"

Phineas nodded.

Engus drew his short sword from his scabbard. "Will you have my sword, sir?"

Phineas took the proffered weapon, savoring the feel of the hilt as it slid into his hand. It had been nearly a year since he'd last held a weapon.

"I'll send someone for the body, shall I, sir?"

"Yes. Thank you, Lieutenant."

"Do you know the way, sir?"

"I believe so." He did not wait for the lieutenant's salute. He followed the long corridor, up narrow stairs, and down another narrow corridor until the passageway widened. He heard the familiar sounds of the end of a battle—mostly the moans of the wounded, the shouted commands of the victors, the sounds of women weeping. At the entrance of the hall, he stopped.

On the dais, Abelard stood before Mortmain, who was held by three guards. Phineas recognized Mondana and Obayana, as well as a few of the other soldiers who stood guard over Mortmain's defeated men.

"Swear!" Abelard pressed the tip of his broadsword into Mortmain's throat.

Mortmain shook his head.

"Then die, traitor." Abelard drew his hand back to strike the deathblow. From across the room, Melisande flew at him, dagger raised.

Phineas saw with sinking heart she was dressed like a boy. "No!" he cried, as loudly as he could, but his voice was lost beneath her scream.

Abelard dropped the broadsword and wrestled the dagger from her grasp as easily as if it were a kitchen knife. He grabbed her by the waist, then stared as he realized she was a woman. "What have we here?" He grinned at Mortmain as he forced Melisande's chin up. "Who are you, sweetheart?"

Mortmain struggled against the grip of his guards and Abelard slowly nodded. "The daughter. Mortmain's heiress. Well." He pinioned her with one arm around her body.

Melisande writhed, but her struggles were futile against Abelard's strength.

"I'll make terms, Mortmain." Abelard's mouth curved in a wicked grin. "Give me your daughter as my Queen, and pledge allegiance, and I'll let you live."

"Not while I breathe." Mortmain spat.

"She's a beauty, your daughter." Abelard's eyes narrowed

and Phineas took a step forward. He gasped as Abelard grasped Melisande's shirt at the collar and ripped it open to the waist. Her thin chemise was all that covered her breasts.

"Swear, Mortmain, or I'll have her now—here—and you'll watch."

Mortmain's face went red and he heaved against his guards.

"No, Father," Melisande cried. "Please, no, it doesn't matter—"

"No?" Abelard's voice chilled Phineas. Before he could take another step, her white chemise hung in shreds, and Abelard pulled her arms behind her back, thrusting her naked white breasts into full view. He turned her around to face the hall. "What do you say, men. Shall we all enjoy Mortmain's heiress?"

The men cheered, and Phineas stumbled forward, hardly believing what he saw.

Abelard forced her back to face her father, rolling one pink nipple between his fingers. "Well, Mortmain? Or shall I have the guards put her on the table?"

"Father—" Melisande's cry was anguished.

"Abelard!" cried Phineas.

But the King's attention was riveted on his enemy, who sank to his knees between his guards, and in a voice choked with tears, recited the words of the Pledge of Allegiance.

Chapter Twenty-Six

~~~

The candles were low when Abelard came to her, his shirt half-unlaced, his trousers carelessly tucked into his boots. His hair was tousled, and his beard was rough on his chin. Nydia eyed him coolly, and when he would have taken her in his arms, withdrew across the room.

"What's wrong?" He sounded genuinely puzzled, though his eyes were hooded and wary.

When she finally spoke, her voice was cold, although emotion simmered through her words like the summer heat. "You come to me, fresh from your bridal bed, and expect me to welcome you? Is your cock dry yet?"

He flinched. He spread his hands helplessly. "Nydia, surely you understand that that was only done to solidify the Union—"

"The Union?" She spat the word back at him with venom. "This morning, I watched you take another woman for your wife—made her your Queen in full view of both armies—and swear fidelity until your heir is either born or named. Have you named an heir in the last three hours? Or did I miss something?"

He looked uncomfortable. "No, no, I've named no heir. But certainly you must understand she means nothing to me. I married her only because—"

"Because she is heiress to an Estate larger than any other except your own. Because by marrying her, you control more land than any other man in Meriga. Because now there is no one strong enough to dispute your right to rule."

Abelard flushed, and his brows knit together. "If you had done as I asked over a month ago, none of this would have happened."

"Me? What have I got to do with it?"

"If you'd used your Magic and leveled these walls, the siege would never have lasted as long as it did, and we'd both be safe in Ahga right now."

She shook her head in disbelief. "Go ahead and blame me! This has nothing to do with me. You married that girl for your own ends—you forced her father to capitulate by the cruelest means—how can you say this is my fault? I heard what happened last night. You stripped her practically naked and threatened to rape her in front of her father. The battle was won, Mortmain was beaten. It wasn't necessary to use her that way—"

Abelard's shoulders went rigid. "I told you, lady, that there are no rules in war—that men do what they must."

"And I suppose it was absolutely necessary to marry her—absolutely necessary to swear fidelity—"

"It means nothing."

"It means everything!" she cried. "You gave your word—your pledge. What more is there? And now, you stand here and offer to break your word with me—fine for you, perhaps, but what about me? You're the King—they'll say I seduced you—I enchanted you—you don't care a fig about me. All you think about is your own pleasure—at your own whim."

He lowered his head and glared at her. "Very well, lady. If that's your mood, I see I'll seek my pleasures elsewhere."

He spun on his heel, but her next words stopped him. "Wait, Lord King," she called a little hysterically, sounding a little drunken. "Don't you want to know what you've sown this day—the harvest you'll reap of this day's work?"

He turned back to her, his face all rigid lines. "Well, witch?"

She smiled, a harsh triumphant smile, and threw her head back. "It's seldom I see so far, Lord King, for seldom does one action have such far-reaching consequences. But this day's

shadow lies long over the years. Your little Queen is barren—
you'll get no son off her, nor daughter. There will be no legiti-
mate heir of Meriga to follow in your footsteps—and your
other sons will tear this country apart after your death like
jackals over carrion. Hear me, Lord King, and remember well.
No son of yours shall reign in Ahga. The line of the Ridenau
Kings ends with you—and the Union you've so desperately
fought to save, will go down into anarchy."

An act of will greater than she had known she had kept her
smiling in the face of his wrath. He opened his mouth, hesitated, then stalked silently away.

Later, when she had finished weeping, she made her way to
the top of the highest tower. A full moon rode low in the sky,
and pale clouds scudded across its face in gray streaks. Only a
few fires flickered in the dark night, and the land lay quiet, an
air of exhaustion hanging over all.

She leaned against a battlement and sighed, her breath a soft
quiver. Her head ached and her eyes were heavy, yet sleep
eluded her. She stared across the land, the soft rolling hills
stretching west to the sea, some hundred miles distant, the fertile fields still heavy with crops. The scrape of leather against
concrete made her jump.

"Forgive me, lady."

She gasped as she recognized the voice, and a tall shape coalesced out of the gloom, a gray ghost against the dark tower.
"Captain Phineas!"

"Lady Nydia."

There was a heavy note of grief in his voice that seemed to
match her own, and curious, she stepped forward, squinting up
at him in the shadows. "How is it with you, Captain? It's been
a long time."

"I am well enough; Mortmain was a gentle jailer."

"So I understand." She gazed up at him in the dark, his profile spare and clean, the lines of his face deeply etched. His
body was thinner than Abelard's; his shoulders lacked the

breadth of the King's, yet he carried himself with the control of a man of great strength.

There was a short silence, and then he said, as if forcing himself to speak: "And you, lady? How is it with you?"

She bent her head while tears welled in her eyes and her throat thickened. She shook her head, unable to speak. A sob escaped, and he said, "I see."

He gave a long sigh and moved to stand a little distance away. He leaned on the battlement beside her. "I saw by your face today how it was with you and Abelard."

"What do you mean?" Her voice was hoarse.

"I knew when I saw you, lady, the first day in that forsaken little village that he would—that you would—" He shrugged. "I tried to warn you."

"You weren't surprised? Today, when he married Melisande?"

In the gloom, she thought he flinched at the mention of the girl's name.

For a moment he was silent, as if considering. "No," he said at last. "I guess I wasn't."

"He doesn't even know her, Captain. She means nothing to him—how could he—"

He looked at her with pity etched on his grim mouth. "I told you a long time ago, that whatever more he might be to you, he was the King—first, and always."

"Yes," she answered bitterly. "I see that now. He came to me—now, just a little while ago. He must have come from her bed—and he expected me to—" She broke off at the savage look on Phineas's face. His hands were clenched in fists and he struck the stone wall, heedless of the pain.

He cursed beneath his breath and turned away. With a few quick strides, he was across the top of the tower, and he kicked at the wall of the battlement with another oath.

"Phineas!" she called, surprised.

He did not respond, but leaned against the wall, every muscle tensed and rigid.

Understanding dawned, and timidly she approached. "Phineas," she said softly. "You love her, don't you?"

He shot one anguished look at her and turned away. She put her hand on his, and he did not shake it off.

"You love her—and you saw what he did to her in the hall last night?"

He nodded. "I wanted to kill him," he whispered. "I wanted to kill my King." He smiled, a thin, brittle smile full of pain, as though his face might break. "He came to you tonight?"

She nodded, unwilling to pour salt on his anguish.

"He'll never love her. He'll only use her to get an heir—"

"No," whispered Nydia. "She's barren—there'll be no heir. Ever."

Phineas sagged against the battlement. "Oh, by the One." His voice broke. With a long shudder, he drew himself upright, his spine rigid as an untempered blade. "And the kingdom?"

"Will disintegrate. Eventually."

He said nothing more. In the east, the sky was touched with the first rays of the rising sun. They stood side by side, not touching, until the light was strong enough to blind them.

Chapter Twenty-Seven

❧

N ydia stared straight ahead, unseeing. The horse's hooves beat a steady, numbing rhythm across the wide surface of the highway. Behind them rose the Saraneva Mountains, darkly silhouetted against the cloudless sky. The noon sun was warm across her shoulders. Liss and the rest had discarded their cloaks, but Nydia did not care.

A curious numbness had settled on her as the little party made its way out of Vada into the foothills of the Saranevas. The land lay ravaged under the late summer sun. Everywhere, people working in the fields and the villages paused in their rebuilding to stare in sullen silence as their horses cantered past. Nydia avoided looking at them, feeling their resentment in the fallow fields, the burned ruins of the farmsteads and the granaries. Fire still smoldered in Yudaw, said the sergeant of the guard, and people everywhere were faced with famine.

They were well-provisioned; Obayana had given orders that they were to be provided with every comfort for the journey back. And so, here they were, six weeks from the Kora-lado Pass, heading east toward Ahga and Abelard's lands.

Not to Ahga though, thought Nydia. Never to Ahga. Not so long as Agara held sway there, even if the Bishop were dead. It was Liss who'd suggested, shortly after her arrival at Obayana's keep, that Nydia might want to accompany her back to her parents' homestead somewhere in Linoys. Liss didn't want to return to Ahga, either.

The thought of Linoys, of Tedmund's holding, of Tedmund himself, seemed comforting. It was far enough that Nydia would be outside the reach of Agara's grasp, yet close enough that somehow she might contrive to get a message to Vere and so retrieve her precious books. And after that? The future was nothing but a heavy emptiness that seemed to grow with every passing mile.

The days following the King's marriage had passed in a blur of pitying looks from the women and sidelong glances from the men, who watched the sway of her hips as she walked and muttered remarks in breathy whispers calculated for her to hear. She no longer felt safe among the soldiers of Abelard's train and knew that Mortmain's men might believe the King's cast-off companion an easy mark. Obayana had offered to arrange her departure, but the thought of leaving Vada without seeing Abelard at least once was more than she could bear. Beneath her anger was bitter pain, and the knowledge that he could never belong to her, nor she to him, was like the twist of a knife in her gut.

Her interview with Abelard had been brief as well as public. There was something humbling about the way he made her state her request to leave without looking at her as he listened. His eyes were fastened on a parchment scroll and his hand moved hastily across its surface. Even when she was finished speaking, he did not look at her.

He rolled the parchment up and placed it inside a wooden message tube. He reached across the desk, poured a little sealing wax on the ends, and fixed his signet ring to seal it. He handed it to the messenger who waited in the background. "To my son, Brand, as quickly as possible. You may need to travel at night, for this must reach Brand—" he looked up at Nydia for the first time since she had come in the room "—within the next two weeks."

"As you say, Lord King." The messenger bent his knee and was gone.

"Lord King—" began Nydia, feeling as though she ought to repeat her entire request "—if you would be so kind—"

He ran his eyes up and down her body, and she swallowed. She felt her cheeks flame as his eyes lingered on her bosom, and she saw all the other men gathered near him rake her with the same violating glance. "You may leave me, my dear, but not because I'm kind."

She made a sound, a little involuntary protest, but he waved his hand as though he would shoo her away like a fly. "Go," he snarled, and she was glad to see the emotion beneath the carelessness he feigned so well.

She had curtsied slowly. When she looked up, he had turned away and was slowly tearing open another message. Phineas nodded, whether in greeting or dismissal, she could not say, but she saw the dark shadows beneath his eyes, the lines etched around his mouth as though carved out of granite. She gave him a brief bow and turned away.

As Nydia reached the door, the King's laugh rang out, echoed in the vaulted ceiling, and she flinched. The guard swung it open for her with a leer. She picked up her skirts and ran.

On the road, Nydia watched Liss with the child. Reginald had grown into a plump sandy-haired baby with fat thighs and chubby arms. He brought everything he could get his hands on to his mouth and seemed to spend most of the time he wasn't asleep greedily attached to his mother's breast. He attempted to nurse from every woman who held him—a phenomenon which was a great source of jokes for everyone in the train. But Nydia could not shake the feeling of detachment, the dull sense that nothing mattered, nothing was quite real. Her life was a series of minutes lived from one to the next, like disjointed beads on a string.

By the middle of Tember they were once more close to Abelard's lands—lands every bit as war-ravaged as those Abelard had left in his wake. "Harleyriders," said the captain of the guard, pointing with a grim face at the ruined farms, the fresh burial mounds which rose like sores from the plundered, uncultivated fields.

Nydia shuddered and turned away. She had seen enough war. The damaged houses and barns, blackened stones, and charred wooden beams lying haphazardly like discarded blocks, reminded her of her father's holding. She kept her head down, her eyes steadfastly on the road.

Finally, near the first of Tober, Liss touched her arm hesitantly. "Lady?" Liss was shy of her, as though she lacked the words to reach Nydia's grief. "Do you see? The shadow on the horizon? That's Ahga, lady. We're nearly home."

Home. The word lingered like a bad taste. She looked up, following Liss's finger to the dark smudge on the eastern sky. Home. Ahga. She had thought she would return on Abelard's arm. She never hoped to be his Queen, but his consort—protected, loved, cherished in the strong circle of his arms. The King's consort—she had imagined it on the long trek through Yudaw and Vada, had dreamt of it in the long nights in Koralado. The people would line the streets, as they had on the day the King had ridden away, and throw flowers, offer wine and toast their conquering King. No woman would have dared throw herself across his saddle, for she would have been there, by his side, basking in the reflected glow of his glory.

Not now. Not ever. Her shoulders sagged as reality pressed her down. She would not enter on the King's arm—rather she came at his sufferance: a beggar, a refugee, like all the rest who had fled in terror at the Harleyrider's advances. She avoided Liss's glances of concern.

At the gates of the toll plaza on the border of Abelard's domain, they were forced to halt. The gates were locked and barred. Nydia sat in her saddle for quite a while, before she roused herself sufficiently to understand that there was some sort of problem. She slid unaided to the ground and walked to the captain of the guard, who stood conferring in low tones with the sergeant at the gates.

"Is there a problem, here, Captain?" Her clear voice brought the conversation to an abrupt end. The man's face was guarded. He did not meet her eyes, as he replied: "There's some question about your return, lady."

"She's coming home with me," interrupted Liss.

"Yes, lady. It seems there's someone who wants to speak with you."

"With me?" She let the hood fall back from her face and raised her face to the captain. "I don't understand—"

"If you'll forgive me, lady," interrupted the sergeant of the city guards, "we were given orders to detain you, if you arrived."

She turned her gaze on the sergeant. He was perhaps of an age with the King and susceptible to her beauty. She tilted her face up to his, lowered her long lashes over her pale cheeks. She heard his quick breath, saw the drop of his eyelids as he ran his eyes as if by reflex over her body.

"I am a member of the household of the King. Who would have me detained?"

The men did not look up. The sergeant scuffed a toe in the dirt, looking like a little boy caught in some quarrel he did not understand.

"Answer me!" she demanded as the silence lengthened.

"Lady Agara Ridenau, the King's mother." The sergeant's voice was hoarse, as though he spoke the name unwillingly. "And the Bishop of Ahga."

"The Bishop of Ahga? We heard last winter she died in the raids."

"Not the old one. The new one—she just arrived, not even a month ago. Her name's Doriunn—she's from somewhere near Ithan, in Tennessy Fall."

Nydia sat at the foot of the bed, her hands clenched in her lap, her feet squarely on the floor of white pine planks laid with painstaking precision. The bed was so narrow it was impossible to lie on it without gripping the sides lest an ill-calculated turn tumble her to the floor. The mattress was hard and thin, little more than a layer of quilted linen upon the crosswork of rope. The sheets were coarse and unbleached.

The walls of her narrow cell were whitewashed, the one window set high in the eastern wall of the Bishop's Palace.

The late summer rain splashed with dull monotony down the rippled glass.

Two weeks had passed since that day outside the gates, although the memory of Agara's thin face flushed in triumph and the cruel smile on the new Bishop's coarse face were painfully, perfectly clear.

She had admitted nothing, of course, though it seemed that she was to be accused of nothing. It was a foregone conclusion she was a witch. She gathered that she was held responsible for the war, and for all the misfortunes which had befallen the city and the people; and she knew with a sinking certainty that both Agara and the Bishop intended to pacify the Deity with a speedy and public execution.

Her feet were cold in the rope sandals they had given her to wear, and the one coarse garment of rough linen, the same material as the sheets, scratched her skin everywhere it touched. The sergeant of the guard seemed content to take his orders directly from Agara, though whether from fear of her displeasure or a genuine respect, Nydia was uncertain. In the King's absence, there was no one in all of Ahga to countermand the lady's orders.

At the thought of the King, she glanced up at the window. The weight of her grief had settled in the pit of her belly like a lump of lead, a constant ballast which exhausted her by its mere existence. At night, her dreams betrayed her, for it seemed that no sooner had she laid her weary head on the hard pillow than he was there—his arms around her, his eyes so vivid and so blue, his body pressed against hers, and all her anger and her hurt, if she remembered it at all, was an inconsequential puzzle without reason. She would wake from those dreams with her heart temporarily lightened, until reality crashed upon her like a relentless ball and chain.

But now, the thought of Abelard made her tremble, for it seemed that he alone could save her from what daily seemed to be certain death.

The heavy wooden door opened silently, and a guard peered

mpassively into the room. He withdrew his head and gestured
o someone unseen. "Five minutes." Then he stepped aside.

Nydia sagged with relief to see Tavia. The girl ran to her.
"Oh, lady, I came as quickly as I could."

"I'm so glad to see you, Tavia—"

The first friendly face in so many days brought tears to Nydia's eyes, and when Tavia saw the tears, she wrapped her
arms around Nydia and hugged her close.

"There, there, don't cry. We'll think of something, it can't
be as bad as it seems—"

The stock phrases of comfort died on her lips as Nydia pulled
back to look into the girl's face. "But it is as bad as it seems."

Tavia's eyes shifted to the floor, though she patted Nydia's
shoulder comfortingly. "There must be something—"

Nydia shook her head and pulled the girl to sit beside her on
the narrow bed. There was no other place to sit except the
floor. "Tell me what's happened in the city. How is Agara able
to do this?"

"My grandmother's let out the rumor that the King is dying.
Some say it was Mortmain who forced Abelard to marry his
daughter so he'd be King when Abelard was dead—"

"But that's lies! How could anyone believe such nonsense?
That's ridiculous—"

"The fighting's been so bad hereabouts hardly any of the
messengers got through. And of those that did—well, Agara's
only let out the information she wants people to have. Surely
you believe that?"

"Go on."

"They're saying you're a witch. That you've brought the
wrath of the One and the Three down upon the city and the
King. The Harleys got all the way into the city. The fighting
was terrible, a lot of people died, a lot of the farms were destroyed—"

"And I'm to blame."

"According to the Bishop."

"How did that happen?"

"When the old one was killed, they called a Convening, I

guess they call it, of all the priests and all the bishops, and every one of them that could get here did. And so they held an election, and Doriunn won by divine decree, they say."

"What about the Congress? Are any of the Senadors here?"

"No. There wasn't a Convening last year—things were too unsettled." Tavia bit her lip. "There's talk of a public trial, lady."

"When?"

"Soon. As soon as they know whether or not you're with child. That's what they're waiting for."

Nydia pressed her fingers to her temples. Her head swam with speculation. "What about Vere?"

"He's disappeared. No one knows where he went."

"Is there any talk of evidence against me of any kind? Testimony? Books—"

"Yes, there's talk of testimony. Some Mayher from some town in Tennessy's been summoned by the Bishop—"

The door opened and the same guard stuck his head into the room. "Time's up."

"Tavia—" Nydia put her hand on the girl's arm as she got reluctantly to her feet, "if you could, try to find out what might have happened to my books."

"Books? You had books?"

"Yes. I left them with Vere—I need to know what happened to them. But you mustn't let on, you know, to anyone who might condemn me. You know what I mean?"

"Let's go." The guard stepped into the room and grasped Tavia by the elbow.

She shook him off with an imperious shrug and a chilling glance. "I'll do what I can. There's my brother, Brand—"

Nydia nodded and shut her eyes so she did not have to see the door shut behind her friend.

The days melted into each other, a blur of gray skies and white walls, tasteless food brought on rough trays, served on hard trenchers of stale bread. Even the water had an acrid sting to it.

Tavia came no more, though on the evening of the twentieth day of her captivity, the guard brought her a note. It was written in a large childish hand, the letters carefully drawn as though the writer was neither skilled at the act of writing nor graced with the gift of written expression.

She unfolded the parchment carefully, noting that the seal had been broken, not once, but enough times to crumble the wax, leaving mostly a smear of color across the back of the note.

The message was brief. "No sign."

She crumpled the parchment into a ball. At least Tavia had understood that if, by some chance, Vere had been able to take the books into hiding with him, neither Agara nor the Bishop must be alerted to their importance. Of course, Doriunn would remember they existed, that Abelard had allowed her to take them when they had ridden from that forlorn little place so long ago. It had begun to seem like a lifetime ago, she thought wistfully, when she had lain safe in the circle of Abelard's arms, secure in the knowledge that none dared threaten her so long as he stood by her side.

But this time, she stood alone.

Chapter Twenty-Eight

How pleads the prisoner?" Rever'd Lady Doriunn, Bishop of Ahga, robed in heavy scarlet silk, peered down from her episcopal seat on the dais of the hall. Clustered around her were priests, all wearing black gowns. Those on the right wore the white, green, and blue surplices that designated the priests of the Three, while those on the left wore the purple surplice of the One.

Agara was seated to the left in a chair only slightly less grand than the Bishop's. Her ladies stood around her, dressed in subdued grays and browns, hair covered with snowy coifs, not a bosom or a bare arm in sight. On the other side of the hall, merchants' wives ranged in strict rank from highest to least. Above, on the balconies, a mostly female audience from the outlying districts pushed eagerly to secure a place close to the railing.

The only men present were the King's Guard, three of whom were grouped around Nydia. A half dozen more were posted at the three entrances.

Nydia's heart thundered in her chest, and sweat stung her armpits. She had not been given water to bathe with in over three weeks, and her long hair hung lank around her face. Her linen robe, the same one she'd been wearing since she had been brought to the Bishop's Palace, was rumpled and stained.

Doriunn's broad face was flushed. Her little eyes gleamed with a hungry light, like a pig scenting slop, thought Nydia. The Bishop's scarlet robes were stained in places, as well, and her large hands clutched at the carved arms of her chair like vises.

"Well?" Doriunn leaned forward. "How pleads the prisoner?"

"I am not guilty," cried Nydia as firmly as her voice allowed.

The Bishop leaned back in her chair. "This is not a court of law. This is a court of the Righteous, who have inherited the earth."

"World without end, amen," intoned the priests to the Bishop's right.

Doriunn ignored the soft chorus and looked at Nydia with something like pity. "Guilt or innocence has no meaning here—for we are all guilty. Do you plead penitent, or not penitent?"

Nydia threw back her head and the guards on either side tightened their grip. "Not in the least," she spat at the Bishop.

A murmur spread throughout the hall, from the priests around the dais through Agara's ladies. It swelled as it reached the ranks of the public gathered on the upper levels.

"Not penitent!" the cry echoed through the room.

Nydia pulled herself as straight and tall as she could. This low-born priest might order her burned, order her tortured, all in the name of a god or gods she doubted cared or existed, but she was a member of the landed nobility and she would not let them, any of them, forget.

Her proud gaze swept over the room. "I have a right to know of what I stand accused, Lady Bishop." She emphasized the title ever so slightly. "I have a right to know who my accuser is and what evidence they have to bring before me. And you may not execute me, or harm one hair on my head, without the permission of the lord of this Estate—who is the King of Meri—"

"Who may be dead or dying even as we speak," interrupted Agara.

"Abelard Ridenau was in no danger of dying when I left him a month ago. You lie, lady—"

"Silence!" thundered the Bishop. "This court answers to no man, nor law of any man, is that clear? As for who accuses you, I accuse you, as if that matters, the mother of the King of Meriga accuses you, the priests of Ahga Castle accuse you— shall I go on?"

Nydia bit her lip. So this was not to be a trial in any sense of the word. She had already been judged guilty—this was simply an exercise to further demoralize her. She glanced up at the guards on either side of her. They stared rigidly straight ahead. There would be no succor from them.

"So." The Bishop settled back in the high wooden chair. "Bring the prisoner forward." There was a new ring of authority in her voice which Nydia did not remember from the village. There, she had cringed just a little when Nydia had fixed her with the cold stare of the nobility, but here in this palace, she did not blink.

It was the authority of the mob, Nydia realized, the weight of all these faces pressing down upon her. The hall was hot and airless and she stared up, feeling as though she were held at the bottom of a great sea, seeing hatred and fear and hunger for her death plain on every face.

The guards jerked her forward, and she stumbled, her foot caught in the hem of the robe. A sudden wave of nausea overwhelmed her. She had had only water to drink that morning and a small heel of a loaf of bread. Bile rose and flooded her mouth and she grimaced, hanging her head, fighting against the swirling dizziness which suddenly engulfed her. She raised her head, gulping for air. Her eyes fell on the crowd, and she blinked at the kaleidoscopic tangle of present and futures overlapping on the faces before her.

The dizziness increased, her head swam, and she sagged against the guards. As though from far away, she heard the Bishop begin an angry tirade, and then all was blessedly black.

When she opened her eyes, Agara was holding up a book. Nydia's heart sank. So Agara had her books. Vere had failed to protect them.

The Bishop seized the book with greedy fingers and held it up for all to see. There were gasps of horror, murmurs of shock as she slowly turned with it held high in both hands.

Nydia looked up at it, suddenly puzzled. The book which the Bishop held was not her book. It was one of the King's, one of the ones kept in the room he used for a private study which adjoined the audience room near his bedchamber. And what was even more curious, it did not pertain to Magic. It was an old collection of children's stories, "Fairy Tales," as they were called in Old Meriga. There was not a numeric symbol in any of the text—except a few page numbers at the bottoms of crumbling pages, and even those had mostly crumbled into dust long ago. Anyone—especially the Bishop and the priests who could read enough to distinguish letters from numbers—could tell that this book, at least, had nothing to do with Magic. So why this one? Why not one of the science or mathematics texts that contained the forbidden equations?

As Nydia tried to make sense of it, Agara's ladies rose, and one by one, brought other books wrapped in white linen—to protect them from contamination, Nydia supposed—before the Bishop. Nydia watched in astonishment. With great ceremony, the Bishop systematically began to tear the pages out of each binding. She cast them into a small brazier set on the floor. Nydia gave a little cry at the senseless destruction. There was no harm in any of Abelard's books—they were simple tales told to children across the ages. Surely the Bishop could see that? Why destroy them forever?

She raised a tear-streaked face to the Bishop, mouth open in a soundless cry of pain. The Bishop smiled down at her. "See, my people? See how the witch laments the destruction of her Magic? See how the flames cleanse and purify the world. See the smoke as it rises—black and foul—as the One and the Three allow the fire to destroy the black filth of man-made power. Hear me, my people! We have been cleansed! We have been purified! We are the meek who inherit this brave new world—and we shall not suffer the witch to live! We are the

Saved! We are the Chosen People—a holy nation, a royal priesthood—and we shall not suffer a witch to live!"

Sweat trickled down her face, and her face was flushed an ugly red, a painful contrast to the scarlet silk. "Lady Agara!" she cried without taking her eyes off Nydia. "Are there more? Is that all of the filth?"

"Yes." Agara's reply was a long hiss.

Nydia turned shocked eyes on the King's mother. Why did she lie?

Agara met Nydia's gaze with a look of triumph. Something cold went through Nydia. It was as though Agara dared her to speak, dared her to ask what had happened to the rest, and by so doing incriminate herself still further. Nydia dropped her eyes. She would not give Agara the satisfaction of seeing her in defeat. As best she could, she straightened her shoulders and lifted her head, although she kept her eyes low. The books burned with a dusty smell of old paper, the hard binding with the acrid odor of ancient glue.

If Agara had her way, she would end on a similar pyre. She closed her eyes and murmured a silent plea that Abelard get home as quickly as he could.

"See, oh, people," intoned the Bishop. The whole company rose to its feet and began to pray. Nydia was forced to her knees.

Nydia listened to the chanted chorus. Didn't they ever think about the words, she wondered. Had no one ever thought that the words were nonsense and meant nothing? She kept her face down, her eyes fixed on the floor.

The long shadows fell across the hall, and the last rays of the dying sun slanted across the faces of the women in the eastern tiers. The "trial" was done. The Bishop pronounced her sentence with a satisfied smirk. Tomorrow at noon, Nydia was to be taken to the central market of the city and there burned—

The Bishop broke off in annoyance as the Captain of the city garrison stepped in front of the dais. "Why do you interrupt this sacred business, Captain?" It was a sneer.

"Sacred business or not, lady, I don't put anyone to death without the proper writ. And you haven't got one, and won't until the King returns to Ahga."

The Bishop rose ponderously to her feet and stood at the edge of the dais. She towered over the Captain, and he stepped back, in the face of her wrath. "I need no writ. The witch slipped away once, Captain, when she should have burned. You will not throw up that same technicality of law. The One and the Three will have their due. They shall not be denied. Fool! Would you have worse fall upon this city? Were the Harleys not enough? Perhaps were the water to rise, or a great wind sweep over the houses and carry away your children, perhaps then you'd believe me when I tell you this woman must be put to death?"

The Captain licked his lips. "I know my orders, lady—"

"Whose orders? Who has the authority to flout the One and the Three? There is no higher court in all the realm—the witch is not only guilty but unrepentant. Who knows what revenge she'll wreak upon us all?"

"Then I can't take responsibility."

"Very well, Captain." Agara rose to her feet and came swiftly to stand beside the soldier. "I take the authority. I will answer to my son when he returns—if he returns. Are you satisfied?"

The man did not answer. He gave both the Bishop and Agara a nervous look and glanced apologetically over his shoulder beyond Nydia.

"People of Ahga," cried the Bishop "whose wrath will you risk—the King's or the One's?"

"The King's!" the crowd roared back, and here and there Nydia heard the high-pitched voices of the women call: "Burn the witch! Save our children! Burn her! Now!"

The Bishop looked around, a satisfied smile on her face. "Tomorrow. At noon. The witch will burn."

Chapter Twenty-Nine

❧

$\mathcal{N}$ ydia shivered. Either the way back to her cell had suddenly doubled in length, or she was being taken to a different prison. The guards on either side gripped her elbows tightly and followed the two black-garbed priests down the winding corridors. She blinked as torchlight guttered and flared in a sudden wind. A door squealed on its hinges.

"This way," muttered one of the priests.

Silently, the guards led her down, down a steep, square staircase that reminded her of the stairs in the high towers of Ahga Castle. At the bottom of the steps, another door swung open.

A man beckoned. "Quickly."

The priests threw the robes back from their faces.

"Liss! Tavia!" Nydia nearly fainted with relief.

"Not now, lady." The man's voice was harsh and not completely unfamiliar. There was something piercingly familiar about the set of the broad shoulders beneath the dark cloak, and her heart leapt. A flickering shaft of light fell across his face, and Nydia recognized Tavia's brother, Brand. "Get back to your post," he said to the guards. "Say nothing. When the guards come to relieve you, complain loudly about their being late. You'll all answer to me if anything goes wrong here— and I promise the doom I'll give you is a lot more certain than the Bishop's. Understood?"

"Sir." The guards saluted smartly and slipped away up the steps.

"Here." Liss was pulling off the soiled robe. "Ugh. You smell like a sewer."

"I feel like a sewer." Nydia shivered.

Brand averted his gaze, but not before he had run his eyes down her body. She felt herself blushing in the dark. Together, Tavia and Liss got clothes on her: boy's clothes. They bundled her heavy hair into a tight coil, whispering as they worked.

"Come on, come on," muttered Brand.

At last they slung a cloak over her shoulders and hustled out the door. Four horses stood saddled and waiting. "Now," said Brand. "Can you ride, lady?"

She was faint and hungry, but the thought of freedom sent adrenaline rushing through her system. She nodded and gripped the reins eagerly and, unencumbered by skirts for the first time in her life, swung herself up into the saddle.

"Let's go." Brand helped Tavia and Liss onto their horses, then mounted his own and pulled at the reins. "Say nothing, none of you. If anyone asks, Tavia, you're my wife; Nydia, you're my son, and Liss—"

"I'm your sister," she said sweetly.

"Fine." With a brief gesture, he indicated which way they should ride. The streets were crowded with people around the Bishop's Palace, milling men and women excitedly discussing the day's events. They passed workmen bringing in loads of wood and faggots tied with cord. As they neared the walls of the city, the crowd began to thin, and the horses moved forward steadily down the darkened streets.

Finally Brand held up his hand. "Here's where we'll see if that fool boy got through."

They touched heels to their horses' sides and slowly walked forward. About twenty feet from the northern gate, the sentry cried, "Halt."

Brand reined in immediately.

The sentry walked up to the four. "State your names and your business."

Nydia glanced up and over the sentry's shoulder, frowning in the meager light. There was doubt and confusion; she saw clearly that the man's superior would be summoned. Suddenly she knew that Brand's messenger had not arrived.

She leaned over and tapped Brand on the arm. "I think there's been a delay with your message."

"What?" He turned to her, startled. "How do you—"

"Leave it to me," said Tavia, who pushed her horse through the rest to the fore. "Now see here." Her voice so accurately blended the aggrieved tone of an overworked farm wife with the rigorous authority of a princess of the blood that all eyes turned to her instinctively.

"See here. My husband and I was summoned to bring our boy home from his 'prenticeship. He's worked half to death, can't you see, and who's to keep the farm if anything happens to him, I'd like to know? So when we got the letter, I says to my man, I said, we'd better ride in and see for ourselves, you know hard work's one thing but they're not to be killing the boy, don't you know? And so, I said to my man, I says—"

"Hold, missis, hold." The sentry peered up at them uncertainly. "This your boy?" He narrowed his eyes at Nydia.

She slumped in the saddle and hoped she looked worked half to death.

"Yes, sir, indeed he is, sir, and a likelier boy there never was, don't you know until that harsh master got his hands on him. Don't I rue the day we ever thought to send him into this den of thieves, it was my man's idea, don't you know, and I says to my man, I said—"

"Yes, yes, missis, I can see that." He frowned at Liss. "Who are you?"

"I'm her man's sister," she replied with the same sweet tone.

He hesitated just a minute longer. "All right," he said, "you can go."

Nydia kicked her heels into the animal's flanks and the horse leaped forward. Tavia and Liss followed. They galloped down the road, and Nydia half-expected to hear the hooves of a company of soldiers sent after them. It seemed to her that they had barely gotten away from the outskirts of Ahga when Brand gave the order to rest.

"Here?" She looked around a little wildly. "Are you sure? So soon?"

He looked at her curiously. "Lady, we've come twenty leagues or more—the night is half gone, and the moon about to set."

She stared up at the sky. The moon was indeed low in the sky, and suddenly she was aware that the horse's sides heaved with effort, and that they all looked very weary.

Tiredly, she slid off the horse and allowed Brand to tether them to a stand of trees. Tavia and Liss led her into a little clearing, where a brook splashed noisily in the starlight. From a pack, Liss produced soap and towels. "Come."

Together, they managed to bathe her. She was tired, her head heavy, her eyes so heavy she could barely keep them open.

They dressed her and wrapped her hair in a towel to dry, then led her to the fire Brand had built. She was so tired, she fell asleep immediately.

Toward dawn, she woke and sat up. Brand was sitting by the fire, feeding it a log every now and then. He smiled a little when he saw her eyes open. She sat up slowly and stretched her hands toward the light.

Liss and Tavia slept side by side on the other side of the fire.

"How do you feel?"

She started. "Free." She watched a faint blush creep up his throat. He was still very young, she thought, surely not much more than twenty, yet he had engineered her escape and brought them this far without mishap. "You haven't slept." It was a statement, not a question.

He shrugged. "It's not the first time, lady. In the field the nights are often long, or nonexistent."

She remembered the long night's retreat across the bridge in Senifay. His gaze was fastened on her face. "Thank you."

He dropped his eyes. "I did what was required of me, lady."

"Required?"

"Are you not pledge bound to my father?"

She looked up, startled. "How—"

"Nearly a month ago, I received a message from him. It was the first I'd had in over a year, and I thought it very curious that my father should have accepted the pledge of a woman. I never really saw you before, lady. When you came to Ahga, I had just been promoted. But now, seeing you, I understand."

"Do you?" She could not keep the lilt of amusement from her voice. "What do you understand?"

"You're the fairest woman I've ever seen, lady, and I doubt I'm the first to say so. My father wouldn't rest until you were his; I imagine you know that, too."

"What did the King's message say?"

"He told me that I was to keep a careful watch on the situation in Ahga, that you were on your way back, and that he was bound by a pledge of allegiance to protect you. And he handed the charge over to me, since as a member of the King's Guard I could not refuse it, and as his eldest son he has trusted me implicitly since the day I put on this uniform."

She sat back, shaking her hair from the towel. It was still damp and she spread its lengths across her shoulders. "So Tavia—"

"To tell you the truth, it would have been weeks before I would have thought to inquire for you. I was not idle in Arkan, you see, the Harleys have completely overrun Missiluse and the Mutens—" He spread his hands and dropped them in a careless gesture. "But that's why I acted as quickly as I did— why I knew I had to prolong your life—at least until he could return."

"He thought of me?" She twisted a damp curl thoughtfully around her finger.

"Why should he not? You are pledge bound?"

She nodded.

"And you have honored your pledge to him?"

She shrugged.

"He is bound by his own word to protect you. Why would he not?"

She stared into the flames. "We quarreled."

"The pledge bond is above quarrels, surely you know that. There is nothing he would not do in its name—"

She looked away.

"Do you doubt that? Then you do not know my father."

The image she'd had of Abelard Ridenau on his wedding night jarred with the image his son so clearly cherished. Had she been saved in the name of honor, or because he wanted something more from her? She looked into the dark eyes of his eldest son and saw there quiet conviction.

She lay down again on her blanket, the damp towel as her pillow, and thought of Abelard. They called her a witch. What magic did the King weave that he inspired such dauntless faith and loyalty in the men who served him? With the firelight flickering across her face, she drowsed.

They arrived at Minnis in the middle of the afternoon, weary, saddlesore, and hungry. The man and woman who hurried from the low building to greet them turned out to be Liss's parents—sent on ahead by Brand to augment the skeleton staff.

The lodge of Minnis Saul in the Great North Woods was a low building, set far back from the road on a slight rise above a long lake. The late summer nights were chilly in the shade of the ancient trees, the shadows deep beneath leaves already turning brilliant shades of orange, red, and yellow. Liss's parents fussed over all four of them, treating Brand and Tavia with special deference and Nydia like a stray lamb.

She woke from a long sleep on the morning after their arrival to find that Brand had already left. Tavia intended to stay until the King returned. "Of course," explained Liss when she brought Nydia's breakfast, "Prince Brand mustn't be missed. But as for Tavia, heaven only knows the outcry which must have been raised when it was discovered you were missing. It would not have been safe for her to return to Ahga, at least not until the King returns. Would you care to face Agara's wrath?"

"Surely they'll suspect that Tavia helped me to escape?"

"Surely they will. Eat."

"But will they not look here?" Nydia struggled to sit up while Liss tucked a large linen square beneath her chin as though she were a baby.

"Who will come? Prince Brand had ordered the Captain of the city guard not to leave the city undefended under any circumstances. The outlaws are certain to attempt the last raids of the year, now that the harvest is almost due in, and they are stretched thinly enough. Do you think any of the soldiers are likely to leave the defense of their homes and their families to go rushing after some hapless woman, even if Agara orders them? And besides, their orders from the King are to protect the King's family, and those take precedence."

Nydia stared at Liss. She dipped her spoon slowly into the thick pudding of oats. Steam circled lazily, and a golden dollop of butter melted in little rivulets, mixed with honey. Her mouth watered. "So what now?"

"We wait here."

"Defenseless?"

"There's nothing to fear, lady. The gamekeeper and his son are handy enough with bow and spear—you'll see." Liss folded her arms firmly across her bosom and stared pointedly at the bowl of steaming porridge. "Eat. Or must I feed you as well?"

With a thin smile, Nydia slowly dipped her spoon into the mixture.

As Liss promised, the days blended into a pleasant blur so different from the nightmare of her captivity they seemed like a waking dream. The gamekeeper and his son were not the only men on the place—the stables housed the King's most prized horses, and the grooms who lived there in attendance amounted to a small garrison. The mornings were misty, the nights were cool enough to warrant a fire, and the afternoons

were spent in simple homely tasks like churning butter, spinning yarn, or sewing. Reginald, Liss's son, was growing fat,
and although Nydia thought him an unattractive baby, Liss
loved him and doted on his every whim.

In the long afternoons, the women sat before the fire as the
days shortened, spinning, while Nydia stitched away at the
endless pile of mending. It seemed like a small enough task to
repay the men who guarded her.

On a warm day in early Tober, a long shadow fell across her
lap. Thinking it was Liss's father come in from the pastures,
she looked up, but her smile of welcome and ready greeting
died in her throat as she met the steady blue gaze of Abelard
Ridenau.

Tavia gasped and ran to him. "Dad!" Her sewing tumbled
unheeded to the floor.

The King acknowledged his daughter with a nod and a
smile, although his eyes did not leave Nydia's face. He patted
Tavia's cheek. "Leave us, child."

"Dad, you're back—"

"Later, child."

His tone brooked no disobedience, and with a faint look of
disappointment, Tavia left the hall.

Nydia rose on unsteady feet and sank into a low curtsey,
while her heart pounded in her chest. Her throat felt thick.
"Lord King," was all she could manage.

"Look at me."

She raised her eyes to his. There was no anger in the deep
blue gaze, only a faint reproach. Her pulse slowed to a steady
throb, as her senses responded to his nearness.

"You need not kneel to me." His voice was soft.

She wet her lips and thought that she might not be able to
stand.

He caught her under one elbow and pulled her gently but
firmly to her feet. He stepped closer and she trembled. Now
that he was here, she was forgetting everything—forgetting all
that she had heard of that terrible day, forgetting everything in
the blur of memories of those strong arms around her, her

head pillowed on his broad chest, his scent, sharp and masculine, the sleek hardness of his body, the texture of his skin and
the thick golden hair which covered his chest and legs— She
swallowed hard and stared fixedly at the flames.

"Nydia." His voice was a caress. "I married Melisande because I believed that I must. I told you long ago, it seems, that
I was no callow lovelorn boy. I hold all Meriga in my hands,
and I will not let one pebble slide away while I am King. I am
sorry if my actions hurt you. I did not act as your lover, that is
true. I acted as the King of Meriga, for that is what I am. But I
swore to you once, and I will swear again, if it will bring the
joy back to your eyes and you back to my arms, that by the
throne of my father, I will love you until I die. And that will
never change—though I marry a hundred women and swear fidelity to every one." His voice was pure, naked need.

"Brand said you sent him a message—"

"That message went out before you even left Vada. I knew
what my mother was likely to do."

"Have you spoken to her?"

"I've banished her."

"Where's she gone?"

"To the darkest pit of the lowest hell, for all I care. I've had
enough of her meddling. She'll not trouble you again."

"What about the Bishop?"

"That's not a problem quite so easily solved, my dear." He
smiled at her sadly. "She cannot execute you without my permission—which I, of course, will not give. But you cannot return to Ahga."

"No." She twisted her fingers in the fabric of her gown and
stared at the floor.

"Do you like it here?"

"Here? At Minnis? It is a pleasant enough place."

"Though somewhat isolated?"

"I have never much cared for a lot of company."

"I have been thinking," he said slowly as he hooked his
thumbs in his sword belt and slowly surveyed the room, "of
making Minnis more than a lodge."

"Oh?"

He crossed the space between them and stood so close the tips of her breasts brushed his chest. "In the next few weeks, before the snows fall, I shall begin construction of a castle. It shall be defensible, and as impregnable as I and my masons and my engineers can make it. It occurred to me over the winter that there should be some nearby place to send my household if Ahga is threatened again."

"Where?"

"Foolish child," he chided. He raised her chin with the tip of one finger. "Where else? And I will garrison Minnis as well as Ahga. No one shall ever do you harm again."

She shut her eyes against sudden tears. Suddenly all she wanted was to lay her head on his massive chest. In the circle of his arms, she would be safe. "Abelard—"

"What is it?"

"My books—my Magic books—I don't know what happened to them. The Bishop burnt yours, and Vere's disappeared, and without my books, I can't possibly do as you asked." The tears spilled down her cheeks.

"Hush, my dear, don't cry. There's nothing to fear anymore."

She leaned into him involuntarily, relaxed against the hard-muscled body. His arms slid hungrily around her, pressing her close. As though of its own volition, her face turned up to meet his, and her mouth opened as his came down to meet her lips. For the first time she could remember, she felt she had come home.

Chapter Thirty

❦

*Prill, 55th Year in the Reign of the Ridenau Kings
(2723, Muten Old Calender)*

$\mathcal{T}$he storm was over. Phineas tugged a clean tunic over his damp hair, glad he had reached the protection of Ahga's sheltering walls before the full fury of the weather had hit. Thunder still echoed in the distance, and a muted flash of lightning illuminated the night sky. Ah, well, he sighed as he scraped a razor over his chin, what did one expect in Prill?

He glanced around the Spartan room. Not much had changed, though seven years was a long time to stay away. A long time to stay in the field, though the One knew it had been necessary. Only in the last year had the Harley grip on the central Plains begun to weaken, and the Muten tribes to withdraw once more into the hollows of the Pulatchian Mountains.

Seven years was a long time for one who used to sit beside the King. Well, Abelard had another to sit beside him, one who graced the place of honor as he never could. . . . He pushed the thought of Melisande firmly out of his mind.

He tried not to think of her. The years had not been long enough to forget the clear hazel eyes and spirited grace, not long enough to forget the stricken face when Abelard publicly humiliated her and forced her father to submit. And never long enough to forget the shadowed face in the days after her marriage to the King.

He reached for a belt, this one of fine-tooled, intricately braided leather. He'd forgotten he'd ever owned such a thing.

When he was dressed, he slicked a comb through his damp hair and tugged his tunic into place. There was a knock at the door.

"Enter."

"Captain Phineas, you may go to the King's audience room." The waiting boy began to gather up the towels and discarded clothing.

"Very well, Tib."

"Will you want supper, sir?"

Phineas hesitated. "Perhaps I'll sup with the King. There's a lot I need to discuss with him—don't wait up for me."

"Yes, sir."

At the door of the King's audience room, the guards snapped to sudden attention and saluted. Phineas returned the salute, satisfied that discipline at Ahga was as strict as ever, and pushed open the door. A small fire burned in the polished grate, and a low table with a flask of wine and two goblets was pulled up before it.

The woman sitting next to the fire smiled. "Please come in, Captain Phineas."

Had it been seven years? he wondered as he walked slowly forward. Surely it was no more than seven months or seven weeks, for by the soft glow of the fire and the candles, Melisande had not changed at all. He went down on one knee and lifted the hand she offered to his mouth. "Lady Queen." He glanced around the room. There was no sign of Abelard.

"It's been a very long time since you honored us with your presence, Captain. I'd understood you considered Ahga your home, and yet, you've not been here at all for over—"

"Twenty months."

"And that last visit you stayed less than a day. Surely conditions in the field are not so severe they demand your constant presence?"

"Until late last autumn, Lady Queen, conditions, as you call them, were very grave indeed."

"I see." She drew a deep breath.

In the flicker of the flames, he saw that her beauty had matured. Her face was thinner than he remembered, her cheekbones more sharply defined. Her hazel eyes were shadowed in the dim light, and there was about her face a look of suffering, as though from a long illness. It was a look he had seen on the faces of soldiers grievously wounded in battle, who'd lived on despite their injuries but kept pain a constant companion.

Her body was thinner, too, he thought, though beneath the bulky dress it was hard to tell. Her fingers were long, the nails smooth pink ovals, and he thought they trembled as she busied herself with the wine. "Will you join me?"

He hesitated. "Lady Queen, I came to see the King. I mean you no insult, but the matter I must discuss with him is one of most pressing urgency. Perhaps after I speak with him, we might all—"

He broke off as she turned away to stare into the fire. "What is it?"

She gave a little laugh, harsh and bitter. "Don't you realize? The King isn't here."

"Not here?" he echoed, confused. "Where is he? Can he be summoned?"

"I imagine he'll return in a day or two—he never neglects the Court of Appeals longer than that, but I cannot say for sure."

"Lady Queen, I don't understand—"

"Don't call me that. Don't use that accursed title. You know my name."

The sudden bitterness confused him. "Melisande," he said gently. "What's the matter? Where's Abelard?"

"At Minnis."

"In this weather? This is no time of year to hunt."

"Oh, you blind fool, he's not hunting. He's with that—that woman. The one they say is a witch—she must be a witch—he can't bear to be away from her for more than a few days and then he's off—"

"So Abelard finally named his heir?"

"No! He won't name an heir—he refuses—" Her face crumpled, and she buried her head in her hands as sobs racked her body.

"Melisande." He spoke harshly and it had the desired effect. She wiped her face and looked at him, mute anguish in her yes. "Abelard has not named an heir, yet he breaks his vow to you in order to lie with Nydia?"

She nodded.

"What about you? Does he ever—" He paused, searching for a delicate way to inquire about the physical intimacy between the King and his Queen.

"Of course. He's not stopped trying to get an heir."

Phineas rose to his feet, gestured to the wine, and downed half the goblet in one gulp. "How long has this been going on?"

"Since before he brought me to Ahga. You really did not know?"

"No. I knew he'd moved the Lady Nydia to Minnis, but I had no idea. He's always been here whenever I've come back."

"You always sent a messenger on before you."

"There was no time." Still reluctant to believe her, Phineas gestured to the door. "His colors are flying from the tower of the city."

"Of course. Do you think the King advertises to all the world when he visits his witch?"

"How long is he gone?"

"Not long. Two, three nights, at the most. Except in the autumn, when he goes there to hunt."

"And you, Melisande? How is it with you?"

"Well enough. Life is pleasant here most of the time."

"Have you written to your father?"

"And humiliate him further? You know Abelard stripped him of almost everything—what does he have left than to believe his daughter is at least the Queen of Meriga? Do you think he needs to know that to Abelard I am nothing but a brood mare—and a barren one at that?"

Phineas nodded slowly. "I understand."

She gestured at the wine. "So, I thought, when I heard that you had come, I thought you might drink a cup of wine with me, for once you were a prisoner and I believe I helped you while away the long hours of your captivity?"

Phineas smiled sadly. "Indeed you did." He sat down besid
the fire. Pity warred with outrage at the King's treatment o
her. Even as he gestured for her to refill his goblet, his min
turned to what he would say to the King. It was as well, h
thought, that the King was a night's ride away, for if Abelar
were to walk through the door in the next few minutes, he di
not trust himself not to wrap his hands around the King'
throat.

He leaned back in his chair and watched Melisande, th
graceful droop of her head, the fall of her snowy coif over he
thin shoulders. He wondered if her hair was still as black an
thick as he remembered. He wanted to lean forward and tea
the fabric off her head, pull out the pins which she must use t
tame it, so that the whole mass of it would tumble, loose an
free about her face. He wondered what she would do if he di
such a thing, and he smiled.

"Why do you smile, Captain?"

"You know my name as well as I know yours," he reminde
her gently.

"Very well, Phineas." He was glad to see the dimple appea
in her cheek and wondered how long it had been since it ha
made its appearance. He wondered if Abelard even knew it ex
isted. "Why do you smile like that?"

He stretched his long legs before the fire with a sigh. "I wa
just remembering the first time I met you."

A shadow crossed her face. "It was very different then, wasn'
it?"

He nodded, suddenly sorry he had brought it up. "I have no
eaten, for I thought to sup with the King. But since he is no
here, perhaps you would do me the honor and the courtesy t
call for some food, and perhaps—" He paused and she leane
closer, color rising in her cheeks. He wondered what she ha
in mind. "Perhaps a chess set? It's been a long time since I ha
the leisure for a game of chess."

If she were disappointed, she covered it well. She rose wit
a graceful swish of skirts. "I will call for your supper."

She disappeared behind the panel that hid the door to th

King's bedchamber. He stared, brooding, into the flames. Was this what his actions had condemned Melisande to? If he had remained more visible at the court, was it possible Abelard might have treated her more kindly?

He thought of Tedmund, thought of Abelard's treatment of Nydia and of Melisande on their wedding night, thought of the ruthless scene in Mortmain's hall when Abelard had threatened to rape Melisande before her father's eyes if Mortmain did not surrender. And he wondered when he had stopped respecting the King's tenacious determination and begun to fear it. But how could Abelard have such callous disregard for the feelings of a helpless woman who was indeed little more than his prisoner?

He managed to smile at Melisande when she returned, followed by servants bearing trays of food and an elaborately carved chess set he recognized as the King's own. But he was careful to keep their conversation impersonal; he told her stories of his exploits during the years of his absence, and he noticed all that long night that she did not mention the King again.

Chapter Thirty-One

❧

*Y*ou forget yourself." Abelard's face might have been carved out of the same granite as the walls of Ahga. The years had treated the King kindly, Phineas acknowledged. The full beard he now wore made him look wise as well as noble. He sat at the head of the council table and stared up at Phineas with the expression he might have worn had Phineas been the lowliest scullion called to task.

But Phineas met the King with equal fury. His eyes were colder than the King's, and he met Abelard's glare with a defiance he had never felt before. "Perhaps I do, Lord King. But the fact remains that Melisande Mortmain is your Queen, not your hostage, and she should be treated with all the respect due her. She is the daughter of a landed Senador."

"That is none of your concern."

"It is my concern when you openly flaunt the breaking of the marriage vow before the entire court. You may be King, Abelard, but you are not above the law."

Abelard leaned back in his chair. "I am the law."

His words hit Phineas like a fist in his ribs. He stared at Abelard as though he might have heard the King incorrectly, but the King only returned his stare without flinching. "I see. Is that what you will tell the Congress, if they should question you?"

"Congress has more important matters to consider than whose bed I sleep in."

Phineas shook his head and backed away. The silence thickened. Finally he said, staring out the windows at the calm blue sea, "Why, in the Name of the One, Abelard, won't you name an heir? You could always change it if the Queen did bear you a son—"

"No!" Abelard's fist slammed down and the whole table shuddered.

"But then you would not be guilty of breaking this vow."

"I care nothing for that vow, do you understand?" the King said through clenched teeth. "I care about Meriga. I care about the realm I will leave after I am dead, and I will not leave this nation divided, is that clear? No matter who I name—"

"What about Everard?"

"What about him? His mother's practically a Muten. There is no one, Phineas, no one; there was no one seven years ago and there is no one now. And that Queen of mine, as you call her, is barren—"

"Just as Nydia said she was. Why haven't you persuaded her to use her Magic to get you an heir, Abelard? Is that why you visit her? You hope to convince her to use the Magic—"

He had struck home. Abelard's eyes were narrowed and his lips compressed. A tic appeared beneath the King's left eye.

"I would prefer to think, Phineas, you had more pressing matters on your mind when you arrived here so unexpectedly. Or did you come deliberately intending to goad me into killing you?"

Phineas hesitated, considering whether or not he should let the matter drop. But what else was to be gained? Had Abelard changed so much? Or had he simply become more of what he had always been? He took a deep breath. "There's serious trouble in the Pulatchian Highlands, south of Ithan. I have evidence that Eldred is working with the Mutens."

"Are you sure about this?"

"My scouts reported that about a month ago a Muten appeared to be in residence in Missiluse Castle. Now, a large number of Mutens have moved into the hills to the east of Missiluse and appear to be arming for war, as is the army Eldred's got surrounding his keep."

"So you think—"

"I think he plans to use Missiluse as a base of operations to launch attacks come the warmer weather. Which, as you know, is just a few weeks away in the south."

Abelard swung around, light in his eyes. "Finally! That wimp-chinned coward shows his hand. I always suspected his whining about the Harleys was an act to gain sympathy. What is the state of your troops at Ithan?"

"Well rested, refreshed. Garrick's planning to leave soon to take up a position in southern Arkan—we don't want to lose any ground we gained last year against the Harleys."

"No. Supplies?"

"Lean, as usual. You'll have to send more, but that's not what I'm worried about. This is not so clear-cut as simply laying siege to an enemy castle. There is, after all, the matter of your mother."

"I wish that witch would die."

"She has Amanander and Alexander—we'll have to move carefully if no harm is to come to your sons."

Abelard nodded. He stared out the window with faraway eyes. "Was I wrong to let her take them, Phineas?" He shook his head. "At the time, I was so glad to be rid of her. I'd have given anything to get her out of Ahga."

"It was a mistake, and I told you so at the time." Phineas was not yet ready to bury the hatchet. "The One only knows what she's filled their heads up with, and if they're involved with the Mutens somehow—"

Abelard nodded, stroking his beard. "Have there here been any raids, any initial attacks?"

"Not yet. At least, there hadn't been according to the latest information I had when I left. That may have changed. I left word that messengers were to follow me with any change in the situation."

"Perhaps I'd better get down there."

Phineas nodded. "Perhaps we can get Amanander and Alexander out before the fighting begins—"

"Don't be foolish, Phineas. You know that's not likely. For all we know, Eldred or my mother intend to use them as

ostages to force my hand. Perhaps that's what this is all
bout. My mother is the most single-minded person I've ever
nown."

Except for yourself, thought Phineas.

It could have been a night seven years in the past, thought
Phineas, as he surveyed the great hall of Ahga from his van-
age place on the dais. Once more, he occupied the place on
he King's left hand. The only real change was that instead of
Agara it was Melisande who sat, pale but composed, on the
King's right. The King ignored her for the most part. Melisande's place could have been vacant, for all Abelard seemed to
care. He seemed almost recklessly jovial, a hungry air about him,
as though he were eager to have an excuse to confront his old
nemesis. He had apparently forgotten all about the quarrel that
morning.

Phineas could barely see her profile with its long dark
lashes. She kept her head down, her attention focused steadily
on her plate. She looked up only when Abelard called for his
harper.

The man obeyed the King's summons instantly. He took a
place on the stool before the King, and Phineas was reminded
with an unexpected pang of the night so long ago when Nydia
had been commanded to play for the King. He remembered
her songs, the poignant pathos of the one which might have
been her own story, and the daring flirtatiousness of the other,
especially beneath Agara's very nose. Had that been the beginning? Phineas wondered. No, he decided. It had begun that
day in the little village when she had dropped the woolen
shroud and stood naked before the King. Abelard had wanted
her from that moment, and the fact that she could work the
Old Magic and foretell the future only sealed her fate as far as
the King was concerned.

The company was quieting, their faces turned toward the
harper with keen expectancy. Phineas did not recognize the
boy. Well, one had to expect some changes in seven years.

"Lord King," His voice was rich, with a tenor's unmistakable ring. "The new music you bid me learn, I would play it for your honored guest tonight, for surely a man so brave as the Captain of the King's Guard has left many a woman weeping when he rides to war?"

Phineas realized with a start that the man meant him. He gave a little bow of acknowledgment.

"Listen," Abelard was saying in his ear. "This is one of Nydia's songs."

The boy's hand rippled over the strings like wind over the water, and the music which rose from the harp was as sweet and clear as a mountain stream. Phineas felt a shiver run up his spine, although he did not recognize the song.

"I must away, love, I can no longer tarry,
This morning's tempest I have to cross,
I must be guided without a stumble
Into the arms I love the most.

"And when he came to his true love's dwelling
He knelt down gently upon a stone,
And through the window, he whispered lowly,
'Is my true love within at home?' "

From the other side of Abelard, Phineas heard the Queen inhale, and a flush crept up her throat. Her fingers tightened on her wine goblet. His heart twisted in his chest. He glanced at Abelard. The King was staring beyond the harper to a point down the hall, into some place Phineas could not see, but he did not doubt it was Nydia's face which held the King entranced.

Melisande's knuckles were white as the boy continued.

"And when the long night was past and over,
And when the small clouds began to grow,
He took her hand, they kissed and parted,
Then he saddled and mounted and rode away home."

Melisande made a little strangled cry, and rising so quickly she knocked her chair backward, she hurried from the hall. Abelard did not even glance after her, or acknowledge in any way that his Queen had left in some distress.

"What do you think, Phineas?" murmured Abelard. "Is it not beautiful?"

"I think you've become the worst sort of tyrant," muttered Phineas beneath his breath. He pushed back his own chair and bowed to the harper. "Well sung, master harper. Forgive me, Lord King," he said, voice pitched to carry down the hall, "I am weary as well. May I have your permission to retire?"

Abelard looked at him with a cold glitter in his bright blue eyes. "Go."

As Phineas left the hall, he heard the first strains of another song, and the men and women in the hall began to sing.

He hesitated in the dark corridor for only a moment, and then, taking the stairs two and three steps at a time, he soon caught up with Melisande. She was weeping, the tears running silently down her face. He touched her arm, and she turned to him, eyes streaming, mouth working silently.

He gathered her into his arms and held her close. Without thinking, he tore the white coif off her head and pressed his lips into her springy dark curls. Her hair smelled like lavender and rosemary and made him think of wide green meadows under a summer sun. She turned her face up to meet his mouth.

Her arms wrapped themselves around his neck, and of its own volition, his body pressed itself on hers, hard and hot and demanding. Dizzy, he sank to the steps, cradling her on his lap, and he laid her against the hard tile stairs, his arm protecting her back from its worn edges. She guided his hand to her breasts, and beneath the fabric, he felt her nipples—hard, pointed peaks. He groped for the lacings of her gown and reached for her breasts, felt the weight, the rough pebbled texture of the tips. She moaned beneath his mouth. Her hands pulled at his tunic, tugged him closer.

His hand touched the cold tile and he pulled back, drawing

the edges of her bodice together. She made a little murmur of protest and arched her back.

"No, Melisande, we mustn't."

She sat up, eyes wide and incredulous. "We mustn't? You say that to me—when Abelard has his harper sing about his witch woman before my eyes? Why shouldn't we do as we'd like?"

He dropped his eyes and pulled away. He felt his erection throb against his thigh and cursed himself suddenly for a fool and a coward. "We cannot."

"Why not?"

"Did you not swear fidelity?"

"Well, yes, of course," she sputtered. "But it means nothing to the King. Why should it mean anything to me?"

"But it does," he said gently. "A vow, a pledge, is a sacred thing—what else is there? And I, too—"

"You?" She gave one of her harsh laughs that made his heart ache to hear it. "You? What do you owe the King? You even less than I—what vow do you stand by? What has he ever done for you?"

"He saved my life," he reminded her, so quietly he spoke almost to himself. "He made me what I am—everything I have, everything I know, everything I ever was or hoped to be, he made it possible. I may live to regret this night—this lost opportunity—but I will not be less than I am because he is less than he should be."

He rose to his feet, and she stared up at him, an expression of wonder on her face. "Why did you follow me? What do you want of me?"

"I cannot bear to see you so unhappy. I hoped that things would be different. I did not want to intrude upon your life with the King."

"That's why you stayed away," she said. "You did love me in my father's house. I wanted you so much then, loved you so much, and yet I was half afraid of you. But when he threatened to kill you, I was—I didn't know what to do. You're so much like him, did you know that?" She shook her head. She picked up her skirts and started up the steps. He followed.

"You thought perhaps I'd learn to love the King if you stayed away, didn't you? And perhaps I could have, even after that horrible day in the hall, when he humiliated my father and me. But when it became clear that there'd be no child, he ignored me ever since." She paused on the step above him. "So you see, Phineas, I could never love him and I could never forget you."

Chapter Thirty-Two

✦

$\mathscr{I}$t was easier once Phineas and Abelard left Ahga. So long as the sight of Melisande's face hovered at the edges of Phineas's awareness, it was difficult for him to even look at Abelard. But once they were well away from the city and far along the highways, he could pretend that everything was the same as it ever was—that they were King and trusted confidant, most faithful of all his advisors.

Eight years of war had ravaged the countryside. Again and again the Harleyriders had surged across the country, spreading out from their hidden fortresses. But slowly, the alliances Abelard had forged over the years, sometimes by diplomacy, sometimes by sheer force of will, had gained the upper hand, and slowly, the tide of destruction had begun to turn.

Although even the outlaws could not obliterate the ancient precision of the roads, the fields and pastures showed obvious signs of the recent raids. Houses and barns everywhere were in ruins; many of the once-cultivated fields lay fallow, flocks that had numbered in the hundreds now barely required even a tenth of the pastureland, and the faces of the people wore the pinched look of starvation. But there were a few signs that prosperity was returning: here and there a family tilled a field, men repaired fences, women sprinkled seed onto newly plowed furrows.

At the border of Linoys, the toll plaza was no more than a pile of rubble, and Sprinfell, Tedmund's home, had been burned to the ground in the second year of the war.

Abelard reined his horse by the bridge that still stretched

cross the river, now leading up to nothing. "I'm sorry every me I see this."

Phineas raised his brow. "You are?"

"Of course. Sprinfell was perhaps the prettiest of all my oldings. A pity those barbarians destroyed it. There's not ven anything left to make it worth repairing."

Phineas tugged at his reins, hardly surprised. He wondered f Abelard ever thought of Tedmund, or for that matter, if Nydia ever did. Probably not. They belonged together, Nydia nd Abelard. Tedmund had been an interlude, a pawn, some-ne who happened to get in the way. Just like Melisande.

His mind veered away from Melisande to her father. What ad happened to Owen Mortmain? he wondered. He still lived nder the thumb of an administrator Abelard had set over him o make certain that Owen never rose against the throne again. Yudaw and Ragonn and Senifay were in ruins. If Abelard's oldings seemed bad, it would take generations for the west to ecover from the wrath of Abelard Ridenau. Chunks of each state had been carved out, given to Kora-lado, Rissona, Mon-lana, and Norda Coda. The west was won.

They skirted the ruins of Tedmund's holding. In the inter-ening years, the Arkan lords had proven to be tough and roud and tenacious. They had held on while the Harleys ipped across the central Plains, held fast even while the Harleys reigned in Arkan. They had been beaten, but they had ever surrendered, and little by little, one square mile at a ime, the armies of the allied Senators and the King had orced them back into the Loma deserts and beyond, into the rid rocky wasteland of southern Meriga, into the region alled Dlas-for'Torth.

He thought of the men with whom he'd fought: Garrick and Brand and young Miles of Ithan Ford. Not so young now, hough. Miles had seen his first real battle at sixteen, had slain is first Muten at seventeen. The young Senator of the Ten-lessey Fall was brave and daring and utterly loyal to the King. Weren't they all?

And then there was Eldred. Eldred of Missiluse, who had

slunk into his swamps in disgrace, stripped of all power after Abelard's men had forced the Harleys out of his estate, who had given succor to the King's mother when she had fled Ahga in the wake of Abelard's rage. It wasn't wise to thwart the King. Phineas thought of Mortmain, of the Senadors of Ragonn, Yudaw, and Senifay. No, he thought, watching the King ride by on his pale yellow stallion, his blue cloak flung over one shoulder, the jeweled hilt of his broadsword glinting in the sun, it wasn't wise to thwart the King.

They reached Ithan in less than a week. They found Garrick still in residence, young Miles—Phineas always thought of him as young Miles—and Brand there as well, still planning the year's campaigns. The goals were clear-cut enough, he knew, although Brand and Garrick had different ideas about how to realize them. It was another good reason to bring the King more directly into this, he thought, as he washed and changed and readied himself for dinner.

He looked around his room and realized with a start that this place felt more like home than Ahga.

As though to confirm his thoughts, Tib spoke up as he handed Phineas a clean shirt. "It's good to be back, isn't it, sir?"

Phineas laced the shirt, rejected a tunic. The night air was pleasantly cool without the sting of winter. He smiled a little ruefully. "I suppose it is, Tib, although I'm not sure any place feels like home to me. Don't wait for me."

"You'll sup with the King?"

"And General Garrick, and Lieutenant Brand. We've a lot of planning to do this night. So rest while you can."

"Yes, sir." Tib saluted.

He found young Miles in the great hall, studying a hide map, fingering a message tube. He looked up when he saw Phineas. "Greetings Captain."

"Lord Senador."

Miles grinned. "I'm glad you're here, Captain. I was beginning to fear if you were away much longer, Garrick and Brand

would call each other out and fight for the glory of the Guard
and the honor of the Army."

Phineas shook his head. "It's getting worse?" There was a
delicate balance to the relationship between Garrick, the
King's General in the East, and Brand, who had been promoted just last year to Lieutenant of the King's Guard. As
Phineas's second-in-command, he wielded a great deal of
power, commanded the most elite troops in Meriga. But Garrick's men were greater in number, and the two must comple-
ment each other, not behave like rivals.

"Well, you'll have to speak to them for yourself, but they
each have a point, you know."

"I think Lieutenant Brand may have been promoted just a
bit too quickly for everyone's good."

"Brand's a good soldier." Miles rushed to the defense of the
idol of his youth.

"Of course he is, and so's Garrick. If they want to disagree
that's fine. But it mustn't go too far, or—"

"Or what?"

Phineas turned to face Garrick. At fifty, Garrick's back was
ramrod straight. "Or we'll have no one left to fight the
Harleys."

Garrick made a noise of dismissal. "Brand's a good boy,
Phineas. There's just too much of the puppy about him yet.
There's a time to go rushing into the desert, and a time to con-
solidate a position—"

"And I say this year is the time to do both," Brand's voice
interrupted smoothly. "Captain." He saluted his commanding
officer. "I trust you and my father had a good journey?"

Before Phineas could reply, Miles was on his feet bowing to
some point past them all. "Lord King."

As the greetings went round the room, Phineas noticed
again the wooden tube Miles held. "Is that for me?" he asked
when the conversation lulled.

"By the One, I nearly forgot. This is for you, Lord King.
Just arrived today."

"Oh?" Abelard broke the seals and fished the rolled parchment out of the tube. "What's this?" Surprise was plain on his face. He handed the parchment to Phineas, who could not believe what he read.

"What is it, Dad?" Brand asked with a trace of impatience.

"It's from Eldred," answered Abelard, looking at Phineas.

"Well, what's he want?"

"Aid." Phineas stared at the King, at the faces of each man in turn. "Eldred begs you to send aid."

"It's a trap." After the initial shock and flurry had subsided, Garrick spoke the words on everyone's mind.

There was a mutter of agreement from Brand, and Abelard nodded.

Young Miles caught Phineas's eye. "What do you think?"

Roused from a reverie, Phineas started. "Me? I don't know. There's something about this that bothers me."

"Come, Phineas," began Abelard, "Eldred's always—"

"No." Phineas shook his head, murmured his disagreement. "I'm not certain, but—" He broke off, looked at Miles. "What do you think?"

The young Senador flushed, and for a moment, he looked like the boy who had come to Ahga after the death of his father so many years ago. "I think you're wrong about Eldred."

Abelard frowned. "You don't know Eldred like I do, boy. He's ever been a thorn in my side in the Congress—it was he who gave the Harleys the foothold which started this mess. You're wrong, boy."

Miles flushed deeper. "I beg your pardon, Lord King, but I don't think so. I spoke with the messenger who brought this, and—"

"Well, where is this messenger?" demanded the King.

"I sent him to the kitchens. Shall I have him brought here?"

Phineas nodded as Abelard rose to his feet and began to pace beside the hearth.

It occurred suddenly to Phineas that they were gathered in the very room in which Abelard had first interviewed Nydia and the Bishop. He unrolled the scroll and studied the shaky handwriting. The ink was blotted and smeared. It had been written in a great hurry, then rolled and sealed before the ink was fully dry. Why? he wondered. And the message was brief: three words. Help. Sons. Now.

A servant opened the door for the messenger. The men looked up. Phineas frowned. The messenger was heavily cloaked, his hood pulled down across his forehead. Only the lower half of his face was visible.

There was something odd about him, so odd that Phineas rose when he was seated by the fire before the King and tore the hood off his face.

"Ugh," cried Miles, who was closest. He leapt to his feet.

Garrick and Brand grimaced, Abelard's mouth narrowed in disgust at the semi-Muten features.

Only Phineas leaned closer for a better look. "You're a halfling."

The messenger nodded, his terror plain at finding himself surrounded by five of the most formidable men in Meriga.

Miles glanced at the King. "He didn't tell me that, sir. I had no idea—"

"Enough, boy, it doesn't matter." Abelard hooked his thumbs in his sword belt. He towered over the messenger. "Why did Eldred send you?"

"I was the only one who could get past the enemy."

"Why?"

"I—I have just enough mindskill to hide from the others, if I need to."

"What others?"

"He means full-blooded Mutens," said Miles.

"Do you?"

The messenger nodded.

Phineas put a restraining hand on Abelard's arm. "Your mother was a human?"

"Yes."

"Raped in a raid?"

He nodded once more.

"We won't hurt you. Don't be frightened. You're Eldred's man?"

Again, a quick, silent nod.

"So why should we believe him?" asked Abelard scornfully.

"What's going on down there?"

At that, the messenger looked even more frightened. "Your sons, Lord King, are in gravest danger." He spoke in a heavy whisper as though he feared even the walls had ears.

"Speak up, man," said Garrick. "There's none to hear."

"You're wrong," whispered the messenger.

"Who's listening?" asked Phineas.

The messenger shook his head, closed his eyes. In the center of his forehead, a depression which marked the place where his third eye would have been pulsed frantically. Phineas shook his arm. "You've got to tell us what you know."

He opened his eyes, staring up at Phineas with mute agony. "I have."

"Is it Mutens?" growled Abelard impatiently.

The messenger nodded.

"Why can't you tell us—"

"Because, Lord King, if I even think his name, he'll hear me. You have no idea. Lord Eldred may even be dead by now, and that accursed woman with him."

"What woman?" Abelard's voice was cold.

"Agara Onrada, Lord King. She who brought the—the—him into my lord's home. For the Magic. He knows, and she wishes to learn—"

"Who is he?" demanded the King.

"I must not—cannot say, Lord King. But something must be done without fail and without delay."

"Garrick, order a company—"

"No, Lord King. It will do you no good, no matter how many troops you bring. They will be scattered—Eldred's own men have deserted, disappeared into the swamps and the poison pits."

The men glanced at each other. "What about the scouts I

sent out before I left, Garrick?" asked Phineas. "What do they report?"

Garrick gave a start. He looked at Brand, at Miles, and back to Phineas. "They haven't returned."

"They've been gone over three weeks."

"No one escapes him, my lord," interrupted the messenger. "Lord King, take only a few of the men you trust the most and go. Believe me, there are no soldiers left to fight you. Only him. You, and you alone, may have a chance to save your sons."

"Where are they?"

"Beyond the foothills of Missiluse, on the other side of the Great Gorge, there is a junction of two old highways. Eldred has a keep there—"

"I know it," said Miles. "That's less than a week's ride from here. By the One, are they so close?"

"This enemy—as you call him—is not Eldred?"

"No, Lord King."

"A Muten."

"Yes, Lord King."

"And he knows the Magic?"

"Yes, Lord King."

Brand guffawed. "Come, Dad, you're not about to believe this, are you? Let's go down with a regiment of the Guards. You don't seriously believe some Muten halfling—"

"I speak the truth, Lord King," protested the messenger.

"Silence," commanded the King. "Phineas? What do you think?"

Phineas looked at the messenger. The story was unbelievable, and yet . . . "It's easy enough to find out if he's telling the truth."

"How?"

"Take a regiment, or two, as far as the border. If the scouts report that all is as this messenger says, we leave the troops on the border and go in alone. Otherwise, we'll have men poised to invade, if necessary."

"Do what you must, Lord King," whispered the messenger. "But go. Please. Soon. Go."

They left Ithan at midmorning, Phineas, Abelard, Miles, and Tib heading south, through the rocky passes of the Pulatchian Mountains. Through green, rolling valleys they pressed on, ever south, into the high mountain country that marked the border between Tennessy and Missiluse.

It was in the mountains that Phineas began to feel uneasy. He shifted in his saddle often, turning quickly, plagued by the feeling that they were watched by unseen eyes. They were too far west for Mutens, and yet the hills seemed to breed unrest. They spent two nights at different places with the Pulatchian Highlanders: sour, grim-faced men, who spoke little and seemed singularly unimpressed by the honor done them by their King.

Yet the leaders renewed their oaths of allegiance to Abelard without fail, and their nights were long with tales of the many grievances done them by the Harleys and the Mutens.

A miasma seemed to hang in the air, and Phineas was glad each morning when it was time to saddle and be on his way. At least on horseback he did not feel so vulnerable.

On the border of Missiluse, they halted. Phineas was not the only one who felt uneasy; there were mutters from the ranks, and the sergeants looked uncomfortable every time there was talk of advancing further into Missiluse.

"The last scout I sent out hasn't returned, Abelard." Phineas squinted out over the horizon. Beyond the foothills, the land flattened out abruptly, giving way to low, swampy fens, marshy flats where oily water lay in deceptively shallow pools.

"And according to the last reports, there were no signs of human life?"

"Human or Muten. No. There's nothing over there."

"What do you think, Phineas?"

"I don't think there's much of a choice. If we lead the men in, and they panic, or end up getting lost in the swamps—"

"What if this Muten really does have the Magic?"

"Then all the armies in Meriga aren't going to make a difference, are they?"

The two men stared at each other, and finally, Abelard nodded. "Very well. You and I will leave in the morning."

Miles and Tib insisted upon accompanying the King and Phineas, so it was late in the morning of the following day when they finally left the encampment. The going was slower, and they were careful not to stray off the old highways. At night, things with leathery wings flapped in the darkness beyond the weak circle of light cast by their campfire, and they took turns by twos keeping the watch all through the long nights.

The air was thick with the stench from poison pits, unseen but ever present. Trees dripped with gray-green moss like cobwebs, and the hair often rose on the back of Phineas's neck. None of them slept well, and they were tense and haggard.

On the morning of the fifth day out of Ithan, the road wound up a slight rise, and the swamps were left behind. Small farmhouses dotted the landscape, and a wide fertile plain lay before them. Green fields lay within a network of complicated irrigation ditches and a toll plaza which flew the colors of Eldred of Missiluse lay perhaps a few hundred yards in the distance.

"Well, gentlemen, there it is," said Abelard.

"Looks peaceful enough," said Miles.

"No," said the messenger. "Things are not as they appear."

There was no one in the toll plaza. They rode through, unchallenged, and Phineas became aware that the fields and the houses were deserted. As they advanced down the road, he held up his hand for the company to stop. "Listen."

As though from far away, there was a dull throb like a great heartbeat through the air.

Miles stared in all directions. "Muten drums."

Phineas nodded silently.

"Do you understand what they say?" the King asked.

"It's a warning," whispered the messenger. "From the east. We're being warned to stay away from the keep."

"Why?" demanded Abelard.

The messenger looked at the King with pity on his face. "You'll see."

As they continued down the road, Phineas gestured to the fields. "Where are all the people?"

"Run off," said the messenger.

"But why?" asked Miles. "I see nothing to be afraid of."

"You're accustomed to the threat of danger, Lord Senador. Lesser men would shudder to set foot upon this highway in the direction of that accursed keep."

"Are you afraid?" Miles looked at the messenger curiously.

"Lord Senador, it's not for my life I fear."

"What, then?" There was amusement in Miles's voice.

"For my very self, Lord Senador. But you'll see."

As they approached, Phineas was aware of something which felt like a hand descend onto the back of his neck, as though he were held in a giant's grip. It was a feeling he could not shake off, and he realized that the closer they came to the castle, the more often he peered over his shoulder and shifted in his saddle. The others grew silent, and all idle chatter had long ceased when at last they rode up to the gates of Missiluse Keep.

"Look, Lord King," said Tib, "the Senador's colors—he's still in residence."

A long banner hung limply in the still air over the gates. Abelard rode up to the gates and pounded on them with the hilt of his broadsword. The sound echoed with dull thuds.

"Open the gates," he cried. "Eldred of Missiluse, open the gates for your King."

Almost at once, the gates creaked. Abelard moved back as the gates swung inward. Phineas peered inside and blinked in astonishment. Eldred himself stood in the gateway, leaning on a broken spear. His face crumpled behind his beard, and he fell on his knees at the sight of the King. "Lord King," he said with a heaving sob, "thank the One you've come."

Chapter Thirty-Three

❦

*E*xcellent." The voice which emanated down the length the darkened hall was soft, almost gentle, and Phineas's ood was instantly chilled. "Come closer, gentlemen."

Eldred writhed, clutching his spear, and Phineas reached for e dagger at his side.

"That won't be necessary, Captain," said the voice. "Come oser. We are all friends here."

They had no choice, for their feet seemed to have acquired a ill of their own. Only Abelard strode resolutely forward, as ough he alone retained the will to move of his own volition. ib and Miles moved with wooden steps, while Phineas strug- ed against the feeling that the grip on the back of his neck ad strengthened and was propelling him toward the shadowy ais.

At the base of the dais, Abelard stopped and narrowed his yes. "Mother!" Phineas suddenly noticed the tall, thin woman ho stood by the one chair in the center, her hands clasped be- re her.

"Greetings, my son." Agara's voice had lost none of its ing. "You knew, of course, that I had accepted the kind hos- tality of your cousin?"

"What's going on here? Where are my sons?"

"Patience, Lord King. All will be revealed in its time. Not our time, however. Mine."

Abelard stared into the face of the Muten who sat in the ntral chair. He grabbed Eldred by the collar and shook him. What's going on?"

"Leave him alone," the Muten directed. "He's been punished enough."

Eldred's lip quivered and two great tears rolled down his cheeks into his beard. He sniffled and sobbed, shoulders heaving.

"Enough!" cried the Muten. "Worm."

"What have you done to him?" asked Abelard. "Who in the name of the One are you? And what do you think you're doing in that chair?"

"My name is not important."

"I want answers, dog." Abelard made as if to step onto the dais, and the Muten held up his hand, gave a queer moaning sound, and Abelard fell to the floor as if pushed. Agara giggled.

"I said you'd have answers, Lord King." The sarcasm was tangible. "When I was ready to give them to you."

"What do you want with me?"

"I want you to name Amanander as your heir," Agara spoke with no attempt at concealing her contempt.

"You think that you and this miserable Muten dog are going to force me to name Amanander my heir? Think again."

"Abelard," his mother said, "we have the Magic."

"I don't care if you have all the Magic ever made."

Phineas felt the grip on the back of his neck lessen infinitesimally. He looked up at the Muten, who sat on Eldred's chair as though it were his. His three eyes gleamed in the firelight and his secondary arms were folded firmly across his chest.

"Where are my sons?" The King sounded suddenly wary.

"Safe." Agara spoke with a silky assurance Phineas instantly distrusted. "And well."

"I want to see them."

Without taking her eyes off the King, Agara called, "Aman! Alex! We have visitors!"

From a side chamber, two tall, thin boys came forward, so identical that Phineas blinked as though to clear his vision. Then he realized that one had rushed forward into his father's embrace, while the other hung back.

"Amanander?" Abelard said uncertainly to the tall boy in
his arms.

"No, Dad, I'm Alex."

"I'm Amanander. Sir." There was hostility in the last word
that made Phineas look very closely at the boy who leaned in
the doorframe. Like his twin, he was tall for his age—their
bones were long and slender, and one could see that when
their muscles had filled out and hardened, they would both be
tall men. Their skin was fair, made to seem even paler against
the dark shock of hair and brows and eyes. But where Alexander's mouth curved in an eager smile, Amanander's lips were
thin and pressed tightly together, as Abelard's did when he
was angry, or as Agara's did, even now, while she watched.

"Are you well?" The King demanded.

Alex nodded eagerly and opened his mouth to speak, but
Agara cut him off. "That's enough. Get back to your tutors.
You'll have time to speak with your father soon enough."

As the boys obediently seemed to melt into the walls,
Abelard swung on his mother. "What do you mean, that's
enough? I haven't seen my sons in seven years or more—"

"Did you think of them at all in that time?" she spat at her
son.

"I've had my hands full in the last seven years, making sure
there would be a kingdom for anyone to inherit."

"I'm sure your hands were full—full of that witch," she
replied.

Abelard's face drained of color, and then flushed an angry
red. "I remember suddenly why I banished you. You still
haven't learned to hold that tongue." He looked at the Muten.
"You lured me down here. Well, I'm here. What do you want
of me?"

"Your will is stronger than any other human's I've ever
met, Lord King. Look."

Abelard followed the Muten's glance to Tib. The servant
shuddered once, twice, his body reverberating as though some
force undulated through it. Phineas tried to step forward,

found he could not move. Eldred fell to his knees, hiding his
eyes behind his fists.

Tib made a muffled, gargling sound deep in his throat. His
eyes widened, closed, and he slumped forward in a heap.

"What did you do to him?" demanded Phineas. His limbs
felt heavy, as though his bones were made of steel, but he
forced himself to move painful step by painful step to stand
beside Abelard at the foot of the dais. Sweat beaded on his
forehead and rolled down his neck, but he fought the Muten's
grip with every ounce of strength he possessed.

"Captain," said the Muten softly, "congratulations."

Abelard stared up at Agara. "You're behind this, aren'
you? You took Nydia's books—you brought this creature
here. Why?"

"Do you think I'd let that witch have the means to disinherit
my grandson?"

Phineas realized that for Abelard and Agara, he and Eldred
had been forgotten.

"What are you talking about?"

"If your Queen bears you a son, you'll make him your heir
and Amanander will have nothing—and I won't let that happen. So I took those books and made certain that she wouldn't
be able to use the Magic for you. And now you grow old. The
kingdom needs an heir—soon you'll have no choice but to
name Amanander heir of all Meriga—"

"Amanander," spat back Abelard, "whom you've corrupted
for seven years? Amanander will never be King of Meriga—
not with Magic or without it. There is nothing you could do to
force me to name him heir—and nothing I will ever do to
leave the kingdom to him. I'd rather give it to the mewling
pup Vere than to a son who's had the benefit of your tutelage
for seven years."

Agara's eyes narrowed. "I will never let that happen."

"You? Woman, who do you think you are? I am the King—
I say who comes after me."

A thin smile curved Agara's thin mouth and made Phineas
think of a predator going after prey. "And who do you think

made you King? Ensured that you had a kingdom to inherit? If your father had lived, he might have signed away half the kingdom to pacify the Congress—because he wasn't man enough to march against them. But you were, you were always my son, and so—"

Abelard stood rigid. "It was you. You were the one who hired the outlaws who killed Dad—"

Agara threw her head back. "Yes. It was me. And you were so far away, there was no way anyone would say it could have been you. No one ever thought that I, a mere woman, would do such a thing. So you came to the throne and made the country even stronger—and you will not leave the crown to anyone but Amanander."

"And so you've tried to use the Magic?" Abelard did not wait for an answer, but she did not deny it. "You? When you would have had Nydia Farhallen burnt as a witch? That's what you've been doing all these years. . . . Just what do you know, Mother?"

Her mouth twisted in a sulk, and Phineas realized that Agara had not been as successful as she wanted to be. Suddenly, it all fit together. "She still doesn't know it, Abelard. But that one—he does."

Agara said nothing.

"So what do you want with me, Muten?"

"You will do as your mother asks."

"What's it to you?"

A smile twisted the Muten's lips, and Phineas shuddered at the sight. And he understood that he was in the presence of something purely evil—evil in a way that surely no human could be. It was the presence of a will bloated beyond all reason, a will which understood no motive, no justice, no goal but its own.

The Muten stared at Abelard, unblinking, and the center eye pulsed with a slow throb. The King stood his ground.

He hasn't the same effect on Abelard that he has on the rest of us, thought Phineas as he glanced at Miles, Eldred, and

Tib's prone body. Because Abelard is so strong-willed himself, he realized. He can't control the King quite so easily—

Behind Phineas there was a loud cry, and Eldred rushed at the King, broken spear pointed at his back.

Abelard whirled just in time, dodged, and pulled his broadsword from its sheath. He swung at Eldred viciously, and Eldred stumbled clumsily out of the way. His eyes rolled back in his head, his face was twisted into a rictus of agony. "No, no, no," he mouthed, even as he lowered the splintered shaft toward Abelard's belly.

He rushed at Abelard once more, a crazy, side-to-side run that made it easy for Abelard to escape. Eldred fell on his knees, the shaft suddenly pointed toward his own throat. Just as Phineas cried out, Eldred plunged it into his throat. He died in a gurgle of blood.

Phineas stared up at the Muten. "What kind of a monster are you?"

"My people have hidden under rocks and underground long enough, Captain, while you humans squabbled and fought and kept everything for yourselves. But we had the Magic, and you and all the priests could not take it from us. And I will use it as it should have been used long ago."

The sound of a sword being drawn from a sheath made Phineas turn. Miles shuddered and jerked, his face taut with effort. "I—will—not—kill—my—King—" The sword slid out of the scabbard as though of its own volition, and Miles's hand closed over it. With his left hand, he grasped his right, pushing against his own arm with all the strength he possessed.

Abelard backed up and crouched into a fighting stance, waiting. Agara smiled, as though she enjoyed the sight of her son forced to fight his own men.

Phineas glanced up at the Muten, and its gaze fell directly on him. Its third eye bore into his brain, as though it reached down, deeper, into the place where his most secret thoughts were hidden.

"Ah!" It was a gloat of triumph.

The grip on Phineas's neck tightened. *You'd like to kill him, wouldn't you, Captain?* said the Muten's voice in his mind. *Kill him, take his Queen? Why not? No one else would want her. Kill him, and she's yours for the taking.*

With a grunt, Phineas pulled his sword from his scabbard. He jerked his head from side to side, trying to ecape the seductive whisper in his brain. *Kill him. He deserves it. You know he does. You could do it. Not these others—they're weak. You're as strong as he is—take a step, now, Captain.*

His legs moved. Phineas gasped for breath, as though by holding his breath, he might force his body into submission.

One stroke and she's yours.

Tedmund's face rose before him, the ruins of Sprinfell holding, Mortmain's face on the night Abelard forced him to submit, Melisande's white breasts exposed to the lust-filled eyes of the soldiers.

One stroke and she's yours.

With a cry, Phineas rushed at Abelard, sword raised. He swung, and the King required both hands to block it. The force of the blow shuddered down his arm. Sparks flew off the metal edge as Phineas attacked, again and again, and again, orcing Abelard back in an ever-tightening circle.

It had been some years since Abelard had taken to the field—he was slowing, tiring. His breathing was becoming labored. Sweat ran down his face. His eyes darted frantically. "Phineas!" It was a desperate plea. "Remember who you are, man!"

Remember, yes, remember, echoed the voice in his head. And the image of Melisande struggling in Abelard's arms as he stripped her clothes from her body rose up to taunt him again. He seemed to possess a nearly inhuman strength. *Remember,* his own voice responded silently. *I pledge allegiance to the King. Your life for his, unto death. Pledged and bound.* He whirled to face the Muten, the blade a steel gray blur, then the force of the Muten's mind turned him back again to Abelard.

Abelard stumbled, tripped, fell on one knee.

Now! cried the alien voice. *Finish him, now!* And as Phineas raised his sword to deal Abelard the deathblow, another voice sounded through his mind, this time like a clean wind out of the north, fresh and pure like snow. *Ferad-lugz,* it called. *Ferad-lugz!*

Like a man awakening out of a dream, Phineas lowered the sword with hands that shook. He tried to extend a hand to help Abelard to his feet, but his arms and legs refused to do his bidding. He tried to breathe, but the air was somehow far too thick to enter his lungs.

A faint luminescence outlined them all. The Muten stood up, mouth open in a snarl.

The floor trembled as though the keep rocked on its foundations, and a current, like the one he remembered from the day in Ahga when the giant wave had crashed against the castle walls, surged through the room. This time however, there were no lights to flicker, no sudden fountains of water. The current seemed to pass over him rather than through him, and the hair on his legs and arms and head rippled and stood straight up as it passed. It snaked its way across his body, headed for the Muten.

The light winked out and the whole room tilted. In the dark, he fell to his knees, blindly groping. The world spun, heaved once more, and Phineas felt himself falling, down, down, down, until the dark dissolved into a void.

Chapter Thirty-Four

*H*e opened his eyes to a night sky where a million stars wheeled in pinpricks of white light. He heard an unearthly music that sent a thrill down his spine and he did not care where he was or who was singing, so long as that music continued. A fire crackled to his left. Half a dozen figures, wrapped in robes of white or pale gray, crouched around it. His head was pillowed comfortably on a rolled blanket, which smelled like woodsmoke and moss: a clean, not unpleasant, scent.

The singer was one of the figures gathered by the fire. He saw a delicate hand pluck something which resembled a many-stringed guitar, and he drew a deep breath and listened, content.

Images of Melisande and Nydia swirled through his mind, for the music called up memories of them both; not ugly, shameful memories as the Muten's voice had done, but images of beauty, for they were both at once so vulnerable and so fair.

The voice faded away into the silence of the night, and Phineas wondered if he had really heard it. He sat up, surprised he felt no pain, no grogginess.

One of the figures looked up, and seeing Phineas sitting up, rose swiftly to his feet. As the others scattered into the dark, he pushed his hood away from his face. "Greetings, Captain Phineas."

"Vere! What are you doing here? Where's your father? Your brothers?"

"Unharmed, Captain, and close by."

Phineas got to his feet, startled to find himself looking up at this tall, spare youth, whose long hair was held back from his forehead by an intricately braided leather band. His face was thin, the bones all jutting angles, just as Abelard's had been in his youth, but the cheeks were decorated with swirls of white and green and blue paint, arranged in a complicated series of markings which seemed at once both random and ordered.

"Please come with me, Captain. There's someone who would like to speak with you."

"Who?"

"Please come."

Phineas glanced down at the fire. Light leaped off the edges of spears lying on the ground before the flames, and fear licked at his heart. "Where's Abelard?" he repeated, and he flinched at the memory that he had nearly killed the King.

"Please, Captain, everything will be explained. If you'll just come?"

There was the faintest edge of pleading in his voice, which reminded Phineas that this was Vere, the outcast and loner, the one who of all Abelard's sons had never mastered staff or sword, bow or spear. Still uncertain, he followed Vere into the night.

His boots crunched on dried leaves, and a scent like newly turned earth, faintly sweet, reached his nostrils. The tang of pine needles was in the air, and suddenly Phineas understood that they had somehow been brought into the hills where the Mutens scraped a living on the edges of existence. Fires flickered here and there in the night, little pinpoints of brightness that seemed to reflect the stars overhead.

The path wound up a gentle incline at the base of a steep hill, and at the crest, Vere paused. "In here, Captain." He ducked low and disappeared into the mountainside.

Confused, Phineas realized that an entrance was concealed in the hillside, so cleverly that it was nearly impossible to distinguish it from the earth surrounding it. He pushed through a curtain of coarse canvas and halted, shocked.

He was in a long, narrow building, clearly of pre-Armageddon onstruction. The floor was wide oak planks, bleached and moothed by a thousand scrubbings. Marble pillars rose to the aulted ceiling, and long wooden benches were arranged in recise rows on either side of a center aisle.

But it was the light which puzzled Phineas. Chandeliers ung suspended from the high ceiling, set with what looked ike candles, but the flames did not flicker. Rather, they urned steadily, casting off a soft yellow gleam unlike any-ing Phineas had ever seen before. Vere touched his arm. Come."

Startled, Phineas followed Vere down the aisle. Here and here, groups of five or six gathered in the silence. Their heads vere bent together, their bodies shrouded in long white cloaks. As Phineas passed one such group, he happened to glance own curiously at one of the Mutens. He sucked his breath in orror.

The Muten was blind, its eye sockets empty except for uckered scar tissue. Only the third eye stared up at him. In its ap lay the handless stumps of its primary arms, bound in loodstained bandages.

Instantly, Vere plucked at his sleeve. But Phineas grasped Vere's arm. "What happened to that one? What's wrong with im?"

"Patience, please, Captain. I promise we'll answer all your uestions."

We. The word burned in his brain. Silently, Phineas fol-owed Vere up a short flight of shallow steps past what looked ike a waist-high block of solid marble. Here Vere paused and nclined his head for a short moment. Then he gestured to the eft. "This way." He led Phineas through a door, down a short orridor, and into a small room lined with shelves filled with nore books than Phineas had ever seen in his life. The floor vas covered with a threadbare carpet of intricate design. A mall fire burned in a low grate, and here there were none of hose odd candles. There were no other furnishings, but the oom was scrupulously clean. Although there were no win-lows, the air seemed fresh. Vere reached into a cupboard and withdrew several cushions covered in much-patched fabric. "Here, Captain. Please be comfortable."

He indicated that Phineas should seat himself on one and spread the rest in a circle. As he took a place beside Phineas, another door opened, and a small white-robed figure entered.

"Captain Phineas. Be welcome."

The woman moved into the dim circle of firelight, small and graceful as a reed in a river. The top of her head would barely reach his waist. She turned to face him, throwing back her hood at the same time, and revealed a smooth terra-cotta face, utterly unmarked, and three dark eyes, the one centered above and between the other two. They regarded him with something like amusement.

He had never seen a Muten female before, though he knew that of course there must be such things, but he had never thought that they could be in any way attractive. And yet, this woman most definitely was small and graceful, perfectly miniaturized and proportioned as if she were a doll or a statue.

She inclined her head. "Thank you."

"I beg your pardon?"

"For the compliment."

"I—I don't—"

Oh, yes you do, said a musical voice in his mind.

She arranged herself on one of the cushions opposite Vere. "You are concerned about your King and his sons. They are safe, and asleep."

"Who are you? How did we get here, and when will you let us leave?"

"You may leave in the morning. Believe me, Captain, we are no more happy about your being here than you are."

"Then why are we here?"

"Where else should we have taken you? Or would you have preferred to have been left in the ruins of that place?"

"Ruins? Missiluse Castle is not in ruins."

"It is now," said Vere.

"Why? What happened? What about the King's mother?"

"I'm sorry to have to tell you that she's dead. Ferad did not rrender easily. It was as much as we could do to get you, the ing and his sons out of that place."

"Ferad? That's the Muten who had us in thrall? Is he here?"

"No."

"Dead?"

The woman glanced at Vere. "That's why we need to speak ith you, Captain. Ferad escaped. We could not find his body. 'e will certainly do all that we can to find him, but—"

"But what?"

"We may need your help, although some of us find the ospect as repugnant as you do."

Phineas glanced from the woman to Vere. "And what part you have in this, boy?"

"Prince Vere came to us more than seven years ago. He me seeking knowledge, and it is thanks to him, and the debt e owe to Nydia Farhallen, that we have decided to reveal as uch to you as we will."

"Nydia? What debt? What are you talking about?"

"Captain." Vere touched his arm placatingly. "Please. Lady Lin will tell you as much as she can. Please be patient."

J'Lin looked from one to the other. She drew a deep breath, esitating. "Many years ago, a young woman and her child ame to this place seeking refuge, following a raid upon her ome by one of our northern tribes."

"Nydia had a child? Why would she come here if Mutens estroyed her home?"

"This place is unlike any other, human or Muten. Concealed ere beneath the mountains, we preserve the old learning. We e the children of the Old Magic, and we never turn anyone ke Nydia or her child away."

"I know about Nydia's ability. What about her child? Could see the future as well?"

"No. The boy had another gift. A greater gift. The child of a rescient is always an empath." J'Lin waited. Phineas did not eact. "I see Nydia keeps her secrets. The two abilities are in- xtricably linked in some way we do not fully understand. mpaths are usually female. In all of recorded history, there

have been, so far as we know, only two males. One may be
mere legend. His name was Jesus of Nazareth, and he die
more than two thousand years ago in an obscure corner of th
world before Meriga was a nation. There are those who dis
pute the truth of his existence. But the other was Nydia's son.

"And he died."

She nodded.

"What has this to do with what happened today?"

She held up her hand and leaned forward. "The empath i
the key to controlling the Magic."

"I know very little about the Magic, lady. And I know noth
ing about this—this ability you call empathy."

"The touch of an empath is sufficient to heal the most griev
ous wounds, cure the most virulent disease. Yes," she nodde
when Phineas drew a quick breath and rocked back on hi
heels, "an empath is a rare and precious gift. But that's not a
an empath can do. The nature of the empath is such that sh
participates in the very scheme of existence on another scale
another level, one unreachable by ordinary mortals. Fo
through an empath, the Magic and its consequences can b
channeled, directed, and predicted. We believe that the empat
is an integral part of the overall order of the universe."

Phineas tried to digest this information. He remembere
Nydia's explanation of the Magic, which Abelard had relate
to him so long ago. "I know that the Old Magic is dangerous
because it is not possible to predict the reactions to its use. Bu
what is this overall order? How do you know what it is?"

It was J'Lin who sighed. He noticed for the first time tha
there was a lid above the third eye, and it slid down so that, i
the dim light, it was easy to think that the woman before hin
was human, that the dimple in her forehead was only a trick o
the light. "Do the words 'fractals,' 'phase transitions,' 'strang
attractors' mean anything to you? I see they do not. In the la
ter days of Old Meriga, before the Armageddon, men—hu
mans—made discoveries which challenged everything eve
known or thought about the nature of the universe. They aske
questions so fundamental that they were nearly unanswerabl

ecause they were so intrinsic to the understanding of the way
e world worked. Their names are lost for the most part—
eep in the mists of time and the wreckage of the Armaged-
on, but a few still resonate down the centuries: names like
instein, Mandelbrot—a few others. What they found, what
ey discovered, were the intrinsic patterns of the universe.

"It is said that Mandelbrot discovered the face of God. He
ound patterns in chaos, chaos in order, and everything
anged.

"Even the sciences changed, as physics and mathematics
nd biology, which had all once been separate disciplines,
ombined in new ways—until all the boundaries were blurred.
nd then the boundaries between philosophy and theology
urred as well."

"Lady," Phineas shook his head, "I don't understand what
ou're talking about."

"Have you ever looked at the stars, Captain? They appear
ndom, do they not, sprinkled across the heaven like so many
rains of sand? But they are not random. In their very random-
ess is an order. A mathematician once wrote that if he had a
ver large enough, and a place to stand, he could move the
arth. If you had a place to stand, Captain, you would see the
attern in the universe—the largest and the grandest of all de-
igns. You would see what we call the axletree of Heaven."

"So there is an underlying order even where we perceive
haos—is that it?"

"The underlying pattern extends into places which we can-
ot necessarily perceive because we stand too close. It is not
ust a matter of pattern, but of scale. The patterns, the order,
ie rationale, as it were, extends into the very mind and will of
ian—human or Muten."

"Abelard said that the Old Magic was the manipulation of
ie material world."

"Yes, that's correct. But our minds are not sufficient to
omprehend the intrinsic order of it all. We, too, exist as tiny
ranches, buds, on the axletree. Knowledge beyond mortal

knowing would be required to comprehend it all. The contemplation of it has driven men mad."

"The Magic," said Phineas slowly, "is dangerous because it interferes with the workings of an order which is beyond the comprehension of those who use it. But the empath understands the order, inherently, and so, if an empath uses the Magic, the consequences can be—"

J'lin nodded. "The empath does not even need to use the Magic herself. If an empath touched me while I worked the Magic, the empath would, by her very nature, correct any imbalance even as it occurred, and the reaction would be harmless, perhaps even beneficial."

"So if someone wanted to use the Magic, an empath would be very useful."

"More than useful."

Phineas exchanged a glance with Vere. "What happened to Nydia's child?"

There was a silence. "He was killed." Vere said finally.

"By whom?"

Vere looked at J'lin. "By the same one who tried to kill you, Captain." Her voice was strained, as though the words were dragged out of her unwilling.

"How?"

"Empathy does not reveal itself until after puberty. Ferad, using the Magic as it is never meant to be used, attempted to force the boy into an early maturation, and in the process, the child died. He was only ten years old. And then, he attempted to force Nydia to bear another child."

"That's when she left you and made her way to the King."

J'lin nodded.

"Who is this Ferad?"

"Ferad was one of our students here. One of the best."

"So what happened? Why did he turn against you?"

"Everyone who comes here is required to take certain vows to ensure that we will be protected. And those who attain the knowledge of the Old Magic are required to make certain sacrifices in order that the secrets are kept."

Phineas looked at Vere once more, and then back at the uten woman. "What kinds of sacrifices?"

"One must sacrifice one's eyes, one's hands, and one's ngue."

"Why?" Phineas whispered, appalled at the barbarity.

"There are two reasons. By the time one attains the level of astery required to understand, one's eyes and hands and ngue are largely extraneous. One communicates almost ex-usively with the mind. The second reason is to safeguard e secrets of the Old Magic. When the first priests came, ter the Armageddon, to try to discover if we were the source the devastation, they could not discover the secrets, for ose who knew them could not be communicated with in any ay they understood. And those who could speak or write ew nothing, or at least nothing which was secret. But Ferad fused to submit. After he left here, he made his way eventu-ly to Agara Onrada in Missiluse—"

"Where he proceeded to try to teach her to use the Magic?"

"I don't know whether he did or not. And that is immaterial ow, since Agara is dead. Ferad would not have needed her lp in any way—he was as skilled as the best of our Pr'fes-rs."

"So why would he have agreed to help Agara?"

"Once Abelard was removed from the throne, Ferad would ve had access once more to Nydia Farhallen."

"And any child she bears would have this ability?"

"Every child."

"And Ferad has escaped."

"Yes. We believe he would have headed into the deep sert, into the region you call Dlas-for 'Torth ."

"There's nothing there; it's a wasteland."

"There's plenty down there, if you know where to look," id Vere.

"Why don't you tell all this to the King?"

"Would the King listen?"

Phineas met her dark eyes. He had no answer, for he knew

that if Abelard had any inkling of this information, he was likely to order every Muten in Meriga put to death on sight.

"Captain." Vere touched his arm hesitantly. "There is the matter of my brothers."

"What about them?" Something in Vere's voice made him feel as though he stood in the dark on the edge of a great precipice.

"Ferad—he did teach them something. I could feel it, not so much in Alex, but in Amanander—"

"What are you trying to say, Vere? That your brothers are a threat to the kingdom?"

"They were always a threat, Captain," answered the Muten woman. "But Ferad has fed them with his own twisted desires."

"So Abelard must not name either one as his heir?"

"Abelard Ridenau has set himself upon a path of his own choosing. We dare not interfere, for we believe that behind and above and beyond the workings of men is the Eternal Will of the Power which created this axletree of Heaven and continually works to keep its form."

"So you won't interfere? While this Muten does whatever he pleases—"

"I didn't say that. We will do everything we can to find him, but that is only part of the problem. Amanander Ridenau has tasted power—power even beyond his father's control—and power, once known, is seldom willingly surrendered."

Someone else had said that to him, long ago. "What am I to do?"

"As best you can, you must guide the King. We wanted you to be aware of the dangers—the system will achieve equilibrium eventually. But before that happens, the potential exists for untold suffering on every scale."

"Ferad must be found."

"Yes, Captain. But that is not your problem."

"And Amanander must be controlled."

"Yes."

"And Abelard . . ." His voice trailed off. Who had ever controlled Abelard?

"Abelard has retrieved Nydia's books and will return them to her."

"Why don't you keep them? Prevent him from ever enabling her to use them?"

"Steal them?" J'lin sounded shocked. "They were not given to us of Nydia's free will. The books are hers—she must choose what she will do with them. You truly do not understand, do you, Captain? The key to this is the will—"

"No, you don't understand," interrupted Phineas. "Nydia is pledge bound to Abelard. She swore to use whatever means at her disposal to uphold the King—and his kingdom—in return for his protection. And he has upheld his side of the pledge. If she has the means to use the Magic now, there's nothing I or anyone else can do to stop Abelard from commanding her to use it. Abelard and I have quarreled—I doubt he will ever listen to me again. Tonight, in Eldred's castle, I nearly killed him. I violated every oath and raised my hand against my King. I fully expect him to send me away when we return to Ahga."

J'lin shook her head sadly. "You are not entirely to blame for that. You were in the grip of Ferad's Magic. He took feelings that you, under ordinary circumstances, control with the strength of your own will and used the Magic and his will to turn them against you. No, Captain. Abelard will not dismiss you. Surely you know that. You are more than a friend to Abelard Ridenau—the people of Old Meriga might have called you his conscience."

Phineas got to his feet. "I am not certain I want to be Abelard's conscience."

"And what of your vows, Captain? Will he release you from your Pledge of Allegiance?"

Phineas looked at the fire. "I hoped that he would. By raising my sword against the King, I have violated my own pledge. He is no longer bound to me by any obligation."

"Captain, you must try to understand. You have a choice—

Nydia has a choice—Abelard has a choice. You may choose to turn your back upon the King and the country. But you will live with the consequences of whatever you do."

"Is that a curse?"

"Curses are for children, who cannot accept responsibility for the consequences of their own actions. It is easier to say that a curse is responsible for what happens to one in life than to accept that it is one's own choices which bring one to a certain point. If you decide to stay and serve the King—if Nydia agrees to use the Magic—if Abelard decides to try to compel her—I cannot tell you what will happen." J'lin shook her head. "All I can tell you is that you, too, have played a part in this. So you, too, are responsible for the ultimate outcome, no matter what you should choose to do."

"Damned if I do, and damned if I don't, eh?"

"I don't believe any of us are damned at all." She rose to her feet with a graceful gesture. "We, too, bear a responsibility for the outcome of this. We are to blame for the death of Nydia's child—not directly, perhaps, but indirectly. We took him, and buried him beneath the tree in Arkan—the Axletree of Meriga."

"Why do you call it that?"

"It does not die, for its roots are nourished by the bodies of the empaths buried beneath it. That's where all the empaths in Meriga are buried when they die."

"That's why you sent Nydia that leaf."

"It was all we could do."

"What about Ferad? What will you do if you find him?"

"Punish him."

"Put him to death?"

"We don't kill—it's against our vows."

"And if you don't find him?"

"Then we shall pray, Captain, that the Power which orders the universe keeps us all in His care. Because this is only the beginning."

She raised her hand in a gesture of blessing and disappeared through the door she had entered, leaving Phineas staring into the dying fire.

Chapter Thirty-Five

*N*ydia always knew when Abelard had come. Even after nearly eight years, it seemed there was an electricity to his presence, as though the very air crackled with potency and expectation. She heard shouts from the watchtowers go up in the middle of the bright summer morning, and wiped her dirty hands on her apron.

She and Liss were transplanting roses, which had been nurtured in the sunny glass enclosure over the winter. Now, finally, the weather was mild enough that the gardener said they might be moved. The central gardens of Minnis were magnificent—the buildings had been built around them so that all the interior rooms looked out, or opened onto, the gardens. The old trees, willows and oaks and elms, soared higher than the walls, and the wide planed paths of gravel meandered through carefully tended beds of flowers and sweet-scented herbs. In the very center, the gardens opened out into a grassy court, where the children played on sunny days, where Nydia and her women sat and sewed.

It was easy to forget that there was another court—for Minnis was a world unto itself. In the summer, Abelard stayed for days at a time when he was not away campaigning, and in the autumn, in early Tember when the days were right for hunting, for two and sometimes three weeks.

There had been many changes in the world, thought Nydia as she gathered up her gloves and her tools, the small rakes and trowels. Tavia married, Vere gone, Phillip married to

Jarone of Nourk's daughter, the twins with their grandmother in the south.

But there was still Jesselyn, who at twelve was a gravely beautiful child, with long dark curls and blue eyes like her father's. And there was Reginald, who had grown from a chubby baby into a chunky seven-year-old, stolid and still, thought Nydia privately, the least attractive of all Abelard's children.

Liss called across the sun-dappled lawn for the children to gather their balls and hoops and bats, and Nydia paused to watch them: Jesselyn, moving with graceful dignity, as befitted her years; Reginald, with his slow deliberate stride, wholly focused on the task at hand; the three others, who were children of her ladies, their fathers men in the regiment of the King's Guard garrisoned at Minnis.

As she watched, she saw Jesselyn, a bright smile lighting her tanned face. "Dad!"

Nydia turned, and her heart leapt. Framed in the doorway that led into the high-ceilinged hall stood the King in travel-stained garments.

He started down the steps toward her, a broad smile on his face, a canvas pack slung over one shoulder. He looked badly in need of a bath and very tired, she thought with sudden concern. More than tired—for the first time since she had known Abelard, he looked older than his age.

He was across the graveled paths in a few long strides, and he crushed her against his chest with one arm while he carefully set the canvas pack gently on the stone bench.

She wrapped her arms around his neck with a little cry of welcome, and his lips found hers. They stood, oblivious to the others, until Reginald roused him with an insistent: "Dad!"

He looked down at his youngest son, swung the heavy child up in his arms with an effort, and gently cuffed him on the head. "You've grown, my boy. Soon I'll expect you to carry me about, eh?"

"Dad, I can use the sword you left for me."

"Can you? Well, perhaps after I've rested, you'll give me a [m]atch, if you promise to be easy on your old King?"

The child's face creased with a shy smile, and he looked al[m]ost appealing, thought Nydia, his features without their usual [su]llen set.

The welcome lasted a few more minutes as Abelard teased [an]d complimented Jesselyn and had a few words with Liss. [Th]en he made a quick gesture of dismissal. "Away, now, all of [yo]u. We'll see each other at dinner. I must wash and rest. [T]ruly, lady, this last trip—I begin to feel my age. It's time, I [th]ink, I left this campaigning to the young ones and stay warm [an]d grow fat by my hearth."

As the others scurried away, Nydia looked up at him with con[ce]rn. Beneath his teasing tones, she thought she detected a weari[ne]ss deeper than simply his return from an arduous campaign.

"You sound tired," she said, and waited.

"I am tired, lady," he answered with a heavy sigh. "Let me [lo]ok at you." He held her at arm's length. "I never tire of look[in]g at you, you know that?"

She nodded happily.

"And when I must leave you, I carry your face before me [li]ke a banner in my mind," he went on. "This cannot be a [ha]ppy existence for you here at Minnis."

He hooked his thumbs in his belt and turned away.

"Abelard, what are you talking about? Minnis is the most [b]eautiful place in the world, you know that. And while I [w]ould rather be with you all the time, perhaps it is better this [w]ay—at least you don't tire of me."

"I will never tire of you," he said with sudden passion. "I [br]ought you a present."

"What sort of present?"

"Look in the pack—gently."

She seized the pack, surprised by the weight, and when she [re]alized what it contained, she sank down on the bench, [st]unned. "Abelard, my books. You found my books."

He nodded.

"Where? How did you ever?"

"My mother had them—took them with her when she left Ahga. She had them all these years in Missiluse."

"But why? What did she hope to do with them? I thought she'd given them over to the Bishop."

"No," he said, shaking his head and sounding wearier than ever. "No, she didn't."

"But, I don't understand—"

"Nydia." He cut her off gently but firmly. "We must talk."

Something about the intensity of the look on his face made her pause. "Shall we go in?"

"Yes. I'd like a bath and something to eat, and then we need to talk."

He took the pack out of her arms and gestured for her to precede him. Puzzled, and a little alarmed, Nydia gave the orders for a bath and food, and while Abelard was bathing, oversaw the laying out of fresh clothes for him.

He walked into the bedroom they shared when he was in residence at Minnis still naked, his hair damp, his face above his beard pink.

"Come here," he said, holding out his hand to her.

She went to him and he drew her close, gathering her in his arms, bending her back to nuzzle her throat. "I missed you so much," he murmured, and he guided her hand down to his pulsing erection. She pressed the hot length of it against his belly and he groaned, low in her ear.

"I thought you wanted to talk," she teased. And then she said nothing else for quite a long time.

The late afternoon shadows had fallen long across the bed when Abelard finally opened his eyes. Nydia looked up from the table near the wide windows overlooking the gardens. He books were spread before her, carefully and lovingly, and she smiled when she saw him looking at her.

"Feel better?"

He sat up, stretched and yawned. "I can't remember the last night I spent in a real bed."

"You didn't stop at Ahga?"

"No. I sent Phineas there with the twins, but I came straight in to you. I brought Aman and Alex north with me—it's one of the things we need to talk about."

She waited. He got out of bed, reached for his clothes where they had fallen in a heap to the floor, and began to dress. "My mother's dead," he said without ceremony.

She tried to keep her face carefully neutral.

"Yes, I'm not sorry either. That's how I got your books back. But—" He pulled the tunic over his head, tugged at the lacings.

"What happened down there?"

He told her briefly what had happened in Eldred's castle. "I'm still not sure how we got out of there . . . one moment I was fighting Phineas while that thing looked on, and the next, it seemed we found ourselves on the road to Ithan with fresh horses and provisions for the trip. But, now—Nydia, I need your help. I haven't asked for your help in years, even though it seems clear that you were right about Melisande—she's barren. I must have an heir. Unless you help me, I have no choice but to leave the realm to Amanander. He's the only one the Congress would accept. His mother was a noblewoman, and all the rest of my sons were born of serving women. That—that Muten got to him, somehow, started to teach him the Magic. There's something about him—I can't explain it, but I don't want to make him my heir unless I have absolutely no other choice."

She swallowed hard, clutched at the closest book. "What do you want me to do?"

"Use the Magic so that Melisande conceives a son."

She shut her eyes, drew a deep breath. "I can't."

"Can't or won't?"

"You don't understand what you ask. When I told you that no son of yours would ever reign in Ahga, I meant it. I do not see how the future would be changed if Melisande bore you a son."

"You're jealous."

The accusation hit her like an icy blast. "What?"

"That's why you won't help me. You don't want Melisande to bear my son—"

"That's why you brought these books back, isn't it?" She rose to her feet, nearly sputtering with anger. "It wasn't to please me, or make me happy, it was so I'd use the Magic for your own purposes—"

"To uphold the kingdom and the King, lady. Have you forgotten the words you swore to me?"

"And if the ultimate result would be to destroy the kingdom, as long as your purposes were served it wouldn't matter, would it? You can't see further than the end of your own nose—and you told me your father lacked vision. You don't want to do what's best for the country, you want to do what's best for yourself."

"There must be an heir," he said through tight lips.

"And what's to say he must be your son?" she shot back at him. "What about Tavia's husband?"

"What about him? He's not suited to rule the whole country. By what right would he rule?"

"By the same right you do," she snapped. "By right of law, by will of Congress. Do you think you're above the law?"

His eyes narrowed and a vein throbbed in his forehead. His eyes were twin slits of icy blue, cold and burning at the same time. "I am the law in Meriga."

She fell back into her chair. "I see. And so whatever you will, must be."

He nodded.

"When I told you on your wedding night that no son of yours would ever reign in Ahga, it was not jealousy or revenge. I told you the truth. What you don't understand is that nothing has changed. You have made no decisions, no new choices which would allow a son of yours to rule. I see what you mean to do—you think if Melisande has a son, then the country will rally around him and the Congress fall in line behind him. But you forget the others—and most especially Amanander."

"I'll send him away."

"Where? Where will you send him that he will never be a

hreat? Or will you kill him? Will you kill your own son? Do you hink the others—Alexander, Brand, Philip—will understand hat? And if he has tasted the Magic and gains the upper hand—" She broke off, shook her head, and bit her lip. "Abelard, don't ou understand? You made a choice that day in Vada—a choice vhich resonates across the years like the echo of a bell across a nountain. No matter where you go, or how you hope to hide, here is no way you can escape the results of what you've done."

"I don't believe that."

"I know. You aren't the kind of man to accept defeat. Even y your own hand."

"I am not defeated." He slammed a fist against the bedpost and the whole frame shuddered. "Damn it, there must be a vay. I want my blood to continue on the throne of Meriga. I vas the one who kept this realm together—I'm the one who ajoles and orders and fights to maintain the peace. Who do hey all come crawling to when the Harleys raid, or the Mutens threaten? Who sends supplies in times of famine, or animals in times of blight? I will not let the Ridenau Kings die with me. My blood will go on—and all Meriga with it."

She sat back, very still, almost afraid to move or call atten- ion to herself.

"And you swore an oath. An oath to uphold the kingdom and the King by whatever means at your disposal. Whatever means. Do you recall it?"

She looked out the window. The shadows were long across he lawns; the grass was dark, even the trees were deep in shadow. "Yes," she whispered.

"I have upheld my part of the pledge, have I not? Even when you left me, went running halfway across the country because I'd done what seemed right at the time, I made sure you were safe, protected. I banished my mother and built this fortress—all for you, lady. No one else. My relationship with the Bishop of Ahga is strained to this day, did you know that? Because of you. But I have honored my pledge. I have never broken my word—"

"Abelard, I've explained this to you before."

"Then explain it again."

"It is not just the question of whether or not there's a son to succeed you. To use the Magic that way would bring the risk of dire consequences, life-threatening consequences. I have no way of knowing or predicting what would happen were I to do such a thing as call a life into existence, where no life should exist. What if you died? The heir would be an infant— Abelard, the end of the realm would be assured. Meriga would indeed break up into factions, for who would be strong enough to hold it together?"

He moved around the bed slowly, warily, as though he did not quite trust himself to approach her. "You said no son of mine would ever reign in Ahga."

"No son. Not ever."

"Then what about a daughter?"

"You'd leave it to Tavia?"

"No. Because then her husband's family would have it— and then the bloodline and the name would be lost."

"Jesselyn?"

"The Congress would never accept a daughter known to be mine—not when there are so many sons."

"No." She was wary now, suspicious of his tone.

"But if there were a son believed to be mine—what about the Queen's son? Is it possible a son of the Queen could reign? As long as he weren't mine."

She shook her head, confused. "I don't understand you. How could the Queen—"

"Answer me. If the Queen had a son, by another man—"

"But as long as you've not named your heir, who—how—?"

"Never mind. If the Queen had a son by another man, yet the child was thought to be mine, and so was accepted as the heir of Meriga by the Congress, and grew up and married my daughter—"

"But if everyone thought this boy was your son, it would look like incest if he were to marry one of your daughters—"

"Unless no one knew that I had this daughter."

"You talk madness."

"Do I?" In the gloom, his teeth were very white. "Think

about it. The Queen's son—everyone would believe he was mine."

"What about the boy's father? Would he keep silent about his part in this scheme?"

"The right man would."

"Who is there who would consent to such a thing—father a child and never be able to acknowledge—"

"Phineas."

"Phineas? You'd use him like that?"

"You forget, lady, he took an oath very similar to yours, and he's never flinched or backed away from anything ever asked of him."

The retort stung, and she clenched her hands together. "So this boy would grow up to be the King of Meriga?"

"Well, he wouldn't be my son. He could reign in Ahga, and if he married my daughter, then both the bloodline and the throne would pass to my grandson. And so any consequence, or any result of any choice I may have made, will be circumvented."

"And which daughter will he marry?"

He looked at her, and in the shadows she saw little but his eyes. "Ours."

"We have no daughter."

Abelard leaned toward her, and involuntarily she shrank back. "Yet."

"You'd put all of us—you, me, Phineas, and Melisande into utter danger. This idea is insane. Think, Abelard. You want to control something that no one man should ever have any control over. Just because something can be done doesn't mean it ought to be. The men of old Meriga learned that to their detriment."

"But this is the only way. Isn't it? Admit it. Tell me you don't see this nation dissolving into chaos after my death, splintering into a hundred pieces—you know the history of this country as well as I do. What was Meriga like before my grandfather unified the estates into a single realm? There were pockets of peace and prosperity in places fortunate enough to be surrounded by mountains or water, but how many countless thousands suffered and died? The Harleys ran free in Arkan, the Senadors quarreled among themselves—tell me Meriga is not better off under the Ridenau Kings, and I'll never ask another thing of you again."

She was silent. She got up, felt for the tinder and the flint, and lighted the candles. "You know I cannot say that."

"And as for the Magic, and the consequences—I don't expect to die in my bed. I never did. I'll accept the risks and take the chance that Meriga might be preserved for our children and their children, and theirs. What do you say?"

She turned her back and gazed out the window. A voice echoed in her mind, the voice of the oldest among the Muten Pr'fessors: *When the will of men is turned upon the axletree of Heaven, it is like a great ax swinging carelessly through the branches of a great tree. Who knows what the blade will sever? Who knows what leaf, what branch, what twig will fall? Who can calculate the cost?*

She looked back at the King. "There's something you must know about me. About any daughter that I bear." Haltingly, she told him about the inevitable nature of the child she would bear and watched a kind of light dawn on his face as she spoke.

"That's amazing," he said with awe.

"Abelard, don't you understand? This child would be in as much danger as I am, more even, because the nature of the empath is so magnetic. People are drawn to empaths, and they to others. They feel the pain, sense the wounds everyone carries. It's almost impossible for an empath to hide her ability. Even when they are very careful and don't heal, others are drawn to them. There's a kind of grace that comes just from being in one's presence—a kind of peace. And besides, if I bear a child, everyone will assume that child is yours as well."

He was silent.

"And the Muten—the one in Missiluse. I know that Muten—he will pursue this child by any means at his disposal. How will you keep us safe from him?"

"Then you must leave here." He spoke slowly. "As much as
-you must leave."

"And go where?"

He walked to the window and looked out to where night had
llen over the tops of the trees. A few stars flickered in the
mmer sky, and a full moon hung high above the forest. "A
w hours' ride from here, there's a tower—it's old, older than
hga, but the foundations are sound. I used to explore it when
was a boy. I'll send you there. The garrison here at Minnis
ill protect it, and—"

"Everyone will think that my child is yours."

"Then we'll let them think you've borne another's child.
nd that's why I sent you away."

"So you are prepared to sacrifice me and our happiness, our
e together—" She broke off.

"I will keep you safe. I will honor the pledge between us,
t—"

"You are the King, first." She finished for him. So he would
deed sacrifice everything they had or might have had to-
ther for the sake of his kingdom.

His expression was unreadable, but he dropped his gaze and
ould not look up. "Tell me what you see in the future."

She opened her mouth to protest that the choice to obey and
de to his demands had yet to be decided, but the sight she
w so clearly over his shoulder stopped the words in her
outh, and she knew that she had already made her choice.

She stared dully ahead. "I see war, and death, and destruc-
on. I see Meriga racked and bleeding—I see a great army rise
p and sweep Meriga before it like a dry leaf in a wind. And I
e a boy, a man, who rules from Ahga, and he does not have
our face." She shook her head. "I can see no more than that."

"Would he marry my daughter?" asked the King eagerly.

"That will be his choice to make. You cannot compel the
ature."

"But I can influence it."

"Oh, yes," she echoed flatly. "Yes, you can do that."

Chapter Thirty-Six

*T*he messenger found Phineas in the practice yard. Tl
midday sun was hot across his shoulders, and he was glad f
an excuse to stop and get into the shade. He broke open tl
seals, scanned the message quickly, and glanced up at tl
messenger.

"Have you any idea why I am requested to join the King?"

"No, sir. He only instructed me to give you the message."

"What's that other?" Phineas pointed to a sealed packet
the messenger's pack.

"This is for the Queen, sir. I believe she is requested to jo
him, as well."

The shock showed plainly on Phineas's face. "I'll deliver i
messenger."

"As you say, sir." The messenger handed him the pack
and saluted.

"Dismissed," said Phineas absently. He fingered the parcl
ment wonderingly. Abelard had never, in nearly eight year
sent Melisande a message even inquiring as to her healtl
What now?

He looked across the yard, where the weaponsmaster wa
busy with a few of the younger guards. He beckoned to th
nearest soldier and handed him the sword he had been usin
for practice. "Take this back to Peddy and tell the captain
shall require an escort of perhaps ten men, as well as prov
sions for a night and a day's journey."

"Yes, sir. Has there been trouble, Captain?"

"Trouble? No, no. I go to take the Queen to Minnis."

Without waiting for more discussion, he went to find the
`een.

Melisande was sewing with her ladies in a sunny corner of
hall when Phineas found her. He bowed, careful to show
` the respect her rank demanded, even if her husband did
`. When she looked up, surprised to see him at that hour of
day, he gestured to the packets in his hand. "May I speak
`th you alone, Lady Queen? There's a message for you from
` King."

The surprise was evident on the faces of all the women.
`elisande caught her breath. "No trouble, I hope, Captain?"

"May we speak privately, Lady Queen?"

She handed her needlework to the nearest of her ladies and
stured toward a private audience room off the main hall.
`hen they were alone, he handed her the message from the
`ng and waited silently while she read it.

"Do you know what this says?"

"I received a summons to Minnis, Lady Queen. I am to
`ve within the hour. He expects me to arrive tomorrow by
`sk."

"He wants me there, too." She folded the parchment and
`oked up at Phineas nervously. "What does he want?"

"He doesn't say?"

"Only that he expects me to be there for dinner tomorrow.
`ineas, what does he want?"

Phineas shrugged. "I have no idea."

"I'd better go and ask my woman to pack a few things for
`e."

"I have already ordered an escort."

"Very well. I shall be ready to leave as soon as possible."

He nodded and watched her hurry off. He smoothed out the
`rchment, stared at the King's unmistakable black scrawl.
`he message was penned by Abelard himself—that alone was
`usual. What was of such urgency that the King would not
`ll for a scribe, write it himself and seal it, not even in a
`ooden message tube, but only hand it to a messenger?

A memory of J'Lin, the Muten woman, surfaced. "Your

part in this is not yet finished," she had said. What part was h
expected to play? he wondered. Nydia now had the books, h
knew, and was able to work the Old Magic, as she had bee
unable to for seven years. Had Abelard convinced her to use
so that Melisande at last would conceive a son? That seeme
the likeliest. Yet Nydia had sworn never to use the Magic—h
had heard her tell the King the Magic was dangerous and mu
never be used.

Yet what would that matter to Abelard? a tired voice aske
in his mind. And the oath she had sworn to the King, th
pledge which bound them both, did it not say by whateve
means at their disposal? Abelard was not the sort of man t
overlook that.

Phineas crumpled the parchment savagely and threw it i
the hearth. He stalked away to the stableyard to see that th
preparations were being made. As he crossed the hall, he m
Amanander coming in from the practice yard. Although h
and Alexander were identical, there was a furtive quality abou
Amanander that made it easy for Phineas to tell them apart.

"My father has summoned you to Minnis, Captai
Phineas?" asked the Prince without preamble.

"That's correct."

"And he has bid you bring the Queen?"

"Yes, Highness. If you'll excuse me, I must see to th
arrangements."

"Why? What's he want with her?"

Phineas paused. The boy was still too young to truly di
semble, he thought, being yet transparent. "She is his wif
There is nothing untoward about a man desiring the compar
of his wife, is there?"

"Not under ordinary circumstances," agreed Amanande
He threw a shock of black hair back from his brow. "But n
father has never desired her company, has he?"

"It is not for me to speculate upon the King's desires whe
the Queen is concerned, Highness. Nor for you, either, Hig
ness." His voice was bland, but his eyes met Amanander
without fear. You don't frighten me, little Prince, he wanted

y, and when you play games with me, you'll play by my
les.

The Prince dropped his eyes and stepped aside. "I mustn't
ep you, Captain. Please convey my greetings to my father,
d tell him I wish him a pleasant interlude."

Phineas bowed silently and left Amanander standing in the
ll. As he strode from the hall, he wondered briefly why he
lt as though he had escaped.

Melisande said little on the road to Minnis. She bore herself
iffly on her little gray mare. Phineas saw her hands shake on
e reins, and he realized abruptly she was very much afraid.

He managed to ride over to her and guided her somewhat
ead of the other riders, so that they had some measure of
ivacy. "Lady Queen," he murmured so softly that she alone
ard him.

She started on her saddle and the mare shied.

"Forgive me for interrupting your thoughts."

"Phineas," she said without any attempt at ceremony, "I'm
raid. What does he want with me? Why does he summon me
ere, of all places? Does he intend to flaunt his witch before
e? Why? I have endured years of humiliation at his hands—
hat else does he want from me? What else can I possibly
ive him?"

"I don't know, Lady Queen."

"I think you do know. You've been very quiet this whole
ourney, and you've got that closed-off look on your face, as
ough you're afraid someone might hear your thoughts. What
 it? Please tell me. Do you—" She hesitated, bit her lip, and
ooked around to see whether anyone else was close enough to
ear. "Do you think he intends to kill me?"

Phineas was forced to utter a laugh of disbelief. "No, my
ear lady, I don't think he intends to kill you."

"I—I thought perhaps, since he had ordered you to attend
e and bring these guards, perhaps he intended to—to do
way with me, and perhaps make his witch Queen. I know he
oves her, and I know she's very beautiful."

Phineas stared at the road ahead. "No more so than you, Melisande." He did not look at her, and he kept his voice low. "When you meet the King, show no fear. Remember who you are, and I'll be with you. I will never let any harm come to you, I swear it."

"Even if he orders you?"

"Even if he orders me." He looked at her, and his gray eyes met her hazel ones with quiet conviction. "You were brave once, lady. You faced ten ruffians for the sake of one young boy, and you faced Abelard Ridenau himself when your father was threatened."

"That seems like it was a very long time ago." She turned away as her eyes filled with sudden tears.

"It was not so very long ago."

"I am not that girl."

"Yes, you are." The intensity in his voice made her turn to look at him. "For it was that which made me love you, and I love you still."

"Do you mean that?" she whispered.

"Yes." And in that one quiet word, he poured all the feeling he had kept to himself for so long, and Melisande smiled for the first time that day.

They arrived at the high walls of Minnis Saul near dusk, as the long shadows fell across the walls. Torches lit on the gates told them they were expected, and Phineas was not surprised to see Abelard waiting for them in the hall.

Nydia was nowhere to be seen. He cast a quick look around the hall as he bent his knee before the King. Abelard nodded a greeting and signaled to a woman standing near the dais. "See to the Queen." He nodded to Melisande, barely looking at her, as though he would prefer to forget she had ever arrived.

When the women had gone, Phineas faced the King. "What's all this about, Abelard?"

The hall was deserted, except for a guard or two by the entrances and a scullery boy sweeping at the other end. Abelard glanced around. "Let's find another place to talk."

"Why?"

"Because what I have to say concerns only you."

"What about the Queen?"

"I'll come to that."

"Abelard, if you in any way intend to harm her—"

The King stared at Phineas, a bitter smile twisting the corners of his mouth. "You don't think very much of me these days, do you? Come out into the garden. It's a beautiful night, isn't it?"

Warily, Phineas followed the King. He caught his breath at the sight of the wide lawn, the ancient trees, and the flowers, whose scents rose sweet and heady in the night air. The dew had not yet fallen, but a cool breeze rustled the leafy branches. Abelard led the way to a secluded bench, where a flagon of wine waited beside two goblets. "Please." He indicated that Phineas should sit. "Wine?"

Phineas wanted to refuse, but he was thirsty, so he nodded grudgingly. Abelard poured the wine, and Phineas listened to the sound of it splash into the goblets over the gentle whine of summer insects. He waited.

"I need your help."

Phineas sipped his wine.

"You know that Melisande is barren."

He nodded.

"Nydia has agreed to use the Magic so that Melisande will conceive."

Phineas set the goblet down deliberately. "Has she?"

"She has." The King's voice was cold.

"Of her own volition?"

"That does not concern you."

"Then what does concern me? Why am I here? Surely my part in this is finished."

"No. Melisande cannot bear my son, for no son of mine can reign in Meriga without a civil war, or worse. Nydia will use the Magic, but it must be your son she conceives."

Phineas picked up the goblet, set it down, and watched the

wine swirl in the depths. "You want me to lie with the Queen and get a child—"

"Not any child. A son. A son who will be King of Meriga when I am dead. Think of it, man. Your son will reign in Meriga after me, when we are both gone."

"What makes you think the Queen will have me?"

"Do you think I'm a fool? I can see how you look at her, how your face changes at the mention of her name. I knew in Vada there was something between the two of you; come, admit it. She'll have you, and you'll have her—with my blessing."

"So in exchange for my seed, you offer me a night with the woman I love?"

Abelard's face was unreadable. "I do."

"The woman who is your wife. The woman who swore fidelity to you—"

"The woman I've been unfaithful to for nearly eight years. I doubt she'll take her vow as seriously as you seem to."

"And what's in this for you, Abelard?"

"Isn't it obvious? I get a son."

"You may lack for many things, Lord King, but sons aren't one of them. There's something about this you haven't told me. Yet."

"There's nothing else to tell."

"Yes, there is. I don't believe you'll pass the throne of Meriga on to the get of a stablehand's son. So what is it? What else do you plan to do with my son?"

"He will marry my daughter."

"Which daughter? Everyone will think—"

"Nydia's daughter."

Phineas sat back. J'Lin's gentle face swam before his. He remembered all she had said. "Nydia's daughter. Conceived at the same time as this son, I take it?"

Abelard nodded.

"And what about the consequences? Don't you realize there's bound to be repercussions of some kind? Amanander—"

"Amanander is bound to rise to take the throne anyway. sn't he? But at least the others will fall in line—and the Congress. If this boy has the support of the Congress, and the Army, and the Guard, what difference does it make if Amanander tries to seize the throne? Who would support him? He cannot stand alone."

"What if this son won't marry your daughter?"

"He must. We'll do all we can to see that he does."

Phineas heard the "we," rebelled for one instant, and thought of J'Lin once more.

"Do you agree?"

What choice is there? he thought bitterly as he drained the wine to its dregs. Is there always a choice? he wondered. A choice between nothing and nothing. Out of simplicity arises chaos, out of chaos, order, and who has seen the shape of Heaven's axletree? J'Lin's words echoed softly through his mind like a summer wind. He squared his shoulders and looked at the King. "Yes," he answered finally, "I do."

Chapter Thirty-Seven

A full moon hung high in the late summer sky like
bloated orange lantern, its light filtered through a haze o
clouds. Phineas turned away from the window, loosened th
lacings of his shirt. Sweat trickled down his back between hi
shoulder blades. The night was windless, only the insect
whined in the summer heat. He threw himself in a chair an
waited for the sand to slip through the hourglass on the man
tel.

Tonight was the night. Abelard had whispered it at dinner
leaning close so no one else could hear. But Melisande ha
overheard, of that he was certain. She started, flushed, the
turned pale. He wondered what, if anything, Abelard had tol
her.

He had not seen Melisande, except from a distance or a
dinner, when the conversation was perforce stilted and forced
Nydia had forbidden close contact—the need must be grea
she had said, and so he had absented himself as much as possi
ble, spending the days crashing through the green forest like
madman, ostensibly at the hunt, spending his nights in a grow
ing fever of anticipation. He had not wanted to admit to him
self his need, his growing desire, yet every time he caught
glimpse of the Queen, or sat beside her at dinner, the sight an
sound and smell of her incited his senses, made his puls
pound and his mind fill with heady dreams of what she woul
feel like, taste like, smell like in his arms. Would she sig
when he entered her? Or would she cry out? Would she gri

is hips to hers, or raise her arms above her head in wild aban-
on?

The delay was necessary, said Abelard, not only to rouse
he men to a fever pitch, but to allow Nydia to bring the
omen to the point of readiness. There had been the charge of
Magic all through the heavy air, like an incipient energy just
eneath the surface. He wondered if Melisande had felt it
orking upon her, wondered if the way she dropped her eyes
nd blushed when she felt his eyes on her was a result of the
elentless force of the Magic, coaxing the tides of her body
nto fullness, warming and softening even as the warm spring
ain acted upon the fertile earth.

Desire thrummed through him. He watched the glass, impa-
iently counting the grains as they slithered through the tiny
pening, falling in a powdery pyramid into the glass chamber
elow.

From somewhere far away, an animal howled, a lycat on the
rowl. He rose to his feet and paced beside the window.

Nydia lay back against the pillows. The full moon cast her
ody in a golden glow so that both she and Abelard appeared
s though they were made of something more than flesh. Her
mind was full of the equations of the Magic, and she was only
alf aware of the man who stripped and lay beside her.

Abelard cupped her breasts between his hands, raised the
aut nipples to his lips. His erection throbbed between her legs.
She lay back, staring at the ceiling, only half comprehending
vhen he thrust into her.

Phineas wet his lips, paused at the threshold of the dark
loorway. The woman on the bed was lying on her side, her
ead pillowed on her arm. She wore a white gown beneath the
vhite sheet.

The floor creaked softly as he approached the bed, and
Melisande sat up, clutching the sheet to her breasts. "Who's
here?" she cried softly, and Phineas's heart clutched at the
aked fear.

"Phineas."

"What are you doing here? What do you want?"

He moved to stand beside the bed and held his hands wide to show he was unarmed. "You know what I want."

"Phineas?" She sounded as if she did not quite believe her ears.

"And I think you want it, too."

"It is you, Phineas." She made a little sob deep in her throat, reached out and clasped his hand. "I've dreamt this would happen—"

Without another word, he clasped her in his arms, pulling her up so that she knelt before him on the bed. Their mouths met in a frantic kiss, and she twined her hands in his hair.

He raised his head and said shakily, "I want to be gentle with you, Melisande—"

She laughed. "Just show me how much you love me."

He pulled the gown down off her shoulders, showering her neck and arms with tiny kisses, cupped her breasts and brought the nipples up to his mouth. She moaned, tearing at his shirt, pushing it off his shoulders.

He laid her back upon the bed and slowly straightened to undo the lacings of his trousers. As he kicked them out of his way, he felt the jolt. It was like a flame bursting in his blood, a thirst which must be quenched, a wind that howled in the night. He fell upon her with a groan and buried himself in her flesh.

Nydia followed the equations into dark canyons lit by a thousand points of light; light which danced and whirled, formed patterns, split, merged, and split again.

The light beckoned, leading her into streams and whirls and vortexes and finally onto a great branch of something which seemed like living light. At some point, the numbers lost all meaning, as though she had entered a place where only the swirling patterns of light and dark seemed to matter. As though from far away, she knew Abelard rode her, knew his flesh pressed deeper and deeper within her, seeking release.

But her mind was entranced, dancing on the edges of the light, and she followed the twisting, turning swirls into a vortex where tiny sparks shot in all directions.

This was the place. Along the edges of reality, where matter and energy merged and blurred. She summoned all the will she could muster and reached, out, and out, until the light flared and sparked. The force of Abelard's will was hers. The two of them together made the light seem to split into prisms of colors which alternated with the pulse of the vortex.

She reached into the vortex, down, down, down, again, until the quality of the light changed, became something not quite solid, not quite liquid. It slipped and slid, and with one mighty burst of will she seized it, forced it, shaped it to her bidding. The light flared, sputtered; a thousand sparks fanned out, flying madly in all directions, whirling like a thousand frantic fireflies on a summer night. There was something horrible in the light, something cruel and hard and grasping, something which flung back her will with a force all its own. Out of the bright halo a vision formed, black and scaled. And it smiled at her. She wrenched the molecules into form, and the aftershock of it shuddered through her mind. It is finished, she thought, and abruptly let it go, clinging to the light of Abelard's will, which still shone more brightly amidst the chaotic fire play.

Her hands clenched on the small of his back, jerked into fists. Her head turned into his shoulder as, at that moment, he stiffened and gave a loud cry.

Phineas felt the Magic like a hot hand on the back of his neck, urging him on, faster and faster, until he pounded into Melisande like a stallion gone mad. She bucked beneath him, clasping him close with legs wrapped around his hips, her arms locked around his neck. The pressure mounted, harder and harder, on and on, until finally, she arched her back beneath him and gave a final, triumphant cry. He felt the pressure ease, abruptly, as his seed flooded into her womb.

* * *

Abelard raised himself away from Nydia. She lay, spent
unmoving, on the bed. The moon had faded; the light was no
longer so golden or so bright. Thin silvery streams edged the
room with faint luminescence. "Nydia?" he said finally
hoarsely.

"Yes?" There was a coolness to her tone he did not expect.

"Well? Are you—all right?"

"In a little while, I'll be pregnant, and so will Melisande."

He reached over, picked up her hand, and kissed it. "Thank
you."

She turned her head then and stared at him tiredly. "I don't
know whether you're going to want to thank me or not. There
will be consequences. We are all vulnerable to it now, all four
of us."

"The children?"

She shrugged. "I don't know about them. We'll have to wait
and see."

He moved away from her, sat up and looked around.
"Would you like some wine?"

"I'd like to be left alone. Please. Just leave me."

He got up uncertainly and reached for his clothes. "Are you
sure you're all right?"

"I'm fine." She looked away as he dressed and did not acknowledge that she heard him close the door softly as he left.
I'm fine, she thought, for someone who's just twisted the stuff
of creation to do one man's bidding. She shuddered to herself
as she remembered the feel of that slippery light throbbing in
her mind. And as she had wrenched it, twisted it and shaped it,
she wondered if the monstrous image she'd glimpsed had been
his future, or hers.

Melisande stirred, and Phineas raised his head, kissed her
shoulder. He touched her cheek; her eyes were bright in the
silver moonlight. She smiled at him. "Why do I feel as though
some purpose has been completed? As though something
which was meant to happen has finally happened?"

He smiled back, wondering what she would say if he told
er the truth. "It has."

"You're laughing at me."

He picked up her hand, kissed each finger, and shook his
ead. "No."

She stretched again, her smile lazy and replete. "Why did
ou come tonight? All day, I've been thinking of you, of this. I
aven't been able to get you out of my mind. And here you
re."

"I'm leaving tomorrow. I must go back to Ahga."

"Will I see you—"

"Then on to Ithan."

"But I thought, after this, surely—"

He touched her mouth. "It's better if we don't see each
ther, don't you think?"

"But—"

"Let's not worry about tomorrow." He leaned over her,
issed her mouth, and this time, he was gentle with her.

Chapter Thirty-Eight

May, 56th Year in the Reign of the Ridenau Kings
(2724, Muten Old Calendar)

The tension in the great hall of Ahga was palpable. Men and women stood by the great hearths in small clusters, whispering among themselves, glancing every now and again to the dais where the King and the Captain of the King's Guard sweated over a chess board. It was a desultory game, because the attention of both men was too easily distracted by anyone who entered the south door of the hall.

For the better part of two days, Melisande had labored to bring the heir of Meriga to birth, and Abelard and Phineas found themselves once more bound by a common concern. If the King was more worried about the child, and the Captain more worried about the Queen, no one noticed.

Abelard gestured to the waiting boy behind his chair for more wine. "By the One, Phineas, I don't remember it taking this long for any of the others."

"I suppose that's because you had other things to think about." Phineas held up his hand against the offered flagon. "And there's more riding on this birth, of course."

Abelard drained the goblet in one long gulp and held it out for more.

"Is there any word of Nydia?" Phineas asked below his breath. Since Phineas had returned from the Arkan Plains, Abelard had not mentioned her.

"She won't see me." Abelard looked away.

"Why not?" Phineas was surprised.

"I don't know," the King replied softly. "But ever since that night—she'll have nothing to do with me. She won't eak to me, she won't return my messages inquiring as to her ealth, and all she says is that she is well. I hope, after all is—" he gestured vaguely in the direction of the Queen's oms "—is over, perhaps it will be as it was."

There was hurt in the King's tone, and Phineas sipped the egs of his wine. So Abelard did care for Nydia, after all, he ought. It was not just her ability, or her knowledge of the agic that he cared about.

"Lord King! Lord King!" They heard the cry before the aidservant burst into the hall. She ran to the dais, tears in her es and on her cheeks. "Please come at once." She bobbed a isty curtsey, and Phineas noticed the stains on her apron.

"Is it born?" Abelard breathed, pushing back his chair.

"The Queen—"

The words weren't out of her mouth when Phineas leapt out his chair and bolted for the door, Abelard behind him, the aid scurrying to keep up. He heard Abelard's anxious flurry f questions about the child and her equally anxious attempts tell him about the Queen.

Phineas did not wait for the midwife's admittance. He burst to the Queen's antechamber, past the shocked stares of the aiting women and the nurses, and bolted into Melisande's edroom.

He took in the scene instantly: two nurses bent over a qualling child in a shallow basin, and four midwives clus-red around the Queen's bed, exchanging bloody linen, mut-ring among themselves. They shook their heads, and the xpressions on their faces were grim.

He pushed past them, and stopped. He had never seen so uch blood—not even on a battlefield. A large spreading stain eched up into the covers on top of Melisande, which told im that the mattress below her was fully saturated. Her face as gray, her lips blanched. He picked up her cold white hand, eling for a pulse, and thought surely she must be dead.

At his touch, her eyes fluttered open, and he bent over her, eedless of the squawking women. He knew Abelard had ome into the room, but he paid no attention.

"Melisande," he whispered, bending over her, to stroke h[e]
hair with his other hand.

"A son," she whispered, so faintly it was hardly a whispe[r]
"Yours."

"Yes." He pressed her hand, hoping for some answerin[g]
pressure, but she was too weak.

She struggled to take a breath, gasping as one does when on[e]
bleeds to death and the lungs are deprived of air. "Roderic."

"What?" He shook his head, thinking that she hallucinate[d]
that she no longer knew where she was, or who he was.

"Brought us together."

And then he understood. The standard-bearer, Roderic, t[he]
boy who had served him so well in the months of his captivi[ty]
in Vada, who had died so that he might live—Melisand[e]
wanted the child named for him.

He nodded and brushed her forehead with his lips. "H[is]
name will be Roderic. I swear."

"Phineas." She smiled, then, and shut her eyes. He felt h[er]
body shudder once, and then she was still.

He waited a moment, bending his head down over her fac[e]
thinking to hold her hand until it cooled, but she had lost s[o]
much blood it was already cold.

He rose heavily to his feet and turned back to an exulta[nt]
Abelard. The women were milling frantically around th[e]
room, trying to retrieve the child from the King, who held hi[m]
up like a trophy, thought Phineas. He straightened his tun[ic]
and went to Abelard. He touched the King's arm. "Let the[m]
clean him up," he said.

Abelard smiled the smile of a man who has won a great vi[c]
tory and turned to Phineas. "See how strong he is already—li[s]
ten to that cry. He'll make them all sit up and take notice—ju[st]
wait."

"Come on." Phineas tugged at Abelard's sleeve, and unwil[l]
ingly he noticed that the boy was long and lean, his skin th[e]
customary blotchy red of the newborn, and yet, already ther[e]
was the ghost of definition in the muscles of his shoulders an[d]

upper arms. He opened his eyes and turned his head, seeking the source of the sound.

The milky gray gaze locked onto Phineas, and Phineas caught his breath. This child was his—his son, born to reign in Meriga. Something in him knew the child, reached out— He dropped his gaze.

Reluctantly, Abelard handed the baby over to the midwife and followed Phineas out into the antechamber. Beneath the noise of the crying baby and the women wailing over Melisande, Phineas said, "I want you to name him Roderic."

"Roderic? Why?" Abelard frowned.

"Because I'm his father, and it is the only thing I will ever give him. I relinquish him to you, Abelard, but I want to give him his name."

Abelard shrugged, considering. "Roderic Ridenau," he said, turning the name over on his tongue. "It is a good name—it has a princely sound." He smiled and clapped Phineas on the shoulder. "Very well. Roderic he shall be. Roderic Ridenau, Prince of all Meriga."

Phineas nodded and turned on his heel. He could not stand to be in that chamber any longer. He left the room and went down to the hall. The faces turned toward him as he entered—eager, expectant.

"Captain?" asked the nearest woman.

He took a deep breath, thinking how ironic it was that he should be the one to announce the baby's birth. "The Queen is dead."

"And the child?"

"The Prince is strong, healthy."

"Praise to the One." The woman closed her eyes in silent prayer as a whisper went round the hall.

"Captain Phineas, sir." A sergeant of the Guard saluted as Phineas stepped past on his way to the dais.

"Yes?"

"A message just come from Minnis, sir, for the King."

Phineas held out his hand for the wooden tube. The seal was a formless blob of wax.

"You'll see he gets it, sir? I don't think I'll get too close what with the new Prince and all. The King's got other things on his mind, I suppose."

"Yes." Phineas saluted and the man marched back to his post. "Yes, the King has other things to think about."

Epilogue

*W*hen the second message came from Nydia, Abelard sent me to take them deeper into the Great North Woods. It fit his plan that anyone who might give the matter any thought would think I was responsible for fathering Nydia's child, and I do not believe he trusted any other to see to it.

I left shortly after the naming of the new Prince—a fantastic ceremony with Senators bowing before the baby and declaring that they would honor the oaths sworn to the King. I watched the ceremony, and when it was my turn, I knelt before the child in Abelard's arms and swore to him the same Pledge of Allegiance I had sworn nearly thirty years before to the first of the Ridenau Kings I had served. He did not look at me, but only yawned and chewed his fist, so I suppose he was an ordinary baby, after all.

I rode into Minnis alone, and Nydia received me immediately. Her daughter, born the night before Roderic, was asleep in a cradle. She showed me the baby with more than a mother's pride on her face.

I opened my mouth to say the appropriate thing and felt the words stop in my throat. Even at six weeks of age, the child in the cradle was extraordinary. It had something to do with her appearance—her head a mass of dark, silky curls, her cheeks like roses dipped in cream.

But it was more than that; I felt it immediately. There was something irresistible about the child, and I wanted to pick her up and cradle her close. I reached out and traced her cheek with the tip of my finger.

Her mother had come up behind me. "You see?"

I turned back to Nydia. Her left hand was wrapped in
piece of white silk, and I wondered what she had done to i
"She's—beautiful." The word was pitifully inadequate.

"Yes." Nydia smiled sadly, I thought. "She is."

"We'd better go, lady." I shuffled my feet awkwardly. "
want to get you settled before dark." I frowned down at he
suddenly concerned. "Are you sure you'll be all right?"

"Yes." Her voice was distant. "Abelard's always kept hi
promises." She took a deep breath. "I should warn you, Cap
tain, that you will suffer for your part in this. But you will b
honored, too. You will be a lord, Captain, and your son wi
love you like a father."

"He's not my son."

"Yes, he is," she said. "And because he is, he will be
greater King than Abelard could ever be."

"Was Melisande's death a result of the Magic?"

"She was the luckiest of us all, I think. But then, she wa
the most innocent."

"What about Abelard?"

"The last years of Abelard's life will be a hell beyond a
imagining."

I started to ask her what she meant, and decided I woul
rather not know. "What about you?"

She unwrapped the white silk on her left hand, and I drew i
a breath of horror. Her hand, once so small and white, wa
covered in thick green scales like a lizard's skin, the last thre
fingers fused into one long yellow claw. "It began with just
patch of scales, shortly after she was born. It grows a littl
more every day."

"Can you do nothing to stop it?"

"No. I don't know what will happen to me. But don't worry
When the time is right, I'll send my daughter to your son."

"Not my son, lady." I could not help sounding bitter, an
suddenly, all the fear, all the misgivings I'd ever had abou
her, vanished like snow on a spring morning, and I looked a

he pure profile before me with regret. And I knew what my
art in this sorry tale had been.

"Shall we go?" She wrapped her hand again in the silk and
icked up the sleeping baby. I led her out of the bedroom. In
he antechamber, she paused—to take one last look around, I
hought.

"Phineas?"

I was surprised to hear her speak. I thought she wanted to be
lone with her thoughts.

"You never did tell me why you chose to send Tedmund of
Linoys into Arkan. Please, tell me the truth."

I drew a deep breath, and all the years of loyalty to the King
ell away like an old skin outgrown. I looked her squarely in
he eyes. He had my life, he had my son, but he would not
ave my honor. "It was done on the order of the King."

"I thought so," was all she said, and then she walked past
ne out of Minnis without a backward look.

ABOUT THE AUTHOR

DAUGHTER OF PROPHECY is Anne Kelleher Bush's first novel. She holds a degree in medieval studies from Johns Hopkins University. She lives with her husband and four children in Bethlehem, PA.